Novels by George Zuckerman

FAREWELL, FRANK MERRIWELL

THE LAST FLAPPER

THE POTATO PEELERS

a novel by
GEORGE ZUCKERMAN

Dodd, Mead & Company
New York

ISBN: 0-396-07018-3
Library of Congress Catalog Card Number: 74-11796
Printed in the United States of America
by The Haddon Craftsmen, Inc., Scranton, Penna.

For Gregg and Laurie

1

The wild hawk eyes read havoc in the Monday morning clouds leading the northwest wind over the mountain into the valley, ripping dry fronds from tall bent palms.

The boy's troubled mind was being drawn to another ghost of sky when he heard his name called. Turning away from the northern window, he rose on his lanky legs, ran an uneasy hand through his tousled sandy hair. Disregarding the grins of his Ojai Prep classmates, he directed his blue eyes toward the frowning physics instructor at the blackboard.

Braced for a reprimand, he heard instead a brusque question: "Mr. Hendley, what makes an airplane fly?"

With ease, Hap Hendley explained the airscrew and jet principles before the instructor continued his own lecture on aerodynamics. Hap felt no relief, no pride. He would have preferred to voice his thoughts about more difficult, more pertinent questions: What turns a turbojet into a fire bomb? What's the pitch of human panic? How do you recognize burnt-away faces? Can gravediggers really bury the dead?

Then, blind to the past, deaf to the instructor, Hap concerned himself with the oncoming storm. He put his father in a jetstream high above the Midwest, eastbound. No danger for him. He estimated that the storm would strike San Fernando Valley in about two hours. Bad for Sally. It would wash out her tennis match.

When the instructor faced the blackboard to illustrate a principle, Hap turned to the northern window again. This time he counterattacked and tried to halt the enemy storm within the battleground of Ojai Valley. For Sally's sake.

By noon the dark clouds had tented San Fernando Valley. In South Oaks, on the Coopers' private cement tennis court, the ill wind played havoc with the tennis ball in play. Suddenly chilled, the four attractive women in smart tennis dresses stopped play long enough to add to their skimpy attire.

Sally Hendley, honey-haired and lissom, the youngest, at thirty, and the prettiest, donned a self-knitted sweater over her self-sewn tennis dress. In the delay, she found time to worry about Hap. She hoped he would not be so foolish as to play golf this afternoon in the rain. Unwittingly recalling her confrontation with Neal in the foul hours before

1

dawn, she hurried back to her position on the court.

Her partner this day, Joan Lawler, pulled a Beethoven sweatshirt over her tennis dress, a bargain from Loehmann's. At thirty-three, she was a skinny Irish girl with flaxen hair. She, too, was anxious to resume play, to block out her postmidnight anguish and torment.

Ilona Belanger added a Saks cardigan to her Saks tennis dress. At thirty-seven, raven-haired, blue-eyed, she was the most beautiful woman in the group. On any other such day, she would have been the first to suggest a retreat to the bridge table. But her most recent nightmares, sleeping and waking, drove her to damn the elements.

The hostess, Dolores Cooper, zippered an I. Magnin white nylon windbreaker over her I. Magnin tennis dress. At thirty-nine, a tall brunette, she looked younger and more attractive than her years.

She was neither disturbed by the bad weather, nor by the strangely bitchy and ill-tempered moods of her three friends. It all fitted in with her design for the day.

The tennis did not matter. Bridge was out of the question. This was the day to take the others into the eye of her own hurricane and lead them from there to liberation.

By way of a sexual conspiracy.

As play was resumed, the sky darkened but never approached the blackness of their postmidnight soul storms.

2

2

One A.M.

According to the day/date clock on the night table between Dolores Cooper's warm bed and its cold undisturbed twin, it was Monday, January 29, 1973.

As so often before, instead of finding sleep, she returned to the black night of Wednesday, April 8, 1970, to pan more of truth's bitterest dust.

It was almost 9:00 P.M. when the telephone rang without alarm. Putting aside her copy of *Psychology Today*, Dolores rose from her den chair to take a call from her husband.

"Yes, dear," she said, her voice warm.

"I'm still at the hospital." Perry sounded more like a sick patient than a doctor.

"You lost the patient."

"On the table."

"Who was the surgeon?"

"Cameron."

"Then you can't blame yourself, dear."

"I always do," Perry said. "Listen, honey, meet me at the Ivy League. Half an hour."

She understood. "Of course, dear."

As she went up the stairs, she was troubled by the elation she felt in the face of death. Her husband was alive, her two children were well, and she was alive, loved, and needed. And Ben was alive.

She opened two bedroom doors to tell Linda and Larry where she was going and why. The mirrors in the master bedroom and bathroom told her, once she had shed her clothes, that she was too much of a matron at thirty-six. There was too much lard on her hips, too much sag to her breasts.

The brassiere and the girdle helped. The new dress from Bullock's Fashion Square helped more, and she was happy again. With herself, her Colonial house, tennis court, swimming pool, and grove of trees. She had everything. Even a Mercedes of her own.

From South Oaks Drive she turned right onto Ventura Boulevard, staying in the outside lane until she came to the walls of the Ivy League.

Roy Sutter, the proprietor, gave her his best smile and made small talk about her tennis as he ushered her to the secluded booth where Perry was sipping a Marguerita, a strange drink for him.

Unsmiling, Perry rose. As she sat down, he did another strange thing. Rather than return to where he had been seated, he sat across the table from her. They usually sat side by side, to hold hands, to touch each other.

"I forgot to ask Roy about his wife," she said, making conversation.

"Don't," Perry said gravely.

She braced herself for more bad news. "What is it?"

"Leukemia."

"Oh, no!"

Perry nodded.

"Oh, God!"

"The flu triggered it," he explained.

"She's so beautiful," she said. "Any hope?"

"None."

She needed the drink, and it was not long before a black waiter appeared with her screwdriver. They made no toast. They touched no glasses and traded no smiles. It was Perry's stage, and she let him set it. She did not set herself for anything more than his melancholy.

"I have something to tell you," Perry said.

"Yes, dear."

Perry sipped his drink before he drank in her empathy. "Something's happened to me."

She held her tongue. She wished to voice no such alarms as leukemia.

"I met a girl," he said. "I'm in love with her. And she with me."

She looked about the restaurant, at the photographs of the sporting scenes mounted on the walnut-paneled walls, at the real people in the real booths, at real tables, at the real flames rising from the open charcoal broiler. She smelled the charred steaks and her own Chanel fragrance. And she saw the familiar black waiters and the personable Roy Sutter. It was all real and it was truly happening. To her.

Another sip of her drink, tasteless now, and a new sigh, deeper and more painful than she had ever known, and she was ready. Never the fainting kind, she easily found her strength in the fonts of her intelligence, her character, and her psychology.

"What's her name?" she asked.

"Valerie Hopkins."

"Pretty name. Is she pretty?"

"To me she is," he said.

"How old is she?"

"Twenty-seven."

"Married? Divorced?"

"Single."

4

She felt better. "How does a pretty girl escape the altar for twenty-seven years?"

"Ambition. Career," he said.

"What sort of career?"

"As a writer."

"I envy her that. What has she written?"

"Nothing professionally."

"She's young—for a writer."

"Valerie won a literary prize in college. Bennington."

"She must be bright. But how did she manage to live all these years?"

Perry told her. "She was a script girl for two years with CBS in New York. Soap operas."

She felt no impulse to laugh, and it pleased her. "And then what?"

"Valerie came to Hollywood, also as a script girl. This time for Fox. Working on television films. There was a cutback at the studio, and she was laid off."

"End of career?"

"Yes," he said. "When her unemployment insurance ran out, she took courses in medical terminology and transcribing. Then she went to work at South Oaks Hospital."

"How long ago was that?"

"About eighteen months," he recalled.

"Did you notice her right away?"

"No," he said.

She waited to hear more.

Perry said, "I was checking over a transcript. There was one word I didn't remember using. And in its place was a word I'd never heard of. I was upset and I went down to find out what the hell was going on there. That's how we met."

"Did you bawl her out?"

"No, she was right. I was wrong."

"How long did it take you to get interested in her?"

"Months," said Perry. "I'd run into her from time to time in the coffee shop. We'd chat. Shop talk mostly. At the beginning. Then we got personal. Serious."

"Very?"

Perry nodded. "I started sleeping with her about three months ago."

Afraid to say anything wrong, she said nothing.

"It was my fault," said Perry. "Not hers."

"Is it a question of fault?"

He hesitated. "I didn't want you getting the idea that Valerie had seduced me, that she was looking for me to break up my marriage to you and have me marry her."

"You are a good catch, as they say."

"It was all my doing," Perry said.

"I forgive you, dear."

Perry winced. "Do you?"

"Yes, I love you, I know you, and I understand you."

"I don't think so," he said.

"You doubt my love?"

He shook his head. "Only your understanding."

"Please. Correct me if I'm wrong. You're thirty-seven. You work too hard, you play too little. You're around doctors who play around and talk about it. You've never known another girl or woman except me. You had to break out. I'd rather you did that than break down. Now what have I said wrong?"

Perry sighed. "You think it's over and done with?"

"Why else would you pick this night to tell me about your affair, if it were not over?"

He sipped his drink. "You're wrong, Dolores. It's not over."

"No?" Her voice was choked, her nerves taut.

"I want a divorce," he said plainly.

She could say nothing for a long while. She had trouble enough trying to keep her heart beating and her mind working. She had more than enough rancor and rage to subdue.

"Perry?"

"Yes?"

"Does Valerie know you're here and why you're here?"

"She does," he said.

"But it's *your* idea?"

"I sold her on it."

"Was it a hard sell?"

"It was," he said. "She's no fool."

"I'm glad for you." She emptied her glass.

"Like another?" Perry asked.

"No, thank you. You look very tired."

"I haven't got your answer yet," Perry reminded her.

"About the divorce?"

"Yes."

She detected a note of impatience. "I do have questions. Only about us. Care to hear them now?"

"Frankly, I'd prefer answers," he said.

"So would I, my dear. And, yes, I'll have that drink now."

Perry summoned the waiter and placed his order. She guessed that Valerie Hopkins drank Margueritas, but she did not ask. She meant to waste no questions.

"Perry, when did you stop loving me?"

"Around Thanksgiving Day," he said.

6

She was thinking that Perry at that time was in love with Valerie. But she asked, "What did I do?"

"Exactly what you've been doing every time I get into a fight with Ben." Ben was a dirty word to Perry. Ben was her father. Her Daddy. And she was Daddy's girl.

"Yes," she said. "I took Daddy's side. He's right. And about the middle of April you'll realize how right he is."

"The hell with him," said Perry. He was angry now.

She refused to match it. "I understand your feelings. But, please, think twice about punishing Linda. And Larry."

"They're smart kids," he said. "I hope they'll understand."

"You might be asking too much of them," she said calmly. "I myself don't understand you."

"Sure you do," he insisted.

"The affair perhaps, the divorce never."

"You'll survive."

"Of course, I will," she said. "I pride myself upon being adult."

Perry frowned but said nothing. The waiter was back with the drinks. When he was gone, it was she who spoke again.

"May I say something about you and Ben?"

"Shoot."

"You've always resented my father. You know he wasn't happy that I married you. Yet he helped you, and you'd like to forget that without Ben's help you'd never be a doctor today."

Perry was forlorn. "Sure, the man owns me."

"Ben loves you now," she told him.

"I hate him."

She winced. "May I say something about the Thanksgiving Day row?"

"It's too late now."

She would not be deterred. "Just this one point. After that, I promise you I won't mention his name. Or Valerie's. We'll just talk about you and me."

"What's your point, Dolores?"

She sipped her drink, trying to compose herself, and trying not to remember that it was too late. "Linda has her own mind. A first-rate one at that. She wants Radcliffe, and if Radcliffe wants her, that's where she'll go. But I don't wish for her to be hurt by disappointment. And neither do you. All right. So when Ben opens his big mouth and tries to make a case for Linda enrolling at UCLA, I don't shut him up. Of course he's an old, selfish man. Of course he's thinking more of himself than of Linda when he tempts her with a sports car of her own, an apartment of her own, plus her own checking account. And, of course, he wants her in town. Westwood is close to Beverly Hills. Cambridge isn't."

"Get to your point," he urged her.

"I knew what I was doing when I sided with Ben."

"Did you know what you were doing to me?" Perry demanded.

"I took a chance, Perry. For Linda's sake. Don't blow up. Just hear me out. Consider this: Radcliffe turns her down. It's a terrible disappointment. At least now she has Ben's tempting offer to fall back on."

Perry looked hard at her. "Is that it?"

She was sick. "You don't understand me."

"I understand that Linda has other choices. Stanford, for one."

"There's more to it," she said. "Linda's more confident about Radcliffe than Stanford."

It made no sense to Perry. "Why?"

"Because her mother's Jewish."

He was angry again. "Who put that in Linda's head? You or Ben?"

"Her peers," she revealed.

"All right, enough of that. It doesn't matter. Not about you and me," he declared.

"I had to try, Perry. I don't know how to give up."

"Are you going to contest the divorce?"

"No," she said. "You tell me what you want done, I'll do it."

He believed her. "I'll tell you what I don't want. I don't want Ben bothering me."

"I'll see to that."

"You file for divorce," he insisted.

"On what grounds?"

"Incompatibility."

"All right."

"You name a lawyer, I'll name mine. You and I discuss nothing about the details. Not directly."

"Done," she said.

"I'll move into the guest room. Tonight. I'll get out as soon as I'm able to rent something."

"Don't rush, we'll manage it."

"I'll manage things," he said. "I'll tell the kids."

"Good," she said.

"That's all I have to say now." Perry brought his drink to his mouth.

She did not touch hers. "I have more to say."

He frowned.

"Am I keeping you?" She said nothing about Valerie.

"Finish your drink."

"I won't be long," she promised. "No auld lang syne. No Carrollton, nothing about the cigar band you put on my finger when I was ten. I don't wish to spoil what we had for so long. Nobody can take that away."

She sipped her drink. "Just a few questions—just for the life I've yet ahead of me."

"You'll marry again," Perry said with certainty.

Her smile was wan. "I hope so. So be candid with me. You can help me."

"I'll try," he said.

"Aside from the truth that I am Ben's daughter, tell me how I lost you."

Perry could say nothing. The manner in which he emptied his glass told her that he wanted an end to the confrontation. She looked for him to rise.

At last he said, "We were too young, and we grew old too soon. My fault. I got you pregnant, married, and turned you into a mother too soon. And I became a doctor too soon. Too much of life. A good life, but I guess we—at least I did—I guess I missed out on the romance."

"Sex?" asked Dolores.

"No, I mean romance. Remember me, the bookworm, the work-horse."

"I remember us," she said. "And I remember it as romance."

"I can't. I don't. I don't know what it is. Maybe I've seen too many people die. And so many of them have said what I'm thinking now: 'God, I can't die. I haven't lived.'"

"Think of those you saved from death," she said.

He shook his head sadly. "No, I have to save myself. I know how alive I am when Valerie smiles at me."

She fought tears. Emotion would not save her. Neither would ridicule. Perry was at least ten years from the crisis of a male climacteric. She wondered if it was the premature graying of his hair, but she dared not pose the question.

All she said was, "Be well. Live."

"That it?" he asked.

She made the smile a good one now. She had to show him and herself that she was brave and strong. "I'll live. Anyway, I came here tonight to cheer you up. You're free. Bring the glad tidings to your girl."

Pleased with herself that her voice did not break, she rose and made her exit. Alone.

The past faded, the trauma passed.

January 29, 1973, 1:25 A.M.

In vain Dolores tried to return her attention to the book in her hands, to the open pages hot with the white light of the Tensor bed lamp. Instead she turned her head to read the emptiness of the other twin bed and to sense the freight of despair and loneliness carried by her nervous system to her distraught mind.

She closed the book. Simone de Beauvoir had nothing to tell her about the coming of age. Suddenly she reached out for the telephone and dialed seven numbers with urgency. The ringing was music to her, a prelude to the one voice able to sing to her.

An unexpected, cold voice chilled her. "The number you have reached has been disconnected. Please check your directory for—"

Dolores dropped the telephone onto the cradle and lowered her father into his grave.

The next sound she heard was coughing. Larry? No, he was in Ithaca, New York, a freshman at Cornell, whose thick envelope had come with the thin ones from Harvard, Yale, and Princeton. Linda? No, she was in Palo Alto, at Stanford, whose fat envelope had arrived with a thin one from Radcliffe. Linda was a junior, married to a medical student and big with child.

The cougher was Perry. In the guest room.

When the coughing died, Dolores left her bed and went to confront the stranger in the bathroom mirror.

It was hardly the face and figure of a soon-to-be grandmother. The new Dolores was but two years old, the work of a noted San Francisco plastic surgeon, the last gift made to her by Ben.

Ben, the jeweler, had pronounced her "a flawless, polished diamond." Linda had looked upon the new Dolores as "my older and more beautiful sister." Larry had pouted and said, "What did you want to do that for? I loved you the way you were."

The change had found the approval of her friends, male and female, particularly the three younger and more attractive members of her tennis group.

As for Perry, the change had evoked nothing but surprise, short-lived and silent. It brought no change to their relationship. He remained the ghost in the guest room. She remained unhappy, unloved.

No more time for biding, waiting, hoping, and dreaming. The time was now. Today. Life was a masked ball and, masked, she was free of everything but her rage to love and be loved by strange, masked men.

3

Two A.M.

Ilona Marton Belanger saw the streets running red with flames and blood. In her dark boudoir, alone in the circular bed, she writhed, kicked away the satin quilt, and knocked her husband's cold pillow with a flailing arm to the deep, crimson carpet. Supine, she crossed her arms and tore at her sheer, short nightdress, gasped, moaned, and at last escaped from the nightmare.

She sighed when she saw that she was alone in America, in California, in South Oaks, in her own silly bed. She was out of Hungary, out of Budapest, and out of the clutches of the Russian soldiers with their rumbling and cannon-roaring tanks.

A yawn, a smile, and a nervous laugh. A nightmare was a nightmare and not a recipe for panic. She saw nothing in the face of the clock but time. And she saw nothing in the absence of her husband but absence itself. It mattered not where he was at this hour. It was not 1956, the year of the revolution.

She left the bed, returned the fallen pillow, and removed the telephone from its base. Still yawning, she slipped into a terry-cloth robe and left the bedroom. She entered two other rooms to remove two other telephones. Downstairs she did the same in the study and in the kitchen, all as a matter of caution.

She did not fear emergency calls from a hospital, a police station, a prep school in Connecticut, or a boarding school in Massachusetts. What she wished to avoid was another obscene telephone call. She had had four such disgusting experiences in the past year, each from a different woman alone with the same man—her husband.

Not wishing to return to bed, or to Budapest, Ilona turned on the lights in the kitchen to take her through the night. She meant to return by a happier route to happier days in Budapest. She was going to bake a batch of Hungarian double-deck cookies with chocolate icing. No problem now about Ronny's pimples since her fifteen-year-old son was at Choate, and no problem about Karen's weight since her fourteen-year-old daughter was at Abbott Academy. She would bring the cookies tomorrow afternoon to Dolores Cooper's house. A nice treat after tennis.

She was rattling in the cupboards and drawers when she sensed she

11

was no longer alone. Turning, she faced an old woman in a woolen nightgown who was scowling at her.

Ilona smiled and spoke to her in Hungarian. "I am sorry I woke you. Go back to bed. I am all right, really, Sonia."

Her scowl persisting, Sonia turned and went back to her room beyond the laundry room.

And Ilona's smile endured as she gathered her ingredients.

She loved Sonia's peasant scowl, for in it was contained all those memories of childhood and girlhood.

Ilona was grinding unsalted almonds when she let her mind wander to Pasadena and to the day in 1957 when the Hungarian conspirators arranged her life and fortune in America.

There he was, the nice young man who came in a Bentley to Mrs. Fodor's bakery on Lake Street every afternoon at four to buy two dozen Hungarian double-deck cookies with chocolate icing. And there she was, by arrangement, in her costliest dress, buying up the last of these cookies. Mrs. Fodor, in her broken English, played her scene. And she played hers, and from then on played all the right cards, and within a month she was, at twenty-one, Mrs. Robert Belanger.

Bobby was twenty-nine, hardly handsome, hardly wealthy. The Bentley belonged to an old Pasadena tycoon, one of Bobby's clients. Bobby was an accountant who drove a used Ford and lived in a bachelor apartment. A French-Canadian boy from Maine, a Korean War veteran, a graduate of the University of Southern California.

But the Hungarians were right about him. Within five years he was driving a Cadillac, within ten a Bentley of his own. They moved to bigger and better apartments as Bobby made the right stock and real estate investments and, at last, ended up building tract houses in San Fernando and Simi valleys.

Never the love of her life, Bobby was a nice boy. He grew richer, but he never grew up. So clever with money, so stupid with love. With sex.

Ilona had no wish to think about that now, and she easily blocked it out of her mind as she measured four cups of flour, two cups of sugar, one-half pound of salt butter, one-half pound of sweet butter, one teaspoon of vanilla, and eight ounces of ground almonds.

She was at the kitchen sink, running hot water over a sealed jam jar top and listening to the wind in the pine trees, when she saw beams of light strike the window. Looking out, she saw Bobby's Bentley. One glance and no more. She meant to say nothing to him, and she hoped he had nothing to say to her. Not in the kitchen, not in that silly circular bed. She hoped he was tired enough to sleep without troubling her—without going into the window seat for his bag of tricks, costumes, and disguises. Someday, she vowed, she was going to burn it all.

Ilona looked out the window again. Bobby had not run his car into the garage. It was parked in the driveway, the lights on, the engine running. Bobby was still behind the wheel, and he was not alone. There was a woman beside him.

More concerned about being seen than in seeing what the woman looked like, Ilona left the window and went to the oven. The dough was baking, the sweetness pervading the kitchen and returning her to Budapest.

In another moment Bobby entered the kitchen and returned her to South Oaks. An English cap on his balding head, a short car coat open to reveal his mod clothes, the clown entered laughing, stuck a finger into a pot of chocolate sauce, blew on it, and licked it clean.

"Boy, is that good!"

"Hello," said Ilona without interest.

"What are you doing up?"

"The Russians came."

Bobby laughed. "Did you come together at the same time?"

She gave the man with the million-dollar brain a bored look. "You left your motor running."

"Well, I don't know whether we're coming or going yet."

"Go," she said with finality.

"I just came in."

"Just go out. The same way."

"Listen, sugar, I want you to say hello to someone."

"I already did."

"Not me. Someone in the car."

"Good night, Bobby."

"She's dying to meet you."

"She will die first."

"Her name's Nicki."

Ilona tried to play deaf and dumb. Again she peered into the oven window.

"Listen, she lives all the way the hell out in Inglewood, and you wouldn't send me back there on a night like this, would you? Would you, sugar?"

"You have my blessings. Both of you, go to—Inglewood."

"Can we wait for the cookies?" He giggled, and to Ilona the giggle was more insipid than the question.

"Drive carefully. Do not get yourself another ticket for speeding," Ilona said, as she searched a drawer.

Bobby pouted. "Look at me!"

Deaf to his demand, she continued to rattle around in the drawer, despite the fact she had located the two-pronged fork she needed.

Bobby came toward her, put a fist under her chin, and forced her to face him. "Look at me and listen carefully. I'm going out, but I'm

13

coming in again with Nicki. And I'm going to take her straight upstairs to our little den of iniquity."

Ilona stared at him and was repelled by his measure of rage. He neither stank of tobacco, liquor, or pot, but he was drunk with the power of his money. And she despised him for it.

Bobby went on. "We'll be in bed waiting for you. When the cookies are done, bring them up. We'll have a little party."

Ilona played deaf.

He turned to leave. "You heard me."

"You hear me!"

He faced her again. "I heard you when you had your way with Ronny and Karen. Okay, you got them out of the house and far enough away from me and my *games*. We're alone again, and after I work my balls off all day, I *need* fun and games."

"Sonia is here," she said.

"She doesn't send me. She had her fun with your old man and his old man, so the hell with her."

"All right, Bobby. You take Nicki upstairs. The two of you can carry the bed out of the house."

"Carry it where?"

"As far as your Bentley will take you."

He held a weak smile. "You're crazy."

"Yes, I am. If the two of you insist on going upstairs, then I advise both of you to be ready to walk through fire."

"What fire?" he demanded.

"While you will be playing in bed, I will be playing with matches."

"No way, sugar?"

"No," she said.

"Some other night?"

"I think we can arrange something for tonight. If you do exactly as I tell you."

Bobby found his giggle. "Anything you say."

Ilona gave him her recipe for the night. "Drive to Hollywood, to the Western Costume Company. If it is open, walk in. If not, break in and find where they keep army uniforms. Select two Russian infantry uniforms. One for Nicki, one for you. Then you and Nicki rush right back here and get in bed. In full uniform, heavy boots and all."

"What'll you be wearing?" Bobby asked.

"Nothing but two sharp carving knives."

Bobby shuddered. Saying nothing, he watched Ilona open the oven door and remove the baked cookes. He reached for one, burned his fingers but held on to it, dipped it into the chocolate sauce, and gave himself a burning, sweet pleasure.

Bobby opened the refrigerator and sipped cold milk from a half-

14

gallon carton. Turning to Ilona, he said, "Good-bye."

"Good-bye," she echoed.

"I wasn't kidding about Inglewood. It's a long drive."

"Call a taxi."

"You have all the lousy answers," he said.

"I did not say I would not take care of you."

Bobby slammed the refrigerator door shut. "You dumb Hungarian! You don't know what sex is!"

"Good-bye, Bobby." She busied herself spreading jam and pouring chocolate sauce.

He made a last try. "Come out to the car and say hello."

"You see how busy I am."

"I'll bring her in."

"All right, if you like her with hot chocolate sauce on her face."

"I want Nicki to see you. I told her you were better looking than the Gabor sisters."

Bobby turned and left the kitchen. Ilona dropped everything and hurried after him. The front door was open and Bobby was gone when she reached it. Without chancing a glance outside, she slammed the door shut, locked, bolted, and chained it.

She stood there and listened as Bobby in turn tried the doorknob, his knuckles, and the chimes. And then she heard a voice which she recalled with disgust.

"Forget it, Fatty," shouted Nicki.

"I told you not to call me Fatty."

"Take me home, Bobby. Come on, if you promise to hold onto the wheel, I'll blow you from here to Inglewood."

Bobby giggled.

Silence, the sound of the car doors, the purring of the engine, and, at last, the wind out of the north, fresh, cold, and singing through the trees.

Returning to the kitchen, Ilona was startled to find Sonia standing at the window, her mouth pursed, her eyes dark with melancholy.

In English, Ilona thought about her own state of mind. I will not be melancholy. I will not be weak. I will not suffer Bobby as I suffered the Russians. I will spill his blood before he drinks mine. I will be free. I will run free. Run wild. Looking for love.

In Hungarian she said to Sonia. "Go to bed. The Americans are gone."

4

Three A.M.

Joan Clarke Lawler lay awake in the four-poster bed, far from her mouth-breathing sleeping husband and very close to the Blessed Virgin.

Gentle Mary, what'll I do? I'm out of sleep, out of patience with the night. I was a bad girl tonight. Frank was out and I hardly missed him. Oh, I watched the clock, not the door. I didn't want him to come home before one in the morning. I wanted to be alone in front of the television set in the living room, curled up in my soft chair and smoking cigarettes, drinking beer, and waiting anxiously for the clock to reach eleven-thirty. Waiting for the late news to end and for the film I so wanted to see and never saw in a theater because Frank has no stomach for such movies. An X-rated film, a shocking, immoral film of sex and perversion among European nobles.

But I was sinned against by those blue-nosed censors who shut their eyes to vaginal sprays, underarm deodorants, and false teeth, but not to those scenes that made this particular film something to be talked out, seen, and discussed to the point of disgust. Especially by women like Dolores Cooper who believe God is dead.

But I tolerate Dolores and all of her quotes from all of those so-called profound books about love and sex. I can take her or leave her, but I do take her on those tennis afternoons—me, Ilona, and Sally. Sally's one of those Protestants who thinks about God only during earthquakes. Ilona's a Roman Catholic, but so unlike the Irish Catholics I grew up with and went to school with in Philadelphia. She says she believes, and she let's it go at that. Unlike me, she has no Catholic conscience, no sense of carnal sin. She lives and lets live and tries not to trouble God or let Him trouble her.

Thank the Lord, I fell asleep before the boredom of the film killed me. "X" marked the places where the hot stuff was cut to make room for commercials. The next thing I knew, it was after one o'clock, and Frank was waking me up. Poor boy, working so late, long hard day, long hard night. Leaves the house at nine in the morning in his Brooks Brothers suit, button-down shirt, narrow tie, and slender attaché case looking like one of the Kennedy Catholics who made it through Harvard Law School.

16

Oh, that poor Irish boy from the Bronx who scraped his way through Fordham. He should have been a priest like his brother Tim. He'd have been such a handsome one, so much more impressive than those fat Italians. And I should have been a nun. Skinny girls look good in habits.

But you know me, you remember me, skinny Joanie Clarke, the girl with the flaxen hair and the wicked tongue, always getting into trouble with the sisters, right through college. Always in trouble with my dear, devout mother, my blustering father, who was never able to get his Irish up in that Broad Street bank where he worked with all those Protestants.

I was skinny at twenty-one, at twenty-six when Frank took me for better or worse, thinner or fatter, and now, at thirty-three, I'm only fat in my head.

Three pregnancies, three miscarriages. No accidents, no carelessness. Just what was it, Dear Gentle Mary? Were those three of the punishments due me on earth? And is Frank my fourth punishment?

I loved him so much when he married me. But that was five years after I had met him and fallen in love, at first sight, with his dearest friend. His law partner. Rian Sheridan. Oh, he was not quite as handsome as Frank. Red hair, freckles, not as tall. But what Irish charm and malarkey! What Irish chutzpah!

They were a year out of Fordham Law School and opening their first office—in Los Angeles, because Rian sensed that Horace Greeley was still right about the West. I answered the ad as I had answered six or seven other ads before it with no success. I did have one offer: to take off my dress.

Frank interviewed me. He was as severe with me as the worst kind of priest. Nothing. It was about all over when Rian waltzed in, took one look at me, and said, "Great, this is going to be an all-Irish party."

Frank tried to explain that I had no experience, and Rian just repeated, "Great."

Oh, it was great all right for four years. Spent the days in the office with Frank, and spent too many nights with Rian. Before and after his wedding at the Church of the Good Shepherd in Beverly Hills to a girl whose father was a prominent Catholic layman, a papal knight, and a corporation lawyer to boot.

Then for a year it was just Frank and me, measuring each other's long face by day. And nothing by night. He was shattered. When Rian deserted him, it was like God Himself had turned His back on him.

Oh, it's to laugh. The wicked tongue that made me so much trouble with the sisters made me Mrs. Francis Xavier Lawler.

Oh, how I taunted him, how I mocked him. And, in the end, I made him see who and what he was and what he had to do to get off the floor. And I kept after him until he did it. He came back to the office from lunch one day and told me he'd been invited to join a Beverly Hills law firm which handled a lot of show business people who needed constant handling. Take it, I said, you're the boy for them.

Frank took it. He tried to take me along as his secretary. I refused. I held out for a better offer. We invited Rian to the church in Santa Monica. He never showed. We read about him in the papers. He's got four kids. Frank and me, we've got trouble.

Oh, yes, Gentle Mary, we do indeed. I'm not complaining to you, just talking the dark of the night away with you. No more praying or looking for miracles. The Lord helps those who help themselves. Off the floor, out of hell, and into—

"What are you doing?"

"Did I wake you?"

"Yes, you did. Good night."

"Good night, counselor." She reached for his penis.

"Let go."

"I think your client likes the touch of my hand."

"Take a look at the clock."

"Turn around and look at me, Frank."

"Forget it, Joan."

"You excited me."

"I was sleeping."

"Who were you with tonight?"

"A client."

"Animal, vegetable, or mineral?"

"You're very unfunny at this hour," he said.

"I wasn't exactly reaching for laughs."

"Let go now."

"The erection's gone, Frank. How did you do it? Did you hold your breath?"

"Good night."

The two monotones were stilled. Joan withdrew her hand and clasped it with her other. In prayer.

"Frank?"

"You're driving me out of the bedroom."

"You can walk—after you hear me out."

"Get to the point."

"I want to try again," she pleaded.

"To conceive?"

"Yes. Tonight."

"Why this night? Did you consult Dr. McLish?"

"No, Gentle Mary."

"Unless She spoke to you, I don't want to hear about it."

"Gentle Mary heard me out. And she smiled. I never have a vision

18

of that smile. I just feel it in my heart. Like I always do when I think good thoughts."

"What good thought?"

"To have a baby sleeping in the other room. Instead of you."

"Talk to Father Madera."

"In the confessional booth?"

"No, in his study. About adopting a Catholic child."

"I'd rather talk you into my vagina."

"Forget it," he said with finality.

"Where were you tonight, Frank?"

"Rita Nash."

"Her house?"

"Madhouse," he said.

"What was the legal problem?"

"Divorce."

"Interesting. Has it been a year since she married her last creep?"

"Just about."

"Was his ass out of the house?"

"By ten o'clock."

"Did her doctor come?"

"Ten-thirty."

"And what time did you come?"

"A double entrendre is not a question," he said.

"What time did you go to bed with Rita?"

"At no time."

"Where did you do it?"

"Do what?" he yawned.

"What I'm trying to get you to do again. Now."

"Forget it."

"How about tomorrow night?"

"Forget it."

"How about a divorce?" Silence. "Let the record show that the witness responded to the above question with a deep, painful sigh."

"Good night, Joan."

"Can you recommend a good lawyer for me?"

Frank sat up, grabbed his pillow, and left the bed.

"I believe I'll retain Rian."

He stopped at the door. "Very funny."

"Isn't it?"

"You wouldn't dare."

"Oh, yes, I would."

"Rian doesn't touch divorce cases."

"Oh, he'd make an exception in my case. In one way, he and I were closer than the two of you ever were."

19

"That wouldn't surprise me."

"Did you ever suspect?"

"I never thought about it at the time."

"It didn't matter that Rian was balling me."

"No."

"But it did matter to you when Rian screwed you, didn't it?"

"You were there."

"Yes, I was. And I saw it all. And it was obscene."

"What was?" he asked.

"The way you went to pieces."

"I have no recollection of that."

"Don't lose your hair or your lean figure. Don't get bad breath, Frank. Once you do, you'll be out of Weil & Tanner and in some safe hole in some federal building. Or wherever it is that untalented lawyers bury themselves."

Frank said nothing. He took his pillow to another room and another bed.

As she ended her own version of a tenth-century Irish prayer, Joan became aware of the heat consuming her body and the dryness of her mouth. Wet-eyed, she left the bed, shivered in the January cold, and made no move for her robe. Instead she opened the door, stared for an instant across the corridor to the shut door behind which her husband had divorced himself from her bed and bitchiness, and went down the cold oak stairs.

A night light was burning in the kitchen and in its dimness the knots on the pine-paneled walls flew at her like bats from a dark cave. Opening the refrigerator door, she took a can of Tuborg, pulled the ring, and took one swig and no more. Then she found and uncorked a bottle of Old Forester. After she had poured the bourbon into the beer can, she carried it into the dark living room.

Curled into the lounging chair, she sipped her boilermaker and gazed at the dark, blank television screen until it caught the purple light of her imagination.

The X-rated foreign film was running again in her mind, without commercial interruptions or excisions by network censors. The star was none other than herself, playing all the female roles: the little molested girl, the full-breasted star with a passion for rape, and the lesbians at play.

Soon the beer can was empty and the mental television screen was again dark. When the sweat of her quieted body grew cold, she left the chair, mounted the stairs, climbed into the cold four-poster bed, and took the stairless way not to Gentle Mary but to Lucifer in hell.

Here I am, wicked Joanie Clarke Lawler. I'm yours. Bring me sin, bring me sinners. Tomorrow and tomorrow.

20

5

Five A.M.

Awake now for hours, Sally Foster Hendley lay in the king-sized bed and watched two faces, one luminous, the other dark with sleep.

The alarm clock exploded like a time bomb. Her husband erupted like a volcano. The day was born for daring and reckoning. For crisis.

By 5:40 she was buttoning her raincoat over her ski sweater and blue jeans. Darkening the banks of light in the warm kitchen, she traded the fragrance of coffee and fried bacon for the cold, foul smell of the attached garage.

A pressed button raised the aluminum door and let in the January chill of the dark before dawn. She started her MG, backed out into the straight driveway, and watched the garage door shield the Ford station wagon.

Parked and waiting, she studied the house she hated. It was a grounded spaceship, a space station, or a house on the moon. Glass and cement blocks, gadgets, and built-in fixtures and furnishings. A dream come true and lost by the aerospace engineer who had designed it, and who had trouble selling it until Neal came along. Alone.

She would not have taken it as a gift, and yet that is what it was—a gift from Neal to his new, young bride. It did not belong in South Oaks, in San Fernando Valley. She would have preferred a rustic ranch house.

There was no heart warmth to the glass house she was throwing stones at. It lacked the feeling of shelter she had known in her clapboard home in Indiana, in a Sutton Place town house, and a Central Park South apartment.

She was thinking of how much she needed to change her address and her life when Neal appeared at the front door with the familiar luggage, tall carriage, and easy lope—the walk of a giant eagle.

He laid his bags on the back seat before easing into the bucket seat beside Sally. Eyes on the rear-view mirror, she backed out into Montana Lane.

The knees of his long legs arched high as he sat back, Neal lit a little Dutch cigar, the kind he favored after a breakfast of orange juice, three fried eggs, five slices of crisp bacon, three slices of buttered and jellied toast, and two cups of black coffee. He had slept well, and the blue smoke drifted past his clear brown eyes.

She let him alone as she drove north on South Oaks Road. She concerned herself with the geography of the neighborhood.

On her left Sally caught sight of the two used-brick posts and the carriage lanterns that lit the long hedge-lined entrance to Roy Sutter's ranch house.

Texas Lane. Right turn to Joan Lawler's Cape Cod home. Arizona Lane, left turn to Dolores Cooper's Colonial home. Utah Lane, left turn to Ilona Belanger's French Normandy home. Idaho Lane.

Sally repressed an urge for a detour, for a right turn that would take them past a house whose "For Sale" sign was a battle flag she soon hoped to capture.

She had crossed Ventura Boulevard and was approaching the Ventura Freeway when Neal lost altitude and found his smile and his voice.

"You're lookin' good, honey."

"Thank you, kind sir."

"You're the only gal I know who can fall out of bed lookin' good."

"Tell me more."

"Tell you what. Come along this mornin'. I'll tell you all about it in Rome."

"I want to hear it now."

"There's no room in this English job of yours for me to stretch out on top of you."

"You have hand room," she said, smiling. Her eyes were on the road, on the ramp climbing and curving into the eastbound lanes of the freeway.

"My hands this mornin' belong to another cute number. Seven-forty-seven."

Sally laughed. The laughter was a better reply than the words and numbers she had meant to throw at him. She knew he had twenty-five million dollars' worth of airplane and some hundreds of lives in his hands.

At this hour the freeway was free of traffic. Sally found the middle lane and ran the speedometer up to sixty—Neal's limit for her.

"Tennis this afternoon?" Neal asked.

"If it doesn't rain."

"Well, it won't rain on your bridge table. You four gals never get bored, do you?"

"Together or singly?"

"Tell me about together."

"We manage."

"And you, honey, you manage best, don't you? Tennis or bridge."

"You've forgotten," she said. "My game is gin."

"That damn rummy game. I see them playin' it when they should be

22

lookin' out the window and seein' what the birds who can't fly that high never see."

"Some of them are frightened," she said.

"Why? Because I'm not in the cockpit?"

"Because they're not on the ground."

Neal blew a perfect ring of smoke. "They don't understand the situation."

"Not all of us are eagles."

"Thank God, *you* understand."

"Do I?"

The smoke ring was gone. Neal looked askance at Sally. "I take back what I said for openers. All of a sudden you don't look good. I see a storm in those red eyes of yours. Didn't you get much sleep last night?"

"Not much."

He was puzzled. "I had nothin' to drink last night so I couldn't have been snorin'."

"You weren't."

"Then what the hell was troublin' you?"

"A sign," said Sally, happy for her opening.

"A sign of old age in me?"

"A real estate sign. It reads 'For Sale.' "

Neal glared at Sally, making her feel like Alice in Wonderland being confronted by the March Hare, wondering if she had meant what she said, and not understanding she had said what she meant. What she had to say.

She refused to desist. "Will you look at the house?"

"If it looks like you do right now, forget it."

"Don't you care that I'm troubled?"

"I love you, and lovin' is carin'. Now shut up and drive. And slow down. You've got it up to seventy."

Obeying, Sally sighed, glanced at the rear-view mirror, slid into the outside lane, and then made the soft turn onto the ramp leading into the southbound lanes of the San Diego Freeway.

The MG was climbing the Mulholland grade before Neal broke the silence between them. But not the tension.

"Damn you, tell me about it."

The tone was wrong, the time was not right, but Sally took her chances. "It's on Idaho Lane. The lowest priced house in the immediate area. And that's good because—"

"Skip the real estate lecture."

"It's on a half acre of ground. Very private. Sycamore trees, lots of roses, fruit trees—"

"Get to the house."

"Twenty-three hundred square feet. A seven-year-old architect-designed ranch house. Three bedrooms and a den. Beamed ceilings, three fireplaces—"

"How much?"

"Seventy-five thousand. That's the asking price."

"You didn't mention a pool."

"There isn't any."

"Why the hell don't you figure what that'll cost you in this inflation?"

"We can use the pool at the country club."

"You don't even use the damn tennis courts there anymore."

"Yes, but you and Hap play golf there."

"I can't skinny-dip in the club pool. Besides, it's too far to walk from the bedroom. Hell, yeah, and what's this about three bedrooms? What the hell do we need three for?"

"One for us, one for Hap, and one for the nursery."

The eagle eyes screamed at Sally. A claw grasped and crushed the still-burning cigar. Turning away, Neal lowered the window and threw the dark tobacco leaves and ash and fire to the winds. Then, raising the window but not his voice, he confronted Sally again.

"When did you find out?"

"About the house?"

"Fuck the house! I'm talkin' about your fuckin' pregnancy!"

Sally was anything but flustered. "I'm not pregnant. Not yet."

"Not ever," Neal vowed. "Not ever by me."

Sally made a tactical retreat. "Will you let me have the house I want?"

He glowered at her. "What the hell are you goin' to do with the extra bedroom?"

"I've changed my mind. Maybe one day soon you'll change yours."

"Not a chance," he said.

"The honeymoon's over," she told him.

"That's not news," Neal said. "That hasn't been news since you talked me into keepin' Hap with us."

"Was that my first sin?"

"I don't believe in sin. I believe in errors. And hell, yeah, that was your first error. Hap was doin' all right, and my sister Martha was doin' all right by him down in Shreveport."

"He's your son. Not your sister's."

"And not yours."

"Why not? He's part of you, and you're mine."

"What song is that from? I don't recall ever singin' that ditty for you."

Sally made her point. "By healing Hap I'd hoped to heal you."

"I'm as fit as a bull fiddle."

"Only from takeoff to landing," she said.

24

"Look, you Hoosier cheerleader, drive me to LAX. Don't ride me there."

"I'm sorry, Neal. I don't wish to upset you. I only want you to do some thinking about us."

"You picked a helluva time."

"I'm sorry. I had a bad night."

"Don't take it out on me now. The rules say I can't fire up my mind with booze for twenty-four hours before a flight. Don't fire it up with a fuckin' spat!"

Sally shut up. She glanced at the unleaning round tower of a hotel near the Sunset Boulevard off ramp before returning her eyes to the near-level stretch of freeway.

His voice still harsh, Neal hit her again. "Do me a favor, do us a favor. Don't bring it up again."

She drew him on. "What does *it* refer to? Us the living? Or them the dead?"

"You're askin' for it." He was seething now.

"Let it all out."

He banged a fist against the dashboard. "You bitch! We made a bargain!"

"I'm sorry, but I want out of the bargain."

"Divorce?"

"No. Marriage."

"And all that goes with it? Everythin' I had once and don't want to have again?"

"Yes, Neal."

He said nothing. Opening the glove compartment, he failed to find what he was looking for. "Try and keep a pack of those Dutch cigars in here for me."

"Consider it done."

"Look, we've had five years. Four of them have given me a second helpin' of marriage I didn't want and didn't need. No such thing as a honeymoon for three. So I think you owe me at least four more years of honeymoon."

"You won't get them from me," said Sally.

"You'd better get used to missin' Hap. He'll never be more than a visitor at home from here on in."

"I'm glad," she said. "Hap's my victory."

"Tell you what. When in Rome, I'll see the Pope about puttin' you up for sainthood. Let me tell you what *I* had to put up with these past fuckin' two years. All the times I had to listen to Hap callin' you *Mom.*"

The revelation chilled and sickened Sally. "Did I ask him to?"

"You didn't ask him not to."

"Did you?"

"Hell, yeah. Two or three times," Neal said.

Sally lowered her window. She was desperate for cold, fresh air to still the nausea rising within her. "And what did Hap say to you?"

"Nothin'. He just looked at me with that same wild look he had the first time I saw him at the hospital after that fuckin' turbojet crashed and burned."

"All three times you asked him?"

"Yeah."

She turned away from him and gasped for air. Eyes on the freeway again, she said, "Didn't you hate yourself each time?"

Neal was distraught now. "I'd hear him, look up from whatever I was doin', and wait to hear my wife's voice. To hear my daughters bickerin' upstairs. And then I'd hear nothin' and see nothin' but myself walkin' through that high school gym and lookin' for the three rubber sheets that held together the bones of my life. Then I'd hear Hap and you. And I hated both of you—and myself—for hatin' you."

Sally said and did nothing but try to blink the tears obscuring her view of the dark freeway and the off ramp to Aviation Boulevard.

The last miles were passed in silence. Once the airport, the hangars, and the planes came into view, Neal seemed to divorce himself and free himself from the earth, and from what was buried beneath it.

Sally stopped the car at the TWA terminal, left the engine running, and kept her eyes from Neal. He opened his door, transferred his baggage to the sidewalk, and came around to her side of the car.

"Look at me," he said quietly.

Sally did and saw his contrition.

"I'll tell you somethin' else. It's been about seven years now, but I still hate my wife for dyin' on me. For destroyin' me."

A taxi stopped at the curb. Two feminine TWA flight attendants alighted. They waved to Neal. He waved back. Smiled.

Still holding his thin smile, Neal bent down and faced Sally, who was not smiling. "Somethin' tells me I'm gonna sleep with the tall gal tonight. That's layin' it on the line, isn't it?"

The anguish came through to choke his otherwise strong drawl. He straightened up, took up his baggage, and never turned back. No smile. No wave. No goodbye. No kiss.

When she understood the design of Neal's leave-taking, Sally found the gear lever, the gas pedal, and the sense of driving away from the scene of a crash in which the bones of her dreams had been crushed.

Once she was northbound on the San Diego Freeway, she pushed the MG up to seventy. She was a girl in a hurry with no place to go.

Up there Neal had his track and his two timepieces, one on his left wrist set on Greenwich time, another on his right wrist set on Los Angeles time. "Stomach time."

She had but one wristwatch, one time, and no stomach for the upcoming day.

6 The advancing storm drove light rain through the chain fence. When it jumped the net, Joan Lawler scowled at the dark sky. "Shit!" To the others she said, "Let's finish the set."

There was no protest from Sally, or from their opponents, Ilona and Dolores.

They did manage to complete the game, a winning point for Joan and Sally, before the rain found its fury. Without a word, Dolores turned and led the running retreat to the shelter of her house. Ilona trailed, Sally followed, and a disgruntled Joan, shaking her tennis racket heavenward, brought up the rear with a defiant heel-and-toe gait.

On the portico of the Cooper house, when Sally said something about rushing back home and into a hot shower, Dolores invited her and the others to come inside. She had four bathrooms and dry clothes.

"I don't feel like bridge today," said Joan.

Dolores smiled. "I have something more interesting in mind."

"Ping-Pong or Parcheesi?" asked Joan with scorn.

"Sex," said Dolores.

Having heard enough, Joan entered. Ilona, who on any other day would have laughed out loud, was amused enough to follow Joan. The last to enter, Sally remained wary of what Dolores had in mind.

For a half hour the Cooper residence sounded like a sorority house on any rainy Monday afternoon. Once the four of them had showered and changed into robes belonging to Dolores and her daughter, they gathered in the breakfast room for coffee and Ilona's cookies. As the rain pounded the bay windows, they seemed to huddle closer together.

Dolores, Joan, and Ilona were candid about revealing their marital problems. Sally—for Hap's sake—insisted that hers was a real estate problem, a failure to convince her husband how desperately she wanted the house on Idaho Lane.

At last, Dolores began to draw them into her cabal. "You know, girls, I took great care in forming our tennis group."

"You're a social climber," said Joan.

Dolores continued. "You're all faithful, attractive, and there's not a divorce among you."

Joan frowned. "Is that what you're selling? Divorce!"

"I'm selling nothing," replied Dolores. "We're discussing sex—"

"I'll take my sex without discussion," said Joan.

"Good for you," said Dolores. "If you wanted a man this afternoon, where would you go?"

"To Dr. Perry Cooper," said Joan.

Ilona laughed. Sally listened to the rain.

Dolores smiled. "Our four husbands are out of bounds."

"Tough titty," said Joan. "Okay, I'll play by your rules. If I were hot for a man, I'd go to a certain swinging bar on Sherman Way."

"What sort of men?" asked Dolores.

"Animals at worst—or at best," said Joan. "Nobody for tennis or tea."

Dolores turned to Ilona. "Where would you go?"

"Back to Budapest."

"Without leaving the city limits," explained Dolores.

Ilona had to think about it. "I would go—all dressed up—to the art exhibits. There maybe I would meet a gentleman—"

"—interested in other gentlemen." Joan again.

Ilona smiled. "I would find one interested in me."

Dolores faced Sally. "And you?"

"I pass," said Sally.

"As you wish," said Dolores.

But Joan now confronted Sally. "What's with you? You probably know more about swinging and men than the three of us put together! Four years as a college cheerleader! Five years as an airline stewardess! Don't tell me you were a virgin when you got married!"

"I was no swinger," said Sally.

"What in hell were you?" demanded Joan.

Sally hesitated. "A lucky girl. I had some nice gentlemen friends."

Dolores again. "Where did you meet them?"

"At work. On a flight from here to New York."

"So much for that," said Dolores.

But Joan wished to know more. "Anybody special?"

"Both of them," said Sally.

"Who were they?"

"A Broadway producer and a songwriter," said Sally.

Joan persisted. "Did you sleep with both of them?"

Sally said, "I lived with the producer for three years. After he threw me out, I took up with the songwriter."

"Why were you thrown out?" asked Dolores.

"I made the mistake of telling the producer that the songwriter was the smartest man I'd ever met."

"You stupid, silly girl," said Joan.

"Yes," Sally agreed.

Joan now asked. "Why did the songwriter throw you over?"

"He went to work on a new musical comedy. And I met Neal."

Puzzled, Joan did not relent. "How could you go from the smartest man you'd ever met to an airline captain?"

Sally smiled weakly. "I guess I'm not the smartest girl around."

"Welcome to the club," said Joan absently.

At this point Dolores asserted her presence. "All right now, may I carry on?"

"Where? And with whom?" asked Joan.

"I'll get to that," said Dolores.

"Say it!" insisted Joan.

"The Ivy League."

Joan laughed at her. "You're mad!"

"Am I? Or is it that you're too blind to see the opportunity?"

"For sex?" asked Joan.

"Yes," said Dolores patiently. "Question. Where can be found the most attractive men? Men of standing and worth? Professional men, business men, men of talent? Where else but in the Ivy League?"

"Why not Scandia? Or the Polo Lounge?" asked Joan.

"We're not that well known there," said Dolores. "No, the Ivy League's best for us. We're regulars there. Roy Sutter knows us, we know him. Our presence, even in tennis dress, is nothing unusual. Wouldn't you all agree that we're attractive?"

"It's hardly a pickup joint," argued Joan.

"No," Sally agreed.

Ilona said. "Not for us. But it happens. I have seen it. It can be as Dolores says."

Dolores took a vote. "Who's interested?"

"Tell us more," said Joan. "I know you, Dolores, you have rules, you have reasons."

"Rules. Don't bring the men home. Don't be late for dinner. Don't invite trouble," said Dolores.

"Are you going to play housemother?" asked Joan.

"No," said Dolores. "We're each on our own. Need I say more?"

"You usually do," said Joan.

"I agree with you, Joan," said Dolores. "From now on I intend to talk less and do more. Much more."

"Are you old enough to do it without support from us?" asked Joan.

"I am," said Dolores.

Joan persisted. "But you'd like company?"

Dolores weighed the question. "One woman alone in a tennis dress —that wouldn't do at the Ivy League."

"Roy knows you," argued Joan.

"He knows I don't drink alone. He'd know I wasn't waiting for Perry. He'd suspect something."

Sally spoke up. "Does that concern you?"

30

"Yes," said Dolores. "Despite what Ilona says, the Ivy League's no swinging bar. I'd rather change nothing except my attitude."

"About what?" asked Joan.

"Extramarital sex," said Dolores.

Ilona had a question. "Are we to sit there like Hamburg prostitutes sit in their windows waiting for men?"

Dolores smiled at Ilona. "In our tennis dresses—or in any of our smart afternoon clothes—we should appear as nothing more than sexually liberated women. We're not about to sell ourselves for money, are we?"

Joan asked, "What price do we put on our souls?"

"That's between you and your conscience," said Dolores.

"You mean God?" asked Joan.

"That's up to you," said Dolores.

Joan did not desist. "You have no conscience?"

"I have something more," said Dolores. "A rage for freedom."

"You mean a rage for sex?" Joan asked.

"Yes," said Dolores.

Joan smiled. "You look and sound desperate."

"So I am," admitted Dolores. "I have to break out of the stupor I've been in these past three years. The new morality's opened my mind, my heart, and my will. I'm free. I'm available."

"And how wild?" asked Joan.

"I intend to find out." Dolores rose. "I believe our tennis dresses are dry now. Think about it. My party, my treat."

When Dolores was gone from the breakfast room, Joan broke the silence with a question put to Ilona. "How do you feel about it?"

Ilona shrugged. "Will she do it?"

"I doubt it," said Joan. "But I'd have to see it to believe it. I'm for tagging along." She turned to Sally. "How about you?"

Sally said. "Let me understand you, Joan. You'd rather take us to a swinging bar, wouldn't you?"

"Just an idea," said Joan. "I'll go alone, but I won't end up alone."

"You expect nothing to happen at the Ivy League?" asked Sally.

Joan smiled. "It's as safe as church. Especially with *our* leader."

Ilona laughed. She believed Joan. Sally did not. She did not trust any of them, herself, or the rage of the rain against the bay windows.

7

One-thirty P.M.

As Roy Sutter walked from the locker room of the South Oaks Country Club to the parking lot, he sensed that the rain was as heavy as the time on his hands. He had no idea how to kill the remainder of the day without chancing the forbidden.

He got into his white Cadillac coupé and drove off thinking back to the morning whose promise had drowned in the rain.

The flashing light cut the dark four times before it pierced Sutter's sleep. The clock said 5:58 A.M. His mind cried fire. At the Ivy League. His left hand brought the telephone to an ear.

"Hello." He heard alarm in his own voice.

"Roy?" A bitter, unfunny voice belonging to Hershey Barnes, calling from Las Vegas.

"Yeah, Hershey."

"Get your ass over here by noon."

"Can't. Got to be at the doctor's office at eight. My yearly checkup. Do it every year on my birthday."

"A lovely way to celebrate your forty-sixth birthday, letting the doctor give you a pain in the ass."

"It's Christie's law."

"Christie's dead," Barnes retorted. "No show, no cake."

"A giant cake," guessed Sutter. "And out of it pops a squealing naked broad."

"No, it's not that kind of a cake. Listen, this is new, fresh. The cake is stuffed inside a naked broad. You get me? Inside her pussy."

Sutter broke up with laughter, and it was not until some minutes after eight o'clock that he surrendered his lingering smile.

The pain was sharp, the terror dull. The windowless walls closed in on Sutter. The examination couch, which he held on to with his trembling hands, seemed to be rising off the cold floor until Perry Cooper withdrew his rubbered finger.

"Well, Roy, you won't die of cancer of the prostate."

Sutter wanted to suggest that Cooper use a sand wedge next time. But he remembered that the good doctor had in recent years relinquished his practice of laughter. He grinned and said, "Thanks."

32

Cooper now handed a small glass slide to him. "A smear, please."

Sutter obeyed, staining the slide and returning it.

"You can pull up your shorts now," said Cooper. "The girls'll do the rest."

"At least they're gentle with me."

Cooper glanced at his wristwatch. "They'll be in in ten minutes."

"You rushing off to the hospital now?"

"No, I'll sit and smoke a pipe with you while you get dressed," said Cooper. "How's your memory, Roy? Can you tell me all the times I've been at your place in the past three years?"

Sutter was quick with recall. "One night late with Dolores. One night with the whole family when Linda was accepted at Stanford. Another night when Larry was accepted at Cornell. That's about it. Sure, I see Dolores and her tennis friends every now and then at lunch time."

"I don't eat lunch out. One of the girls brings back something."

"Where do you go for dinner?"

The question saddened Cooper. "A place I like better than yours."

"Scandia?"

"Leo's."

Sutter grinned at the mention of a coffee shop on Ventura Boulevard.

"There's a particular booth in the back," said Cooper, "and in it I find a particular ghost."

"How particular?"

"It's mine."

"One of your ex-nurses?"

"No."

"A patient you lost?"

Cooper blew smoke before he spoke again, and his words and his mood were bluer than the smoke. "A love I lost."

Sutter was incredulous. "No."

"You don't believe me."

"I thought I knew you, Doc."

"Nobody knew me. Not till Valerie came along."

"The ghost?"

Cooper nodded. "Met her at the hospital. A medical transcriber."

"What's that?"

"A person trained to listen to doctors' tapes and type out all those medical reports for the hospital records, the insurance companies, and Medicare. One day I went to question her about the use of a word. 'Gymnophobia.' I seemed to have remembered dictating the word 'nudophobia.' She was right. I'd used the wrong word. But she had a face, smile, and a voice I couldn't put out of my mind. About a week later I asked her to have a cup of coffee with me. That's how it began."

"And how did it end?"

"I was like a kid again. Like I was with Dolores before either of us was sixteen. Well, not quite. Dolores and I used to pet to climax till we went off to college together. The first time we went all the way I got her pregnant. But, getting back to Valerie, I took her to bed. Not in any sordid motel, but in her apartment, with her books and music, and a warmth and a feeling for things and life that I thought was long gone. Do you understand what she meant to me?"

"No," Sutter said frankly.

"What are you thinking?"

"About Dolores and Linda and Larry, and about how much I envied you."

"Before or after your wife died?"

"Before."

Cooper shook his head with bewilderment. "You were married to one of the most beautiful women in the world. I'll tell you something else, Roy. There was something about Valerie that reminded me of your Christie. And I'm not referring to physical beauty. Valerie didn't come up to her, and Dolores doesn't come up to her, even with her new face and figure. It's just an effect—I can't think of a better word—a feeling that you're in the presence of—of soft femininity. Am I coming through to you?"

"No. What's wrong with Dolores?"

"She went to the wrong surgeon. I wasn't consulted. I would've sent her to a man who knows how to cut the balls out of a woman like Dolores."

"Would you cut the balls out of your daughter?"

"Who said Linda has them?" asked Cooper.

"I wish Christie had them."

"Roy, is there a profundity in you I've missed?"

"The word is horse sense. Now, don't get me wrong, I'm not pushing for unisex or anything like that. But a little bit of balls—not too much —is what every girl and every woman living in California in 1973 had better have if she wants to make it."

"Tell me more," Cooper urged.

"Only what I know. Christie failed as an actress because she had no balls. She failed me as a wife for the same reason. Balls give you guts. Drive. Balls get you off the floor when you're down and out. Balls get you pregnant, balls get you babies and get you up in the middle of the night to take care of 'em."

"You weren't happy with Christie." Cooper was shaken.

"Yes and no. We could've had more."

"Did you play around?"

"No."

"Do you play around now?"

"In Vegas. Hershey Barnes fixes me up."

"What about here?"

"I'm married to my restaurant."

"Is it enough?"

"Enough, pleasure and trouble."

Cooper blew more pipe smoke. "I do understand your thinking about women and balls, but I don't believe I made myself very clear."

"I interrupted you to make a speech," said Sutter.

"No, you made sense. Now let me see if I can do the same. Do you remember Dolores's father?"

"How could I forget him? My severest critic and Scandia's drumbeater."

"Think back a few minutes ago. Think of me in the position you were, and think of my father-in-law with his finger up my rectum from 1945 till the time he died in 1971. Got that picture?"

"Don't remind me."

"Now get this one. And forgive me for being crude. Dolores rubbing up against me, rubbing me the wrong way, and giving me a sick feeling that her Daddy's balls are beating the hell out of my own. Clear enough?"

"Sure is," Sutter said.

"From the time I was eighteen, that man had me in bondage. Of course, without him I never would've been a doctor. But I might have been a man. I was such a man with Valerie."

"What happened?"

Cooper's smile was sick. "This might hurt you more than my finger. But the truth is Valerie's balls destroyed me. Her career came between us. Show business. New York. Television. Story editor."

"Does Dolores know?"

"You'll forgive me, but I used your place to tell her."

"That's what it's for," said Sutter. "Infighting. Plotting. Scheming. Cheating. Murder. You name it."

The wall telephone lit up. Cooper took the call and responded to the urgency of the caller. When he turned to Sutter again, he said, "Got to rush to the hospital. We've got to talk some more. I'll come in some night for a steak sandwich. And more of your insight about women and balls."

"Do that," said Sutter.

Cooper opened the door and held it open. "About Valerie. I just want to say this now. I made a fool of myself over a girl sweeter than my life. It was beautiful while it lasted. The most human thing I ever did."

For almost another hour Sutter underwent the series of tests administered to him by both of Cooper's nurses. In all of that time he forgot to indulge in his usual kidding around with the girls, his form of grave-

35

yard whistling. For he was unable to forget Cooper's eyes, voice, and last words, and he was given to wondering about the sweetness and folly gone from his own life.

Christie was dead. The house that for so long had almost been a home was now Christie's mausoleum and his own cold grave. The restaurant, alive and well, was not quite the same without those occasional afternoons when Christie waltzed in wearing one of her I. Magnin tennis dresses and tearing out the eyes of the beholders of her grace and beauty.

The morning air was cold as Sutter went to the South Oaks Country Club. When he drove off the first tee, he was feeling good.

Have a nice day, Roy, he told himself. Have a nice birthday. You're in a good foursome today. Nice guys, pretty fair golfers. No son of a bitch like Neal Hendley.

His Cadillac, moving like a milkman's horse, found an eastbound lane on Ventura Boulevard. Finally, still haunted by Perry Cooper's last observation, he decided this was the year to break the second of Christie's laws: forbidding him, on his birthday, to enter the Ivy League.

That seemed more rational than Hershey Barnes's last suggestion to him: "Suck both barrels of your Winchester and jerk both triggers."

8

By way of the back door, Sutter came in out of the rain. Stealing glances into the dining room and cocktail lounge, he shivered when, in the soft light, he saw the ghost of his wife rising abruptly from a table near the blazing fireplace.

A second glance revealed it was none other than Sally Hendley. A drink had been spilled and she had risen to escape wetting her tennis dress. He watched her sit down before he identified her three similarly clad companions. Suppressing an urge to go over and greet them, he turned away. He had taken three steps in the direction of the stairway leading to his upstairs office when he was accosted by the good face and warm smile belonging to Police Lieutenant Vincent Fonte.

"Happy birthday, Roy."

They shook hands. "Hello, Vince."

"I'll buy you a beer," said Fonte.

"Sure, at Ziggy's."

"Here," insisted Fonte.

"Against the law today."

"I'm the law." Fonte put a strong arm on Sutter and led him to the bar. Getting head bartender Rick Kelley's evil eye, he said, "Draw two, Rick."

Kelley said and did nothing.

Sutter repeated Fonte's argument. "He's the law."

Kelley moved. Setting the beers down, he stared at Sutter. "Drown." Turning to Fonte, he found mock venom. "Choke, you dago pig."

Fonte gave Kelley his winning smile. The latter blew him a kiss and went about his business.

"Listen," said Sutter to Fonte. "I got to tell you what Hershey Barnes had in mind for my birthday."

Smiling, Fonte listened.

Dolores Cooper, who was seated facing the long bar, was so interested in the dark handsome man with Roy Sutter that she played deaf to Joan Lawler's taunt to wake up and tell the waiter whether or not she wished another martini. Seeing Fonte rock with laughter, she asked the waiter to take a message to Mr. Sutter; she would like a word with him. And, yes, she'd have another.

Sally Hendley, who was having J & B on the rocks, confronted

37

Dolores with her concern. "What do you have in mind?"

"Something Italian."

"What?" asked Ilona Belanger, thinking of food.

"Who?" asked Joan, who knew better.

"We'll soon know, I hope," said Dolores. Her smile faded as she saw Fonte leaving, but it bloomed again when the waiter whispered to Sutter. He nodded and came toward her.

Sutter's eyes went first to Dolores and then around the table. Proper smile, respectable greetings. Mrs. Cooper, Mrs. Lawler, Mrs. Hendley, Mrs. Belanger. Comments about the rain. Tennis. Golf.

At last Dolores asked, "Who was the gentleman with the good smile and the fresh laughter? Is he an actor I should recognize?"

"No, he isn't," said Sutter. "His name's Vincent Fonte. And I hope you never meet him."

"Mafia," Joan guessed.

Sutter turned to her. "Police. Robbery–Homicide, Van Nuys Division."

"Well," said Dolores, "it's so very nice to see a detective laughing. How did you do it, Roy?"

"Easy," said Sutter, smiling. "I told him a funny story."

"Please, tell us," said Dolores.

"Happens to be—I guess you'd call it a locker room story," he said, trusting that would be the end of it.

"You lead the way," said Joan.

Sutter was confused. "I beg your pardon."

"To the nearest locker room," Joan explained.

Sutter smiled. "I think that day isn't far off, the way you girls are stirring up things these—"

Dolores broke in. "Clean it up a bit, but tell us. Please."

"That's an order," said Joan. "Or we'll take up picket signs outside."

Ilona was warmer. "Sit down and have a drink with us."

"I'll take a raincheck on that," Sutter said.

Joan again. "All right, but we won't take one on the dirty story."

Sutter turned to Sally. He saw that she was not Christie, not amused, not comfortable. "Mrs. Hendley, you don't want to hear it, do you?"

"I trust you," Sally said.

This was enough for him, and he made the attempt. "A friend of mine called me early this morning to tell me he had a birthday offering for me. Not a girl inside a cake, but vice versa." He waved. "Good-bye, girls." He turned and left the four of them unlaughing and perplexed.

"It's a riddle," said Dolores.

It was to her, to Joan, and to Ilona. Not to Sally and her Broadway education. She veiled her smile and said nothing.

Suddenly Joan laughed.

Unlike Dolores, Ilona voiced her bewilderment. "Please, Joan, in English."

"The cake is stuffed inside the girl's pussy!"

Ilona laughed harder than Dolores and Joan. Sally unveiled her smile. The laughter had died when the waiter returned with the second round of drinks.

Joan spoke up. "What kind of cake do you have today?"

As the waiter served the drinks, he said, "Strawberry cheesecake, pineapple cheesecake, chocolate rum cake."

"The rum cake, please," said Joan.

"Two, please," said Ilona.

"Mine's for stuffing," said Joan.

Ilona laughed. Dolores and Sally frowned. For different reasons.

"We'll draw straws," said Dolores. She turned to Sally for support.

"No," said Sally.

"Why not?" demanded Joan.

"Be smart," said Sally. "Think."

"It's time for acting," said Dolores.

"Wisely," said Sally.

"It'd be a nice birthday present for Roy," said Dolores.

"True," said Sally. "And he deserves the best."

"So?" asked Joan.

"Ask yourself," said Sally, "who Roy favors."

Dolores said, "I've known him longer than any of you."

"You're the oldest among us," said Joan.

The taunt shut up Dolores.

Ilona faced Sally. "You surprise me. I did not think you were in favor of all this."

Sally hesitated. "Roy's no stranger. We belong to the same club. He likes me. I like him."

"Good enough," said Joan. "Besides, you're the youngest. You're the *virgin* to sacrifice today." She ended with laughter.

Ilona laughed. Dolores did not. She was miffed by the ease with which Sally had challenged her leadership. Moreover, she was not as sure about Sally as she was of Ilona and Joan. She was thinking that perhaps Sally had nothing more in mind than betraying them to Sutter. This suspicion was somewhat allayed when she saw Sally seemingly drink courage from her glass.

"Need another before you go?" Dolores asked Sally.

Sally smiled. "I'm all right."

"Excited?" asked Joan.

"I'm hardly a virgin," said Sally.

"I'd be," said Joan. "Nothing like this has ever happened to me before. Am I understood?"

Sally and Dolores understood her.

Ilona did not. "I do not understand."

"It's like Barbra Streisand sings, people eat people," said Joan.

"Like Bobby's movies!" Ilona exclaimed.

Joan would not quit. "Not like you and Bobby?"

Unabashed, Ilona replied. "Not with cake." She laughed.

Now Dolores turned on Joan. "Not like you and Frank?"

"No, I'm sorry to say," said Joan. "But I'll get mine."

The waiter appeared with two forks, and two plates of chocolate rum cake. Ilona wasted no time picking up her fork and indulging herself. Sally took her plate and rose. Deftly Dolores reached up and removed the fork.

"You won't need this," she said.

"Smile," said Joan. "You're not going to the dentist."

Sally smiled and went on her way.

Dolores sensed the pleasure, vicarious though it was. She drank to the beginning of the masked ball. Her turn, her man would come along. Soon.

While Ilona kept stuffing cake into her mouth, Joan poured a jigger of whiskey into her beer glass. As she drank, she let her eyes roam the cocktail lounge until she met the stare of a man whose chiseled face and stone eyes seemed to grow larger and larger until they had filled a motion picture screen.

Cake in hand, Sally climbed the stairway. She stopped to catch her breath before she rapped gently on the door to Sutter's private office.

"The door's open," she heard Sutter call.

Sally turned the knob and entered to find Sutter sitting at his rolltop desk, reading a letter. She read the warmth and coziness of the office: the rain-wet window looking south to the hills, the redwood walls with the framed photographs and sports pages with Sutter's younger faces and faded fames, the red carpet, the black matching desk chair, barrel chair, and couch.

Turning his head, Sutter again saw Christie before he was stunned by the reality of the girl in the tennis dress bearing cake.

"Hi," he said. "Excuse me, I thought it was Jasper."

She recognized the name of the old black headwaiter. "Are you expecting him?"

"No, but Jasper has a gentle knock. Kelley kicks the door in. He— what's the cake for?"

Sally smiled, held out her offering with both hands, and said, "Happy birthday from all the girls."

Rising, Sutter looked at her with boys' eyes, and took the plate from her. "Thanks, and thank them all for me."

"Can I stay a minute?"

"Longer. Try the barrel chair."

She sat down. He set the cake down on the highest level of the desk, reached for his Camels, and held out the pack to her. She smiled and shook her head. He lit his cigarette before he returned to his desk, sat down, and faced her.

"Forgetting about the cake?" Sally said.

"You forgot the fork."

"I think you forgot the story—"

"The story!" He tore through his bewilderment to find the right laughter, the proper laughter. "Very funny. You girls have a great sense of humor. I like that."

Sally let her words come as cleanly as the rain against the roof and window. "It wasn't my idea, and it wasn't meant to be funny."

"I don't believe it," Sutter said.

"Think about it."

"In what light?"

"Women's lib," said Sally, finding a calm that came with Sutter's ease of manner. "The sexual revolution."

"Not you," he said.

"How would you explain the cake?" asked Sally.

He drew heavily upon his cigarette. The smoke streamed from his nostrils and through it came his explanation. "One of the girls took the story seriously."

"Three."

He shook his head. "Mrs. Cooper?"

"Shocked?"

"No, I sensed something was wrong at their house, but I didn't find out what until this morning."

"That's when we girls found out," Sally said.

"Helluva story, isn't it?"

"It's getting worse," said Sally. "Witness the cake. And me."

"Yeah," he said with understanding. "Only I'd be lying if I didn't tell you how glad I am—right now."

Smiling, she said, "Shall I lock the door?"

Sutter shook his head. "No, I'm thinking of opening another door."

Sally's smile widened. "I like you. I don't know what you mean by *another door,* but I definitely like you."

"That's sweeter than the cake," he said, smiling. "And that makes three gifts you've given me today."

"Three?"

A sad, bittersweet nod. "The other two times, at first glance, I saw you and thought I was seeing my wife come back from the dead."

"The tennis dress."

"Right."

"But there are four of us."

He shook his head. *"One* of you."

"Now you're flattering me."

"Wrong," he said.

"Christie was one of the most beautiful girls in the world."

"What world?" he asked.

"Magazine covers. Movies. Those TV commercials."

"That's the other world," he said. "Christie's world. The one she lost. The only one she belonged in."

Sally doubted him. "How about the world she made with you?"

Sutter said, "I gave her nothing but a hiding place."

"Yes, but a beautiful one."

"The house?"

"And yourself," she said.

"It wasn't that way at all."

"Didn't Christie love you, and didn't you love her?"

Sutter hesitated. "It's hard to explain."

"Try, please," Sally urged him.

"We didn't make the most of the twelve years we had together."

"Why not?"

"It was just the way we were," he said. "Look at it this way: Christie was dead when the cameras and the lights weren't on her. And there wasn't much I could do about that. My love? The house? I guess they were small comforts. Never enough to make her happy."

Sally asked, "Why didn't you have children?"

Trying to make light of it, Sutter smiled and said, "Christie was always expecting."

"But what? Miscarriages?"

"No, never that. It's a bad joke. Yeah, Christie was expecting the telephone to ring to take her back to the lights and cameras." Sutter's voice died away.

"Did you ever talk about having children?" Sally asked.

"Before or after we were married?"

"At any time."

"After."

Sally prodded him. "And what did Christie say?"

He conjured the key phrases. "Not now. Tomorrow. Next year. And, in between, there were those parts she was up for at Warner's and Fox. Yeah, she was up, she was down. I finally gave up. I just had to admit to myself it was no damn use. No sense troubling her—making her feel guilty."

"Did you stop loving her?" asked Sally.

"No," he said. "I tried harder. With both of my total commitments."

"I don't understand," said Sally.

Sutter smiled at her. "You in a hurry?"

Sally returned his smile. "Remember? I go with the birthday cake."

He laughed. "I won't forget." He blew smoke and found again his blue mood. "I wasn't smart enough to make the most of the first real chance I had to make something of my life. I came to the pro tour with a smooth swing and a lot of cockiness. But I didn't know about total commitments. Guys like Hogan and Snead did. That's why I never really made it. Sure, it was fun, and I had a ball, but when I should've been concentrating on my game, I was fooling with country club women. Any town, any time, any place. And then, one day I was out of it. My game soured, my backer soured on me. You follow me—Sally?"

"Yes, Roy," said Sally. "Go on."

"The Ivy League was my second chance, probably my last. And I made a total commitment to it. I made a go of it, and it was going strong when I felt confident enough to take on my second total commitment: my marriage to Christie."

Uneasy, Sally rose from her chair. "I'd better go."

"And do what?"

"Get the girls out of here," said Sally. "Before they wreck the only total commitment you have left."

Sutter did not share her concern. He smiled. "Sit down, please."

"Restaurants can be ruined, can't they?" she demanded.

"Happens every day. It's that kind of business. But I can't believe your friends—and mine, in a way—can do me in."

"I don't trust them," she said. "They're in a rage. Doesn't it mean anything to you that my friends were of a mind to come up here and seduce you?"

Sutter did not buy it. "I told a joke, I asked for it. I'm sure they were joking."

"I think not," said Sally. "And I think I'd better go down and—"

"Sally, they're not hookers," Sutter insisted. "If they were, they wouldn't be here. We look out for that sort of thing. Me, my staff. We know what's going on. We can handle it, believe me. Please, don't go."

Relenting, Sally sat down again. "A few more minutes."

Sutter asked, "How long has this been going on? This *rage*."

"It began today."

"For you also?"

"No," said Sally. "I came along to check the rage. Which is why I'm up here with you."

He was intrigued. "How did you manage it?"

Sally balked for a moment. "I said you've long had an eye for me."

"It's the truth," he said. "It was true even before Christie died."

Sally looked askance at Sutter. "While she was dying?"

Sutter shook his head. "Before the tests, before we knew. Can I explain?"

"Please."

"It goes back to the first time I saw you at the club," Sutter remembered. "You were on the tennis court."

"And I reminded you of Christie," Sally concluded.

"Did *you* ever see Christie on a tennis court?"

"No," she admitted.

"Nobody ever did," he said. "She wouldn't play. She couldn't. As beautiful as she was, she had no coordination, no muscle, no tomboy in her. If she couldn't do anything gracefully; she wouldn't dare do it. Sure, she had a closet full of tennis clothes and rackets, and she'd give the appearance—that's the secret word for Christie—*appearance*. At her best she was never more than an appearance of reality. Of life. And that's the pity of it all."

Sally sensed he had more to say.

"Am I getting through to you? Can you understand how I felt when I first saw you? I said to myself, there's Christie, there's what she should be and isn't: alive and stirring, swinging and sweating, beautiful, graceful, dancing around the court, eyes afire. Yeah, you were beautiful, and I wanted you."

Sally tried to catch the sound of the rain and let it lead her back to reality.

Sutter went on. "And then, that day, I did something I hadn't done for a helluva long time. I said to nobody but myself, but actually to you: I love you."

Sally made an effort to smile. "When was the first time you said that —before that day?"

"Dallas," he said. "1950. I was coming up the fairway toward the green and I saw this brunette standing behind the green." He laughed. "I three-putted the green. Failed to make the cut by one stroke."

Sally joined in the laughter that gave her easy release from her tension. "Have you done it since *that day?*"

"Three-putted?"

More laughter. "No, said 'I love you' to a pretty face."

"No," he said, beholding her with love.

Sally turned to face the window. "I wish it hadn't rained."

Eyes upon her, he said, "It's a beautiful day."

"Yes," Sally agreed. "And this is the best moment of it."

"Where do we go from here?" Sutter asked.

"I believe I'd better go downstairs," said Sally, smiling.

"Don't. Not just yet."

"I am worried about the girls."

"Not about me?"

Sally shook her head.

"They're big girls," he said. "So are you."

"Yes, but I don't like the game they want to play."

Sutter smiled. "I'm glad. Can I suggest another for you?"

"For me alone?" asked Sally, sensing his line of thought.

"For us," he said uneasily.

"What is it?"

"A more dangerous game than the one your friends have in mind," he said.

She shivered, and not from the cold. It was more like excitement, like fear. "Is there anything more dangerous than becoming involved with strange men?"

Sutter nodded. "Sure there is. All you got to do is get yourself mixed up in a triangle. You, me, and Neal. That's trouble."

When she shivered again, Sally rose and retreated to the window. She observed the rain for a long moment before she faced Sutter again. "You confuse me. Are you warning me? Or are you inviting trouble?"

"Both, I guess," he said solemnly. "If you play the game, you have to go into it with your eyes open."

"Tell me more about it," she said. "Are there other rules I should be aware of?"

"Yeah, several. I'll be playing for keeps. To win you away from Neal."

Sally took note of his determination. "I know what I may win, but what can Neal possibly win?"

Sutter said, "He might win you back."

"He already has me," she contended.

"Has he still got your love?"

"Why do you believe he hasn't?"

"If he had," said Sutter, "you'd never have come here with the girls. And you'd never have come upstairs with the cake."

"You're wrong," she said.

"Do you love Neal—now?"

"No."

"You're unhappy, aren't you?"

"Yes, but I had no games in mind. Not Dolores's, not yours."

Sutter smiled again. "I believe you. And I wish you'd believe me. I have more than a game in mind for you and me. Things like life, happiness, marriage, home, kids."

"And love?" asked Sally.

"It's there. Just open your eyes."

She did, and she saw. And then she lowered her head and shut her eyes.

Sutter turned away from her. On a slip of paper he wrote down his unlisted home telephone number. Rising, he came to Sally.

She opened her eyes in time to accept the slip. She studied it for a while before shredding it.

He thought he understood, and he accepted her decision. "You're right. It's too dangerous."

Sally demonstrated to Sutter that he was wrong. She rattled off the seven numbers she had committed to memory.

And there was no need for further words. There were only looks of pain and pleasure, happiness and unhappiness, right and wrong, dream and danger.

He took her hands and squeezed them. She freed them to walk to the desk, finger some crumbs of cake and bring them to his lips. He drew them into his mouth before he drew her into his arms and kissed her.

Going down the steps, Sally was deaf to the restaurant's din, and blind to everything but her alternating visions of Roy and Neal, of love and hate.

It took Dolores's voice to return her to the less dangerous game. "Ah, Sally, so lost, so quiet, and so ringing with ecstasy."

Seated, Sally looked blankly at Dolores and at Ilona. The blankness gave way to bewilderment when she saw that Joan's chair was vacant. "Where's Joan?"

Ilona laughed.

Dolores confronted Sally. "Am I wrong about you?"

"Yes," said Sally forlornly.

"No ecstasy?" Dolores was crestfallen.

"Nothing but a few laughs," Sally lied.

Still laughing, Ilona asked, "Did he like the cake?"

"Nothing happened," said Sally. "No sex." It was no lie.

"Oh, no," moaned Ilona.

Dolores again. "Did Roy understand what you—?"

"Yes," said Sally.

"Did we misunderstand the riddle?" Dolores asked.

"No," said Sally.

Dolores sighed. She was contrite now. "I was foolish, Joan was foolish."

Ilona begged to differ. "No, not Joan. She is quick. She is smart."

Sally faced Ilona. "Where *is* Joan?"

Ilona said, "Joan has done it! She smiled at a handsome man. He smiled back and he came over to the table. And then she left with him —just like that! Just like Budapest!"

Dolores frowned as she turned to Sally. "A real estate agent. He's showing her a house."

Ilona laughed. "A castle in Spain!"

Dolores said, "I was wrong."

"Very handsome," said Ilona. "Almost as tall as Neal."

"His eyes were dead," said Dolores. "I don't like it. I wouldn't have gone with him."

"I would have," said Ilona.

"Roark Bennett," said Dolores. "Doesn't sound like a real name. I don't like it. Shall we go?"

They went, Ilona smiling and dreaming of being in Joan's place, Sally remembering seven numbers she could not forget, and Dolores troubling her conscience with forebodings about Joan and the man with the dead eyes.

9

The man with the dead eyes held the wheel of an Impala sedan moving westward on Ventura Boulevard. Beside him sat Joan Lawler, her eyes on the windshield wipers fencing the rain and fanning mystery and fantasy.

Failing to find the frames of motion picture film buried in her memory, she turned to the man himself. The porkpie hat and trenchcoat seemed to suggest a foreign correspondent or a secret agent in an Alfred Hitchcock film. Not a star like Humphrey Bogart or Richard Burton. Just a character actor in a supporting role, a killer who appears to menace Bogie, only to be shot out of the movie, out of her memory.

Or, perhaps, he was a killer in real life, a sex fiend now luring her to a deserted place where he would rape and strangle her, leaving her blood screaming in headlines: CATHOLIC SCHOOLGIRL RAPED AND SLAIN! *Little Joan Clarke, a skinny Philadelphia girl, honor student at Sacred Heart, was today discovered brutally slain in an abandoned castle in Spain.*

Joan tried laughter and failed. She tried a smile. It also failed. When she tried her eyes, she saw the gooseflesh on her bare legs, down to the white socks and tennis shoes, and up to the white dress, and underneath to the white panties.

The day was cold, the car was cold, the eyes of Roark Bennett were cold. And the tennis sweater brought no warmth to her. Only the name of the stranger beside her warmed her, until she found herself writing "Roark Bennett" on a blank wall of a room in the castle in Spain. In her own blood.

The car was slowing down, easing into the right lane, turning into a driveway, into the parking lot of a liquor store. Stop. Into "park" went the lever. Engine running, wipers working, the quiet man never once glanced at Joan as he left the car and stepped into a store without class. A stucco shanty. The right place for the wrong kind of things. Cheap beer and whiskey, girlie magazines, and maybe condoms. Was the son of a bitch on his ass? Was this the one place in the valley where his credit was good? Gentle Mary, they had passed a dozen liquor stores, the kind that had wine cellars and looked so much like castles in San Fernando Valley if not in Spain.

Escape.

The word struck her and took her right hand to the cold metal of the door handle. She could get out and run away with the rain. Better yet, she could slide over, shove it in reverse, and stick the son of a bitch with a car stolen for a half hour. She would leave two dollars on the seat. Thank you, Mr. Hertz and Mr. Avis. And I'll thank you, Mr. Bennett, not to rent my garments.

But only her eyes moved. They saw the pot-bellied man behind the counter slip a six-pack of beer and a pint of something harder into a paper sack. The quiet man made no move for his wallet or money clip. Taking the sack in hand, he returned to the car. Into gear, onto the boulevard, westward, ever westward. And not a word, not a look.

The little girl who wasn't there made a noise at last, her fingers rattling the paper sack. The quiet man heard nothing but the voices in his hard head.

"Kind sir?" Her voice was there. Almost.

He only had eyes for the traffic.

"May I please take a peek at the goodies?"

He nodded. She waited for his severed head to drop into the basket. When it did not, she went into the sack. A pint of Old Overholt rye whiskey. A six-pack of Budweiser.

"Boilermakers! Thank you, Mr. Overholt."

Another nod, another empty basket.

"Shall I be on the lookout for the land birds?"

Not so much as a nod.

"Shouldn't we be off the coast of Spain by now?"

No laugh, no smile, no reaction. And so another comedienne fell dead.

Into the bag once more, dear friend, dear little, nasty little pain in the ass to all the sisters at Sacred Heart. Strong fingers, the strength was in the stress of the moment, and the thirst of it. Up came one chilled can of beer. Sticking her forefinger through the ring, she did with ease what usually was so difficult for her.

Happy with herself again, she now saw the quiet man as a box of Cracker Jack. Somewhere inside his boxed-up heart there must be a hidden prize. A secret smile.

She drank to it. One good swig, followed by one better idea. Into the bag again and out with the whiskey. She ran a long fingernail around the tax stamp, twisted the cork, and had no need to twist her own arm as she poured rye into the beer can's open vagina. Presto, a boilermaker.

Eureka, a left turn off of Ventura Boulevard. Good, wonderful, excellent. She wouldn't want her ravaged body found north of Ventura Boulevard. The drink was good. So good, she thought as her mind's eye read tomorrow's newspaper: *The fiend, according to the coroner, had*

*obviously forced whiskey and beer down the child's burning throat,
possibly rendering her unconscious and unaware of the sexual horrors
he practiced upon her. The girl's brain, according to the coroner, was
the size of a pea.*

Or was it a pee? Gentle Mary, the next time she was abducted she
hoped it would be done by a nice man in a camper with a john under
the same roof.

"No yonder yet?" she asked aloud. Having to answer herself, she said,
"Yonder lies the castle of my fair lady. Or are you taking me up into the
hills, Nature Boy?"

There was an edge to her voice. For all the quiet man cared, he could
have been listening to a hemorrhoid commercial on the car radio.
That's the way it looked to Joan, until she saw both of his hands and all
ten of his fingers grip the steering wheel. The narrow, two-lane mac-
adam road was a running brook, running downhill toward Ventura
Boulevard, or Ventura Lake, where engines would stall and die, as
traffic stood by and snarled.

But, look now, a turn, off the brooky road, through an open narrow
gate, and onto a narrow driveway flanked by tall pines. Beyond it came
an open expanse of lawn and hedges and bushes, and, at last, the house.

Castle in Spain, hell! It was a deserted English Tudor mansion. This
is where she was going to die; this is where her body would be found
by the police. No, not the police, they enter later. First comes the
caretaker, cast with care by Alfred Hitchcock. An old, odd character
who goes around with his old cock smelling like a good red herring. Ah,
lovely. Drink up, Joanie. Here comes Roark Bennett.

What a name! The son of a bitch *must* be an actor. Nobody's born with
a name like that. Agents and lawyers make them up for their clients.
Didn't Frank—? Oh, the hell with him. Who the hell wants to remember him now. Here.

The engine was killed; the wipers played dead. The quiet man came
alive, taking up the burden of the sack, taking leave of his storm-tossed
vessel, and coming around to the starboard side to assist Mary Queen
of Scots into the White Castle, and not for a hamburger, either.

"Thank you, m'lord," said Lady Joan, a little unsteady on her feet, as
she ran from the last rain she would ever feel this side of purgatory.

In Lord Smilin' Jack's face she saw the look of the lord of the manor
as he used two keys to open two locks and one imposing door. She heard
no creaking of rusty hinges, but, as she stepped inside to draped darkness, she felt the chill of death. She would die in this tomb. Happy.
Drunk. And screaming for more heat from the sinister lord's loins.

When the quiet man hit a switch and lit up a series of lamps, she
danced from the foyer into the spacious living room, bare of furniture
and other dancers. As she whirled about, the room spun and she under-

50

stood just how drunk she was.

"Make a fire, my good man," she commanded.

The quiet man made no move, no sound.

"No wood? No coal? Burn the furniture!" She laughed and skipped to the staircase. She climbed the impressive staircase to the dark of the upstairs corridor. Looking right and left to more darkness, she went left, stopping to open doors to darkened, empty bedrooms.

At last she opened a door and saw daylight, rain, a disheveled double bed, an easy chair, a lamp, a table laden with books, magazines, and newspapers, and two cold electric heaters. When she moved inside the room, she heard the door being shut behind her.

Joan spun about in time to watch the grim man set down his sack before switching on both heaters.

"Do you live here?"

He nodded as he shed his wet trenchcoat and hat.

"Is this what life after death is?" she jested.

He turned away from her to open a door, revealing a bathroom.

"Just what my kidneys ordered." She moved past him and shut the door behind her. On went the light, off went the sweater and tennis dress, the socks and tennis shoes.

She was trembling with cold and excitement before she emerged and hurried to the bed. Unable to help herself, she entered laughing. He reminded her of the TV commercial in which a handsome, bare-chested actor sat up in bed and extolled the power of a male deodorant. But he was her man and he held an open beer can in his left hand, and the uncorked bottle of whiskey in his right.

She bothered to explain her laughter; he did not bother to smile. Instead, with a steady hand, he poured whiskey into the beer can before he set the bottle down on the floor.

As he sipped his boilermaker, she pulled the comforter over her shoulders and moved close to him, rubbing her own legs before she began to rub his. When she reached between his thighs to fondle his limp penis, he brought his free hand down and withdrew hers.

He kissed her mouth with increasing ardor, with deep, open-mouthed tongue kisses, as one of his hands pressed and crushed together her hardening breasts. With her own hands, she touched and explored him everywhere but the forbidden zone.

At last he came away from her mouth to free his own for a swig from the beer can. After kicking away the comforter, he returned to her, his mouth going now from breast to breast, one of his hands digging into her nates, the other sliding down her belly, over her mons veneris, until one sure finger found her clitoris.

No, he was not Frank, not overwhelmed by his own, frantic needs. There was a vast difference between them. Unlike Frank, he was able to make the sex act an act of love.

And when her orgasm came, she cried out. His finger came away and she turned to fall away, to rest and listen to her mind sing huzzas. But his hands were on her again, positioning her supinely, spreading her legs, coming on top of her.

There was no objection now when she took hold of his hard penis and guided it gently into her vagina. He paused to place a pillow under her buttocks before he began to take up his rhythm. No hurry, no rush, no frenzy. He was all love, all discipline.

He was there, the rhythm was there, almost inhuman, quite unreal. A dream? No, she told herself, this was real, and she was aware of the reality. Her fingernails dug into the flesh of his arms the instant she sensed his perceptible quickening and tensing. This time her cry accompanied the telling thrusts of her lover's orgasm.

Oh, Gentle Mary, this is what I was born for. This is a rainy afternoon in Philadelphia. This is the daydream born in musky classrooms, in front of the sisters frowning on my secret smiles. This is the daydream come true.

In a while, as she was listening to the rain music, he spoke at last. "More to drink?"

She faced him and the beer can he had in hand. "No, I want nothing more."

She watched him drink, from the can, from the bottle. She wished he would talk to her, but she sensed it would be a mistake to prod him. She quietly drank in the nearness of him, the reality of him. He was with her, body and mind.

The minutes passed uncounted. The beer can was emptied, the whiskey bottle corked. He stirred, returning the pillow to her head.

"Sleep in my arms," she said, arms outstretched to him.

He merely shook his head and let a finger trace a course down her forehead, between her eyes, down the bridge of her nose. She tried to bite his finger as it passed over her mouth. When she failed, she lay back and felt the finger move down her chin, her throat, between her breasts, across her navel, and down to her clitoris.

She responded, twisting toward him.

"Don't," he said. "Don't you dare move."

Bewildered, she obeyed.

His head slid down the bed before he brought his face to where his finger had been, to where Frank's face had never been.

The cry that soon ensued from her drowned out the rain music. Her eyes were shut to everything but ecstasy and her mouth was open when she felt something brushing her lips. Opening her eyes, she saw that she was straddled, confronted by his loins. By his erection.

She took it. Her last outcries found no escape from her mouth. The

52

muffled sounds came from her nose, ears, pores, her mind and heart. When her mouth was free again, her soul flew out, screaming through the cold, empty rooms beyond this Eden.

And then to sleep, gently to sleep, she and he.

The awakening was rude. There was a shutter slamming in the wind and rain. Joan opened her eyes to find her lover awake and far from her.

"What time is it?" Joan demanded.

"Nearly four-thirty," he said.

She bolted from the bed. "Got to go. Got to get back and peel the potatoes before Stupid gets home."

He neither laughed nor smiled.

Joan went to the bathroom to wash and examine herself for telltale marks. There were none. She thanked God and Roark Bennett.

While he was in the bathroom, Joan tried to play detective, looking for shooting scripts among his books, magazines, and newspapers. She found a copy of *The Hollywood Reporter,* and it confirmed her belief that she had seen his image on a movie or television screen.

As she left the room with Bennett, she began to fear that it had all been a filmy dream, a scene played on a movie set soon to be struck. To reassure herself that the house was real, she banged her fists against the solid walls along the upstairs corridor.

In the Impala, as Bennett kept his wary eyes upon the traffic and the flooded intersections of Ventura Boulevard, Joan saw only him.

"I have seen you in some picture, haven't I?" she said.

He remained silent. She gave up.

He asked, "Did you get a good picture of the house?"

"It was too good to be true."

"It's off the market. Some kid put a deposit down on it. We're holding it till March first. Would you believe two hundred and thirty-five thousand?"

Joan could not care less about real estate values. "I'll believe anything you tell me."

"The kid's twenty-four. Made a fortune in records. Country and western."

"Why are you living there?"

"My way of getting in good with the boss."

"How's that?" She was pleased that he was opening up. At long last.

"An empty house like that, it's a big invitation to high school kids. They had quite a party there last New Year's Eve."

"We had quite a party, too."

The real estate man went on. "Your house, without seeing it, I would guess is worth about seventy-five. When do you think it'll go on the market?"

"Is it inevitable?"

"It's in South Oaks. That's the history. Up and down the social ladder. Divorce. Heavy turnover. Statistics."

"Fascinating," said Joan, who was anything but fascinated. "What statistic do you fall under? Divorce?"

First a perfunctory nod, then more real estate. "Tell me about the other potato peelers. What kind of—?"

"Potato peelers?"

"There were three girls with you. The tennis players."

"Oh, them."

"What kind of houses do they have?"

"You're mine," she said.

"I like you, too. But I'm broke and I've got to sell houses to stay alive."

"Out of bed, what do you do to stay happy?"

A good question, a bad question he refused to answer save with a grimace of despair.

Joan made a guess. "You an actor?"

A sad nod, heightened by the rain slamming against the windshield and the struggling wipers. He spoke again. "Radio's coming back. So they tell me. Might be work this summer. I've been promised."

"Where are you from?"

"Radio."

"Where's that?"

"Wisconsin. Madison. Disk jockey."

"What picture did I see you in?" Joan inquired.

"It was TV. 'The Spacemen.' "

It all came together for Joan. "Of course. You were the radio operator on the spaceship."

"I did better than that. Off-Broadway. An Arthur Miller play."

"How old are you?"

"Thirty-seven."

"How old are your children?"

Silence again. He had to maneuver the Chevrolet through the flooded intersection at Ventura Boulevard and turn east. The children he had no wish to talk about were much farther to the east, beyond the greatest divide: failure.

Having deduced that, Joan directed the not so great profile—at least in professional circles—to a matter of more pressing concern to her.

"You lunch often at the Ivy League?"

"Can't afford it," he said.

"What were you doing there today?"

"Boss's treat. I had a pep talk coming. I tried to quit this morning."

"Lonesome for your actor buddies on the long lines at the state unemployment office?"

"What do you know about it?"

54

"Stupid is a lawyer. He handles show business people for Weil & Tanner."

The revelation depressed him. "Nothing but stars."

"I'd like to keep in touch," she said.

"Don't lose my card."

"I could find my way alone to the castle."

He shook his head.

"Never again?"

"The next time we meet it'll be at your house."

"When?"

"The day you decide to put it on the market."

She pouted. "I can't wait that long."

"Keep an ear and eye open for me. You hear of one of your friends or neighbors talking about selling a house—"

"That's nasty."

"Open your eyes. You saw where I had to go to get some beer and whiskey on credit. That's the way things are."

"Do you like me?"

"You're beautiful," he said.

"Smile when you say it. Please."

He said, "I'll tell you the kind of character I am. I smile when the script calls for it. Or when I see someone sign a real estate contract, and I can see all the way to summer and radio. That's what it's come down to."

"Why don't you go back?"

"I am. As far back as radio. No farther." His voice ebbed away.

She wanted to cry. "I've got a part for you. A star role. You're Max de Winter, living alone in Manderley."

No smile, no comment. He opened his mouth again only to ask for directions. When he let her off, it was apparent he was more interested in the Cooper house than he was in her. And so farewell.

As she ran to the portico, Joan noted her own red Datsun, Ilona's white Porsche, and the absence of Sally's green MG. She rang the bell.

In turn, Dolores and Ilona were happy to see her. Alive. For them it had been a long, terrible afternoon.

Over coffee Joan asked about Sally. There was nothing to tell. Nothing had happened. And how about her?

Joan responded with a romantic tale about Manderley, Max de Winter, and the love play on a lovely rainy afternoon.

"Beautiful," said Ilona. She was happy for Joan.

Dolores was smiling again. "I wasn't wrong. It happened. You did it. We can do it. I can't wait for tomorrow."

Following some quick exchanges about tomorrow's plan, Joan left.

The sight of her own Cape Cod house was a reality that did not sit well in the rain. It was not Manderley, and it would not be until the planting of a "For Sale" sign on the lawn.

Once inside, she resolved to shower and to prepare dinner for Frank. She did shower and dress, but she lingered in the bedroom. She had to talk to Sally.

Joan told Sally everything, leaving out nothing, the good or the bad. Sally never once interrupted with any kind of comment, good or bad.

"Say something," said Joan.

"What happens now?" asked Sally.

Joan pouted. "I don't like the way you said that, Sally. If your voice were a few octaves lower, I'd believe I was talking to my priest."

"I'm sorry," said Sally.

"What happens next is that we're having lunch tomorrow at the Ivy League. This time we're dressing up. Are you with us?"

"I'll call you in the morning."

"Don't hang up on me."

"I wasn't about to," said Sally.

"Good. Now it's your turn. I want to hear what happened between you and Roy."

"Didn't Dolores tell you?"

"Only what you told her," said Joan. "Now tell me what you didn't tell her."

"Believe me, Joan, nothing happened."

"Sally! This is Joanie. You and me, we're closer. In age, in what we want out of life. You know what I mean? And you know what I'm thinking—what I'm praying for. Are you at all interested?"

"Yes, Joan."

Joan sighed. "I'm praying I'll have a wise child who'll know its father is Roark Bennett."

"I believe you," said Sally. "Will he be there tomorrow?"

"Not a chance," said Joan painfully.

"Then why go back?"

"Why not? Who knows who the next man'll be? Maybe he'll be the one for me. Bennett isn't. I know about actors and what possesses them."

"I follow you," said Sally. She knew about actors, too.

"Anyway, we did break out today. I dared and you dared to go upstairs."

"Yes."

"Now, for heaven's sake, tell me what went on in Roy's office."

Sally hesitated. "Talk."

"If I have to pull teeth, I'll pull them," said Joan. "Good or bad talk?"

"Both."

"Does he like you?"

56

No reply from Sally.

"This is between us. I won't blab a thing to Dolores or Ilona."

"Yes," said Sally. "Roy likes me."

"And you do like him, don't you?"

"Yes."

Joan said, "I'll tell you something. I'd trade my afternoon for yours. Yours has promise. Maybe a future. Roy's a widower, and not an actor."

"He was married to an actress," said Sally.

"Shit," said Joan. "Christie Adams couldn't act her way out of a paper bag. The point is—don't you like Roy enough to want to see him every chance you get?"

"Perhaps," said Sally.

"Then we're all set for tomorrow. You see Roy, and Dolores, Ilona, and I look around and be looked at. All right?"

"I'll call you in the—"

"Not so fast," interrupted Joan. "What's the problem now?"

"I was thinking of the dangers," said Sally.

"Divorce? Rape? Murder? Who the hell cares any more? What's an Eden without snakes and apples? And tell me, Sally, where's a worse hell than the dark of night when you can't sleep and you lie awake asking yourself, 'God, where am I? What am I doing so far from home?'"

Sally pondered the questions.

Joan said more. "Look at your house. Right now. Look around and listen. Do you see anything, do you hear anything that sounds like the home you were born in? I'm looking, I'm listening. I see and hear nothing of what my heart cries for. I don't hear you, Sally."

Sally could only say goodbye. Joan, speaking to herself, said to hell with peeling potatoes, to hell with fixing dinner tonight. She would let her fingers do the walking, the Chinese do the cooking. Up the Irish, up the potato peelers.

Joan laughed and remembered how Dolores and Ilona had laughed at Roark Bennett's description of their group.

10

In the midnight dark, Sally Hendley was listening to the rain when the telephone rang like the alarm clock. It told her the time in Ojai, in New York.

"Hello," she said in the key of fear.

"Sally?"

Her aroused mind failed to match the voice with that of Hap or Neal. "Yes. Who is this?"

"Roy Sutter."

Fear still with her, she said, "Hello. I thought I was supposed to call you."

"I was scared you wouldn't. Scared I scared you off. Do I make sense?"

"Yes, Roy."

"I've got the coffee on, and some fresh Danish."

"Have your clocks stopped?"

"No, it's Tuesday. My birthday's over. Another crisis past."

"Isn't *trauma* the word for it?"

"Whatever. Anyway, I'm smiling, the house is smiling. And I was thinking maybe you'd like to see it."

"When?"

"Now. I've also got a fire going."

"I'm in bed, Roy."

"Get out. The same way you got in."

Sally hesitated. "Is it that simple?"

"No, Sally. I know better than that. You do, too."

Uneasily she asked, "Can I get out of your house the same way I get in?"

He thought about it. "Let's find out."

"Do we dare?"

"*I* have to. You think about it. Don't call back. Just do what you have to. I'll understand. Fair enough?"

"Yes, Roy."

Sally's telephone was long in its cradle before she stirred. Out of bed, a lamp burning now, she opened drawers and closet doors for underwear, socks, pants, sweater, boots, and raincoat. Her mirror gave her the same answer Dolores Cooper's mirror had given her: it was time to dare.

58

She brought soap and water to her face. No perfume, no makeup, no mask of seduction. Coffee, cake, and talk, nothing more. She had to see the house, she had to see Roy again.

There was no traffic, no oncoming headlights to betray the low-slung MG as it stole past the sleeping houses. She knew the way.

Leaving South Oaks Road, Sally guided the car to the amber coach lights outside the white craftsman door. Lights out, engine off, window up, she emerged to behold the charm of the used brick, the shuttered wood windows, and the heavy shake roof. Wood and brick, this was a house, a home belonging to the hill, a home rooted to soil and soul.

Before she could bring her hand to the brass knocker, the door was opened from the inside. She entered into the warmth of Sutter's smile, into the warmth of the house. He took her raincoat.

"I lit up the house. Look it over," he said.

She took off alone. He lingered to hang up the coat in the foyer closet. She went from room to room, and it was all so right in design and decor. She loved the fireplaces, the beamed ceilings, the Early American furniture.

At last, she returned to the kitchen where Sutter was pouring coffee into two mugs.

"It's beautiful," she told him.

He smiled. "You did something to it when you walked in."

"Did I?" She had to say more. Beauty called for truth. "As much as Christie did?"

"I think more."

Rejecting his flattery, she asked, "Isn't Christie still here?"

Sutter asked, "Sugar? Cream?"

She shook her head. "Aren't you going to answer me?"

He handed a mug to her. "I'll do better. I'll let you see for yourself. Follow me."

His own mug in hand, he led Sally back to the master bedroom. "Look around. Do you see anything of Christie's?"

Emboldened, Sally slid open closet doors and saw emptiness. Not even a feminine scent, not in the dressing room, not in the bathroom.

"What did you do with all of her things?" Sally asked.

"Shipped it all off to her mother in England."

"Everything?"

"Yeah."

"What about her photographs? Press clippings, and things like that?"

"England."

"Why, Roy?"

"I can see her. Any time I want to look back," he said.

"Do you watch her old pictures on TV?"

"I don't make a habit of it. I'm not a morbid guy. Except on my birthdays. Seen enough?"

"Roy, when was the last time you built a fire in here?"

"The night before Doc Cooper gave us the bad news."

Sally understood. Cold again, she left the bedroom and went straight back to the living room to find the fire. Crossing her legs, she sat down on the floor facing the fireplace, but her eyes took in the paintings on the paneled walls: striking California landscapes and seascapes.

Sutter came into the living room bearing a plate of pastries. "Dwight Tuttle found 'em in the attic of his old man's mansion in Brentwood. Before the wreckers came," he said, sitting down close to Sally.

"I've heard of Mr. Tuttle," she said.

"From Neal no doubt."

"Yes, Roy." She was uneasy.

"I say something wrong?"

"You brought Neal into the house."

He frowned. "Tell me more. Tell me what Neal says about me and Tuttle."

"It's not pleasant," she told him.

"I didn't expect it to be."

Sally opened up. "Neal claims you hustled Tuttle. He says that's the basis of your success."

"Sure, Neal never lets me forget it."

"I'd like to hear your version," she said.

"No, you tell me what you've heard. I'll give you the real lowdown. The truth."

"You fought the war on a golf course."

"True, but not by choice," Sutter said. "I was only sixteen in 1943. Living in Marietta, Georgia, with my married sister. I dropped out of high school to enlist in the Air Force. I wanted to fly, but you had to be a college man to get into the Aviation Cadet Corps. Well, they put me in the motor pool, driving a truck. And they shipped me only as far as Maxwell Field, Alabama. There I ran into Major Tuttle. Yale and Harvard Law, like his old man. Captain of the Yale golf team in the early thirties. He asked me to join him in a game, and he got interested when he saw how I hit the ball. Then he asked me a lot of questions about myself."

Sally said, "Tell me what you told Tuttle."

"No, you must've heard plenty about me in the last five years. Tell me what you've heard."

Sally burned her tongue on the hot coffee. "Neal says—as a kid, as a caddy—you stole clubs and balls from golf bags."

Sutter smiled. "Not so. I'd find the balls in the woods. Lost balls. Broken clubs. I never stole a dime. Hustled, yeah."

"Neal says you're a born bastard."

60

No smile now. "My old man married my mother when he came out of a veteran's hospital after the First World War. He was gassed pretty bad in France. Never got over it. He never did any better than get to be a greenskeeper. I'd tag along with him whenever I could. That's how I learned about golf courses and golf."

"Neal says you're hustling Hershey Barnes in Vegas."

Sutter smiled. "I give him lessons. Free. On the golf course, and on the skeet range. He's my friend. Did Neal tell you Hershey hustles show girls for me?"

"No. Is it true?"

"Yeah," he said sadly. "Since Christie died."

Sally said nothing.

"I don't remember their names," he said.

"I understand. Now tell me what you know about me, Roy."

"I will," he said. "But first I'd like to know what Neal says about the matches between the two of us."

Sally thought about it. "Neal believes he can fly rings around any-body. He proved it in the war, and as an airline pilot. At least to himself. He feels the same about his golf. He says he was an All-American, not in football, but in golf. And he thinks—if it hadn't been for the war—he would have been up there with Nelson, Hogan, and Snead. He's bigger than you, he's stronger. He says you swing like Palmer. Betsy Palmer."

Sutter laughed.

"And he refuses to concede you're better than he is."

"I'm six years younger," he said.

Unmindfully she said, "He believes you're always cheating him, somehow or other. Are you?"

"Nothing I do with Neal'd get me disqualified by a PGA official. I play by the rules, but I also play my opponent's weaknesses in match play. Neal gets himself in trouble by paying too much attention to the club I'm using. Say it's a four-iron shot to the pin. I can take out a four wood and make it work for me. He takes out his four wood and knocks it over the green. Things like that. A lot of things like that."

"Yes, I understand."

"Understand this, too, Sally. He comes looking for me. I don't look for him. I don't need his money."

"Only his wife?" Sally was not jesting.

"Neal failed you," said Sutter.

"Not really." Again a sad smile. "You could say I *hustled* him."

"The hell I would," he said.

"It's true. I wanted children. Exactly what Neal did not want again. I knew that, but I thought I could make him change his mind."

"Hap was the big problem, wasn't he?"

"Not anymore."

"Sally, I want what you want. I want it bad. And I wish you'd think about going from Neal to me."

Sally met his stare. "How much time do I have?"

"All you need. You say the word. You make the moves. After you think hard about them," he said.

She reached for a piece of Danish. It was good, and she ate it facing the fire and listening to the rain coming down the flue and sizzling the logs.

At last she turned to Sutter. "Did Christie love you?"

"In her own way."

"Dolores Cooper says Christie married you on the rebound."

Unabashed, he said, "That's what Hedda Hopper or Louella Parsons —or maybe both of 'em—said in the columns."

"But it's not the truth."

"The truth's not pretty," he said. "And only Vince Fonte and I know all of it."

"I'd like to hear it," said Sally.

He grinned. "Tell you what. On my next birthday—when I get morbid and down—I'll let it all hang out."

Sally shook her head. "Now. Please."

The grin widened. "Come to think of it. If you're here *now*, it must be my birthday."

"Tell it, please," she urged.

"One night back in 1959," began Sutter, "Vince Fonte walks into the Ivy League with the most beautiful girl I'd ever seen. He's uneasy; she looks like a sleepwalker. I play it cool and say nothing. All the time I'm asking myself what the hell is Vince doing? Is he playing around and got the gal in a jam? Later, Vince comes to me after he shows the gal to the ladies' room.

"He tells me her name, which I recognize, and then he tells me the story. A murder story. Lloyd Stennis, the movie director, was found dead in his bed. Naked, mutilated. The gal—an actress named Christie Adams—walked in and found him. Called the police. Vince's boss makes a few calls from the house and tells Vince to get Christie the hell out of there before the press shows up.

"Seems Christie was the mistress of a front office executive at Warner Brothers. Big Catholic layman, big family man. Anyway, the director was a fag. And he covered for the executive by *romancing* Christie in the gossip columns and at those parties where the executive wanted to see Christie, when he wasn't seeing enough of her at the studio.

"After a while, the telephone rang for Vince. He got his orders from his boss, and he asked me to do him a large favor: take Christie to my house and keep her there—hide her out until he came for her. She

62

understood. Didn't mind. Liked the house, got to like me, and me her."

Sally asked, "How long did she stay?"

He smiled sadly. "Twelve years."

"But when was Christie free to go?"

"In about forty-eight hours, after they picked up the murderer outside of Barstow. Anyway, Christie was dropped by the studio. Her agent stopped returning her phone calls. And then, some weeks later, we drove to Vegas and got married."

Sutter rose and held out a hand. Sally took it and let him bring her to her feet. "Follow me."

"I love the fire, Roy."

"I'll take you to another one," he said.

She smiled. "The bedroom?"

"The den. Some music I want you to hear."

From the floor of the den Sally watched Sutter use a match and the gas jet to enflame three logs, and then place two records on the turntable of his stereo console.

The first lilting piano notes lit up her face. "Scott Joplin! Who told you I was crazy about piano rag?"

Sutter smiled. "You just did."

"Takes me back seven or eight years."

"How about a Scotch or brandy?" he asked, as he went behind the bar.

"I'll have whatever you're having."

Sutter poured Courvoisier into two inhalers and brought the drinks to the carpet before the blazing fire. After he had turned off the gas jet, he sat down close to her. They tapped glasses.

"Happy birthday, Roy."

He grinned. "Maybe I should've saved the cake and brought it home."

"Is that your sexy grin?"

"My loving smile," he said, and made it so.

"Talk to me," she whispered.

"Dream talk?"

She did not understand. "What dreams?"

"The daydream I was having when you knocked on my office door this afternoon. I was reading a letter from a great guy. A Frenchman, a real restaurateur. Had a place on Sunset Boulevard until he sold out, said goodbye to the smog people, took his wife and kids and went north. He's got a restaurant now in Carmel and a new home in Carmel Valley. And he's in love with America all over again."

Sally was ahead of him. "And now you're dreaming the same dream?"

He nodded. "More seriously than ever. That's what you do to me." The words flowed along with the piano rag.

"Are you and I *smog people?*" asked Sally.

"Yeah, but we don't have to be."

"I don't feel like one. Not now, not here. I love this house."

"I can build another like it. In Carmel Valley."

Sally was interested. "How soon?"

"You tell me."

"And what happens between now and then? Do we play what you call the more dangerous game?"

He nodded. "That's the hazard."

She winced. "And what if we don't play?"

"We've got to do something," said Sutter. "The most dangerous game of all is doing nothing."

Sally was perplexed. "How so?"

"Once you stop reaching out for what makes life worth living you begin to die. And you're a long time dying—and dead to dreams. Do I make any sense to you?"

She reached out for him, he for her.

11

Roy Sutter had a warm smile for Ilona Belanger when she came in out of the rain. It was five minutes before one o'clock. The reservation was for one. For four.

Alone at the table in the dining room, Ilona did not face the two men at a nearby table sipping their coffees. Both of them studied Ilona and were vocal about their impressions of her beauty. In French.

Ilona listened, smiled, and made her move. *"Merci beaucoup."*

The younger man was embarrassed. The older and more interesting-looking man was not.

He matched Ilona's smile. "Ah, French, but spoken like an Austrian."

"Hungarian," she told him.

"Class of '56?"

Ilona nodded. "And you?"

"Vienna. You miss Budapest?"

"So much," Ilona said.

"So do I." He paused. "You're waiting for someone, no?"

"Yes. Friends. Visiting here?"

He shrugged, produced a business card, and handed it to her. "Paul Klauber, Ph.D." A Manhattan address.

"Psychology," Klauber explained.

Ilona heard enough. "Where are you staying?"

"The Hilton. Down the boulevard. Such as it is."

"Yes." She understood. It was not Vienna or Budapest. Seeing Dolores, she hid the card in her purse and came up with the right smile. She was not about to introduce the psychology major to the psychologist.

Klauber played his role, too. He called for a check, and he and his friend were gone before Joan arrived.

Sally entered. She and Sutter were guarded in their exchange of smiles. At the table she was content to let Joan and Dolores carry the conversation. Ilona was silent and preoccupied.

They had the same drinks as yesterday, but also a fresh complaint from Dolores, seconded by Joan. The dining room did not serve their purpose as well as the cocktail lounge. No dissent from Ilona, indifference from Sally. She knew where her man was.

Sally had the gumbo and shrimp. Dolores had a Salad Niçoise. Joan went for a steak sandwich. Ilona had strawberry cheesecake and coffee.

The ears had it with Manderley. Enough of yesterday, enough of Joan, enough of envy. The eyes had no prospects, only aspects of some interesting men blind to everything but the beauty of the dollar, the mark, and the yen.

Dolores and Joan joined to make a strategic move to the cocktail lounge, where the yen had another meaning. Sally gave Sutter a good-bye-for-now look and went home to wait for midnight. Ilona went "down the boulevard."

It was easier said than done. Caution caused her to turn her rack-and-pinion steering wheel the wrong way—the way home. But resolve turned enough corners to put her on the course to the Valley Hilton. It was time, Vienna time.

Her Porsche exchanged for a ticket, she entered the modern, bustling lobby and made her way to the house telephones.

"Dr. Klauber, please," she said to the switchboard. She waited for her heart and the ringing to be stilled, and for the gentle voice from Vienna.

"Hello." Nothing gentle, rather a terseness bordering on terror if not panic.

"Dr. Klauber?" Suspicion, doubt.

"Yes." At the least, anxiety.

Meaning to give him balm, she spoke in French. "The lady from Budapest."

"Who?"

Back to English. "The Ivy League. The lady in—"

"Oh, yes, of course."

"Ilona Belanger."

"Yes, Mrs. Belanger."

"I am downstairs."

"Downstairs?"

"You are not alone," Ilona deduced.

"Yes, very much alone. As a matter of—"

"And your room number is?"

A pause. "One moment." A longer pause. "802."

Wasting no effort on the formality of an invitation, she took an elevator and a correct turn to the correct door.

When it was unlocked and opened, Ilona was chilled by the failure of Klauber's smile. Fear was naked on his face, robbing it of handsomeness, maturity, and charm. His lean body, so well groomed in his sports coat and slacks, appeared soft and almost feminine in his silken robe.

He seemed to accept her presence as a lesser of two evils, the greater one being his aloneness. As he shut the door behind her, Ilona glanced about. No flowers, no candy, no liqueurs, no music, no Vienna high

66

above Ventura Boulevard. Only an asexual air of tension, of a terror that could touch her.

Ilona said, "I have lost my way. I was looking for Kartnerstrasse. Ringstrasse."

Klauber heard the incantations of Vienna and tears filled his eyes. "Stay, please stay."

"I am a fool," she said.

"No," he protested. "That is my role this day. The fool. You are the angel of mercy. Stay with me. Sit down. We will sit together."

At a loss at what to do, Ilona did nothing. Klauber fumbled with the buttons of her raincoat, kissed her hands, and then withdrew to the sofa to wring his own hands. Laying her coat aside, she sat down beside him.

"What is it?" She was asking about those Russians who were running through the house of his terror.

"The telephone," he said awesomely. "I wait for it to ring. Life or death. When it rang moments ago, I thought, ah, now I'll know which way to dance. Out the door, or out the window."

Ilona winced. "A call from whom? A doctor?"

Klauber laughed nervously. Gallows laughter. "I'm the doctor; he's the power. The last resort, the last hope, the last terror."

"Who is the power?"

"A name like an apple, a poisoned apple. Emory MacIntosh. A vice-president of Victory Industries, Incorporated. A conglomerate of companies, manufacturers of those trifles that must be produced for Americans, and for export to those markets in the world where American trifles mean more than holy water from Lourdes."

Ilona was confused. "But you are a psychologist. What do you have to do with all of this?"

Klauber sighed. "I am what you call an industrial psychologist. A troubleshooter, as the Americans say. An efficiency expert. A member of the management team given to employee and production problems. Thirty-five thousand dollars a year. America! A fortune for the misfortune of leaving the peace of a university and taking up the perils of employment and unemployment." He sighed again, and his head fell. "At the moment I am unemployed."

"And where was your last job?"

"New York. I was fired."

"Why?"

"If I would tell you, you would run from this room."

"Tell me," she dared him.

"Of what use to you is my misfortune? Stay with me, comfort me. If the telephone rings, if Mr. MacIntosh's voice rings with good fortune, I will tell you and we will laugh together."

"Is there a wife and children to laugh with you?"

"*At* me," he was quick to retort with sorrow. "My wife has a job, an important job as a buyer for Macy's. She loves America and despises me. As success, indeed, must despise failure. Not only did she liberate herself, she flew away from me like a balloon."

"Divorced?" asked Ilona.

He laughed. "A slight separation, by only a continent. Such a big country, such opportunity, so much terror. Look at me, look how nervous I am. Look how beautiful you are, and here I am sitting before you —castrated."

"You lie," said Ilona.

He touched her knees now, absently, gently.

Ilona did not protest or stir.

"What did you think of the boy I was lunching with? Boy! He's thirty-eight. Anyone three or four years younger than I am is a boy. Nice boy, smart. We met in New York. On the job, as the Americans say. Also a psychologist. He's going to be a millionaire."

"You said that so sadly," said Ilona.

"This boy," said Klauber, "is the *president*, no less, of a peculiar American enterprise which goes by the name of Dialog." He spelled it. "Short spelling, short name. You heard of it?"

"No," said Ilona.

"You will. Nonsense is always heard in America. And so profitable. People who are frightened by encounter groups, rap centers, and who cannot contribute to the largesse of your psychiatrists and psychoanalysts who charge too much for fifty minutes of listening. No, these people want bargain rates, convenient places around the corner. Pay your ten dollars, go into a little booth, and talk your head off to some stranger who has nothing on his mind but the money. It's a franchise business. The boy is dreaming of offices all over the country. A tremendous fortune to be made. I, my dear, sweet lady, was offered the franchise rights for the city of New York."

"Did you accept?" asked Ilona.

He shook his head.

Ilona tried again. "Then why are you so nervous about a thirty-five-thousand-dollar-a-year job?"

He shuddered. "My wife, as the Americans say, *pulls down thirty grand*. So how could I pull her pants down on less than thirty-five thousand a year?"

Laughter came readily to Ilona. "That is nonsense. American nonsense."

"My alternative is what? Russian nonsense?"

"You are a European. A Viennese." Ilona smiled with a kindness that melted him.

"You are my dream of Europe. Sweetness, softness, and a beauty that brings out the beast in me," Klauber said, parting his robe with his free hand and revealing himself. "See the spire of St. Stephens. See the Matterhorn."

Ilona flushed before he bent toward her, finding and kissing her mouth, caressing her breasts with one hand and tugging at silk with the other. She stirred to accommodate him, and soon he was over her, and into her, first with a gentle finger and then with his pressing penis.

It was so good, so right for both of them until they heard not the bells of St. Stephens, but, rather, the ringing of the telephone. America was ringing. A third and perverse presence was in the room. Fear.

And Klauber died in her arms, and within her. The handsomeness of his soft face decayed to ugliness.

The second ring evoked a groan from him, a shiver and chill from her. He slipped away from her and responded to his American urgency. The shame of his unmanly terror caused him to turn his back on her, and to command courage from his blood and nerves to take up the burden of the telephone.

Ilona observed Klauber with compassion. The voice she heard was frightened; the voice he alone heard was menacing. Too many "ahs" and too many pleas for mercy. Too many "thanks" for nothings. And then down went the telephone, and the hand that had brought it down seemed unable to rise. The legs wavered.

She was thinking of rising and catching him before he collapsed. Instead she voiced her concern. "Are you all right?"

He reacted not with words, but with a slow turn of his body, followed by the slow step of the walking dead. Making it back to the sofa, he seemed to have eyes only for the upholstered softness. His body slumped, his head fell, and his eyes shut.

Moving toward him, Ilona cradled him in her arms, rocked him, and spared him her voice and her pity. When he spoke again, he did so with his hands. Absently, gently, and then with design. She did not deter the dead, blind man feeling his way back to life.

At last, his voice hollow, Klauber said, "There is no ocean, no sky, no planet for a man to escape his past."

Not knowing what to say, Ilona said nothing. She had no wish to penetrate the mystery of him. She meant to leave him with his past. His pride. There was not enough room for more shame. The hotel room was sick with it, and the rain seemed to wash it from sewer to sewer.

"I am nothing," Klauber said. "I am nowhere. Where is your husband?"

Her mind boggled by the non sequitur, Ilona asked, "Why think of him?"

"He could be my savior."

No comment, no laughter.

"Telephone him now. Marvelous invention, the telephone. Most lethal invention of man." Klauber laughed the laughter of agony, of irony. "Tell the good man where you are. Tell him you are with an evil man. Tell him to bring his American security blanket. His revolver."

Ilona said, "He has no revolver."

"A baseball bat will do. I will—like the French kings—hold my head ever so still. Anything but defenestration."

"What is that?"

"Leaning too far out of windows. Away from life."

Ilona lifted Klauber's head. Smiling, she said, "Keep talking. English, German, French. Anything but suicide."

He found a trace of a smile. "We cannot escape history. Only ourselves." The smile faded. "Madam, you are not addressing an esteemed doctor of psychology. Before you sits an infirm man. A patient. A case history."

"Please," she implored him.

"And you are not yourself as you are now, but as you were when you were but a girl."

"I have a daughter fourteen."

"As beautiful as you?"

"More beautiful."

"What is her name?"

She told him.

"I dub thee Karen. I am named Mark."

"Who is Mark?"

"My son. The lone heir to my misfortune. But now I am Mark, and you are Karen." He said more with his hands. With his eyes, his lips, and his tongue.

He stirred, she stirred with him. No more dying, no more ringing telephone, no shame, and no thought of shame. There were just the two of them, there was the Danube, and there was a boy with a girl.

He spoke in German now, some of which she understood and some of which she cared not to understand. Vocal frenzy, tactile frenzy, tooth and nail. The gentleman from Vienna was dead beside the killing telephone, dead eight stories below the window. The boy was alive and well and snaring her. Freeing her.

Later, when Ilona was dressed again and ready to leave, Klauber made his apologies, but only for his failure to provide any wine, any liqueur, or any continental chocolates. The visit had been a surprise. A beautiful one.

Ilona erred in not believing him. "Why were you undressed?"

Without a smile, he said, "Defenestration is honorable. Ruining good Bond Street clothes is not."

She persisted. "You expected me."

"At first, I hoped. But when I saw those three lovely ladies joining you, I gave up all hope. Four American women. I foresaw a bridge game."

Ilona smiled.

"The truth? I brought the four of you back to this room with me. That was to be my amusement. My fancy to flee the fate the ringing telephone would bring me. Beauty is in the eye of the psyche. Also sex. Do you understand me?"

"I am trying," she said.

"Ah, but you succeeded. You are a miracle girl, and the next time I am in Budapest I will remember you."

"Leaving America?"

"Who knows? There is always Dialog, Incorporated. Perhaps a fortune. Or more misfortune, of my own making. You do understand?" When he saw that Ilona did not, he added, "They are playing a new game in London, I hear. A game I might have invented. Grown persons getting together for parties—making love in children's clothes. Does this excite you or repel you?"

Ilona answered with laughter.

Klauber frowned. "Is it to laugh? Or are you laughing at me?"

"No, at my husband," she said. "He is always saying, 'There is more to sex than love.'"

He was slow to understand, but he did not laugh. "How true." He turned away and went to open the door for her. The interlude was over.

Ilona had enough presence of mind to visit the bathroom, at least to arrange her clothes and her makeup. When she emerged, she found Klauber at the telephone. He was blind to her, and so different from the man who had smiled at her in the Ivy League.

She said, "Good-bye." He said, "Hello, darling." Into the telephone.

By the time she had turned her Porsche into her own driveway, Ilona understood the terror of the day. The Hilton was no Manderley. The man from Vienna was no different from Bobby. The hotel room was no different from her own bedroom. Same obscene telephones. Same obscene games. All that was missing was a window seat containing clues to the punished man's crime.

12 Drink in hand, pipe in mouth, the man of distinction stood with his back to the bar, surveying the framed photographs on the walls of the Ivy League's cocktail lounge.

Joan Lawler, viewing him as another Max de Winter, observed him as he moved about the room for a closer inspection of the photographs. Dolores Cooper, seated with her at the table for two, had her eyes and ears open to four men huddled together in a sober discussion of the stock market.

The man of distinction drew near. Settling into a chair at a vacant table, he eyed the photograph on the wall above and behind Joan and Dolores.

Joan smiled at him in vain. Dolores turned to her, followed her smile, found her own, and then twisted her head toward the picture of the 1916 Yale football squad.

Facing the man again, Dolores found courage and her voice. "Yale?"

Joan reacted. The man did not. His eyes were slow in climbing down from the wall. He fanned away pipe smoke and studied Dolores and Joan for a long, unsmiling moment. He brought his whiskey to his mouth before he shook his head, stilled it, and allowed his eyes to climb up the wall again.

Dolores tried again. "Harvard?"

No reply. His reaction was to rise. Dolores's heart sank until she saw him take his chair and place it before their table. Sitting, glass on the table, he faced Dolores.

"Vassar?" he asked.

"Georgia," said Dolores.

"Chestnut Hill," said Joan, naming her college.

His blue eyes never left Dolores. "Bulldog, bulldog," he said, alluding to the mascot of both Yale and her alma mater.

Dolores beamed. "Yes. Who's in the picture?"

He frowned. "Daddy."

"Which one?"

"The least impressive one," he said to the photograph.

Dolores turned her head. "They're all so impressive. Like young gods."

He said, "The skinny boy in the black suit and black bowler with the

72

thick glasses on his pimply face is no god. That's Daddy."

"Oh, the manager," said Dolores.

"Then and now."

"Is he still alive?"

"Bow, wow, wow," he said.

Joan was heard from. "What class are you?"

He ignored her. To Dolores he said, "Yes, Daddy's very much alive. The past lives on. And on."

Joan showed her class. She emptied her glass and rose. She said something about having to run, and walked away slowly, leaving the field to Dolores. This, to her, was an afternoon for mindfuckers like Dolores and sleepy-time pipe suckers. All smoke, no fire.

"I'm Dolores Cooper."

"What is a Dolores Cooper?" No introduction, no smile from him.

"Doctor's wife. Mother of a pregnant but married daughter at Stanford. And a son at Cornell."

"My condolences."

"On all three counts?"

He thought about it. "Cornell's better than Yale. Not as good as Dannemora or Attica."

Recognizing the names of the Upper New York State prisons, Dolores laughed. He neither laughed nor smiled.

She said, "My son got a thin envelope from Yale."

"Lucky boy. Who wished to condemn him to New Haven?"

"His grandfather," she said.

"Your father-in-law?"

"No. My daddy."

"Yale man?" he inquired.

"Businessman."

"You're a daddy's girl," he surmised.

"Daddy's dead."

"Lucky you," he said.

Dolores said, "You chased my friend. Are you now chasing me?"

"Not here," he said. "You have your choice. Around a desk. Or around a bed."

Dolores had to smile. "Lucky me."

"The offer expires in five minutes."

"Where's the desk?" she asked.

"Top floor of the bank building west of here."

"Where's home?"

"I live with Daddy. Fifth Avenue. Bar Harbor. Palm Beach."

"Where's the bed?"

"Bel-Air Hotel. Daddy's in Santa Barbara, which is encouraging. A high death rate there for septuagenarians."

"You're a bachelor."

"Definitely. Despite three arrests."

"Morals charges?" She was reminded of Ilona's suspicions about Paul Klauber, the man from Vienna.

"My inability to kiss Mammon's ass," he said.

"Picturesque, but obscure."

"I failed three times. As an entrepreneur and as a benedict. But it was the red ink on the ledgers that did me in, not the lipstick on my laundry."

"How are you living now?"

"Daddy gives me allowances."

"And how old are you?"

"I was born old. Daddy's younger than I am."

"What's the secret?" Dolores asked.

"Yale," he said forlornly.

"Tell me more. I'm fascinated."

"At Dun & Bradstreet I'm known by the name of Whitney Callender the Unwise. Now, I believe you owe me an answer. The desk or the bed?"

Dolores hesitated. "One more drink?"

"Not here," he said, and at last he smiled. "Daddy is looking down upon us."

"I like your smile."

"You must see the rest of it. The desk is closer."

"The bed," she said, making her decision.

The sky was blue. This Friday was not. Her Mercedes raced behind his blue Lincoln Continental with the Maine license plates. The arrangement was not to his liking, but she never bothered to explain her caution, her rules of conduct and misconduct. The parking attendants at the Ivy League knew her by name. Roy Sutter, perhaps, knew her game.

East on Ventura Boulevard, south on the San Diego Freeway. The fast way, the fast lanes, the freeway and the freedom. The Mercedes chased the Lincoln up the Mulholland grade.

Dolores chased the dream over the hill. It was all so beautiful and so correct. Yale, Bar Harbor, Palm Beach, Fifth Avenue, Bel Air. And Whitney Callender was so beautiful. The afternoon, the sun, the wind, and the nakedness of him and her.

The Mercedes was doing seventy. Dolores's heart was racing, her blood was running. The outer eye on the Lincoln, the inner eye on a bedroom at the Bel-Air Hotel. Prescience. Foreknowledge. Passion warming her, chilling her, warming her again. A tension of nerves and muscles, twisted by fantasy.

She now saw nothing but red, felt nothing but heat. She cried out above the hum of the engine and the singing of traffic. No, no, she told herself, not here, not here, please, not here.

Damn, it was beginning for her, the tightening, the stirring, and the choking. Gasping for breath, she only got the fetid air of fear. It was happening. It happened. The bell of her had rung, the tremors widening from her excitement-filled vulva and vagina.

Was she asleep and dreaming? Was she awake and conscious? Did it happen, really happen, as it once, and only once, had happened not long after puberty. Both hands had remained on the wheel, her left leg on the floor of the car, her right leg on the accelerator. She had not commanded her body. No, it was the other way around. She was lost, out of control.

What was it? Was it an angst she had exorcised? The bell? The ball? The masked ball? What was it? Was it nothing more in grandeur and splendor than a return to a time long past?

She never answered the question, for another fear now possessed and overwhelmed her: this was a dream, no, a nightmare, out of which she had awakened too soon. Too late.

The Lincoln was gone! Where in time, where in place, was she? Where was the Lincoln? Where was the Sunset Boulevard exit?

Damn, she had passed it. She was lost, he was lost to her. Wilshire Boulevard was coming up. Blind to the traffic, she swerved the wheel to the right, found sight and terror, and swerved back in time to miss the trailer truck passing her on the right. Damn, she could have been killed.

She was dead by the time she eased the Mercedes into the right lane, off the freeway. Bound east, she found herself on the westbound ramp. Sick at heart, mind, and body, she drove past the Veterans Hospital. She was a lemming running toward the sea.

Red light, left turn, U turn, right turn, back onto Wilshire Boulevard, bound east. Which way was faster? Which way was surer to the lost dream of Bel Air? Traffic was heavy in Westwood, probably heavier in Beverly Hills.

A sign, a swinging turn, and back onto the San Diego Freeway. Northbound. Bound for home, for defeat, for shame. Sunset Boulevard. Eastbound. Last chance, the very last moment of the very last time.

She made it. Along Sunset Boulevard, she searched the streets for Stone Canyon Road. One more turn. She found it and made it, and the hotel signs eased the last half mile.

And then the beautiful turn into the hotel parking lot, into the ken of Whitney Callender. He was standing there alone, smoking his pipe and grinning like a little boy after a game of hide-and-seek.

All-knowing, he asked no questions. As he led her along a lawn and through the trees, she understood that her delay had served him. The key to the suite was in his hands. No lobby, no desk clerk, no stares.

Sitting room and two flanking bedrooms. Flowers, fruit, candy, liquor, newspapers, magazines. Very correct.

"Martinis?" he said.

"Please. Which bedroom is yours?"

He pointed. She went into the bedroom and straight into the bathroom. She stripped hurriedly, showered, and emerged in less than ten minutes, still drying herself with a Turkish towel. She was surprised not to find him in the bedroom. In bed.

Opening the door to the sitting room, Dolores saw Whitney Callender lounging in a soft chair, very much at ease with his martini.

"May I have my drink?"

Shortly he entered the bedroom and handed her a fresh martini. "And so to bed?"

"Yes," she said.

He smiled. "Cheers. Remember, anything I do or say is to be taken as good, clean fun."

"You don't have to say anything at all."

"Don't deny me. Sex without an outpouring of words is no sex at all."

"What is it?"

"Ill breeding."

"You're funny," she said.

"The best is yet to come. No double entendre intended. I don't talk dirty. I talk funny. Not ha-ha funny. Well, you'll see, you'll hear."

So saying, he began to undress. Dolores, putting her drink on a night table, removed the bedspread, dropped the towel, and found the cool of the pillow and the cool between the sheets.

Callender drifted in and out of the bathroom, appearing again naked, carrying her Bali bra and hip-huggers, and handing them to her with a smile.

"Master's orders?" Dolores asked.

"The word is fetish," he said.

He went around to the other side of the bed, entering in time to snap brassiere hooks for her. When it was done, she turned, clung to him, and waited to be kissed. He did so, once, a hello kiss, that and nothing more. She had questions, but she dared ask none. No probing, no analysis this afternoon. No, not today. If there was to be talk, it would be his and his alone. She would do nothing more than answer questions, she would do nothing less than to seek and secure the ecstasy and the remembrance of it in treasureless times.

"You may kiss me," he said. "Anywhere, everywhere but my silver-tongued mouth. That, for the time being, is programmed for the fun of my pent-up words."

Obediently, Dolores lowered her head. In darkness she planted his

76

body with kisses. She tensed only momentarily when he flung away the darkness and left her cold and exposed.

"I must look at you," he said, sliding a hand inside her panties. "I dislike talking to walls."

The warm hand and tender fingers stayed with her, and she stayed with him. The difficult part was hearing his voice. Her body was open to him, her mind was shut to him and herself. And, mindlessly, she touched and felt him, kissed and caressed him.

He said, "Isn't this novel? Having sex and improving your mind and character at the same time? So love and listen, daddy's girl, while I tell you the dirt about Yale and daddies."

Dolores never heard him. She was listening for the true ringing of the bell within her, sensing his finger on her clitoris, and the fingers of his other hand on the nipples of her breasts, as she used her mouth to ring his bell.

The bell rang for her, but not for him. She withdrew, pillowed her head on his flat belly, and beheld the rock. Unfallen.

His voice returned. "The year is 1912."

For whom? For what? Where is he now? Is he impotent? Unvoiced questions. Catch your breath, Dolores, catch his time. Silence, sweet silence. Listen. Sweetly.

"Horace Callender comes down from Hartford to the New Haven of his dreams. And the dream soon dies aborning. Yale for Skinny Callender is a cold, cold failure. A Phi Beta Kappa failure. Lost among the football heroes and the beautiful, rich boys from St. Grottlesex. Graduation. Honors. Failure. Skinny goes off to teach English at Poly Prep in Brooklyn. Exile. Poor old Skinny, probable pedagogue, possible pederast. Dying in Brooklyn, and not allowed to die in France with the heroes and scions. Yale is dead, better forgotten."

Dolores cradled the rock between her breasts.

"The year is 1920. Skinny, watching a prep school football game, sees Ward Whitney, classmate. Hello. Blank look. Skinny recites his name. Slow take. Of course, Skinny Callender. Nice seeing you again, nicer to say good-bye. Skinny dies again. Two weeks pass. Telephone message at his Bay Ridge rooming house. Ward Whitney called. Actually left his number. Skinny calls back. Ward has a problem. He's the class secretary and he's got these damned notes to write up for the alumni magazine. Skinny volunteers. Are you with me?"

A nod from Dolores. Back to work for her. Back to the story for him.

"The year is 1922. Ward Whitney hires Skinny as his secretary. Writing his speeches, making his reports, news releases, to Yale, the *Times*, and the *Wall Street Journal*. High finance, the big money. Growing reputation, the man behind the man, watch out for Skinny Callender. Class of '16. Helluva guy. In 1926, the helluva guy marries Eunice

Whitney. Dear old mother."

Meanwhile, Dolores was not succeeding, not conceding. She straddled him, and fitted him into herself.

"I came along in '32, following a sister act that didn't thrill Daddy. I had Yale banners all over my nursery. I was taking in football games in New Haven, Cambridge, and Princeton at a time when I didn't know how to tie my shoelaces. Of course, I was sent to St. Paul's. All the Whitneys went there—our branch anyway. I was imprisoned there to keep me from molesting my two darling sisters. And when it came time—"

Whitney Callender was interrupted by another cry, another spasm. The bell was again ringing for Dolores. A school bell was tolling for him.

"The year is 1950. Yale, without suspense, accepts me. I, without much ado, take a train to Baltimore. St. John's College. The Great Books. The college of my choice. Your life, says brave Daddy, going on to tell me a funny Yale–Harvard story he heard in the White House from F.D.R. I laughed, Daddy didn't. His heart was broken. First break. More and more to follow. The failures of my marriages, my enterprises. Not counting the fact that I failed to finish St. John's, Cornell, or—"

"Cornell!" It was an exclamation, but Callender accepted it as a question.

"Nice place, if that's what you're looking for."

"What were you looking for?" Dolores asked. She was lying face down on the bed, touching linen, and waiting for her breath.

"A good, steady, purposeful job. Which I found seven years ago, when Daddy broke his hip. I became his male nurse, his constant companion, and his secretary. I even began to write his class notes for the Yale alumni magazine. Now Skinny Callender is remembered by some score of survivors as the wittiest man of his class."

Dolores turned to face him, to study his asexual gratification. "That pleasures you, doesn't it?"

"It does," Callender said. "And the victory's Daddy's. Not mine. For me it was a kind of final defeat. This morning Daddy was abducted in a chauffeured Rolls-Royce by good old Gilbert Halsey, who couldn't wait for Sunday. I can see them laughing, talking, and singing of those days when Yale was Hefelfinger, Hinkey, Stover, and Merriwell. Sweet times, sweet medicine."

"Why did you remain behind here?" Dolores asked.

"Things to do," he said. "Calls to widows, sons, and grandsons. Graves to visit and decorate with flowers."

Dolores asked, "Is that why you hate him?"

"I hate him because he refuses to drop dead. Because I want to stop dreaming about killing him."

Dolores could say nothing.

"Be glad your Daddy's dead," he said.

"My father was my best friend."

"Your lover, too?"

She frowned. "No."

He studied her. "You haven't buried him, have you?"

"He's buried in Georgia."

"No, you are. Your Daddy lives in you. As mine still lives in me. And that's the evil in us. Think about it and you might come to know what's wrong with your life."

Dolores hit back. "Are you impotent?"

He smiled. "Yes. But never in bed."

Speaking with his hands now, he took her bewilderment, her hips, and maneuvered her buttocks toward him.

Facedown upon his belly, Dolores felt his lips, the penetration of a finger in one orifice, a tongue in the other. Soon her mouth opened and closed upon his rock. After a desperate but pleasurable while, the rock was split, her own body was sundered, and the bell, the loudest bell of all, was ringing.

This was the climax, she knew, his and hers, now and never more.

Dolores lay there on the bed, quieting herself, forming herself with time, geography, and those spirits of pervading evil and doubt. A question for him. What time was it? A question for herself. Was she glad Ben was dead?

The answer was nausea.

She sat up, green and cold. He took note at once, he took action. First he covered her damp nakedness, and then he left the bed to bring her a glass of ice water. And more.

He washed her and dried her as she lay back on the bed like a corpse being readied for shroud and coffin. Then she came alive to dress herself and take herself home. She was all right until her mind faced the freeway back over the hills to home.

It was not the bell she now feared, but, rather, the missile rush of traffic, and her own weakness. She voiced none of these fears to Callender. But he read her. Whitney Callender, male nurse, his arms about her, held her up, and led her to the parking lot. To the Mercedes, to the wrong door. The steering wheel was on the left side. He was behind it. He was driving. Sunset Bouevard west, San Diego Freeway north. The pipe went from his coat pocket to his clenched teeth and back to his pocket, without being lit. Consideration personified. The windows were open, and her nausea went out like a discarded candy wrapper.

He held on to her, one strong hand in one weak one, two eyes darting smiles at her intermittently. And down the hill, exit to Ventura Boulevard. Wrong turn, or was it? No questions asked. She was in good hands.

Bewilderment and concern returned to Dolores only when Callender made a left turn into the Ivy League's driveway.

"No!" she said aloud.

"You can make it home from here."

"Yes, yes. But what about you?"

"I'm going inside, drinks and dinner. Inside the picture on the wall."

"How will you get back to the hotel?"

"Time machine and taxi," he said.

Unmindful that the parking attendant had opened her door, Dolores continued to face Callender. "I'd like to see you again."

He smiled. "Do you enjoy turning green?"

She pouted. "No, I don't. It won't happen again."

"Not if we exorcise our evil fathers. Meanwhile, please tell Chestnut Hill to call me tonight."

Green now with envy, Dolores pouted. As soon as Callender had left the car, she slid behind the wheel and drove off.

En route to her empty house, she heard another kind of bell: a warning bell ringing out questions.

Should she call Joan? Were fathers evil? Could she exorcise hers? Was Callender evil? Was the pleasure he had afforded her worth the pain she could not exorcise? Where now? What next? What price sex? Who pays the piper? When? How?

At home, when she came naked to her mirror, she saw that her mask had been ripped away.

13

For Sally Hendley it was a day of daggers.

The gray sky over the Los Angeles International Airport was pierced by ascending and descending jet daggers. Her past as an airline stewardess, the good times and the bad, stabbed her.

As she waited for Neal, she dared not muse about Roy Sutter and the promise of the future. She stayed with the past, with the present, and braced herself for a gray reunion.

Out of the skies, out of Rome and New York, Neal came to her, as she had feared, with daggers in his eyes.

Her hello went unanswered. Her attempt to kiss him failed. Questions about the flight went unanswered.

Neal took the wheel of the MG. She took to silence. He drove hard and fast. Eyes on the traffic, he cursed other drivers and complained about the performance of the MG engine.

Sally only heard a strident song of rage without guilt. Certain the trouble lay not in the skies, but, rather, in beds in Rome and New York, she put no questions to him. She bided her time. The day would darken to night, the drinking would bring on Neal's unwinding, and the time of revelation and accusation would come. Daggers from him, and, perhaps, a dagger from her.

And it came late, in the magician's box of the bed, slitted to accept the dagger thrusts. From the outside by the unwound magician. From the inside by the wary magician's assistant. No good-night kiss, no touch of love. No room, no air for love. Only the sweetened air of bourbon, the scent of garlic from the broiled, double-thick Porterhouse steak. No candles for dinner, no intimacy, no warmth. No sense of time, space, or distance. And the anger came to bed with them.

They were lying not two feet from each other, but their voices came to one another via relay stations in Rome and in New York.

"Happy?" His voice was cold.

"Yes," she said defiantly.

"You're full of shit," he said.

"I'm happy there was no hijacking. No crash."

"You know fuckin' well there was a crash."

"Between Rome and here?"

"Louisiana's between Rome and here," he reminded her.

"You're here," she said.

"See any change in me?"

"No," she said.

"Good guess, mighty good," he said with scorn. "How'd you do it? Female intuition?"

Sally said nothing to the nonquestion. She sensed he was only warming up. He could kick higher and farther, footballs and enemies.

Neal did not disappoint her. "Or was it a nervous twitch in your cunt?"

"Hardly," she said.

"That's hardly an answer."

"Or an argument."

"I've come out fightin'," he said.

"I haven't."

"Knock the chip off," he dared her.

"Which shoulder?" she asked, knowing the question and the inanity would not save her.

"I only got one crotch. And don't ask me which one of my nuts. The chip's on my one and only cock."

"Good trick."

"Feel me," he said.

She entwined her fingers, hand in hand. "For love or money?"

"Never paid for it in my life. Not by the trick."

"You heroes, you have it soft."

Her borrowed New York cleverness satisfied her, not him. The hoped-for laughter was never heard.

"Wrong guess," he said. "Feel me."

"I take your word for it."

"That's not what I told you to take."

It was time to obey, to submit, and to take her punishment. Unclasping her hands, she reached for and found the full measure of him.

"Any change?" he demanded.

"No." She withdrew her hand.

"Take your fuckin' time. I want you to be sure."

She returned the hand, freeing it from desire, and leaving it to simulate the act of stroking, and caring not if it stirred him from anger to desire.

"Are you sure now?" he asked.

"I am," she said.

"You're wrong again. You're losin' your touch."

"Sorry." She tightened her fingers.

"Not now. Touch—feel around the insides of my thighs."

Sally obeyed.

"Forget the nuts."

Forgotten, abandoned. Left thigh, right thigh. She felt nothing but the flesh of him, and nothing but her own remorse. It was far from Rome, and so much farther from Dijon. From the love they had found there, so far from New York, so far from Louisiana.

"Any change?"

"No." None in the question, none in the flesh. Only in the voice. It was now closer to the cracking of truth.

"Wrong again," he said.

She had enough. "All right, Neal. Something's wrong with you. Tell me what."

"I was knifed in Rome," he revealed.

"The tall one?" she asked, alluding to the statuesque stewardess she had seen at the airport last week.

"No, some tight-cunted, fuckin' cheerleader from Indiana. She and some fine Italian worked me over."

The burning was there, contained by her fevered skin and her charred bones. "With a knife?"

"Some fuckin' kind of stilleto. English translation: scalpel."

The understanding fed the fire. It was no joke, not any joke about an Italian Jack the Ripper plying his madness in the company of a madwoman.

"Vasectomy." She breathed the word.

"Right."

"And you blame me."

"Right again."

Her hands together and clasped again, Sally said, "I never have uttered that word to you."

"You pushed me into the scalpel, you and your fuckin' wet dreams about babies and families and homes."

She hesitated and lost nothing more. She had lost him last Wednesday, on the freeway, at the airport. Before takeoff, before the crash, the hijacking, and the vasectomy. Before the peeling of the first potato. Before Roy Sutter and Scott Joplin.

She said, "I'm sorry."

"I'll never let you forget it," he retorted.

"How long is never?"

"Well, you can pray for me to be killed."

"You? You're the prize escape artist. A million bombs, a million miles."

"Everybody gets killed. In the air, in bed."

She knew what she had to say, but she decided it was time to put some light on the matter. Touching a button among buttons, she threw lamplight against the overwhelming darkness.

"What the hell—?"

He said no more as he watched Sally throw off the blanket, free his pajama bottoms, and study the insides of his thighs.

It was there, a half-inch scar, encircled by discoloration and some fine Italian stitches. All true, all done, this deft killing of what he called a wet dream.

"Satisfied?" he asked.

Saying nothing, turning away from him, darkening the room, she returned the blanket to the ice around her heart.

"It's done," he said with pain. "The fuckin' scalpel was hangin' over my head. To New York, to Rome. In Rome, in bed. The next mornin' I took a walk. Walked to the doctor's office and back. Short walk, long walk. Like the time I walked behind three coffins—" He said no more.

Sally's eyes said tears.

"It's gonna be tough to forgive you," he said.

"Don't try," she said.

"I have to."

"Why, Neal?" she implored.

"You know fuckin' well why."

"Hap?"

"Right."

"How long do we wait before we do divorce?" Sally asked.

"Just as long as it takes you to get Hap into college."

She considered the time element. With luck, with hard work, Hap might be graduating from Ojai Prep by June, 1974.

She said, "A year from April? Upon notice of his acceptance?"

"No, a year from September," said Neal. "When Hap's there—in college. No earlier. Not April, not June."

She hesitated. "What do you and I do in the meanwhile?"

"The honeymoon goes on."

"Honeymoon?"

"You heard me."

"I hear the hate in your voice. I see it in your—"

"So what? So I've got hard feelings against you. But it doesn't go down as far as my cock."

She shuddered. "I'll sleep in Hap's room."

"Like hell you will."

"The den."

"Don't you dare move your ass out of this bed."

Those were the last words, and they hung in the silence. Sally moved only to turn her back on Neal. In a moment she heard him quit the bed. She heard him in the bathroom, in the bar. Before long she felt his weight upon the bed.

She tensed as she felt her nightgown being raised by an untender hand. She tried to escape him until the other hand clutched the hair of

84

her head. He came up behind her, ripped the nightgown, arranged her, and daggered her until he had spent the passion of his hate.

Neal slept well. Sally's eyes remained open. She watched the alarm clock until she understood she had to measure time by her calendar.

Meanwhile, there was the dark and the shapes she saw in them. Daggers. Triangles. Playing with each other the more dangerous game. Love and hate. Life and death.

14

The wild party at the Belanger house did not break up until about three o'clock Monday morning. The scavengers' luncheon began at one o'clock that afternoon for the potato peelers. They gathered around the dining room table to drink champagne, eat Polynesian food, and pick at each other's bones.

Joan Lawler, the only one of them in a party mood, smiled at Ilona Belanger. "Well, tell us about the bash."

Sighing wearily, Ilona said, "What can I tell you? It was Bobby's kind of party. An American party. Tax deductible. Maybe a hundred people, counting the guests, the hired help, and the musicians."

"Did the men bring their wives?" asked Joan.

"Some yes, some no," said Ilona. "There were eight girls in grass skirts. They must be black and blue today."

"How about the wives?" asked Joan.

"I shut my eyes to everything," said Ilona.

"No fun for you?" asked Joan.

"Ha!" Ilona pouted.

Dolores Cooper spoke up. "Wasn't there at least one man who interested you?"

Ilona turned to her. "I was not looking. Not in my own house."

Dolores persisted. "Why not?"

Joan said, "She had to take care of Bobby."

Ilona shook her head. "No, Bobby took care of business. Strictly business. He got what he wanted: investors, men with money for some of his real estate schemes. And what I want was not at the party."

Dolores understood. "A man?"

"Yes," said Ilona, smiling at last.

Sally Hendley, preoccupied with her husband and Roy Sutter, now found interest in the revelation.

"You're in love, Ilona," said Dolores.

"Very much," she said.

Dolores asked, "Not the Austrian psychologist?"

"No," said Ilona. "He is an artist."

Joan laughed. "So are you. When did you meet him?"

"Last Tuesday," said Ilona.

"At the Ivy League?" asked Dolores.

"No. Gelson's."

Dolores frowned. Joan laughed harder. "Romance at a supermarket! Marvelous! That's the kind of supermarket special I go for!"

Sally said, "Tell us about it, Ilona."

Ilona went into her report. "I was shopping—and not for a man. I was wheeling my cart around, picking up this and that, when I saw this man. Alone. Tall, slim, big mustache, corduroy jacket. Lots of hair, lots of eyes. Beautiful. I just follow him and his cart. He stops, I stop. The frozen foods. And then I see he picks up a package of frozen Hungarian goulash, looks at it, and drops it into his basket. The next thing I know I am doing what I do best. Opening my mouth. That is terrible, I say. He turns and gives me a look. Not good. I talk some more, about goulash. He listens, and then he returns the package. I talk some more. Where do you live? Do you live alone? Soon he is talking, and he is telling me he is an artist. A college professor. Back east. He is here on a—what is the word? Saturday?"

Dolores helped her out. "Sabbatical?"

"Yes! *Sabbatical.* From his university, from his wife and daughter. They are in Europe, and his house—well, he and an artist-professor who has this house near here—well, they exchanged for a year. That is all I had to hear. I told him I would bring him some goulash for lunch. He gave me the address."

"And what else?" asked Joan.

"What more can I tell you?" said Ilona. "I am ready to begin scrubbing floors for him. To drink his cheap Chilean wine. To walk the streets for him if I have to."

"But?" Dolores again.

Ilona was sad. "He loves to make love with me. But this year, this is the year for painting. Not painting. He does etching. Very big, very important. A big deal with a book club, big business. America." Her voice died away.

"What's his name?" The query came from Dolores.

Ilona held a Mona Lisa smile. "Ask me in Hungarian."

"You're not telling," said Dolores.

"You are not hearing," said Ilona. "I told you I love him."

"I shared with Joan," said Dolores.

"True," said Joan. "And I told him about you, Ilona. And Sally."

Sally turned to Joan. "Told who what about me?"

"Pardon me," said Joan to Sally. "I forgot you've been out of touch in your spaceship." She turned to Dolores. "You begin it, I'll end it. First chapter at least. I hope."

Dolores needed no further prompting. Only more champagne. She had waited long days for this moment, this chance to tell her story, withheld and deferred for a good reason: she meant to tell it once and only once, for the pleasure and the pain were both too great to withstand the stress of repetition.

Also she had designed her story to ring out a kind of truth that could withstand the omission of the bellringing on the freeway. But now, given more purpose by Ilona's reluctance to share the artist, she decided to omit nothing, to confess all. One for all, all for one, good enough for three musketeers, or four potato peelers. Freedom was a march of the many, in step, in time with the times. With the new morality.

Dolores held her audience from beginning to end, and when she was done she made some judgments. "The sex was wonderful. I was so hungry for it. And he gave me more than release. He gave me love."

"And jealousy," added Joan. When Dolores turned to frown at her, she said, "You didn't call me. I called you."

"I did give you the message," said Dolores.

"I had to drag it out of you," argued Joan.

"True," Dolores admitted. "By the time you called, I had second thoughts about Whitney Callender."

"Like what?" Joan demanded.

"How dangerous he was," Dolores said absently. "The things he said about fathers. How much he's troubled me."

Sally asked, "Would you see him again?"

"No," said Dolores.

"You're a liar," said Joan.

"It's the truth," said Dolores. "He could drive me to the analyst's couch. I've been unhappier than ever. I don't know anymore what's right and wrong. Good or bad." She faced Joan again. "Didn't he trouble you in any way?"

"You told me not to call you and tell you anything about my weekend," Joan reminded her.

"Yes," admitted Dolores. "But we're face to face now. I'll be able to see if you're telling the truth."

Joan helped herself to more champagne, smiled at Ilona and Sally, and faced Dolores without a smile.

"I called him that Friday night," she said, "and he was quick to tell me how many hours I had to live. Forty-four, he said. Frank was downstairs listening to Walter Cronkite's sweet nothings. And I said to Whit, 'In the morning,' and said no more. I went to work. Went downstairs and told Frank he looked bushed. I suggested he take up the standing invitation to spend a weekend down at Palm Springs at his boss's place. 'Alone?' he asked. 'You work hard, you've earned it. Enjoy, enjoy, you don't have to be Jewish to enjoy.' Frank didn't like that. I almost blew it with my smart-ass talk, which he took for a crack at his boss. Anyway, he was soon on the phone to Palm Springs, and off early in the morning. So much for Frank."

Joan took more champagne before she flung her truths at Dolores. "I saved my all for Whit. No masturbation in bed that Friday night. No bells ringing for me on the freeway. And no time wasted once I got into that lovely suite at the Bel-Air Hotel. Into bed with that lovely man. What a morning! What an afternoon! What a night! What a weekend! We ran out of nothing but time. I never laughed and loved so much in all my life. God, I wept when it came Sunday afternoon, time for me to go back to South Oaks, time for him to take off for Santa Barbara. But he says he's coming back. And this is the good part for you, Ilona, and for you, Sally. He's going to find time for both of you—separately, of course—even if he has to trip his old man and put him in a hospital for a few days. Now, how's that for a short, sweet story of love and life in beautiful Bel Air?" She was staring at Dolores when she ended.

"And what did the great talker talk about with you?" Dolores asked.

Joan said, "Catholic schools and schoolgirls, monasteries and nunneries—and then girls like the four of us."

"In regard to what?" demanded Dolores.

"Take your choice. Autoeroticism. Onanism. Masturbation. Psychic coitus. Or what theologians call *delectatio morosa*," said Joan.

Dolores's eyes and her skin cried havoc.

Neither Sally nor Ilona understood. It was the latter who complained. "In English, please."

Glad to be free of Dolores for a moment, Joan turned to Ilona. "It means the morbid brooding on sexual images. The kind that may lead to spontaneous orgasm."

"In American, please."

Joan was quick to oblige Ilona, and to irritate Dolores. "An orgasm without moving your body, without touching yourself."

"I don't believe it," said Ilona.

"Didn't you believe Dolores?" Joan retorted.

As Ilona turned to her, Dolores said uneasily, "Yes, darling."

"America!" Ilona exclaimed in wonder.

"The hell it is," said Joan. "It's universal, catholic with a lower-case 'c.' It can happen to a girl who hasn't a dirty thought in mind. She might be watching the sea, studying a painting—"

"Etchings, too?" Ilona wanted to know.

"Buy one of your artist's prints and find out," Joan suggested.

Ilona laughed and laughed. Sally, quietly sipping champagne, felt no pain. All of this reminded her of some evenings in Manhattan when her producer and songwriter would cross their swords of erudition, with the latter usually winning the duel with a reference to a source of erotica as yet unknown to the former.

But now Dolores returned to make her contribution, her show of education. "That's all very rare. What's more prevalent is the use of motion, the delight of motion. The—"

Joan interrupted. "A Mercedes on a smooth freeway?"

Dolores glowered at her. "Thank you, dear Joan. I was about to forget that. I was thinking of trains, streetcars, buses, horses, swings."

Resting an elbow on the table and her chin on her fist, Joan looked wide-eyed at Dolores and said, "Tell us more."

"Did *Whit* leave something out?"

Joan smiled and shook her head.

"Pretty smug, aren't you?"

"Dear Dolores, tell Sally and Ilona how long it took you to recuperate from your quickie affair with Whit."

Dolores was chagrined. "I had a touch of the flu."

Joan did not quit. "Hong Kong? London? Or Whitney Callender?"

"One last question," said Dolores. "Did he ask you about your father?"

"Yes—my Father who art in heaven." Joan laughed.

Dolores surprised her by smiling. "Thank you. For the truth."

"Are you happy now?" asked Joan.

"No, I'm not. But you are. Ilona is." Dolores faced Sally. "How about you?"

Sally underplayed it. "Nothing much has happened to me. Only rape."

Ilona shuddered. She knew too much about this. Dolores winced. Joan, intrigued, said, "Tell us more."

Sally said, "Avoid it."

"Did you fight it?" asked Joan.

"No, I'm down to fighting for my life," said Sally.

Joan again. "Who raped you?"

Sally chose silence.

"A stranger?" asked Ilona.

After some hesitation, Sally said, "Are rapists anything else but strangers?"

"Yes," said Ilona uneasily. "There is Bobby."

Joan beamed. "This I'd like to hear."

Ilona turned to her. Perplexed, she asked, "You would like to hear me scream?"

"Yes," said Joan. "I'd like to see if I could detect a note of delight in your scream. There must've been such a note. Why else are you still with Bobby?"

Ilona shrugged. "In the end he laughs. The Russians didn't. You try screaming with a dirty hand—a man's hand over your mouth." She paused to sip champagne. "I will leave Bobby. Soon."

Joan returned to Sally. "Did you scream?"

Sally shook her head.

"Was there a hand over your mouth?" asked Dolores.

"No," said Sally. "I kept talking to myself, saying, 'jam tomorrow and jam yesterday—but never jam today.' "

"What is that?" Ilona asked.

"Through the Looking Glass," said Dolores.

"In English, please."

Sally translated for Ilona. "I remembered another man and how happy he'd made me yesterday and would—please, God—make me happy again tomorrow."

The reply afforded enough understanding to Ilona. Dolores, on the other hand, needed a better reckoning of time. "How soon does tomorrow come?"

The champagne having taken down her defenses, Sally said, "Perhaps tonight."

The others understood at once. Each of them knew that Neal Hendley had departed this morning for New York, for Rome. Nobody said a word.

At last Joan said, "Sally, are you interested in Whitney Callender?"

Sally smiled. "He's all yours, Joan."

Dolores changed her mind. "I must see him again. Only to talk to him."

Joan brightened up. "Tell you what, Dolores. We'll go together. You do the talking, I'll do the rest. Make a very interesting *ménage à trois.*"

"No," said Dolores glumly.

"The masked ball over?" asked Joan.

"Perhaps." Dolores refilled her glass. "You can't wear one mask over another. That's what I tried to do. I now believe my salvation—if I dare call it that—is to be found in my own unmasking. I've got to find out the truth about the *ménage à trois* I did indulge in for too long."

Ilona faced Joan. "Do you understand her?"

Joan said, "I don't know if Dolores understands herself. Let's ask her. What the hell *ménage* are you raving about?"

"Perry, Ben, and me," said Dolores to herself.

"Ben who?" Joan again.

"My father."

"Oh," said Joan. "I see. You're in trouble, and I'd like to help you. I could say, 'Get thee to a nunnery.' Or, 'get thee to a shrink's couch.' Or maybe, 'get thee again to Whitney Callender.' Without me. I'll fix it for you when he calls me."

Dolores was interested in the last suggestion. "When will that be?"

"Next week," said Joan. "Or next year."

"What do I do in the meanwhile?"

Joan smiled. "We carry on, just you and me. I think our rape victims have deserted the potato peelers."

Ilona laughed and nodded. "Yes. As long as my artist loves me."

Sally remained pensive.

Dolores talked to herself. "No, no more waiting. I must be doing. Dancing."

"The masked ball's over," Joan reminded her.

"I was thinking of another kind of dance," said Dolores, her face darkening. "In a Nazi concentration camp, there was this young, beautiful girl. A great ballet dancer in Poland, but now a sick, starved animal. A new officer in camp remembered seeing her on stage in Warsaw and ordered her to dance for him. With each step, each movement, she found her humanity returning to her. She drew the officer into her dance and so entranced him that she was able to lift the pistol from his holster and shoot him dead before the guards killed her."

Sally and Ilona were awed, and it was Joan who spoke up. "How does that relate to you?"

"She dared," said Dolores, "and she died a human being."

"That's beautiful," said Sally.

Joan was concerned about Dolores. "And who are you going to dance with?"

Dolores bared herself. "The man who loved me most. My father."

"You're mad," said Joan. "Or soused. Your father's dead."

"No, he's not," Dolores continued. "He lives in me."

"*You* believe in ghosts!" Joan was incredulous.

"In possession," said Dolores. "And I believe I must dance myself free of him."

"Ghosts follow you everywhere," Joan said.

"Not if you kill them," said Dolores. There were tears in her eyes now.

It was Ilona who broke the ensuing silence. "Nobody talks about tennis. About clothes. We have changed."

"For the better," said Joan. "We're human. We're dancing." She faced Dolores. "I'm with you. Shall we dance over to the Ivy League?"

Dolores tried to find her smile. "Why not Gelson's?"

Joan laughed. "We can't cook and bake like Ilona, but we can dance, kill, and be killed."

Ilona laughed at Joan's nonsense. Dolores and Sally heard neither nonsense nor laughter.

15

She lay naked, her head resting on his hairy chest, her eyes open to the blazing logs, her ears open to the piano rags. She was musing how much she loved Roy Sutter and Scott Joplin when the record broke, and with it the spell.

Sutter stirred. He pillowed Sally's head, and left the couch to free the trapped needle.

"Well, we've worn that one out," said Sutter. "I'll buy another."

Uneasy now, Sally said, "Buy us more time."

He smiled. "It's been a good week. Five straight nights."

Sally could not smile. She was listening to the Red Queen saying: "Sometimes in the winter we take as many as five nights together—for warmth, you know."

"What's wrong?" Sutter asked her.

"I'd rather all the clocks broke," she said forlornly.

"Not now. Let 'em run fast. Don't break 'em until the next midnight rolls around for us."

Sally sat up. It was time to dress, time to leave.

Sutter sat down beside her. He kissed her before he said, "Look, we did as we agreed to. We kept Neal out of this house all week long. Now it's time to let him in—and let me in on what's going on in your house."

"*This* is my house," she protested.

"*His* house," he prodded.

"Yes, his house, my problem. Not yours."

"Come on, Sally. Out with it. Neal's my problem, too."

She said nothing. Instead she rose and reached for her underwear.

"How bad has it been?" he asked.

"Not bad enough to spoil anything for us," she responded.

"You say one thing," he said. "Your eyes tell me another. I wish you'd spill it all out."

"I'm all right, Roy. I'll be all right."

He could not believe her. "Does Neal suspect anything?"

"No."

"Has he mentioned my name?"

Sally thought about it. "Once. He said something about you avoiding him. At the club. He's looking to play golf with you. He misses not playing with you."

"I don't miss him. I was avoiding him even before you and I started up."

She glanced awry at him. "Is that what we did?"

"Don't look for a fight," he warned her. "You won't get it from me. You can't distract me from what we've got to talk about."

She went to him and kissed him. "I'm sorry. I had to try."

"Try the truth," he urged her. "It might save us."

Sally paled. "From what?"

"I think I'll be a broken record," he said. "I'll say it again. We're playing a very dangerous game. A long game, two years maybe. We've got to look out for you."

"Just me? Not you?"

"You can't avoid Neal. I can't avoid being afraid for you."

"It goes both ways," said Sally.

"Want some coffee?"

She shook her head.

"Brandy?"

"Nothing but a good-bye kiss," she said. She retrieved her sweater and pants.

"What kind of kisses has Neal been giving you?" Sutter demanded.

"Don't, Roy," she pleaded.

"I'm not just asking out of jealousy. Please, you're wasting lies on me. I know you, we know each other. The only things that scare me are the things I don't know. I can handle everything else. Anything."

Sally understood. When she believed she could be selective about the truth, she said, "Neal doesn't kiss me anymore."

The revelation surprised Sutter. "Since when? The last time he came home?"

"Yes," she said.

He winced. "Then he did see the change in you."

"No, he didn't," she said with certainty.

"What changed him?"

Sally told him about the spat on the freeway en route to the airport. About the tall stewardess.

"Is that all?"

She frowned. "That's a strange question from you. I thought you shared my dreams about a home and children."

"You know I do," he retorted. "But I know there's more you're not telling me."

Sally offered a weak defense. "That's the kind of girl I am."

Sutter persisted. "What else changed Neal? Did he fall in love with that stewardess he had his eye on?"

"No such luck," muttered Sally. She sat down to put on her socks and boots.

He sat down beside her on the couch. "Then what was it?"

She hesitated before she gave it to him straight, without the metaphors about the daggers. "Neal had a vasectomy in Rome."

"Jesus!" Sutter saw it as an act of violence. A first act. But he remained silent about his own alarm.

Sally said what she was thinking. "He's a fool. A sick fool."

"I'm sorry for him," he said painfully. "I never liked Neal, but I never hated him. I was always either sorry for him or envious of him."

Sally was more intrigued than bewildered. "Why were you sorry for Neal?"

Sutter found and lit a cigarette before he responded. "You got to feel for him when you remember what he lost. And how they were lost."

"I don't understand," said Sally.

"The crash, the airplane. I remember hearing him say an airplane was as much a part of him as his flesh and bones."

Sally shivered. "Yes, he keeps dreaming he's putting his wife and daughters on a train instead of a plane."

Sutter blew smoke and nodded.

"And why do you envy Neal?"

"Mostly because of you. Hap. College. The war."

She had nothing to say about the strange measures men took of each other. She meant only to afford Sutter a better understanding of the man he envied. "Neal has another recurring nightmare. He dreams of *four* graves in Louisiana."

"Hap?" asked Sutter.

"Yes. And there's more," she said. It was easier to talk about the past rather than the imminent present. "Do you know the story of 'The Monkey's Paw'?"

"Yeah, I do. Caught it on TV. The three wishes."

"Catch Neal's version. *He* has the monkey's paw. His first wish returns Hap from the fourth grave. When he sees how mangled Hap is, he makes his second wish. And Hap is returned to his grave."

"And the third wish?" asked Sutter.

"A fifth grave beside the other four. For himself."

Sutter coughed, and it was hardly a cigarette cough. "When did Neal tell you this? Before you married him?"

"After."

"Why? What brought it up? Does he get drunk and morbid?"

"He was angry," Sally said. "Very angry."

"At you or Hap?"

"Both of us."

"What happened?"

"It's been four years and I don't—"

"Please." He touched her.

She relented. "Hap took three shots at the television screen in his room."

Sutter tensed. "With what?"

"The pistol from the drawer of Neal's night table."

"What kind of pistol?"

"A target pistol. A .22 caliber."

"Where is it now?"

"They're both gone. I'd—"

Sutter was confused. "Both?"

"There were matching pistols," Sally explained. "The one still in the case had been kept in Neal's closet. I asked him to get rid of them."

Not assuaged, Sutter asked, "Do you know that he actually did? Did he tell you he'd sold 'em?"

Sally shook her head. "Is it important?"

"It is," he declared, "if Neal still has the case hidden somewhere in the house. That possible?"

"Yes, but there's no danger now. Hap's all right now. He's well again."

Sutter said, "I'm not worried about Hap. It's Neal. From what you tell me, he's not well."

Sally frowned. "You're frightening me, Roy."

"I just want you to take care."

"I will," she promised.

He grinned and held her coat for her. She slipped into it. He buttoned it for her.

Placing an arm about Sally, he led her out of the warm house and into the cold night. She was behind the wheel, warming the engine and letting her wipers slap the mist from the windshield, when she turned to Sutter.

Her voice choked, she said, "I love you."

"I love you." He brought his face down toward hers and kissed her waiting mouth.

"Soon?"

He nodded. "Take care."

She released her parking brake and shifted into reverse.

"Hold it," he said with sudden concern. "Put the brake on again."

"Roy, you'll catch cold. If you have something more to say, come in the car."

"I'm all right." He did not tell her he had no wish to leave his tracks or his scent for Neal to detect. There were two places he had to avoid: the car and the Hendley house. "Listen," he said, "are you and Neal still sleeping together?"

"Yes," said Sally.

"Is he still making love to you?"

"Yes. *To* me."

96

"Taking it out on you?"

"I'm his wife."

"Can you take it?"

"I'm all right, Roy, Really I am."

"Maybe now you are," he said. "You weren't when you came here last Monday night. I didn't see any black-and-blue marks on your beautiful body, but there was a beat-up look in your eyes."

"Please, Roy, it's been lovely this week, don't say anything to—"

"I have to," he interrupted painfully. "You're running into a tough week. Into a bad guy. We've had our time together for now, and nothing I say now can change it or spoil it. I just have to know what the score is."

"I mean to be your wife—as soon as possible," said Sally.

He took her left hand from the steering wheel, kissing it before he held onto it. "I know that. That's why it's important for you to level with me. And me with you. And I have to tell you I believe Neal's been letting you have it. In the worst way. I don't know if rape's the right word—"

"It isn't," Sally protested.

"What is?" he demanded.

She studied the rage in his eyes. "I don't know, Roy. I do know I'm not fighting him." She paused. "I don't intend to."

The rage gave way to agony. "How much can you take?"

"As much as I have to," she vowed. "I know what I'm fighting to save. You know what it is, too."

"Yeah. Any cigarettes in the car?"

"No, I'm sorry. Oh, there is a pack of those little Dutch cigars Neal smokes."

"Forget it. He can count."

She smiled sadly. "You're so careful."

"I'll tell you how much," he said pensively. "I've been thinking maybe we're taking too many chances."

"What chances? My coming here?"

"Yeah."

"Have you a better idea?" Sally asked.

"No, a terrible one—but maybe the smartest. We can talk on the telephone. We can see each other at the restaurant."

"Upstairs or downstairs?"

"Downstairs."

Sally looked toward the house. "I don't know if I can stay away."

"Think about it," he urged her, squeezing her hand. "Think about Carmel Valley."

She turned to him again. "What'll you do when you need me? Run back to Vegas?"

Sutter laughed. "Only for some golf, and some shooting."

She smiled. "I believe I'd rather have you play around with girls than with guns."

"You're kidding."

"No, I think not. You have to live with the fact that I'm Neal's wife, and I have to live with the fact that you're a handsome bachelor. Have and eat your birthday cake. It won't kill you. And I won't kill you."

Sutter laughed again. She drew his hand toward her. He bent and kissed her mouth for a long, lingering moment. And then he withdrew to stand in the cold dark and watch her back the MG out of the long driveway. He waved to her and to darkness.

Sally drove slowly. She was in no rush to return to Neal's house. The windshield wipers now stilled, she listened for Roy's laughter and looked for his bright, smiling eyes to give her the light to see her way from San Fernando Valley to Carmel Valley.

Sutter did not go directly into the house. There was a disadvantage he had to correct. He could not know whether Neal had hidden or sold his matching pistols, but Neal did know where he kept his shotgun. One afternoon on the country club parking lot, Neal had come upon him when he was returning his golf clubs to the trunk of his Cadillac. Neal had spied the weapon, had insisted on handling it while the two of them shot the bull about hunting and shooting.

Sutter went into the garage, into the trunk. He removed the shotgun and the boxes of shells, concealing them in an old steamer trunk resting on a high shelf. He locked the trunk, the garage door, and locked out the threat of Neal Hendley turning the shotgun on him.

16

To Dolores it was déjà vu. To Joan it was the luck of the Irish. There were now two Whitney Callenders.

The girls were sitting pretty at the table under the photograph of the 1916 Yale football squad, sipping their drinks and believing in the prospects of this Tuesday afternoon.

The boys were seated at the adjacent wall table on the girls' right. Both seemed under forty; neither was as handsome as Whitney Callender. Nevertheless, they had good, swarthy, rugged faces and bright college eyes more interested in the pictures on the walls than in Dolores and Joan.

As the boys talked football, the girls noted their bankers' suits, the gold cigarette cases and lighters, and the Wild Turkey they were drinking neat.

The boys were studying the photograph above and behind the girls and chatting about drop-kickers and drop-kicking when Dolores smiled and said, "Yale?"

"Hai Karate," said Ted Nichol, identifying his aftershave lotion.

Burt Grant said, "How did you guess? You must be a real Yale football fan. I'm Clint Frank."

Nichol got his cue. "And I'm Larry Kelley."

The names of the two All-Americans who had made their fame at Yale in the thirties meant nothing to Dolores and Joan. They only smiled and introduced themselves.

Nichol and Grant turned out to be glib and amusing. They told funny football stories, and at times they sounded more like a comedy team than Yale men, more like characters from a street corner tavern than like college men. But the laughs and the drinks were coming, and neither Dolores nor Joan cared to be bothered by their suspicions.

In the end the boys picked up the checks. And the girls. The party was being moved to their suite.

"We have our own cars," said Joan. "We'll follow you."

And they did. On foot. The Travel House Motel was three short blocks west of the Ivy League, on the north side of Ventura Boulevard and on the poor side of taste. A neon sign flashing in the sunny February afternoon, weather-stained stucco walls, asbestos shingles.

Joan frowned. "You guys are kidding us."

"We own it," said Joan's man, Ted Nichol.

"Bought it yesterday," said Dolores's man, Burt Grant.

"Another investment for Chicago, Incorporated," said Ted. "That's us, Nichol and Grant."

"The Bentley's ours," said Burt.

Among the battered, muddy Fords, Pontiacs, and other junk heaps, Joan and Dolores saw the clean, polished Bentley. That did it. They followed the boys who were not Clint Frank and Larry Kelley up a cement stairway to a place that reminded neither of them of the Bel-Air Hotel.

The only signs of class in the otherwise tawdry suite of rooms—two connecting bedrooms, hot beds, cold TV sets—were the attaché cases, luggage, and portable bar.

Burt was the bartender, Ted the entertainer, and the spirits and hijinks flowed from them. All in fun, all for laughs. Joan with her boiler-makers and Dolores with her martinis were soon caught up in the comedy.

"Now listen to this," said Ted. "I'm in my dry-cleaning plant one July afternoon. Five years ago. It's hot and I'm hating myself and my life." Ted took more Wild Turkey. "The phone rings. 'Hello. Who? Yeah, I'm Ted Nichol. Who are you? Judy Karlstein? No, I never heard Rosetta talk about you. Oh, the hospital guild.' Then she tells me she's out at the Starlight Motel in Evanston. She gives me the address and tells me she'll be waiting for me."

Burt laughed. Dolores and Joan waited to hear something to laugh about.

Ted went on. "Now I'm getting hot where a guy ought to get hot, and I say, 'What do you like to drink?' And this Judy Karlstein blows her top. 'Get right over here,' she says, 'I just took the air outa your tires.' I figured—tell you the truth, I don't know what the hell I figured. My car was over in the filling station across the street. My beat-up Falcon. Then I hear her say, 'Your wife's Olds!' I'm thinking maybe the fucking heat's got her, and then I hear her again. 'Rosetta's in the motel with my Sylvester! My husband!' Jesus Fucking Christ! Now she thinks I'm crazy because I'm laughing like mad. I tell her, 'It's your ball game, honey.' I hang up and get the hell to the bank before it closes, and I clean out all the accounts, checking, savings, even the kids' Christmas clubs."

Now Ted and Burt laughed. Dolores and Joan did not.

Ted again. "Sold the fucking business, kissed off Rosetta, the kids, Chicago, and came west to find my old buddy, Burt the bum. Between us, we—Burt, tell 'em—tell them—how much are we worth today?"

Burt was proud. "We passed our first million. We're solid. All real estate. Solid as the ground under us."

"We have earthquakes," Joan said.

Funny. Everything was funny to Ted and Burt.

Ted turned to Burt. "Good-bye, Burt. See you in church."

Burt laughed, grabbed the gin bottle and one of Dolores's hands and led her into the other room, kicking the door shut behind them.

Burt talked. "You're not used to this, are you?"

"What do you mean by this?" Dolores asked, standing at the window. The wind was up, the smog gone, and the snow was high on the mountains to the north.

"Dives like this. We're going to fix things up. Do the whole place over. Studio beds, paintings, piped-in stereo. Make it like a pad. No TV and none of this borax furniture. Changing the name, too. Something classy, something priced right, if you know what I mean."

"Do I have to wait?" asked Dolores.

"I made my apologies."

"Are you married?"

"To my money," said Burt.

"And to Ted?"

"I wouldn't divorce my money. Ted and I—we're a good team. We go way back. That counts for something."

Dolores came away from the window and sat down on the edge of the made bed. "Does Ted mean that much to you?"

"Money. Laughs. Hard to live without them."

"And a wife?"

"Not in California. The first thing I learned out here was that the standing joke was marriage."

"Haven't changed your mind?"

Burt smiled. "I'm sure you read more than the funny papers. The only ones serious about marriage today are the fags and the dykes."

"Never been in love?"

"Time and again. How long have you been divorced?"

"I didn't say I was," said Dolores.

A better smile now from Burt. "You look more beautiful than ever. If you know what I mean."

Dolores emptied her glass. "Demonstrate," she said. She was drunk enough now to say it.

Finishing his drink, Burt took the glass from Dolores, and then returned to take off her shoes, stockings, skirt, pearls, sweater, slip, bra, and hip-huggers. He was very neat in laying her things across a chair before he stripped.

Meanwhile, through the closed door, Dolores heard Joan's low cry of release. Ted was not heard from. The bed was.

Using her eyes now, Dolores saw Burt in another light, as an emperor without clothes. Or, on second glance, as a naked, uncircumcised Mediterranean fisherman.

"Greek?" she asked.

Burt put down his carefully folded trousers and faced Dolores. "That a request or a question?"

"Your ethnic—?"

"I know that word. Syrian. Ted's Italian. We both went to court to shorten our names." He grinned. "Just that," he added, fondling his erection.

Dolores laughed and welcomed him to bed with open arms and with an open mind that put her on some sun-baked Aegean isle. Burt brought grapes of kisses and treated her much like a virgin princess until he shattered the mood with a question.

"Which way would you like it?"

Dolores knew at once. "The way you did it with your ex-wife."

"Exactly?"

"Yes."

Burt released himself from the vise of her legs, left the bed, and returned with a condom, which he unrolled onto his penis. Without further ado, he mounted her, kissed and fondled her breasts, penetrated her. His passion soon spent, he collapsed beside her.

Dolores fell to despair. Damn the imposters. Yale men, indeed. No Whitney Callender he. No ringing of bells for me.

She gave Burt some moments to regain the rhythm of his breathing before sliding live fingers across and down his body. Suddenly the shut door connecting to the adjoining room burst open. In rushed Joan and Ted.

Four in the bed. The name of the game was Ted and Joan, Burt and Dolores. Joan went for Burt, Ted went for Dolores, and Dolores went for nothing of the kind.

"No!" she wailed.

"We're all friends," Ted said, laughing. "Come on, the name of the game is four-handed fucking."

Joan and Burt voiced no opinions. Their mouths and hands were engaged in a more primordial language.

"No!" Dolores again, as she tore herself loose and tumbled from the bed to the floor.

Ted laughed and came off the bed to pin Dolores on the floor.

"No!" she cried.

"Ted! Come to bed!" It was Joan calling.

As Ted turned to Joan, Dolores got up in panic, grabbing garments and shoes and pearls. Intercepting her, Ted struggled with her until the string of pearls became as unstrung as Dolores was.

"Shit," said Ted, watching the pearls dance on the plank floor, but not for long. He never turned to Dolores again. A glance toward Joan and Burt told him where he belonged. He went there. Dolores went out, taking a backward look to the bed before shutting her eyes and the door.

In less than five minutes, she was out of the room, down the stairs, through the parking court, and out again on Ventura Boulevard.

The sun was warm, the wind cold, the air clean. She was hot and dirty, body and mind. As she began to walk to the east, to the Ivy League, she saw nothing in the streets, everything in the bed.

Four in the bed. Including her.

And then it began to happen, as it had happened to her on the San Diego Freeway the afternoon she trailed Whitney Callender to the Bel-Air Hotel.

"No!" she cried out, and no one heard her.

No, no bell, the bell must not ring. No, not here, not again, not here. Please, God! Daddy! She let her mind dwell on her daddy, lying in his coffin, the coffin being lowered into the open grave. Fire with fire, morbid thought with morbid thought. She fought the fight and, this time, she won.

The sight of her Mercedes warmed her. The smile of the parking attendant returned the fear of the bell. But she won again, making it back to her house without losing control of the car or her mind.

The loneliness, the empty quiet of the house, was now a comfort to her. Going straight up to the masterless bedroom, she was quick to turn on the bath water, slow to undress, and quick again to return to Ted and Joan, Burt and Joan.

Out of this fire, she went into boiling, scourging water. Anything, anything to take her from the hot-as-hell bed in the Travel House. Anything. Cold water. Anything. Back to the freeway, to the Bel-Air Hotel. To Whitney Callender.

Her mind and her blood still boiling, she released a laugh the hysteria of which chilled her. Damn, she thought, did a man have to go to medical school or Yale to learn the secret and the source of the clitoris?

No more thoughts, no more thinking, a finger can be a tongue. Yes, yes, yes. Darling Whitney, darling Whitney, darling.

Spent, depressed, bone- and soul-weary, she left the bathroom and faced the inviting bed and the lure of sleep. But the bed was not empty. A game was in progress there. Ted and Joan, Burt and Dolores. Ted and Burt, Joan and—

Dolores found fresh underwear, warm socks, ski sweater, and wool pants, and went downstairs to read. A soft chair in the den, a hard drink of brandy, and a harder book to read: Simone de Beauvoir's *The Coming of Age.*

Wandering eyes, wandering mind. Palo Alto. Linda pregnant. A hard laugh. Grandma's back from the motel. Yes, yes, oh, yes. Desperation born of aging and dying. The orgasm as pleasure, as pain. As guilt.

An automobile horn sounded, through the wind, through the walls. Again. Recognizing the sound of the Datsun horn, Dolores froze. Again and again.

Slamming the thick book to the carpet, she rose and went to the door. There was the Datsun, there was Joan behind the wheel. Glassy-eyed, guiltless.

The wind was cold, Dolores's voice also. "I'll call you tomorrow."

Joan waved an envelope. "I've got something for you."

"A note of apology?" Dolores demanded.

"Your pearls!"

Dolores hurried out to the car. She caught the heavy envelope flipped to her by Joan. "Thank you."

"Thank the pearl divers, Ted and Burt." Joan smiled. "We missed you. I missed you. You could have dived down on me, and I—"

"Good-bye."

A limp wave, a roar of the engine. "Bye now!"

Dolores rushed back into the house, slamming the door shut against the cold and the dirt. Joan's exhaust. Out of the mouth shaped by missals and rosaries.

She did not trouble to count the pearls or to consider restringing them. She had really never wanted to see them again. The meaning of them was gone, the memory was not. They were meant to be lost, stolen, or surrendered in partial payment to the piper. But now the piper was dunning her again, not for payment in pearls, but in pornographic pictures of Joan and her, in perversely sounded bells.

17

In the dream he was a boy again in Placerville, panning gold with his father, until the running stream sounded like a ringing telephone. Roy Sutter opened his eyes, his mind now panning terror, his right hand shooting out for the telephone.

He never lifted it. There was no ringing, there was no alarm on the face of the clock. It was 4:42 A.M., and all was not well with him.

At one o'clock in the morning he had telephoned Las Vegas. Unable to reach Barnes, he had left a message: a storm was coming, he was not. And he had gone to bed certain Barnes would be anything but understanding. Barnes did something about weather; he ignored it.

The imagined ringing had led to the imagined fear that Vince Fonte was calling him to report a shooting at the Hendley house. With light, fire, and smoke he was able to blame his tension on Neal's target pistols and his own Winchester. He killed the cigarette and the lamp, accepted night's blindfold, and waited for dawn.

He meant to beat back his depression about Sally and her predicament. He meant to be the early bird beating Neal Hendley and anyone else to the first tee. He wanted to be a boy again playing alone on the lonesome course winding through the rolling hills. That, for him, was the next best thing to panning gold with his father.

The dawn sky was gray and threatening, the rain clouds advancing out of the north, as Sutter drove to the country club. It was warm in the clubhouse, and it was deserted until the door leading from the pro shop opened. The first to enter was a man he liked, Fitch Young, the club's director of golf. Behind him came an ogre, lightning in his eyes, thunder in his voice.

"Roy!"

The sky fell, crushed the day, and trapped Sutter. As he went to join them at a table, he thought that Neal Hendley on this black morning looked older than Fitch Young. And yet, at closer inspection, it seemed to Sutter that Hendley's smile was sun bright.

"Glad to see you, Roy. I can't get Fitch out on a mornin' like this."

Young chuckled, recalled a match with Paul Runyan in a hailstorm, and left the "rain dancers" laughing.

"If we're lucky," said Hendley, "maybe we'll get hail."

"I used to hit stones," said Sutter.

"Stony to the pins, you mean." Hendley laughed.

"Stones. Pebbles. Back of my house, when I was a kid." It was a good memory for Sutter.

Hendley frowned. "Hell, all I can recollect this mornin' is how fuckin' old and tired I feel."

Sutter struck the rock of a question. "Why didn't you forget to get out of bed this morning?"

"Jet lag. Fatigue. Fuckin' nerves," said Hendley forlornly. "Can't sleep. Not more than a few hours at a time. And then I wake up more fuckin' tired than before. I got to play this mornin'."

A waiter brought two coffees. Sutter took his black and hot, and it was good. The morning, he was certain, would be cold and black. Hendley's nerves would fuck him yet.

The waiter soon returned with a stack of cakes and pig sausages for Hendley, ham and eggs for Sutter. He took care to be himself. His question was straight down the middle. "How's Hap?"

"Fine," Hendley muttered without interest.

"And Sally?"

Hendley hesitated. Unsmiling, lying in his teeth, he said, "Fine."

"Good."

Hendley looked up from his plate, swallowed his mouthful of food, and weighed Sutter's honest comment. "You and me, we got things in common."

"The Air Force," said Sutter. It was a shank of a remark.

"Hell, what did you ever fly but those eighteen fuckin' greens at Maxwell Field?" Thunder again from Hendley.

Sutter said it all with a wide grin. This ground had been covered by them, once too often. No duel there.

"Somethin' deeper," said Hendley sadly. "Like the graves where our wives are buried."

"Yeah," Sutter agreed. "But you've got Hap and—"

"The graves are still there. Three of them for me."

Sutter nodded and ate.

"Where do you get your action?" Hendley asked.

Sutter chose not to understand the question. "From pigeons like you," he said, grinning.

Hendley frowned again. "I'm talkin' about sex."

"Vegas."

"Long way to go for it."

"That's where it's at."

"And what about L.A.?"

"That's where I work. Hard, too."

"Not you," said Hendley. "You do everythin' easylike. You and Julius Boros." He laughed at Sutter. "Fitch says—behind your back, that is—

106

he says you and Boros, when the two of you played together, it was like two sleepwalkers comin' down the fairway. Swing, yawn, swing. And the birdies sing."

Sutter allowed Hendley to conclude his encore of laughing. "Old Jay," he said, referring to Boros, "has won himself two U.S. Opens and one PGA. He was awake. I was the only sleepwalker. The only day-dreamer."

"Dreamin' about what?"

"The shots I fell asleep on."

"Don't tell me about Hogan in Tucson," said Hendley, with a sausage in his mouth. "On a mornin' like this, I'm just liable to bust out cryin'."

"Save your tears, Neal. I'm gonna whip your ass."

"How many pops you givin' me?"

"All you can take without embarrassment."

Hendley laughed. "This mornin' I'll take three a side."

"For how much?"

"How's business, Roy?"

"This is pleasure."

"Hundred-buck Nassau. Three ways, no presses."

"I'll take your check."

Hendley laughed. "You're daydreamin' again." He rose. "Take care of the tab. I'll get my cannons."

"I'll get the cart," said Sutter.

Stopping short, Hendley wheeled about. "The hell you will. We're walkin' this mornin'."

"I'll get the caddies," said Sutter.

"No caddies. Just you and me, and the rain."

"You thrill me," said Sutter, smiling.

He fell asleep on the smile as soon as Hendley had gone through the door leading to the locker room. And he was saying nevermore to himself, over and again, until another kind of truth woke him up. He was not playing Neal this morning, not playing golf. This was just another round in the more dangerous game he was playing with Sally.

The wind drove the clouds, the mist, and the February chill over the dew-bound fairways and through the rustling trees. Sutter was ready for it. He wore thermal underwear under his warm slacks and turtleneck sweater, and he had rain gear packed into his golf bag.

Hatless, wearing only a cardigan sweater over his cotton golf shirt, Hendley swung a fistful of irons to limber up, to warm up. His pro-sized Kangaroo golf bag rested against the staunchion of the ball washer. With each swing, he seemed to drive the jet fatigue from his eyes, his brain, and his body.

As he swung his driver, Sutter daydreamed about the lost days when he was caddy-toting two such heavy bags for some country club duffers.

107

He considered playing like a duffer today and sending Neal home happy. For Sally's sake. But he also remembered that Neal—despite some tight matches—had never taken a nickel from him.

Sutter dropped the idea of throwing the match. He knew he had to forget Sally. Today had to be like any other day. This was no morning to be cautious or careless. He had to be himself. Alone. Separate and apart from Sally. No hustling. In Neal's lexicon hustling translated to cheating. No cheating. Not this morning. Not until the first night Neal blew town again. Forget it, forget Sally. Think of Neal blowing the match. As always.

Sutter surrendered the honor of teeing off to Hendley. The latter stepped up, set up his Titleist, took a smooth, practice swing, and then muscled the ball into the face of the wind. Sutter's swing drove his Maxfli on a lower arc, the ball skidding through the wet grass and stopping about ten yards beyond the Titleist.

"Son of a bitch!" cried Hendley. "You slept all the way through the swing!"

Sutter was deaf to him, blind to him. He intended to play his ball, and his ball alone. Despite Hendley, despite Sally, he meant to have his kind of morning. He was alone, and the lone burden was the golf bag.

Hendley talked to himself, cursed himself when he hit a poor shot, and carved humor whenever he made a great shot. And he made several of those. His jabbering did not come close to Lee Trevino's. His humor fell far short of Hershey Barnes's.

A gallery of clouds came lower to watch the match. The mist continued to fall, the minutes fell, and the successive holes played longer and tougher.

Sutter and Hendley were equally as tough. Hendley played the front side in one over par, his best performance ever against Sutter. He needed it. At the turn he had Sutter one down.

"This is great!" Hendley was beaming, color in his face, light in his eyes. "I love you, Roy. Son of a bitch, you're bringin' me back to life."

"I'll bring flowers," deadpanned Sutter.

Hendley, who was teeing up his ball, looked to Sutter. "For your funeral. Not mine."

He was not laughing but there was joy in his swing, distance and direction to the solidly struck ball. Sutter yawned, shut his mouth, kept his left eye open and behind the ball, and skied his shot. It fell fifty yards short of Hendley's drive.

Hendley laughed his way down the fairway. He was singing an LSU football song until Sutter was ready to hit. It was not Hendley who sang when the ball was struck by the face of Sutter's three wood. It was the ball, singing all the way to the green, to the pin. Sure birdie.

Despite his one-stroke handicap on this hole, Hendley blew it by muscling his following shot into a yawning trap and ending up with a bogie. No more laughter, no more song. More yawning traps, more yawns from Sutter.

And then rain, first as soft as Sutter's swing, and then as hard as Hendley's. The snakes came out, and Hendley was there to beat them with his woods and irons, with his temper and rages.

Sutter heard only the rain. He had been quick to don his rain jacket and pants, quicker to wear his rain hat, and to open his golf umbrella. But Hendley, whose bag contained similar equipment, refused to believe it was raining anything but shit, lucky shit for the lucky, yawning son of a bitch parading around under his red umbrella. He gave more concern to his clubs, drying the woods before hooding them, and drying the irons and his putter before using them. He himself was soaked.

Sutter, trying to keep his mind on the game, was thinking that the bastard was being killed two ways: the match and the one life he had. A sure case of pneumonia.

At the fifteenth tee, with Sutter three up on the back side, the rain struck with fury, puddling the fairways and greens.

Sutter looked to Hendley for a sign of humanity, a shiver, or a hangdog look. He saw waterproof rage. But then, abruptly, Hendley went into one of the pockets of his bag. He came out with a pint of Old Taylor.

Before Hendley could open the bottle, Sutter said, "Good idea. Only let's do it right. In the clubhouse."

"Fuck you! Shoot! The fuckin' match isn't over yet."

"All bets off."

"Shoot!"

Sutter shut up and shot. The ball went straight and true, burying itself at first impact within the soaked fairway. Like a bullet. Hendley had better luck. Landing was his business and his ball landed on firmer ground. Sutter had no shot. He waited for Hendley to make an observation about casual water.

"Shoot," said Hendley.

"From casual water?" demanded Sutter.

"Casual water, shit! Nothin' casual about this fuckin' rain. Shoot!"

Sutter took his sand wedge and sent a mudpie some thirty yards down the fairway, a rain forest away from a lost hole.

On the seventeenth hole the situation was reversed. This time Hendley's ball buried itself alive and left him for dead until Sutter, without a pause or a word, dug out the Titleist, cleaned it, and tossed it to him.

Hendley's wet face reddened. "Showin' me up?"

"It's in the book," Sutter said.

"The hustler's handbook?"

"Shoot," said Sutter, walking away from him and listening to the rain pommel his umbrella.

His rage subdued, Hendley struck a three-iron shot that won the hole for him. He was now only one down on the back side. Tied on the match.

The finishing hole at South Oaks was the longest and toughest par four on the course, 432 yards uphill to the green, beyond which loomed the Spanish tiles of the old clubhouse. The number one handicap hole.

"Tell you what, pro," said Hendley, "I stand to win two hundred or lose one hundred, but the hell with that. Let's play for the works—three hundred bucks on this last fuckin' hole."

"No," Sutter said.

"Forget the stroke." Hendley played it tough. "We'll play even."

Sutter was equally tough. "We made the bets on the first tee. You get a stroke here."

"You son of a bitch, you're sore!"

"Shoot," said Sutter.

"By the book," announced Hendley.

"By the bottle," said Sutter to himself. He watched Hendley take a long, deliberate backswing before shifting his weight and driving the ball high, hard, and far. His own drive had too low a trajectory, the first bounce being its last.

Sutter's second shot was a three wood that screamed into wet sand, into the trap to the right of the green.

"Beautiful," said Hendley. He saw no rain, no Sutter, only the flapping flag. He throttled a four wood. The ball flew for the flag, overshot its landing on the green, and crashed into the trap behind it.

"Son of a bitch!" protested Hendley. He could not understand why the ball had not buried itself in the soft green.

Sutter was away. He took a long chance, using his pitching wedge instead of his sand iron. The difficult shot came off, the ball skidding and spinning back to within twenty feet of the pin.

Hendley, aware of his one-stroke advantage on the hole, played it safely. Or so he had hoped. The ball barely reached the green. He was about eighteen feet from the pin. Cursing himself, he flung his sand wedge against his bag, reached for his blade putter, and marched up to the hole. He removed the wet flag and moved out of Sutter's line of sight.

The rain was coming down in torrents as Sutter stood over his putt, set himself, and delivered his best putting stroke. The ball ran straight into the cup, giving him a par.

Giving Hendley occasion for epithets, and for heroics. He now had to sink his long putt to win the hole and pocket two hundred dollars. He had to get down in two putts to break even. He gave no thought to three putts as he took his time lining up and figuring out the speed and the break of the green.

110

Sutter, under his umbrella and carrying his bag, moved about twenty yards away from the green's apron. He stood there and grimly watched Hendley go into action. He wanted to get the match over with, one way or another. He wanted to get the hell away from Hendley.

At long last Hendley took a bold putt. The ball, well struck, well aimed, caught the lip of the cup and spun to rest about three feet away.

"Shit!" thundered Hendley.

At this point Sutter turned his back on his opponent and started up the hill to the clubhouse, never once looking back. He had not lost, and he cared nothing about winning. All that mattered now was his reaction. It had to be truer than his own putt had been. Otherwise the losers would be Sally and himself. And so, in character, on course, he set out for the parking lot.

Meanwhile, Hendley was blind to the rain and to Sutter's retreat. He saw nothing but the putt still confronting him. Before he struck the ball again, he saw defeat. After he had struck it, he saw disaster. The ball rolled toward the middle of the cup, only to die at the lip.

He swung again. The blade of the putter cut the wet grass and buried itself.

His rage spent, Hendley again became aware of the rain, the defeat, and the shame. The most difficult move he had to make that morning came when he turned his body and raised his head to face Sutter.

But Sutter was gone, out of sight, bag, umbrella, and body.

Confusion hit Hendley, and then understanding and shame. The putter was drawn out of the green with ease. The green was repaired with ease.

Nothing else was easy, not the last climb up the hill, not the fruitless search for Sutter, not the warm water in the locker room shower, not the whiskey in the bar, not the drive home.

Getting into bed with a bottle of bourbon was easy. Sally was not at home. A note on the kitchen table explained her absence.

When she returned from the supermarket, Sally was concerned to find him in bed.

"Are you ill?" she asked.

He seemed deaf and blind to her.

She tried again. "Did you play in the rain?"

"Yeah, we played. Me and that prick Roy Sutter."

Sally tried not to wince, not even when she saw the blood in his eyes.

18

The Porsche was singing along the rain-swept Ventura Freeway. Behind the wheel, Ilona was singing a happy Hungarian song. In the bucket seat beside her, Bobby Belanger was listening to the storm's rage.

"You picked some lousy day for it," he complained.

Ilona laughed. "Rain is so romantic. Even Americans sing in the rain."

He looked askance at her. "Not when it's costing them money."

More laughter. "I am your wife. I come free."

"How much do you want to turn around and go back home?"

No laughter, no smile. "That is what I am doing."

Bobby did not understand her. "Good. Take the next off ramp."

Ilona did nothing of the kind.

Bobby now glared at her. "Where the hell are you taking me?"

"To Pasadena."

"The hell you are! You're headed for Ventura!"

Unmindfully Ilona went on. "I am taking you back to the bakery. To
the sweet girl I was when you met me."

Bobby did not buy her nostalgia. "That's something you do alone. If
you have the time, which I don't."

"No time to save your marriage?" Ilona asked.

"Is that what we're doing?"

"Yes, Bobby."

He winced. "You're not taking me to your mother, are you?"

Ilona smiled. "No, this is not the way to Leisure World."

"Then what's it all about? Who says our marriage needs saving?"

"I do," said Ilona. "I have been thinking about divorcing you."

He understood. "We could've talked this out at home."

"Talking will not help."

"What will?"

"Love," she said.

"Turning back the clocks?" He was sarcastic.

"No turning, Bobby. Just facing each other and seeing if we can make
love to each other—like we used to."

He tensed. "In bed?"

"Yes. Just you and me."

He shook his head in dismay. "Then what the hell are we doing way

112

out here in the rain? The best damn bed in California is in our own house."

"Not for me," said Ilona.

"What the hell do you want? A feather bed?"

Calmly, Ilona said, "Just wait and see."

He glowered at her. "This kind of surprise—this kind of situation doesn't turn me on."

"Please, Bobby," she implored. "Do not spoil this chance. There will not be another."

"You're threatening me, you dumb Hungarian. That's no way to go about it."

Knowing he was right, Ilona said, "I was singing. I meant only to sing and laugh. And make love to you."

"Don't bust out crying," he warned.

Ilona found her smile.

"Let's just get it over with," he said now.

She dared not ask him whether he had meant the day or the marriage. She intended to follow her design and to accept the result. All she knew for certain was that she was not about to endure more unhappiness with Bobby.

Eyes on the road and on the windshield wipers moving like metronomes, she sang aloud to herself. In Hungarian. A happy song about young lovers.

Bobby came alive when the Porsche drifted off the freeway and climbed toward an overpass leading to Westlake Village, or to the freeway's eastbound lanes. When the car shot straight ahead, he cried out, "No! What the hell's in Westlake Village?"

"A motel," said Ilona innocently.

"Is that what we came twenty-five miles in the rain for?" Bobby protested. "Why didn't you tell me? I could've taken you to one in town!"

"Is it as beautiful as this?"

Bobby knew better. He had admiration and envy for the city in the country. It was the kind of real estate development he hoped one day to match or exceed. It was all beautiful, the plateau with its artificial lakes and golf course, its smart homes, its exciting backdrop of the Santa Monica mountains, and its proximity to a modern, light industrial park.

He said, "No, but it's more fun. It's got X-rated movies piped into the TV screens in every room."

"That is not for me," said Ilona. "This is. And do not look like you did the time I took you to the hospital for your hernia operation."

"Shut up," said Bobby.

Ilona did.

The motel was beautiful in the rain, as was their upstairs corner

113

bedroom. Still looking sick, Bobby went to the windows overlooking the deserted golf course, the rain-pebbled lake, and the mindless ducks swimming in it.

"Fuck a duck," he said to himself.

The door shut and locked, Ilona got busy. She set up the bottles of Cherry Heering and Cutty Sark on the night tables flanking the double bed. She shed all of her clothes and was in bed and under the blanket and between the fresh sheets before Bobby had removed his hat and raincoat.

"Darling," she beckoned.

"This is dumb," he said.

"Come to bed."

He gave up. A promise was a promise. Bobby Belanger had a reputation for being as good as his word. Might as well get the operation over and done with, the sooner the better.

But in bed he was no good. This afternoon the Scotch tasted like medicine for a sick man. And he was sick, suffering from impotence.

"Have another drink, Bobby."

"An aphrodisiac wouldn't help me."

"No?"

"Wrong place, wrong time."

"Wrong woman?"

"It's too early, too late."

"Which is it?" Ilona asked. There was no edge to her voice, no impatience, no disappointment.

"Too early in the day," Bobby said. "Too late on the calendar."

"Darling, you can be more direct than that. Say what is on your mind."

"We've been married too long," he declared.

"I do not excite you anymore?"

"At this hour, business excites me."

"Have another drink," she insisted.

"Uh-huh, just as soon as the cocktail waitress comes this way again."

"Think anything you want, darling. Make yourself relax. Want to nap awhile?"

"No."

"Want to try another woman?"

"What?"

"You heard me, darling."

"What did you have in mind?"

Ilona suppressed her sense of failure, or the vanishing of her impossible dream. Determined to try as hard as she was able, she left the bed.

Bobby misread her. "Are we leaving?"

114

"No, the party is just beginning."

"Party?"

"Shut your eyes, Bobby. Do not open them until I tell you to. All right?"

Bobby pouted. "And what'll that do for me?"

"It will bring you another woman."

"From where?"

Ilona did not answer him. She went to the closet, took up her valise, and carried it into the bathroom.

Bobby did not close his eyes. He drank more Scotch and kept staring at the shut bathroom door, wondering what the hell Ilona was doing in there. What he wanted to believe was that his dumb wife had been smart enough to fill her valise with some entertaining items from the window box in the bedroom of their own house.

When he saw the doorknob turning, he turned away, lowered his head to his pillow, and shut his eyes.

"Open your eyes," said Ilona, first in German, then in English.

Bobby did, and he turned to Ilona and disappointment. She was wearing a crimson Merry Widow, black stockings, red garters, and high-heeled shoes. Her cheeks were rouged, her lips heavily painted, and a blonde wig crowned her disguise.

"Who am I, darling?"

"Sonia," he said without smiling.

Ilona laughed and went into her act. One foot positioned on a chair, she began her schoolgirl imitation of Marlene Dietrich, singing huskily in German, and snaking her body in a manner the great Dietrich was never permitted to do in the days before X-rated movies.

Bobby studied her as if she were a blueprint of a floor plan for a house that could bring him no profit.

"Who am I, darling?" Ilona repeated.

"Some nut who escaped from Camarillo," he said, alluding to the state mental institution located some miles to the west.

Ilona laughed and came to the bed, to Bobby. She came at him like a Hamburg whore. Nothing.

Leaving Bobby and the bed, she said, "Shut your eyes again, darling."

"What now, Marlene?"

"You knew me!" Ilona said, saying nothing about his inability to know her.

Intermission. Act Two.

The bathroom door opened again. Ilona came out dressed as a cancan girl, dancing, kicking her legs high, and singing in French.

No applause. No interest. "I know who you are," said Bobby. "One of those Beverly Hills housewives practicing up for the SHARE benefit."

Ilona laughed her way into the bed, and out of it again. So much for the cancan.

Act Three.

Out of the bathroom came Ilona, booted, her black raincoat unbuttoned but held closed by crossed hands. She moved like a streetwalker, leapt into the bed, onto Bobby. Her raincoat flew open, her hands flew at him, her mouth came at him. Her free breasts and buttocks danced over him.

It was a dance of death. Nothing.

Act Four. Last act on the program. Last effort, last chance for Bobby. The one chance Ilona had misgivings about, a chance not born in her memories of girlhood in Budapest, of games designed for giggling. For making believe.

She came out of the bathroom now dancing like an American schoolgirl. Like her own daughter had one afternoon by the swimming pool while Bobby trained his movie camera on her. Wet body, wet red bikini and bra, white T-shirt.

Bobby was watching, she was dancing. And, as she did, she directed the action of her body, advancing toward him and retreating from the edge of the bed. Her hands reached under the T-shirt, undid the wet brassiere, and flung it to Bobby.

He caught it and studied it with dark recognition.

"Look at me!" Ilona called to him.

Bobby looked and saw that Ilona had pressed the T-shirt against her wet body and breasts. A few moments of this, and then Ilona took her time as she wiggled the bikini down her legs, stepped out of it, rubbed herself with the wet bikini, and returned to the bed. To Bobby.

He was dead on arrival, and he remained dead while Ilona dared anything and everything before she fell beside him. She let the heat go out of her, she let the last of her love for Bobby die.

"Bobby," she said forlornly, "I tried."

He had no shame or despair about his own failure. He had only contempt for his wife. "You're dumb."

Ilona hit back. "Did *you* try?"

"This was your dumb idea, not mine."

"Have *you* an idea?"

One was not long in coming. "Let's check out."

Ilona was quick to reply. "If you do, it is all over between us."

The contempt endured. "What's your next act?"

"In here? Or away from here?"

"What more can you do in here?" he demanded.

"Anything that comes to your mind," she hinted.

116

"You mean anything that makes me come?"

Ilona smiled. "Be as crude as you like."

Bobby took her at her word. He reached for the telephone.

"Anything but that," said Ilona, knowing what he had in mind. "It has to be between you and me. And nobody else."

Slamming the telephone down, Bobby turned his anger on Ilona. "You bitch! Between you and me, hell! Didn't you bring Karen in? Weren't you suggesting I have a thing for my own daughter?"

"No," said Ilona, giving Bobby some balm and the benefit of her doubts. "But I keep remembering a day last summer—"

"Forget it," interrupted Bobby. He was brusque.

"You know what I am talking about."

"I know you were imitating Karen and the way she danced by the pool while I took those movies."

Ilona did not back off. "Did you know that you had an erection?"

"No," he lied. "I was too busy with the camera."

"I cannot blame you," said Ilona. "Karen was not behaving as your daughter. She was wild. You were wild."

"You're not remembering all of it," Bobby retorted. "Karen's big-titted friend was there. What was her name?"

Ilona shrugged. "What is the difference? What counts? The names? The ages? The Lolitas?"

"Shut up and I'll tell you!" Bobby was loud.

"Tell me," said Ilona. "Not the people in the next room."

He glowered at her. "I'm older now. Things are different. I'm not the sex-starved kid who married you. I'm a businessman whose business is screwing the guys I'm up against before they screw me. I've made a lot of money but I've paid for every dollar. And I've earned my right to pleasure, my kind of pleasure, the kind I need now, the kind I always wanted maybe, but the kind I can buy now. To me there's no pleasure in sex without some kind of perversion. You know the words."

"You like lesbians," said Ilona coldly.

"I need—I like at least two women in bed with me, lesbians or not. I need the books, the movies, the gimmicks. I need what's in the window seat. The dirtier the better. That sends me. That delivers me, that brings me back to the rat race the next morning."

Ilona sighed. "All right, Bobby. Be happy."

"Thanks." He left the bed and went to the window. "Lousy rain. Costing me money. Labor. Interest. I ought to get in another business."

"Bobby?"

He did not turn to her. "What now?"

"Tell me what will make you happy."

Bobby faced her. "Take me back to the office."

"Good-bye," she said with finality.

"What does that mean?"

Ilona poured more Cherry Heering. "Good-bye is good-bye. I am staying here."

He frowned. "How the hell am I going to get back to my office?"

"Not in my car. Not now."

"What the hell are you going to do here alone? Play with yourself?"

Ilona was not about to reveal her plans, present or future.

"I'll tell you what," said Bobby. "I'll take your car and have somebody pick you up in the morning."

Ilona shook her head. "I am driving down to see my mother in the morning."

"I'll have somebody drop the car off tonight," he said.

"No. Get a taxi. Rent a car. Blow your money."

Bobby scowled at her before he went to the telephone. He called his office and arranged for someone to pick him up at once.

No more conversation, no more rebukes. Bobby showered, dressed, had one Scotch for the rainy road, and left without a good-bye or a backward glance.

Ilona waited fifteen minutes before she placed the first of her two telephone calls.

The artist was at home, and she told him where she was and what she had in mind. Politely, he asked for a raincheck. He was behind in his work, he had a deadline to meet. At once, she came up with another plan to save the day. She offered to check out of the motel, pick up food and drink at Gelson's, and cook dinner for him. Politely, he declined. And so did the day and Ilona's dream of the future, at least with the artist.

She did remember to call Sonia. To alert her.

It was a wise call. At about one o'clock in the morning Sonia heard Bobby Belanger entering the house with two strange women. As the three voices died climbing the stairs, Sonia shut her eyes and waited for sleep to take her through the night.

She was not afraid. The Americans, unlike the Russians, burned down nothing more than their own lives.

19

Dolores Cooper had one martini for the long ride. To her it was as far from South Oaks to San Marino as it was from Los Angeles to Carrollton, Georgia. The long storm, gone from the skies, had moved into her heart, and tonight, under the roof of an elegant sixteen-room mansion, she meant to deliver its thunder.

Behind the wheel of the Mercedes, Perry Cooper was quiet and distant from her, trapped in his lane as the Saturday night traffic thickened near the downtown Los Angeles freeway interchanges. Unable to make time, he made polite conversation to tune his and Dolores's voices for the joyless conversations confronting them on this dutiful evening.

Dolores turned her mind to the Hawleys. Dr. Malcolm Hawley, psychiatrist, was Perry's closest friend in medical school. Denise Babcock Hawley, a Ph.D. psychologist, was her oldest friend. San Marino had been close to South Oaks until, at the age of four, the Hawleys' only child, a daughter, was committed to a home for the mentally retarded. She was now twelve going on five. A "gifted" child, in Denise's lexicon.

From the tragic time onward, the Coopers and the Hawleys "entertained" each other only on their respective wedding anniversaries. It was not that Denise dwelled upon her daughter. In truth, she never spoke about her anymore, at least not to the Coopers, and she never inquired about the healthy Cooper children.

Dolores felt that tonight she could not abide more of the same.

Same menu, same pleasantries, same dinner conversation, and the same remembrances of "our town" in Georgia. It was dull, predictable, meaningless. The sadness was in the passing years. The joy was in the clock conspiring to free each of them from a ritual none of them wished to honor.

Out of conversation, off the freeway. Pasadena. She thought of Ilona Belanger in Pasadena and at Westlake Village. A tale told on the telephone with laughter and tears. Ilona's.

San Marino. Magic name for rich, beautiful streets, lovely houses, unlovely smog too much of the time. No smog today. No more of the same tonight. She was bringing a storm to the Hawleys.

Perry and Malcolm were the same age. The latter was slighter, balder, and looked much younger. His two remaining advantages were his aristocratic South Carolina forebears and his wife's Coca-Cola stock. Her inheritance.

In Carrollton, Denise had been considered the prettier of the two, Dolores the smarter. Now the reverse was true. Denise was an associate professor at the University of Southern California, an author of a book on parapsychology, a celebrity in the news. Dolores was an empty nester, a potato peeler, a plastic beauty.

Denise greeted her warmly, said all the right things and meant them. All was well until Dolores refused the ritual sherry and insisted on a martini.

When Dolores had emptied her martini glass, Denise said, "Shall we go into dinner?"

"I'll have another," said Dolores.

"Oh, really?"

"Oh, yes."

"I do believe that the salad's on the table."

"I'll have a double martini," insisted Dolores. "At the table, if you please."

"We do have an interesting bottle of Burgundy."

"A double, Denise. School's out."

"Yes," said Denise, holding her smile and herself together until she backed off to convey the order to the butler.

Perry and Malcolm were making small talk about internal medicine and psychiatry as usual at this juncture of the evening. For the first time in many years, Dolores came over to join them. Perry was surprised, Malcolm was not delighted. He missed Perry, and he had not yet made his most brilliant observation, one of the two a year he managed.

Dolores butted right in with a question of her own, "How has the new morality hit your haughty patients—the women, I mean?"

Short of humor, wary of divulging confidences, Malcolm made generalities that were about as weak as the butler's martinis. A waste of time and words. Perry remained silent. He played the interested bystander and masked his concern for Dolores. He had a sick feeling about the dinner. More than the roast would be carved tonight.

At the candlelit table in the walnut-paneled dining room, Perry played his role, offering a toast to the Hawleys on their sixteenth wedding anniversary, four short of the Coopers.

Denise and Malcolm were delighted with the toast Perry had made up while shaving earlier in the evening. But the delight died, at least for Denise, with the tapping of glasses.

Ignoring her glass of Burgundy, Dolores used her martini glass, and her advantage. "You'll never catch up to us," she said, laughing.

Not to be bested, Denise said, "We may pass you yet."

Dolores had not expected this. She emptied her glass, her eyes never leaving Denise. Long ago they had competed for attention, for compliments, for grades, and for boys. Now, at long last, the old rivalry that had weathered time and circumstance better than their friendship, was renewed.

"You doubt my marriage," said Dolores.

Denise tried to flee the dueling grounds. "Oh, no, my—"

"Oh, yes," Dolores insisted. "Drink your fine wine, but, please, remember this: *in vino veritas.*"

Denise smiled. "You remember your Latin. In wine there is truth. Yes, indeed. As for our respective marriages, there are at least two happenstances to be considered."

"Such as?" asked Dolores.

"Death and divorce," said Denise.

"Choose one," Dolores dared her.

"Divorce, naturally." Denise sipped her wine. "Something's terribly wrong in South Oaks, I fear."

"You're warm," said Dolores.

"Something between Perry and you."

"Yes, but what?" Dolores held a martini grin.

"Why must I guess? I've done enough of that, in those times I've thought about you two," said Denise.

"Often?" asked Dolores.

"No, not too often," said Denise.

Dolores turned to Perry. "You first."

"No," he said coolly. "You, first and last."

Dolores frowned. "Don't you care to tell your side of the story?"

"It's not a dinner story," said Perry.

The frown gave way to laughter. "Out with it, Perry! Bring back free speech and free association to San Marino!"

Perry picked up his salad fork and stabbed a leaf of romaine. Malcolm and Denise did likewise.

Not Dolores. "Denise?"

Denise looked at her without concern, almost without interest.

"Perry's lying," said Dolores. "He has a beautiful story to tell. A love story."

It was a good beginning, securing Perry's, Malcolm's, and Denise's attention. There was wonder in her voice, and a sadness unmarred by jealousy or hate.

Dolores went on with it. "Unfortunately, for Perry, the ending was sad. The lovely girl had an unlovely flaw. She succumbed to it. *It* being a drive stronger than love. The unwomanly drive for a career of her own. Interesting?"

"Yes," said Denise uncomfortably.

"No questions?"

"I believe I've heard quite enough," said Denise.

Dolores, ignoring Perry, turned to Malcolm. "How about you, Malcolm?"

"I'm listening, Dolores," he said.

"As a psychiatrist? As a friend? Or as a man who has his own love story?"

Denise answered. "Dolores, you're being—"

"I wasn't talking to you." Dolores was sharp.

Malcolm said, "As a friend."

Denise faced Dolores. "Your daddy—"

"What about my daddy?"

"He was a wise man not to—"

"Daddy wasn't wise."

"Dear, you've had too much to drink—"

"Just enough," said Dolores.

"You're not letting me finish a sentence, dear."

"I'll do just that. As soon as you begin to make sense. As soon as you stop patronizing me."

"I'm sorry," said Denise.

"Daddy was a fool," said Dolores. "I'm glad he's dead."

Denise and Malcolm played deaf and dumb. Perry regarded Dolores with awe. He could not believe his eyes or ears, and he waited to see and to hear more. He was not denied.

"My *daddy*," said Dolores. "I wish he had died in Georgia and had never followed us to California. Never *dogged* us."

Malcolm picked up the questioning. "Have you considered, Dolores, that it's quite normal, quite human, for the living to hate the dead?"

"You're my friend," said Dolores. "Not my shrink. Friend to friend, I don't hate my father for dying. I hate him for killing my marriage."

Malcolm again, as a friend. "In concert with the career girl?"

"No. Daddy killed the marriage before the girl dazzled—forgive me, Perry—that's a poor word. Let me try again. Before the girl was someone Perry had to find—to again find his—his *manhood.*"

Perry continued to eat his salad: leaves, croutons, oil, vinegar, salt, grated cheese, and pepper—ground in the mill of Dolores's mouth. Coarsely. He drank wine to suppress his coughing.

The Hawleys were stunned, particularly Denise. She said, "You were always so close with your daddy. I used to envy your relationship with him."

Dolores was not moved to nostalgia. *"Envy?* Since when have you taken to speaking that forbidden word aloud?"

Denise shrugged. "Your candor must have exorcised it."

"You envied me because Perry chose me over you."

Perry winced. Malcolm smiled.

122

Denise paled. "True."

"You envied me because of Larry and Linda."

"Also true."

"Yes," said Dolores sadly. "And I envied you because you were richer, more attractive, and not Jewish. Now I envy you—and Perry's erstwhile girl—for having careers. Self-esteem. Identity."

"Thank you," said Denise. "But, tell me, what has happened to your pride in your children?"

"It's gone," said Dolores without care.

Malcolm again. "Linda's pregnancy?"

"That's another story. The more important one is that *my daddy*, damn him to hell, stole my pride in my children."

"I don't follow you," said Denise.

"Daddy usurped Perry's authority. Daddy's money, daddy's decisions —those things came to rule my children. Where did that leave Perry? Left out, overruled, shunted aside. And where did that leave me? Without Perry's love." She faced her husband. "Interesting?"

Perry hesitated. "When did you find out?"

"Recently."

"Miracles do happen," Perry said. "But how?"

Malcolm made a guess. "Analysis, Dolores?"

Dolores shook her head.

Denise tried. "A book you read?"

"By whom, Denise?"

"Sorry—" murmured Denise, confused.

Dolores repeated the question.

"I have no idea what you're reading these days," said Denise. She rang her brass bell. It rang in laughter for Dolores. It brought to mind the bell that had rung for her on the San Diego Freeway. It all seemed funny now. Only to her.

The others held to their bewilderment until the butler entered. Dolores took no meat, no potatoes, no green peas. She asked for another martini, minus the olive, minus an argument.

She got it. And she sipped quietly while Perry and the Hawleys ate the entrée, sipped the fine wine, and made dinner conversation: safe, tired, familiar subjects. When she could bear it no longer, Dolores confronted Denise.

"Break out, Denise. Ask me about Larry."

Perry and Malcolm silenced, Denise asked, "And how is your son?"

Dolores told her. "Poor Larry! Unhappy at Cornell. More unhappy at home. Never writes home anymore, but I call from time to time. It's easier for us to communicate when he's not staring at me and wondering who I am." She drank more.

"Coffee?" suggested Denise.

"Not for me, darling. What is it your sorcerers drink in Mexico?"

"Oh, you don't believe in my sorcerers," said Denise.

"No, not yours, Denise." She laughed. "But I've found one of my own. He prescribes martinis, lovely man."

Denise refused to pursue this. Malcolm did not. "Who is he, Dolores?"

"Whitney Callender." It was an incantation for her.

Perry took note. Malcolm persisted. "I've never heard of him." He turned to his wife. "Have you, dear?"

"No," said Denise, again ringing her brass bell. She had had enough. She was ready to ring down the evening.

Dolores said to Malcolm. "He's from the Yale School of Sorcery and Bellringing."

Having his wine to savor, Perry seemed to be indifferent to Dolores's prattle. Denise seemed more concerned with the butler's entrance and exit. Malcolm, however, was interested in delving into Dolores's psyche.

He asked, "Is this Whitney Callender a lecturer you've recently heard?"

Dolores smiled with cunning. "Yes, at a masked ball."

"In a dream?" asked Malcolm. "Or in a fantasy?"

"In the Bel-Air Hotel," said Dolores. "In his bed."

Denise was embarrassed, Perry stunned.

Not Malcolm. "And what was the nature of his sorcery?"

"A different kind of sex," said Dolores. "One that offers a bellringing beyond orgasms."

Denise coughed. Perry sipped his wine.

Malcolm smiled. "Very interesting—if esoteric. And I believed I'd heard everything. Could you explain?"

"Can sorcery be explained?" asked Dolores. "I'll try." She took more of her martini. "The sorcerer not only gave me the ultimate in sexual satisfaction, but also the ultimate truth about my daddy and me."

Perry was intrigued. Denise became flushed.

Calmly, Malcolm asked, "Incest?"

"Worse," said Dolores. "The truth is my daddy was my enemy."

Denise reacted to the slander. "That's absurd."

At last Dolores faced Perry. "Ask my husband."

Perry said to Denise. "Please, don't."

Malcolm again. "Dolores, where did you meet this sorcerer?"

"In a bistro. The Ivy League."

"He's not a palm reader or a fortune teller, is he?" asked Malcolm.

"Nothing of the sort," said Dolores. "He's someone I picked up. He took me to his hotel room."

"She's joking," Denise said to her husband. "Enough of this."

Unmindfully Malcolm confronted Dolores again. "When did—?"

Denise broke in. "I'm sure Perry doesn't appreciate this."

Perry contradicted her. "I always appreciate the truth."

Malcolm tried again. "Dolores, when did you begin to pick up strange men?"

For the following, uncomfortable minutes, Dolores minced no words as she recounted her role in the formation of the cabal that came to identify themselves as "the potato peelers." She omitted nothing: not the Bel-Air Hotel, not the tawdry motel on Ventura Boulevard, and not the terrors, heterosexual and homosexual.

In the end she turned to an ashen-faced Perry. "Shall we thank the Hawleys for the use of the hall and get out of here?"

Perry said, "They're not yawning. And neither am I."

Denise was disappointed by Perry's response.

Malcolm was not. "No, don't go. Tell me, Dolores, what now?"

"I don't know," Dolores said forlornly. "Perhaps Perry has an answer for you."

Perry shook his head. "No one's asked me anything."

Dolores accommodated him. "Are you going to put up with me?"

"At least for as long as you've put up with me," said Perry.

Dolores pouted. "Don't be noble. I'll understand."

Perry said, "I promise not to be noble. Nothing else."

"Dolores?" It was Malcolm. She turned to him. "What happens now? Do you intend to call off your rebellion?"

"Should I?" she asked.

"I'd suggest," said Malcolm, "that you don't."

Denise frowned at her husband. "Malcolm, how dare you?"

"Quiet, Denise," he said. "Hear me out." He faced Dolores again. "Don't retreat. It was well that you rebelled. Frankly, I was afraid for you. Afraid you were headed for a breakdown."

Dolores winced. "And now?"

"Do something, anything. Act," Malcolm prescribed.

"As recklessly as I have been?" Dolores demanded.

"Anything but quiet desperation," Malcolm explained.

Dolores felt nauseous. "Including lesbianism?"

"Only as a last resort," Malcolm said. "Leave suicide to the hopeless."

"Aren't I hopeless?" Dolores asked.

Malcolm smiled. "Not you. You're brave." He turned to Perry. "Isn't she?"

Surprised, Perry could say nothing.

Malcolm persisted. "Wasn't Dolores brave to put up with you these past three years?"

Perry said, "She had no choice. But she has now—now that she's free of her father."

All eyes turned to Dolores. She rose and went to the powder room.

There was nothing more she wished to say or hear. She meant to open her mouth only to give up the sickness she felt.

Denise glared at Malcolm and Perry. "You male chauvinist pigs! You both make me ill. I would be less annoyed with you if you unzipped your flies instead of opening your mouths. Doctors, indeed!"

Perry rose. "I'm sorry. I'll take her home."

"Now, honestly, will you?" asked Denise. "Can you accept that what your wife did was only a sick, long-deferred reaction to what you did to her?"

Perry winced. "This is your house. I won't give you a fight on it here."

"Don't," said Denise. "Just remember what Dolores has given you, and what she now needs from you."

Malcolm reminded him. "She did a brave thing, killing Ben."

"She had to," said Perry.

"Why?" demanded Denise.

Perry hesitated before spilling the sour wine of his truth. "It was the only way she could bear her shame."

Malcolm studied him with disappointment, Denise with foreboding.

She believed there would be no more invitations to South Oaks for the Hawleys. The Coopers, she sensed, would only invite disaster.

20

Armed with her boilermaker, Joan Lawler dared to invade the territory of the king of beasts, the terror who stood alone and apart from the awed host and hostess and all of their guests.

A graying, balding man with a dour grimace, he confronted the pinball machine set up in the paneled barroom especially for his diversion.

His regal disdain became evident the moment Joan had taken her bold stance, her body leaning against the machine, her eyes upon him rather than the action of the wild ball.

"We haven't been introduced," said Joan.

"Who are you?" he demanded, his cold eyes on the ball.

"A fool who walks in where agents fear to tread."

The pun went unappreciated. "Answer my question."

"I'm a call girl."

The machine lit up, the man did not. "I didn't call."

"I like strong, silent men," said Joan.

He scowled at her for an instant before returning his passion to the pinball machine. "And whose little wife are you?"

"Frank Lawler's."

The name did not register. "Who's he?"

"One of your new lawyers. In charge of hand-holding."

"Oh. So you know who I am."

"Of course." Joan sipped her drink. "Lewis Donald, the mad producer."

"I happen to be not quite so mad about you."

"You seem to be mad *at* everyone here," she said.

"I can afford to be," Donald retorted.

She taunted him. "With your good looks—"

"Listen, Mrs. Lawler—"

"Yes, Lewis."

He checked his temper, put the metal ball in motion, and watched the new game in progress. "What are you drinking?"

"One boilermaker. I'm on my good behavior."

"I'm not," he said.

"You're the guest of honor."

"I'm bored."

"I offered you a solution."

Donald considered it. "What'll it cost me?"

"Your boredom," she hinted.

"Where's your husband now? Point him out."

Joan looked through the open doorway leading from the clubby bar-room where she, Donald, and the pinball machine were standing, to the living room and the swarm of peacocks and chattering magpies. She spotted Frank with Rita Nash.

"Do you know Rita Nash?" she asked.

"Yes, I see her."

"That's Frank with her. Tall, dark, and stupid."

"He *is* holding her hand," said Donald.

"For openers," said Joan. She turned to Donald. "How are your ulcers? I see you're not drinking."

"You may drive me to it," he said.

"Your place or mine?"

"Where do you live?"

"Nowhere. Not until you smile at me."

"One boilermaker, carefully nurtured?" Donald said.

Joan smiled at him. "You're the most fascinating man here."

"Weren't you warned about me?"

"Everyone was briefed about you," Joan said. "But I'm a Chestnut Hill girl."

"So I see," he said, staring at her small breasts. "Philadelphia Irish?"

"Main Line," she said. "Welcome to the party. Your party."

Donald frowned again as he surveyed the scene in the living room. "Wrong setting, wrong set. Should be in Burbank instead of Century City. Ground level instead of ten stories high. Needs a lying-in room at Forest Lawn, with me lying, smiling in beautiful death, on some couch."

"Even as a corpse, you'd be the hottest thing in the room."

Donald faced the living room. "How's the temperature in there?"

Joan looked and spoke out. "That group on the left, they're hot. That group on the right, they're cool. No longer hot, no longer current and in favor. And you know what Mr. Tanner says: 'A cold talent is a dead talent.' "

Donald smiled. "You Micks have a way with you when you hit the bottle. Are you a dipso?"

"No, a Mick potato peeler."

"I'll bet."

"You'd lose," she said.

His smile fled. "Don't look now, but I think you've just been struck dead by Maurice Tanner and—what's his wife's name?"

"Kay," said Joan, unconcerned. "You must know her. She was born on a sound stage, the daughter of Jesus Christberg, King of the Nickelodeons."

"Nevertheless, you're dead. You and your husband," he said seriously.
Joan laughed. "It feels good."

"I'll have to resurrect you."

She fluttered her eyes. "Oh, thank you, king of the Nielsens. I swear my fealty to you. May your ratings never fall."

"Shut up," he said, leading her to the bar.

Donald ordered two boilermakers from the bartender who, upon seeing him approach, had reached for the guest of honor's brand of Scotch. Then, arm in arm, glasses in hand, they made a regal return to the living room.

Joan was pleasured by the turning of eyes. Napoleon was back from Elba, and little Joanie Clarke of Philadelphia had him.

They approached the Tanners and the Weils, and Donald was prompt to declare that it was a marvelous party and that he was having a marvelous time. The pinball machine was a delight, and so was Mrs. Lawler. Wonderful, wonderful. Dear Joan, dear, dear Joan. And have you met Frank?

Frank was summoned, and he came with the unshakeable Rita Nash, who was not about to miss her opportunity to move from the cool to the hot side of the room.

Donald said the right things and made the correct jests with Frank, about the law, about their future relationship, and added some deft but flattering words about Joan.

A few chosen minutes of this, and then Donald chose his own way of getting off stage. An urgent matter. Confidential. Maurice Tanner took Donald off to a private corner. The Weils found another hot group. Kay Tanner had someone hot she wanted Frank to meet.

Joan was left with the cool, burning Rita Nash. Chestnut Hill versus Miss Hotshot of 1966, not so large at the box office anymore, but larger than life in the mountains of her breasts.

Rita Nash hated the boilermaker she had earlier requested of a passing waiter, but she was not about to let on.

Joan fashioned a lie. "I was telling Lewis Donald what Frank says about you."

"Frank?"

"My husband."

"I know that."

"Did you also know how much Frank thinks of your beauty and talent?"

"Tell me," urged Rita Nash.

"Well, the important thing is what I said to Lewis Donald and what

129

he said to me. But tell me, does Frank—after all he's only a lawyer—does he really know about beauty and talent?"

"Yes," said Rita Nash with impatience.

"You think he's bright?"

"Lewis Donald?"

"Frank," said Joan.

"Quite so."

"Charming?"

"You're exasperating, Joan."

"Oh, I'm sorry. It's just that—does Frank turn you on?"

Rita Nash took more of her boilermaker. She was livid. "He's candid, quite so."

"Forward, too?" asked Joan.

"Now what has that got to do—?"

"I'd hate to think he owed you any flattery you didn't deserve."

"Don't." It was a threat.

"Is Frank a good hand-holder?"

"You were telling me about Mr. Donald."

"You're *not* telling me about Frank. If we're going to be candid with each other—"

"Frank's nice. Period," said Rita Nash.

"How's he in bed with you?"

Before Rita Nash could explode, a cool leading man passed by alone and greeted her. She responded with a cool remark that chased him.

Confronting Joan again, she said coldly, "My husband's name is Henry."

"Not talking about Frank?"

Rita Nash glared at her. "I've nothing to say."

Joan smiled brightly. "Nice chatting with you. Bye now." She turned to leave Rita Nash.

The latter quickly grabbed her hand. "Where are you going now?"

"Oh, I'm just going to skate around on the thin ice of this slippery rink."

"Not so fast, sister. You have something to tell me."

"You have nothing to tell me."

Rita Nash's eyes were burning. "We have much to say to each other."

"You first, you're the star," said Joan innocently.

Rita Nash hesitated. "Can I trust you to be understanding?"

"Yes, *sister.*"

"Frank's good. Good for me. These are hard times in Hollywood."

"How nice for you," said Joan.

Rita Nash frowned. "I see where your mind is."

Joan smiled. "I am understanding."

Sadly now, the actress said, "There are days when you wait for the

130

phone to ring. When you die waiting to hear if you're dead or alive. If you're going to get the choice role you'd kill your mother for. That's when Frank helps."

Joan eyed Rita's breasts. "You do give him big helpings."

"Frank comforts me," confessed Rita Nash.

"I'm so glad," said Joan, smiling. "I couldn't be happier if you suddenly grabbed a starring role at Paramount."

Unmindfully Rita Nash said, "Now what did Mr. Donald say about me?"

"Oh, yes, Mr. Donald! He had some very interesting things to say—when I told him what Frank thought about you."

"Such as?" The tenterhooks were there for Rita Nash.

The lies came readily to Joan. "He—Mr. Donald—said you were, without a doubt, the most despoiled talent in town—"

Rita Nash looked sick.

"—the most misunderstood talent in town. Misguided, misdirected. He said you were wrong as a sex symbol."

Rita Nash was turning green.

"He said," Joan went on, "he'd wager his mother's Sunday dishes that he could put you in a picture and get you an Oscar for best actress of the year."

The sickness went, the green went. The blue eyes popped, the body twitched, the breasts shook.

"Tell me more," the actress begged. "What kind of part?"

"He said something about a French novel written—"

"What's the title? Where can I get my hands on a copy?"

Joan said, "I don't remember. But he did say it was a comedy tragedy. A better part than—I forget who. Anyway, you play a whorehouse madam."

"A what?"

"A sure-fire character," said Joan. "Big box office. Boffo. Smash. Top of the world."

Having heard enough, Rita Nash smiled nervously and excused herself. Joan sipped her boilermaker and watched the bitch hunt down and trap Frank. Satisfied with herself, she began to pick canapés, hot and cold, carried by serving women. She picked them as if they were daisies grown in the garden of her deceit.

And so the time and the afternoon went. It was all quite boring and anticlimactic until the word got around that Lewis Donald had done his vanishing act. The hot guests left first, the cool ones lingered, and the very last to leave were the Lawlers.

At a moment when Frank was busy nodding to the whispers of his high command, Joan found herself confronted by a contented Kay Tanner.

"Joan, how are you?" Girl to girl.

"Just fine, thank you."

"How are you keeping busy these days?"

"In the best of all possible ways," said Joan brightly.

"Charity work? Church? Politics?"

"No. A little tennis, a lot of—"

"Ah, tennis! That explains your figure, and your girlish looks. When I was a girl, my father had Bill Tilden and—oh, that was so long ago. Maurice complains that I live too much in the good old days." She smiled. "Enough of that. The party went well, don't you think?"

"Very well."

"I must confess," said Kay Tanner, "you had us worried for a while."

"I'm so sorry."

"This Lewis Donald, strange man. Strange demands, but talent, as they say, must be served."

"Scary, isn't it?" said Joan with empathy.

"The times. Not like the good old—but you were remarkable. You completely won the man over."

"I was just being myself," said Joan.

"Don't change, Joan. Don't allow yourself to ever grow hard. You understand me. If you don't, let Rita Nash be a warning to you."

"I like her," said Joan.

"I don't mean to put her down, poor thing, but she was nice to you because our guest of honor—our prize client of the moment—smiled upon you. And, oh, heavens, were we afraid when we saw you accosting him."

"He seemed so sad and lonely."

"He hates cocktail parties. As a matter of fact, he hates Hollywood."

"Then," asked Joan, "why is he in Hollywood, and why did he show up at your lovely party?"

Kay Tanner beamed. "Maurice is also a talent. And Lewis Donald knows it. The association profits both of them. And this day could profit Frank and you. I dare say it shall."

"I'm so glad," said Joan. "I'm only unhappy about one thing. Not for me, for you."

With motherly concern for Joan, with no concern about herself, her position, or her party, Kay Tanner said, "What is it, Joan?"

"I think I hate Joyce Haber," she said, naming the Hollywood columnist for the *Los Angeles Times*. "For not showing up."

Kay Tanner smiled. "Joyce Haber? I'm very fond of her, but she was not invited. No members of the press were."

"The others don't count. Joyce Haber does. If she doesn't show up, I'm sure everybody goes home thinking it was a "B" party. I'm afraid she'll call it that in her column."

Kay Tanner was annoyed. She had no doubt she had hosted an "A" party. She did doubt the sobriety and the innocence of Mrs. Frank Lawler.

"Did I say something wrong?" asked Joan.

The telephone rang, the bell saving Joan from hearing what Kay Tanner's eyes had already said to her. The hostess excused herself, turning and marching to the nearest telephone.

Joan, standing alone now in the emptied, cooled-off living room, watched Kay Tanner's eyes light up. Lewis Donald calling, thanking her for a lovely party.

When Joan and Frank left, Maurice Tanner was there with a kiss for her and a smile for him. Kay Tanner was elsewhere. In the hell where Joan Lawler had put her.

Down the elevator, up from the basement garage, and onto the Avenue of the Stars.

Frank, driving his Riviera, smiled. "Name the restaurant."

"Is the car radio on?" asked Joan. "I could swear I heard a human voice say, 'Name the restaurant.'"

"You heard me."

"Was that you with all that exuberance, all that happy-to-be-alive—"

Frank laughed. "Chasen's?"

"What happened to your monotone? Why are you laughing?"

"I feel good. I feel hungry."

"Hungry enough to eat me?"

"You're funny."

"Don't you eat Rita Nash?"

Frowning now, Frank said, "Don't spoil the day."

"Oh," said Joan without caring. "I already did that."

Frank had the last word. "You were great."

"Everything coming up roses?"

"Looks that way," said Frank, beaming again.

Joan decided to be kind to him. Chasen's he wanted, Chasen's he got. Roses he was expecting, thorns he would get. As sure as tomorrow was Monday.

In Chasen's Frank was at his Irish best: poetry and romance, about Century City and his own career rising from the bulldozed ashes of all those acres where Tombstone was around the corner from Camelot, cowboys on one street, knights in armor on another. Kay Tanner's good old days. Before television, before Lewis Donald, before the hard hats riveted four-walled buildings to angry skies.

Nice imagery, Frank, Joan was thinking. A far, far better thing you have done than I have done. I, dear husband, have done you in, done you dirt. Ashes to ashes, venom to venom, Kay to Maurice, Rita to Lewis, me to you—I have fucked thee, darling, in my fashion.

Yes, Gentle Mary. Oh, yes.

21

The sun blinded Dolores Cooper as she waited for Joan Lawler to serve. She could not see Joan, the fence behind her, or her house. She heard the sound of a racket striking a ball, she heard the bounce and felt the ball smash her face. Joan's ensuing laughter unblinded her.

She now saw that she was no longer on her tennis court. She was in Ilona Belanger's bedroom, in the circular bed warm with sunlight streaming in the undraped windows.

With her in bed was not Ilona, but Joan, nude, beautiful, dazzling, and suddenly ugly as she strapped on a dildo and attacked her. Dolores struggled against two strong hands, two strong legs, now four strong hands and legs. Another face, not Ilona's. Denise Hawley, with her feet straddling Dolores's face. Denise above, Joan below.

Dolores cried out loud enough to pierce the walls and frighten the sun out of the sky. She sustained the outcry until a third pair of hands came upon her and thrust her into darkness.

"Wake up," said Perry.

"Yes, yes," murmured Dolores, clutching Perry's pajamas and bringing him down upon her bed. She embraced him and wept. He put his arms about her, quieting her trembling, warming her chilled, perspired body, and putting together her sundered mind.

"I heard you," he said. "I was reading. I came running. What kind of a nightmare were you having?"

Dolores balked. She neither wished to recall nor reveal it.

"Do you hear me?" he prompted.

"Yes. Please, stay with me."

From the other twin bed, Perry uncovered the pillow and removed it. Dolores moved body and pillow. Down came the other pillow, down came Perry, close beside her, arms about her.

"Easy now. It's all right," he said tenderly.

Dolores clenched her teeth to stop their rattling. She hugged him to subdue her trembling.

"Easy," he lulled her. "Easy."

"Light," she begged, "please, the light."

Perry twisted his body, reached out and touched lamplight. Dolores straightened up, crossed her hands, and peeled the damp nightgown from her cold, wet body. And then her hands were over Perry, buttons, drawstring, a tug here and a tug there until they lay naked together.

No words, no pleas, nothing more than a desperation of flesh and soul. Perry was understanding, compliant, male and masculine, real and true.

The bell of her heart rang out, without tremor, without agony. It rang in a peace too long gone from her, it carried off the false, nightmare light, it returned her home, and him to her. All that lingered was the dark, long nightmare of their separation from each other.

Perry remained quiet, and Dolores was content to listen to the quieting of his heart, to pick up the proper beat for her own pounding heart.

"Perry?"

"Yes, dear."

"The light, please."

He found the lamp and darkness. "Sleep?"

"Talk."

"Fine," he said.

"Did you miss me?" she asked.

"Yes."

"Am I the same?"

"No."

Fright rode on Dolores's question. "What does that mean?"

"You're a new woman," explained Perry. "New face, prettier, younger. New body, thinner, younger."

"Dirtier?"

"You weren't this sweaty the first time—"

"I wasn't troubled as much then. But that's not what I meant. Am I dirtier in mind?"

"We all are," he said.

"You said nothing last night at the Hawleys," she complained. "You said nothing in the car."

"I was stunned."

"Outraged?"

"A little, but mostly stunned. What you said about your father."

"Did you believe me?" Dolores asked. "Or did you believe I was drunk?"

"Both."

"Please, Perry, the truth. And, please, no monosyllables."

"Shall I tell you what I've been thinking?"

"Everything," she said.

"I think you've been through some kind of fire," he said. "You've been burned. Tempered."

"Please," she urged. "Don't be Malcolm. Be yourself, be harder with me."

"All right," he agreed. "Tell me about the nightmare."

"Must I? Now?"

"Now," he insisted.

Steeling herself, she returned to the nightmare, hoping the released words would fly from memory and conscience.

"Good," said Perry at once.

Puzzled, distraught, she demanded, "What's good about it?"

"The telling. Now interpret it for me."

This was more difficult. "I'm a latent sapphist."

"No," said Perry. "You had a nightmare, not a dream. You screamed."

Quick to accept the balm as truth, Dolores embraced her husband. "I love you."

Perry held her tenderly. It brought her no comfort, for he also held his tongue.

Now she dared to ask, "Do you love me?"

Without emotion, he said, "No, Dolores."

She withdrew from his arms. Her mind screaming, her voice not, she asked, "Haven't we just made love to each other?"

"Was it love?" he wondered. "Or was it sex?"

"Love," she refused to give way.

His truth punished her. "I rather think it was sex—born of terror."

Dolores fought tears. This was a time for truth without tears. Tears were lies. Evasions. Supplications, soft and weak. "Yes, you're so right. I needed a man—any man to reassure me I was a woman." She took Perry's silence for assent before she braved another question. "Can I hope that someday soon you'll love me again?"

"Hope won't do it," he said.

"Can anything?" She was desperate now.

"That's up to you."

"What must I do?"

"The first thing is to forgive me," he said. "If you can."

Dolores came into Perry's arms again. "I do. I do forgive you."

"Too quick," he protested, "too desperate. I want you to think about what deserves forgiveness, and what doesn't. I'm not asking for a blanket pardon."

"I'm confused," she confessed.

"Think," he urged her. "Separate love from sex, necessity from folly."

"Help me, Perry."

He hesitated. "Consider these questions—but don't answer me now. First, can you forgive me for giving my love to Valerie Hopkins? Second, can you forgive me for forsaking you and the kids? Third, can you forgive me for hating you and your father?"

Tethering the three yesses that wanted to flee from her open mouth, Dolores asked, "Do you hate me now?"

136

"I hated you in San Marino last night."

She flinched. "I'm sorry. I only meant to open your eyes to see how much I've changed, for good and bad."

"What do you consider good?" he demanded.

"My liberation from my father," she said at once.

"Obtained at what price?"

"Pardon me, I don't understand you."

"Think about it," he said.

"No, please. What did it cost me? What did I have to lose?"

Perry thought about it. "For one thing, your mind."

Dolores lost her head. "Was I out of my mind to make—to have sex with you now?"

He was cool. "Think about that, too."

"Didn't I pleasure you?" She knew that he had had his orgasm.

"I prefer love," he said pensively. "If I had to choose between the sex we just had and the sense of love and well-being I used to get from Valerie—"

"Don't," she implored.

"—just sitting in a coffee shop and touching her hand."

Abashed, Dolores hesitated until she found something to say. "It's been three years. What have you done for love since?"

"Nothing," he said with a sense of shame. "I died and buried myself a little. Medicine was my medicine."

"And what have you done for sex?" she asked without rancor.

"Paid for it," he said.

"Prostitutes? Call girls?"

"A masseuse. One of my patients."

"And what about your pretty nurses?"

"Never them. When I find one of them exciting me, I call the massage parlor down the street."

"Japanese or Swedish?"

"As American as cherry pie."

"Who Frenches you," Dolores coldly concluded. "If she's ever too busy for you, call on me. I come cheaper."

Perry's comment was not what she had expected. "You're not busy enough. That's your trouble."

Putting sex aside, Dolores said, "If you could be happy with me again, I'd be happy to be a busy grandmother."

"Forget it," he said. "Grandmothers and grandfathers are *out*. We're in South Oaks, Linda's in Palo Alto, and who knows where after that. Expect little more than phone calls and snapshots, occasional visits, and that's about it."

Able to accept the times, the distances, and the mores, Dolores was unable to accept his sufferance of these truths. "What remains for us?"

137

"Life," he said.

She accepted that. "Is there anything I must undo?"

Perry considered the grave query. "I'd tell you—if you could undo them. Which you can't."

Warily she asked, "Such as?"

He had his answer ready. "I'm not referring to the harm you've brought upon yourself—only that which you've brought on others."

Dolores tensed. "I take it you're speaking of Joan, Ilona, and Sally."

"I am," he said. "What's happened to them since you involved them in your own desperation?"

"They had their own desperations," retorted Dolores. "And their husbands were responsible for that—not I."

He said, "My question remains unanswered."

She tried to be responsive; she meant to be candid. "Joan's having a ball. No qualms, no problems. Ilona—she's considering divorce. A healthy solution for her, I believe."

"For her alone?" asked Perry pointedly.

"At least, not for me," she said.

"And Sally?"

"I don't really know about her. Sally doesn't confide in me—not like Joan and Ilona."

"Is she having an affair with Roy?"

"I suspect that," said Dolores. "Perhaps you know better."

"All I know," he said, "is that on the morning of Roy's birthday I told him about my affair with Valerie."

"As far as I can tell," said Dolores, "Roy and Sally appear to be happier than I've ever seen them."

"I hope you're right. I hope it stays that way. But, then, hoping won't help much, will it?"

"Oh, it's all speculation," said Dolores. "We'll have to wait and see."

Perry now brought up another point. "From what you tell me, the others did well—at least so far. Are you still hoping to do as well or—?"

Dolores interrupted him. "I told you I loved you."

He saw no need to remind her that he did not love her. Instead he went to the core of his question. "Does that mean you're through as a potato peeler?"

"I swear it."

"Why were you the first one to drop out?"

She searched the dark of her mind for the truth. "You open secret doors, one upon the other, led on—lured on by the promise of more and more ecstasy. And then you open a door and come upon something your mind can't accept."

Perry understood her and her horror of lesbianism. "Very well put.

You'll be all right, despite the nightmares."

Dolores frowned. "You expect me to have more?"

"Nothing worse, I hope," he said.

"What can be worse?"

Without a word, Perry turned on the lamp, got out of bed, and began to slip into his pajamas.

"Tell me," begged Dolores.

He held a sardonic smile. "No, that's my nightmare."

"Tell me, please."

As he noted the depth of her agony, he sensed he had to open one more door for her. Not for entering, but for one telling stare at the specter he himself had seen.

"What can be worse," he said, "is a possible consequence of your rage for sexual freedom. A consequence demanding a victim."

Her voice hollow, her eyes wide with horror, Dolores asked, "Who?"

"Anyone of the four of you. Anyone involved with the four of you," he said calmly.

Another kind of rage possessed Dolores. "Who the hell are you? One of Denise's sorcerers?"

Perry laughed at himself, but the laughter mocked Dolores.

It also kindled her rage. "The four of us are fighting for our humanity! We were victims before we took up the fight!"

More laughter from Perry. No scorn, no rebuttal, no concession. He gave her a pleasant but unpleasing "Good night."

The light went out, and he went out the door.

The darkness fell upon Dolores, smothering her with dread as she hosted a confusion of nightmares and victims. Name upon name, face upon face, fate upon fate. Missing from the list was the name of Perry Cooper.

He stood apart, alone, unmasked as the piper come for his payment in blood.

22

Late Friday afternoon a Bentley left the Los Angeles International Airport and soon found bumper-to-bumper traffic crawling in the crowded northbound lanes of the San Diego Freeway. Bobby Belanger pouted as he held the wheel with one hand. Ilona gave him a running report of Karen and Ronny before she hit him with her bombshell.

"Bobby, I'm going to divorce you."

There was no explosion. The loudest sound in the car was the ticking of the clock.

"What's it going to cost me?" Bobby asked quietly.

"All I want is my freedom," Ilona declared.

"Have your lawyer put that in writing. When I see it, I'll believe it," he said.

"You can believe me."

"I want to keep the house," he said.

"No argument," she said. "I am going to live in the East."

He did not like that. It cost money to live in New York. "That's not living."

"I am in love. I am going to be married."

This was good news. "Who's the sucker?"

She told him the man's name and the name of the corporation he headed.

Bobby was pleased. "Good. You won't need a property settlement or alimony."

"I want none," she assured him.

"What about child support?"

"That is up to you, Bobby."

"They're my kids," he said. "I'll take care of them."

"As you wish," she said. "Anything else?"

"Yeah," he said. "Did you tell Karen and Ronny?"

"Yes. They are happy for me."

He flared up. "What the hell did you tell them about me?"

"Nothing to shame you."

Bobby calmed down. "California divorce?"

"Any kind you wish."

"I'll talk to my lawyer." He said no more.

140

She held her tongue until the Bentley was parked in the driveway of their home and her luggage was transferred from the car trunk to the foyer.

"What would you like for dinner?" Ilona asked.

"You and Sonia decide. I'm moving out right now. I'll move back in after I have the house fumigated to get rid of the Hungarian stink in here."

Ilona thought about the stink left by Bobby's lesbians. She let it pass. Within a half hour, his own luggage filling his car trunk, Bobby drove away.

Ilona went to the telephone to spread her good news. There was no need to tell Sonia more. She knew all. Dolores, Joan, and Sally knew nothing.

Dolores was at home, but in no frame of mind to share her happiness. "If that's the way it has to be," she said distantly.

Ilona was disturbed. "Dolores, you do not sound like yourself."

"Good-bye, Ilona."

"Tennis tomorrow?"

"No, I frankly don't feel up to it. I'll call you soon."

And that was the end of it. At once Ilona telephoned Joan. She would know what was wrong with Dolores. No answer.

Sally did answer her ringing telephone. She gave all the right answers, all of her blessings.

"Tennis tomorrow?" asked Ilona. "At your club?"

"Neal's still home."

"Is he still in bed with the flu?"

"Out and about, but not well enough to fly."

"And Joan? Where is she?"

"I've no idea," said Sally.

"No tennis? No luncheons at the Ivy League?"

"I wouldn't know," said Sally. "We've all been out of touch, out of sorts. But I'm delighted about you. You've made my day."

So much from Sally. Something was wrong in South Oaks. Ilona tried Joan again. Still no answer, nothing but a ringing of regret and of alarm. She wondered where Joan was, and how she was.

Joan was in an upright glass coffin. A telephone booth within sight and sound of gasoline pumps. A corner Texaco filling station whose lights had formed a beacon guiding her out of strange, dark streets, down which she had stumbled.

She was a tearful fright as she dropped a dime into the proper coin slot and dialed a telephone number read off of a business card she held in a trembling hand.

"Arrow Answering Service, good afternoon."

"Mr. Walston, please." There was a sob in Joan's voice.

An inquiry about her name. She gave her name. An apology followed. Mr. Walston was occupied in his office and could not be disturbed. Did she wish to leave her number?

"Wake him!" She was frantic. "It's a life-and-death emergency!"

The secretary got the message. "One moment, please."

The moment was too long, the voice too cool, too distant. "Yes, Mrs. Lawler."

Gentle Mary, cried Joan to herself, was this the interesting man with mod hair and clothes she had encountered early that afternoon outside of Safeway, in front of the sex newsracks? Was this the would-be swinger she had followed into hell, into the old, dark house north of Ventura Boulevard? Was this the man who had made love to her and the little turned-on blonde? Was this the man who had disappeared and left her to the grotesque characters gathered for a "party" advertised in one of the sex newspapers?

Answering the executive of a telephone answering service, Joan said, "Listen, *Mr. Walston*, I'm giving you twenty-four hours to see to it that a red Datsun is left parked in my driveway. Understood?"

"No, I don't understand," Walston replied.

"My car's been stolen!"

"Did you look on the right street?"

"Yes! And I also looked in my handbag when I couldn't find my car. My car keys are gone! Now do you understand?"

Walston thought he did. "This is a matter for the police."

"Traffic division?" Joan demanded. "Or the vice squad?"

No immediate response.

"Think again, Mr. Walston."

"I don't know what I can do to—"

She broke in harshly. "Shut up, and I'll tell you. That little blonde works for you—so must some of the other slobs. True or not?"

"True," he said uneasily.

"What time did you leave?"

"Before three."

"Had all you could take?"

"Too much," he said.

"Why did you run out on me?"

"You had your own car."

"I want it back!"

"What's the license—?"

"A red Datsun 240–Z. I can't remember the numbers on the license plate. You remember the car, you probably know the two fat dykes—"

Joan slammed the telephone down on the hook. She had no wish to remember what had befallen her.

142

In another minute she made another call: for a taxi. As she waited on the sidewalk outside the filling station, she found herself reviewing the long, terrible days from last Monday night to this moment.

On Monday morning Frank had left the house smiling, only to vanish. The mystery had been heightened when her detective work failed at Weil & Tanner, where she ran into a conspiracy of silence, delivered in daily installments.

Her own deductions had led her to these conclusions: She had, indeed, fucked Frank with Weil & Tanner. The shit must have hit the fan some time Monday. Frank was out on his ass. If not, then Frank had walked out on her.

But where? She preferred to believe he was in Las Vegas with Rita Nash. Better that than her fears that Frank was holed up in a motel drinking himself to death, or that he was in a hospital, or a morgue.

On this Friday morning, after a nightmarish night, she had left the house seeking respite from her torment. She had driven to the Corbin Theater to see *The Devil in Miss Jones*. But the box office had not opened, and she had no wish to join the few dirty old men on the outside. From there she had gone for some groceries, only to run into Mr. Walston.

Some relief came with the realization that the taxi would be returning her to an empty house. Not to Frank, or to questions about the missing Datsun, or the shame and hell in her eyes. All she wished to do now was drink hard enough to forget the unforgettable.

The taxi's headlights found the Lawler driveway, played upon the raised garage door, and the rear of an automobile parked inside. At first, false sight Joan saw her Datsun. Second sight revealed Frank's Riviera.

She moaned. Frank was home. A threat.

As the taxi left, Joan walked blindly to her front door until she heard the tumbling of ice in a glass. Her sight returned to behold Frank sitting on the steps, sipping a highball.

"Hello," she said. No sob, no sarcasm.

Frank raised his glass in greeting, not to the sight of her, but to the sound of her voice. He was blind, not from drink, but from his dark hell.

Joan escaped his presence, going into the house, the house beautiful, straight up the stairs, straight into the bedroom, into the bathroom, and into the shower. Off with the dirt, off with everything but indelible guilt. Hot water, warm water, cold water.

She came downstairs again. Her underwear was fresh, her blouse and slacks were fresh, all fresh to Frank's nose and eyes if not to her own. Her torn mouth was hidden behind a layer of lipstick. All that had to be hidden was hidden.

Frank was in the kitchen, fixing himself another drink.

143

"Like some dinner?" she asked.

He shook his head. "Ilona called. She said to call back."

The message meant nothing; the relaying of it meant something. "A sandwich?" she asked.

Again Frank shook his head. Dead-eyed, he left the kitchen. Joan took a Coke, two aspirins, and then sat down at the kitchen table to have some cheese and crackers. Her jaw hurt.

She was thinking of sleep as an escape from guilt and from Frank's dead eyes. She would take a book to bed with her, any book but the Holy Bible, not for reading, but as a cover for sleep.

Leaving the darkened kitchen, she came into the living room to find a book and to bid Frank good night. She found him sprawled on the couch.

"Sit down," he said.

Joan took the easy chair.

"Mr. Tanner took me to lunch Monday. Hillcrest."

Today was Friday, long day, long week, long story.

"You hear me?"

"I'm listening, Frank."

"You sound like you know it all. What do you think he told me?"

"Good-bye," said Joan.

"Wrong. He told me to go away for a few days and do some serious thinking."

"You went to the Serra Retreat," she guessed. Frank went there once a year.

"No, it's closed down. The fire. I checked into a motel room in Malibu."

"Did Rita help?"

"Don't get any ideas. I was alone all the time."

"All right, you wrestled with a problem," said Joan.

"A decision."

"About us. What—?"

"About divorce." The words came hard for Frank. "A choice of divorces. That's what Mr. Tanner gave me, a choice."

"Nice man," said Joan.

"Simple as this—"

"Simple man," said Joan.

"—either I divorce you—or divorce myself from the firm."

"Congratulations," said Joan, certain that Frank had cast his lot with the law firm. No bitterness, no sarcasm, no sobbing. Dolores Cooper was right: the piper had to be paid. And this was her second payment of the day. No, the third, counting the stolen Datsun.

Frank turned to her with bewilderment. "I haven't told you my decision."

144

"It's obvious you chose Weil & Tanner," she said.

Frank lowered his head and shook it.

"You chose me?"

Frank nodded.

Joan laughed hysterically. "Oh, no! You're such a fool! Have you told Mr. Tanner yet?"

"In the morning I will."

"You fool! You can't think straight in a motel!"

"Makes no difference," he said dolefully. "I'm not that much of a fool. It came to me last night. Mr. Tanner, I now realize, was letting me down easy. Asking for my resignation."

"Did he mention me and the party?" Joan demanded.

"We talked about it."

"Who blew the whistle on me?"

"Mrs. Tanner, Rita Nash, and Lewis Donald."

"Bingo," said Joan forlornly.

"Did you stand up for me, Frank?"

"No, how could I defend—?"

"Just for the record, what happened? Did Rita Nash call Donald and get him angry enough to call Mr. Tanner? Did Mr. Tanner discuss my transgressions with his wife? And did she spill her own beans about me?"

Frank stared coldly at her now. "No surprises, huh?"

"Just one," Joan said. "Your deciding to stay with me instead of the firm."

"I really had no choice," said Frank dismally. "I had no real future there. I'm no rainmaker."

Joan understood. She wondered what they called partners whose wives cost them clients. She put the question to Frank.

He ignored it. "All I know is I'm no great brain. Just a dumb—"

Joan interrupted him. "Dumb? You sound smarter than you ever have. Really. And not because you chose to stay with me, but because you now know the score. You know who you are."

"About time," Frank said.

"What are you going to do now?"

Frank said. "I think I better look for a civil service job. A safe place for a lawyer who can't cut the mustard."

"You sound thrilled about it," Joan said.

"Cut it out!"

The anger did not faze Joan. "Why the hell didn't you come home and discuss all of this with me?"

Refusing to answer, Frank rose and headed for the kitchen, for the bottle. Joan went after him.

"Answer me, Frank."

The anger returned. "You smartass bitch! If I had come home Monday night, the police would've come right behind me!"

"And what would the police have found?"

"You," he said, "with a broken head."

Joan believed him. Holding her tongue, she watched Frank pour whiskey like water into his glass. He turned away from her, his head bent, his feet leaden. A moment after he had left the kitchen, she heard his footfalls on the steps. The ascent that was a descent. Up was down, down was up. The next sound Joan heard was the slamming of a door. She guessed it to be the door to the guest room.

Joan slumped into a kitchen chair and stared vapidly at the whiskey bottle. She considered having a boilermaker or two, or three, until she recalled the drinking of the boilermakers at the Tanners' party, and the drowning of Frank's second and last dream.

She sat there, doing some crucial thinking.

Frank had spared her, and it now called for her to spare him. To give him a wide berth, a safe harbor, far from violence.

An idea in the shape of self-sacrifice formed in her tormented mind. She could act now. She could go to the telephone, call Mr. Tanner, and add a white lie to her list of sins. She could tell the bastard that Frank had decided to divorce her, not the law firm.

She rose and rushed to the telephone in the living room. She had dialed four digits before a truth paralyzed her and caused her to put down the phone. No good, too late, Frank the fool was no longer a complete fool, no longer deserving of her disdain. He knew who he was. No rainmaker, no partner, no great brain. A government bureaucrat? God, that was not Frank's dream, that was his dread, his nightmare. Oh, Gentle Mary, the evil I have done.

The tears came. The easy chair was not easy. The night and the day were hard on her. The dildoes were piercing her, spears between her ribs, nails through her hands and feet.

The telephone rang. It rang four times before she found courage and muscle to accept the latest news from hell.

"Hello," she said without heart.

"Joan? This is Ilona!"

She was unable to respond to happiness.

"Joan? Are you there?"

"Here," said Joanie Clarke to a smiling sister taking the class attendance.

"I have wonderful news! I was visiting Ronny at his school and I met this man who was visiting his son, a friend of Ronny's. And, well, I was going to take the train, but this man had his car and he offered to drive me back to New York. That was the beginning. His name is Roger Brennan and he is a widower with two children, just like me, and he

146

is in the textile business, wealthy, and nice looking and not yet fifty. I am in love and he is in love with me, and Bobby has agreed to a divorce."

The last word locked Joan's jaw. The preceding words had bounced like hail against the closed wall of her mind.

"Joan?"

"Yes, Ilona." Bad voice, bad form.

"Are you not happy for me?"

"Very." Not much, not much better.

"You do not sound like yourself," said Ilona.

"I'm stunned," Joan lied.

"I called you before. You were not home. Anyway, after I put the telephone down, I thought maybe I should talk to Frank and ask him for the name of a lawyer to take care of the divorce. The only lawyer I ever talked to—the only one I really know is Bobby's lawyer and Bobby tells me it would not be right for his lawyer—"

"Ilona!"

"Yes, Joan."

"Come by here in half an hour."

"I feel like I am imposing myself—you do not sound—"

"Come over, Ilona. Please."

"Yes, Joan." Ilona sensed her urgency.

Frank did not respond to Joan's rapping on the closed door to the guest room. Joan entered and touched a switch. Lamplight revealed Frank sitting in an upholstered chair, the glass of whiskey in hand, a look of defeat in his eyes.

"What the hell do you want?"

"Take a fast shower," said Joan. "You're in business. Francis X. Lawler, attorney-at-law."

"And who the hell are you?"

"Your rainmaker."

"Hurray for women's lib," Frank said bitterly.

"Hurray for divorce. Your first client's on her way over. You're going to represent Ilona Belanger in a divorce action against her husband."

"Who says I am?"

"You're going to say it. To Ilona." Having said enough, Joan turned to leave.

"Hold on!"

She turned to him. "Yes?"

"What's the address of my law office?"

"Century City. Best address. I'll give you more details tomorrow after I talk to the leasing agents."

"Takes more than one client to pay the rent, to furnish—"

"Tomorrow," she interrupted, "I'm also calling a real estate agent.

We're selling the house. We'll rent an apartment—"

"Century City?"

"Close by. Something we can afford."

Frank thought about it. "Where's your car?"

The new heaven fell upon Joan. "Being fixed. It's been stalling. I left it overnight. That's the way the mechanic wanted it. Anyway, I may sell it."

She shut up. Frank was on his way, past her, into their bedroom. Drink aside, clothes off, and into the shower.

Fast. God, how fast, God, how sudden. How close heaven was to hell, life to death, victory to defeat. Ashes scattered, ashes swept together.

Together again, Frank and she, husband and wife, lawyer and secretary. All this or nothing. Last chance, the very last. A desperate chance.

Joan went downstairs to open a fresh can of coffee and to unfreeze a Sara Lee cake, only to be chilled by the thought that her enterprise was being built on a foundation of corruption.

23

The four of them came off the tennis court glad to be alive and together again. Their sweat was clean, the March air was warm and free of smog, a good Friday to remember.

In the shade of the Cooper patio, they sat down at the round table for cold drinks, for awareness.

"That was so good," said Dolores.

"Yes, even for the losers," said Sally, who had been Joan's partner. Ilona laughed.

"No losers today," said Joan. "If I seem sad, it's because I have a funny feeling—like being at a class reunion. The first and the last."

Dolores said, "We'll do it again."

"Century City," said Ilona, "is not as far away as New York." She faced Joan. "By the way, Joan, I passed your house yesterday. I saw no 'For Sale' sign."

"Too many such signs in the neighborhood," said Joan. But it's on the market. Cardwell & Company. Roark Bennett."

Dolores remembered the name. "The actor! Manderley!"

"The same," said Joan wistfully.

"More of the same?" asked Dolores.

Joan shook her head. "No, I'm no longer a potato peeler."

Dolores persisted. "Then why ask for trouble?"

"Roark was good," said Joan, "and goodness should be rewarded."

"You sound like a pillar of the church," said Dolores.

Joan smiled. "I'm far from being blessed. Just lucky. Dumb Irish luck."

"You and Ilona," said Dolores.

"I am Hungarian," said Ilona, laughing.

"Aren't you lucky, Dolores?" asked Joan.

Dolores thought about it. "Is it possible to be lucky and unhappy at the same time?"

"What are you so unhappy about?" Joan again.

"Myself. My big mouth, my big idea for a small sexual revolution," said Dolores. "Wrong word, revolution. The correct word is revulsion."

"It was all for the best," said Joan. "At least for Ilona and me. We're starting new lives."

"Better lives," agreed Ilona.

"Joan remains with the same husband," observed Dolores.

Shaking her head, Joan said, "No. Frank's not the same, and I'm not. New dreams, old selves. Good-bye to the false dreams of baby Lawlers crawling around the Cape Cod house and to Frank ever becoming a big partner in a big law firm. We know who we are and we're pleased with our peanut stand."

Ilona was confused. "Peanut stand?"

"A one-man law office," said Joan. "One man, one woman, me. Me the secretary, the rainmaker—the one who brings in new clients. Like you, Ilona. And like a man named Kenneth Walston."

"Who's he?" asked Dolores.

"My second client, my last adventure as a potato peeler."

"You're remarkable," declared Dolores. "But are you sure it was your last fling?"

"I'm cured," said Joan absently, and without a smile.

"I'd like to hear more," said Dolores.

"No, you wouldn't," argued Joan. "It's quite sordid."

Sally spoke up. "It's too nice a day for that."

Ilona agreed. Dolores persisted.

"It can't be all bad," she said. "It has a happy ending."

In turn, Joan asked Ilona and Sally to waive their objections. When they had, she went on to recount her tale of the dark house north of Ventura Boulevard.

It was Ilona who noted Dolores's discomfort. "Darling, are you going to be sick?"

"I've been sick," said Dolores. She turned to Joan. "You didn't say, one way or another, whether you enjoyed the little innocent-looking blonde."

The query unsettled Joan. "Why do you ask?"

"It's important to me," said Dolores. "It has to do with nightmares."

Joan sipped her drink. "I didn't mind sharing Walston with the blonde. I did mind her touching me. I fought her off of me at first, but I was too far gone with Walston to fight her off the second time when—"

"You told us," said Dolores sharply.

Joan shut up—for a moment. "The reunion's over, the encounter group's meeting again. Subject: group sex."

"Lesbianism," said Dolores, correcting Joan.

"Enough," pleaded Ilona.

Sally glanced at her wristwatch and looked for an excuse to leave.

Matching Joan's candor, Dolores recounted her own nightmare, preceding it with the causes: the two gentlemen from Chicago, the cheap motel, the broken string of pearls, Joan's laughing, perverse suggestion, and the fiasco in San Marino.

150

Sally and Ilona listened with horror, Joan with cold interest.

It was Joan who spoke up. "You're lucky, Dolores. Yours was a nightmare. Mine wasn't."

Dolores was not mollified. "Interpret the nightmare for me."

"You're the psych major," said Joan.

"Please," urged Dolores.

"I'm sorry I said what I did—that afternoon I returned the pearls to you. I guess I'm the swine linked with pearls."

"No jokes," Dolores pleaded.

"What I learned in that dark house," Joan went on, "was that women aren't as uptight about homosexual relations as men are. The men are scared of each other; the women aren't."

"Including you?" Dolores asked.

"No," said Joan. "Excluding me." She turned to Sally. "You were a bit of a tomboy; you know what I mean."

"Yes, I do," said Sally with compassion.

Dolores prompted Sally to say more.

"About what?" asked Sally.

"Anything," said Dolores. "Puberty. Schooldays. Your years as a stewardess. No lesbian temptation? No dykes making passes at you?"

"All passes went incompleted," said Sally.

Joan explained to a bewildered Ilona. "Football talk."

"Some football," observed Ilona. "Nice—very nice the way you Americans kick each other."

Joan laughed. Dolores and Sally did not. Joan followed by repeating Dolores's questions to Ilona.

"I always laughed at them," she said. "That did it."

Dolores faced Sally again. There was more. "Were you ever a potato peeler?"

"No," said Sally.

"Are you having an affair with Roy Sutter?"

Sally lied. She believed the lie served her. And Roy.

Dolores persisted. "Have you slept with him?"

Again Sally lied. She remembered what Roy had told her about the more dangerous game. For now, truth was a danger.

"I don't believe you," said Dolores. "Do you, Ilona? Joan?"

Joan spoke up. "Let's get back to me. Did you believe me?"

"Yes," said Dolores. "And I thank you for the truth. You don't know how much your candor has helped me."

Joan grinned. "Enough to do me a favor?"

"What kind of favor?" asked Dolores.

"Get Perry to throw a little business Frank's way."

"Wouldn't Frank prefer to defend me in a divorce suit?"

Ilona interceded. "You, too?"

"I haven't ruled it out," Dolores admitted.

Joan said, "I meant things like collection cases. Nothing's too small for us."

"I'll mention it," Dolores promised. "The next time Perry's receptive to talk."

"Thanks," said Joan. "And next time I hope you get more than talk. Forget about divorce. Perry's not Bobby."

"No," Ilona agreed.

Joan said to Dolores. "Well, you're losing Ilona and me. You and Sally'll have to carry on. Play singles."

"I have a list," said Dolores. "Other women interested in—"

"You'll never replace us," said Joan. "Get smart. Get two men. Mixed doubles. Group sex."

Joan and Ilona laughed. Sally smiled. Dolores heard other sounds. Her name was being called by her cleaning woman. Telephone. Long distance. Her face dark, Dolores got up and ran into the house.

"Is it time?" asked Joan.

"Not for two weeks," said Ilona.

"Lucky girl," said Joan. "Lucky Linda. I wish it were me."

"Our time'll come," said Sally, dreaming of Carmel Valley.

"For you, maybe," said Joan. "Not for me. I've made a pact with God —to be happy as a rainmaker delivering clients to Frank. And I will be."

Ilona had not listened to them. She was looking and listening for a sound from Dolores. She soon heard it.

Dolores reappeared, smiling, weeping. "I have a grandson. I'm a grandmother. Isn't it remarkable?"

As her voice broke, the others came running to her, hugging and kissing her in turn and voicing their congratulations.

Ilona beamed. "What a lovely day to remember!"

It was a few minutes past four o'clock. The lovely day had a little less than eight hours to run.

24

Sally did what the Mad Hatter had told her—she whispered hints to time. But the clock did not go round in a twinkling.

It had been a very good morning, a varied afternoon, with welcome tennis, an unwelcome experience reported by Joan, the death knell of the potato peelers, Ilona's farewell, and Dolores's happy news.

From twilight onward, however, the hours for Sally seemed reluctant to pass to midnight. The night cried for a warm fire, for piano rags, and for Roy's dream music of Carmel Valley.

There was no ease, no smile. And no laughter, save from television sound tracks. The sound that delivered her first smile of the evening came some minutes after ten o'clock with the ringing of the telephone.

She rushed to it, believing Roy was calling her from the restaurant to set up their belated reunion in his house.

"Hello," she said, full of cheer.

"Mom!" It was Hap, matching her cheer.

Although she was happy to hear from him, Sally had to struggle to keep disappointment from her voice. She succeeded.

Hap did most of the talking. He was calling from the Ojai Valley Inn, reporting that Neal and he had enjoyed a great day. Sally listened as the boy described in detail the golf match, the dinner, and the good talk he had had with Neal about colleges and careers.

Sally wore out the word "wonderful" before she inquired about Neal's whereabouts.

"Dad's in the hotel bar," said Hap, "having a nightcap. I'm ready for bed."

"Good," said Sally. "I'm glad you called. Glad you're enjoying yourself. And look out for Dad. Don't let him play thirty-six holes tomorrow or Sunday."

"I won't," said Hap. "He's driving the cart. I'm walking, and don't worry, Mom, I'm looking out for him." He laughed. "If he doesn't get back to the room by midnight, I'll drag him back."

"But you're going to bed," Sally reminded him.

"To read. Study."

"Good, Hap. Everything all right at school?"

"I'm okay. I'll make it."

"I'm sure you will," she said.

"Good night, Mom. Miss you."

"I miss you."

"Love you."

"I love you, Hap. Very much."

Good-bye, good-bye. Sally replaced the telephone and tried to find a place for herself. In the end, she decided to go to bed. Back to the bed she had shared with Neal and would continue to share with him because she loved Hap and would do nothing to hurt him. Not now, not for a long while.

Aired all day long, the master bedroom was fresh, the bed strangely comfortable. Sleep overcame Sally and took her from the night, the telephone, and the house on South Oaks Road.

No nightmare disturbed her, no telephone rang, no alarm clock went off. Yet, at midnight, she was awake again, searching the dark for sleep.

She touched the switch for lamplight, the telephone for dear life.

Sally dialed the numbers with deliberation. The ringing at the other end of the line seemed to come from the sunny side of the earth. The voice came upon her like a thunderclap. "Hello."

"Roy?" Her own voice was wary.

"Hello, Sally." He was solicitous now. "How are you?"

"Lonely for you," she said.

"Same here."

"What are you doing?" she asked.

"Nothing."

"Waiting for me?"

"No," he said.

"Roy, what's wrong?"

"Nothing. It's good to hear your voice."

"I sound better in person," she hinted.

"No," he said. "Ojai's too close."

Sally was bewildered. "Who told you?"

"Dolores Cooper. She and Perry had a celebration dinner at my place before he took her to the airport."

"What else did Dolores tell you?"

"That you wouldn't admit you and I were having an affair. But that she suspected otherwise." He was not pleased.

Sally frowned. "How did that come up?"

"Out of the blue. Dolores was a little high."

"You aren't, are you?"

"No. Tell me, when is Neal due to fly off again?"

"I really don't know," said Sally. "He won't be examined until late

154

next week. I have no idea when they'll pronounce him fit to fly." She heard him sigh into the telephone. "Roy?"

"Yeah?"

"I'll be over in ten minutes."

"No," he protested.

"Just for a cup of coffee, nothing more." She went on to tell him about Hap's telephone call.

"Coffee," he said. He had things to tell her, to show her.

Sally said no more. Off of the telephone, out of bed, nightgown off, into pants, sweater, loafers, and coat, and out of the house, lights left burning.

Sutter also left the house, for the garage, for the shotgun. It was time for preparedness.

Sally had no trouble starting the MG and no trouble with the roads leading to Roy's long driveway. The house was lit. The garage door was shut, no Cadillac in sight. But there, at the middle window—stationary, unscreened, twenty-four lights—stood Roy, smoking, waiting, and watching out for her.

He moved to open the front door for her. Sally came into the house and into his arms. It was Roy who halted the kisses and broke the embrace.

"You feel good; you look good."

"I need a drink," said Sally.

"Coffee's all," he told her.

"Just a touch of Scotch."

He did not bend. "Bar's closed."

They sat down together in the living room. The coffee and cake were on the table.

"Can we have a fire?" asked Sally, glancing at the cold fireplace.

"No," he said. "You're not staying that long."

"I could stay till tomorrow night," said Sally.

"Not here, not with me."

"Just coffee and cake?"

"And pictures." He stood up and took a manila envelope from the mantel.

"From Las Vegas?" asked Sally.

"Wrong." He handed the envelope to her.

From it Sally withdrew a batch of large glossy prints, and another batch of smaller Polaroid prints. She studied interior and exterior shots of a quaint restaurant before she turned to Sutter.

"Carmel?"

"Yeah, I was there on Monday," said Sutter. "Went up to look at this place, and stayed to look at some houses in Carmel Valley."

Excitedly, Sally turned to the smaller photographs, exterior and interior views of a house very much like the one they were in now. "Beautiful!"

"Same architect," said Sutter.

"Have you bought it?" asked Sally.

"I intend to."

"When?"

"Drink your coffee and listen," he said. "A real estate company has approached me. They want to put a high-rise office building on the property where the Ivy League now stands. It means a hefty profit for me and—why the funny smile?"

Sally explained. "I'm sorry. I was remembering how afraid I was that the potato peelers were going to bring the Ivy League tumbling down. Now it's the potato peelers who are gone first. Go ahead, please."

Sutter was interested in hearing more about the potato peelers, but now was not the time. "Anyway, they tell me I can remove all the fixtures I choose."

"And you've chosen Carmel," Sally guessed.

"Just about. How does it sound to you?"

Sally hesitated. "What can I do to help?"

"Be patient. Take care. The problem's Neal. You handle him, I'll take care of the rest."

"No deadline for me?"

"No rush, no risk. It's gonna mean a long separation for us."

She tried to accept it. "When does all this begin to happen?"

"Tomorrow, today," he said. "There's a lot to do, here and in Carmel. Lots of plans, lots of decisions—"

"Outside of our own?" Sally asked.

"You have just one to make," he said. "Want me to buy this house, keep looking around, or do we build one of our own?"

She studied the pictures of the house again. "Buy this one. It's real; it exists. It's something I can reach out and touch when the waiting gets rough."

"Done," he said. "I'll call the agent in the morning."

Sally looked around sadly. "And this house?"

"It goes on the market."

"When?"

"Sometime this summer," he said.

She smiled. "We'll make the most of it."

Sutter did not smile. "No."

"Not even when Neal's in Rome?"

"Never again," he said. "I'll take only those risks I have to. No more."

It was all too severe—his demands, his demeanor, and his voice.

Upset, Sally rose from the couch. She paced the floor, holding back anger and trying to find the right question if not the right answer.

At last she spoke quietly. "Roy?"

"Yes, Sally?" The severity was gone from his voice.

"Are you risking too much? Must I worry that one day, long before I'm free of Neal, you'll find you've rushed into things too quickly, too haphazardly? You can't easily forget that the Ivy League's been your total commitment, can you?"

Sutter considered the questions. "No, I'm doing it this way because I believe you and I've made a total commitment. We'll make out—even if I have to turn you into a topless and bottomless waitress."

She was pleased to laugh with him. The laughter returned her to Carmel Valley. She came to him, kissed him, and took up the photographs of the house. Walking back and forth again, she studied the pictures and put herself within the frame of the future that was hers for the enduring, abiding, and dreaming.

Still seated on the couch, Sutter observed the light in her eyes until he was drawn to the dark beyond the windows.

He saw a darkness deeper than South Oaks, deeper than Ojai. A forest dark where a bear walked like a man. A bear with the face of an old, angry eagle. A hand thrust out, a pistol—

"Sally!"

She heard Roy's cry of agony—a cry of death. Her head jerking toward him, she heard the sound of shattered glass before she felt the blow at the back of her neck. She felt nothing else as she fell to the floor.

At the same instant Sutter flung his coffee mug at the middle window, shattering another pane. A third pane was soon shattered, a bullet tearing into Sutter's right arm and momentarily halting his dash toward the light switch.

Using his left hand, Sutter darkened the room and flooded the outside darkness with light. He saw no one at the window.

Blood running down his arm, Sutter, in the dark, found the hall closet, and the shotgun. He unlocked the safety, listened for sound. Hearing none, he did what was most urgent. He picked up the telephone and called for an ambulance, for the police. He was heard. Not by Sally, who lay unconscious and bleeding like a stuck pig. By the operator, and by the killer outside the house.

Eyes on the windows again, Sutter identified Neal Hendley kicking in the middle one, knocking aside splintered glass and sash bars to make an opening for himself.

Hendley had one foot on the sill and was swinging up his other foot when he heard Sutter's agonized warning.

"Neal, I've got my Winchester on you! Throw in your pistol!"

Hendley could not believe his ears. Unable to see anything in the dark but a flash of memory that put the Winchester in the trunk of Sutter's Cadillac, unable to believe anything but that Sutter was using the dark to sucker him, he decided to keep coming, to break into the room and kill off Sutter and Sally. He was in motion and about to bring one foot down on the carpet when the world blew up.

Out of both shotgun barrels flew a plague of lead pellets, devouring glass, wood, cloth, skin, flesh, cartilage, bone, and teeth, tearing away Hendley's face, ripping open his body, freeing gore and entrails, and slamming his carcass back to the damp grass.

Out of Sutter's sickened sight.

He hit the light switch. Not bothering to examine the extent of his own painful, bleeding wound, not bothering to see how dead Hendley was, he went straight to Sally.

He saw the blood still spurting from the wound on the side of her neck. Understanding that an artery had been severed by a bullet, he took a handkerchief from his trouser pocket and pressed it to the wound. To stem death.

As soon as he detected the sound of an ambulance siren in the distance, he turned his head just in time to see a bloodied face rising like a red moon above the window sill.

An animal cry issued from Sutter's gaping mouth. He would not go for his Winchester again. He could not leave Sally. Shielding her body, he made himself the target as he waited for the face to rise higher, for the pistol, for the bullets.

When the face remained immobile and he was able to read the blank eyes, he loosened another animal cry, this one rising out of hell.

The bloodied face at the window was not Neal Hendley's. It was the boy. Hap.

25

The Bentley swung into the Belanger driveway and came to a quick stop at the front door. The engine left running, Bobby pressed the horn to separate the living from the dead.

The sustained sound did nothing to rouse Ilona from sleep, but Sonia was quick to respond to it. Leaving her bed, trusting the darkness more than the alarm, she hurried from her room into the kitchen. As she parted the curtains, she saw the Bentley and cursed Bobby.

In another moment she heard blessed silence. It was short-lived. Bobby stormed out of the car, slammed the door shut, and ran to the front door. The instant he was gone from her sight, Sonia heard the soft sounds of key and lock, followed by the jangling of the chain barring Bobby's entrance.

She left the kitchen for the entry hall when she heard Bobby trying to break the chain free of the door and the jamb. The next sounds came from Bobby's throat and fist as he shouted and banged on the door.

While Sonia remained steadfast but mute, the tumult finally took Ilona from sleep and from the bed. Confused, distraught, she rushed out of the bedroom, down the stairs. She gasped when she saw she was not alone.

Sonia whispered in Hungarian, informing her who was banging on the door, warning her not to open it.

Trusting Sonia, Ilona did nothing about the chain, did not dare to show herself in the narrow opening. She did make her presence known.

Bobby silenced his fist and shouted out his dark tale. He had been returning from a good time in Inglewood when, absentmindedly, he found himself on South Oaks Road, headed for home instead of the Hilton Hotel on Ventura Boulevard. Siren-screaming police cars and an ambulance forced him to the shoulder of the road. When they had passed, he remembered where he was and followed the vehicles all the way to the Sutter house.

He got out of his car, ran up the Sutter driveway, and ran into hell. Neal Hendley was dead. Sally Hendley was dying. Roy Sutter was wounded. Hap Hendley was all covered with blood.

Ilona had to open the door now. She had to unlock the nightmare. When she did, she found Bobby returning to his Bentley. She called for him to come in. He told her to go to hell and sped away.

159

He did not drive far. He had to stop the car, step out, and vomit into the road.

Ilona went to the telephone. She had to tell Dolores.

Perry Cooper came up from sleep to answer the ringing telephone. She asked for Dolores. Told she was in Palo Alto, Ilona repeated Bobby's report.

Perry hung up and immediately called the South Oaks Hospital. He was on his way.

The instant she heard Joan's drowsy voice, Ilona hit her with Bobby's eyewitness report. Joan screamed then controlled herself and told Ilona that she and Frank would be at the hospital.

Frank, shaken by the report, was nevertheless reluctant about rushing to the hospital, lest he give the appearance of being an ambulance chaser. Joan put him wise: they were going to give blood.

Traffic was heavy on South Oaks Road, most of it crawling southward toward the scene of the shooting. Police cars, press cars, television trucks, the morbid and the curious. To the Lawlers, driving northward, it appeared worse than the night two years ago when an earthquake had cracked windows and walls—and the Van Norman Dam at the north end of San Fernando Valley.

In the hospital lobby, the Lawlers ran into Perry Cooper. When Joan informed him of the reason for their presence, Perry asked them about their blood types. They matched Sutter's. He did not know about Sally. They were told to stand by.

Perry dashed off to the emergency room. He got there in time to see Sally being wheeled in. His stomach climbed into his mouth when he saw the death signs on her face.

He checked with the X-ray room and found Sutter there, alive, conscious, and able to recognize him. He gripped Sutter's arm and told him to hold on. When Sutter weakly inquired about Sally, Perry told him one sweet fact: she was still alive.

Not lingering there, Perry went to wash and change. He meant to join the surgeons in the operating room.

In the lobby, Joan came out of her stupor when she heard the public address system paging Lieutenant Fonte. She recognized him when he came to the reception desk. Waiting until he was off the telephone, Joan moved to intercept him.

Fonte scowled at her and answered none of her frantic questions until she identified herself as Sally Hendley's closest friend.

He had some questions for her. How well did she know Hap Hendley? She told him. Could she get the boy to talk? Of course.

At once Fonte led her to a room guarded by a uniformed policeman. Inside, on a hard chair, Hap Hendley sat and stared blankly at a young detective. The boy's face was washed clean of the blood still on his sandy hair, sweater, Levis, and sneakers.

The sight and smell of blood assaulted Joan before she confronted the boy. The blank horror in his blue eyes further shook her. His own eyes never leaving Joan, Fonte opened a window. The younger detective pulled up a chair for Joan.

She sat down, steeled herself, and tried to reach the boy with her eyes, her hands, and her voice. But the boy remained blind, deaf, and mute. Joan burst into tears and fled from the room.

Fonte caught up with her. She apologized for her failure, her weakness, before she went on to recall the boy's history of trauma: the crash in Louisiana, his ensuing silences and rages. Sally, she said, had saved him, cured him. Only Sally, she believed, could reach him.

Fonte was glum. He told her how Hap had been found by the first policeman to arrive at the scene: lying beside his father's shattered face and body, his head resting in the gore as he whimpered like a dog beside its dead master. As for Sally, the chances were she would never have the chance to make the boy talk and tell them what only he could tell. It would take a psychiatrist to bring the boy around.

Having heard more than enough, Joan fled from Fonte. She went searching, not for Frank, but for the nearest ladies' room. She was going to be sick.

When she returned to the lobby, Joan found Ilona with Frank. Quicker than Frank, Ilona understood what had happened to her. Frank wished to take Joan home, but she refused. She had to give blood for Sally.

The Lawlers gave blood and returned home. Ilona also gave blood. And more. She was not alone when she drove home.

And the night wore on, measured in the hospital not so much by clocks but by gauges, soundings, readings, and by life and death signs.

Dawn came with unrosy fingers tearing tape from Roy Sutter's left arm.

He opened his eyes to life and light, to the sight of a strange nurse withdrawing a needle from one of his veins. The needle was connected to a tube leading to a now empty jar of whole blood suspended from a portable stand, which the nurse pushed aside.

He now became aware of a cold coin being pressed against his exposed chest. Turning his head, he followed the stethoscope to a familiar gray face with unfamiliar bleary eyes.

"Perry," he muttered.

"Good morning, Roy."

"How's Sally?"

"Fighting hard."

Sutter read crisis in the voice. "Will she make it?"

"She's got a chance."

161

Sutter took it as the best light of dawn. The nurse silenced him by placing a thermometer in his mouth. Seeing he was in a private room, he understood his own life was not in danger. He tried to understand more about Sally by studying Perry as the latter took his blood pressure. It was good to know he needed no more blood. He was not sure how good life would be with Sally dead.

When the nurse removed the thermometer, he wasted no time in confronting Perry with other dark questions.

"Where's Neal?"

"The morgue," said Perry uneasily.

"And Hap?"

"The Belanger house."

No understanding from Roy.

"Ilona was here, with the Lawlers. They all gave blood."

"Is Sally still getting blood?"

"Oh, yes. The left carotid artery was severed."

Sutter shut his eyes only to see how Sally's blood had spurted. When he opened them again, he saw Fonte standing beside Perry, also ashen and bleary-eyed.

"Hello, Roy," said Fonte.

"Vince."

Fonte faced Perry. "Can I have five minutes?"

Perry nodded. When he and the nurse left the room, Fonte came around to the side of the bed, brought out his notebook and pen, and faced Sutter.

"Do you remember what you told Detective Phillips about the shooting before you were brought here?"

"I remember talking to him," said Sutter. "Not the exact words."

Fonte recited the sequence according to his notes. "That about right? Leave out anything?"

"Yeah." Sutter related what he had shouted to Hendley before he fired the Winchester.

"How did he answer you? With his mouth or his weapon?"

"Neither. He just kept coming at me. He didn't believe me. Not in the dark." Sutter went on to tell him about the transfer of the shotgun from the car trunk to the hall closet.

Fonte frowned. "You were expecting Hendley."

"I was taking no chances. I knew he was in Ojai. I knew he had a pair of matching target pistols. Not that I knew where he kept them."

Fonte had another thought. "Could the boy've heard you shouting?"

"I can't say. I didn't know he was out there. I didn't see Hap till after the shooting. Did anybody ask him?"

"The boy's in shock. Hasn't said a word. I hope to hell he did hear you, and that he says so."

"How important is it?" asked Sutter.

"I can't say," said Fonte. "About Mrs. Hendley—if you were that concerned, why did you let her come over?"

Sutter appeared pained. "I tried to keep her away."

"What made you give in?"

"I had some pictures to show her." Sutter went on to explain about Carmel Valley. "I told Sally we'd only have coffee."

"No sex?"

"Not last night," said Sutter sadly. "Not ever again, until she was free of Hendley."

"Did she buy that?" asked Fonte.

"She bought Carmel Valley."

Fonte turned his head away to cough. Facing Sutter again, he asked, "Did Hendley know what was going on? I mean, between the two of you."

"Sally didn't tell him. They'd agreed to divorce—after Hap got through prep school and into college. A year from September."

Fonte sighed wearily.

Sutter said, "I sure loused things up."

"You're alive," Fonte now said. "Don't give up."

"Will Sally live?"

Fonte studied Sutter's sick face. "I hope so." He pocketed his pen and notebook. He had other questions, but they would have to wait. What mattered now was whether or not Sally Hendley survived.

26

There was no Sunday for Sally. There was a Monday, and its dawn came about an hour after midnight. It came as a blind man tapping his cane for life's solid ground.

The air around her was cool, clean, and strange, unlike the earth's atmosphere, unlike anything in the universe.

Where was she? Where in time, where in place? Where was memory, where was past, present, and future?

She reduced the universe to the dimensions of her own body, and she made kinetic and tactile explorations of it.

She felt the touch of cotton beneath her head until her senses read the softness of a pillow. Out of the pillow she reconstructed a bed with sheets and blanket and mattress. A bed without legs tossing about on an unknown sea.

And she was not alone in this bed. No, she was in bed with snakes. In her nose, down her throat. Another biting into her left arm. She screamed silence and stirred nerves and muscles. Pain coursed through her neck, the agony causing her to twist her head from side to side and to sense wadded cotton rubbing against the cotton of the pillow.

A bandage covering a raw wound. She had been hurt. She was asking herself where and how when another snake came with a rustling and bit her high on her right arm.

The air was poisoned, she was poisoned. The snake was crawling over her face, licking it with its forked tongue.

The snake fled. Her own mind fled, up from the bed. She held onto the bed, the idea, the being, and the clue of the bed.

Whose bed? A bed in Indiana? Mother, she cried in silence, certain her mother was able to hear silence. No answer, no mother. The airline captain's bed? Neal Hendley's bed! Yes, Hendley! Her name, Sally Foster Hendley. California, South Oaks. Where was Neal? Ojai. With Hap. The telephone ringing. Hap. Midnight. Dialing. Roy. The MG. Carmel Valley. The scream was in Roy's voice. Her name. The awful scream she heard and then she heard—what? What was it? Had the earth trembled? Had it quaked and brought down the roof of the house upon her? Where was she now? In what hell or what purgatory? Was she outside of nothingness and only aware of questions whose answers were questions?

164

She heard the Red Queen. "Off with her head!"

No, no Wonderland, no Alice, not down the rabbit hole, not through the looking glass. Yes, glass. There was a sound of glass shattering in Roy's scream.

The scream, the scream, she told herself, stay with the scream, with the shattering of glass. She asked herself what would make Roy scream.

Neal!

It was all so clear now. Oh, God, yes.

Roy was dead. Neal was alive. Memory and mind slipped from her. Muted voices reached her.

"Dr. Timmons!" A woman speaking.

"Yes, Miss Olsen." A man.

"Mr. Mantley's gone."

"Yes." From far off.

A flurry of activity. Sounds of motion, rolling wheels. Mr. Mantley was gone. Dead. His bed—yes, the bed was being wheeled out of—

God, she knew where she was. A hospital. Intensive care unit. The dying room.

It was her last thought. Everything was slipping away: the voices, the sounds, the tubes, the needles, the pain.

The day broke before awareness crawled back to her.

The bed was moving!

She was dead at last and they were taking her out of the dying room. Terror opened her eyes. She saw light and life; she saw Perry Cooper smiling at her. The smile brought tears to her eyes. The touch of his hand returned her communion with the living.

She wept all the way to a private room. The nurse and the male attendants were gone and she was alone with Perry before she dared to try her voice.

"Hello, Perry." A weak effort.

Perry smiled again. "Hello, Sally. Good girl, you made it. You're out of danger."

"And Roy?" Barely audible.

"Discharged this morning." The smile persisted. It died when Perry saw that he was misunderstood. "Roy's all right. An arm in a sling, but all right. Sally, do you understand me?"

"Yes."

"Roy never had us worried. You did."

She dared not ask about Neal, or about what had happened. She preferred not to implicate Neal. She knew nothing, had seen nothing. No one.

Perry, at this time, wished only to reassure her. "Hap's all right, too."

"Hap?" Sally was confused.

"He's at the Belanger house. Been there since early Saturday morning. He's being taken good care of by Ilona and Sonia. With Dolores and Joan Lawler pitching in."

"Dolores? Didn't she go up to—?"

"She came back Saturday afternoon. I just called her with the good news about you. I'm sure she called Ilona to tell Hap."

"How did Hap get back here?"

"With Neal." No smile.

No question from Sally. Not about Neal. "How did Dolores know what happened?"

"It was in all the papers. She was shopping for Linda when she saw the headlines."

Sally was about to shut her eyes when she saw Vincent Fonte enter the room.

Perry advised Fonte not to stay too long, squeezed Sally's hand, and left. Fonte, appearing weary, drew up a chair and sat down close to the bed.

"Vince Fonte," he introduced himself. "Maybe you heard Roy talk about me."

"Yes," she muttered. She knew. The detective.

"Am I rushing you?"

She could not say. She could not send him away. What had happened would never go away.

"Roy sends his love," he said.

She wept.

"I'm sorry. Just a few questions." Fonte extended the Kleenex box to her. She took two tissues and wiped her eyes. "How much do you remember?"

"I can't tell you what happened," Sally said. "I was standing, moving, excited. Roy screamed my name. I heard glass shattering. I felt pain. And then nothing."

"You were shot," Fonte said plainly. "By your husband."

"No," she protested.

"Then he shot Roy."

"No! Where's Neal? In jail?"

"No," said Fonte. He was careful.

"In this hospital?"

"No."

"Where is he?"

Fonte told her before describing how Hendley had met his death.

More tissues, more tears, more patience from Fonte.

"Want me to ring for a nurse?"

166

Sally shook her head. "I want to die."

"I want to bring Hap here tomorrow morning," Fonte said.

"Why?"

"He hasn't been able to say a word since we found him."

"Where did you find him?"

"With your husband—"

Sally's mouth flew open.

"—with his body."

"No!" she screamed.

Fonte rang for a nurse. One soon came running.

"You'd better stay with her," said Fonte. "I'm leaving."

"Don't go," Sally pleaded.

Fonte drew near again.

"Does Hap want to see me?"

"Like I said—he's not talking, not to anybody. I'm hoping it'll be different with you."

"It will be," Sally said. "Or will it? What did he see? How does he feel?"

"I looked in on him this morning. He's eating, he's sleeping, he's reading all the time."

"The newspapers?"

"Books," said Fonte.

"Good day, lieutenant," prompted the nurse.

Fonte turned and left the room.

The nurse said something about orange juice and sleep. Shutting her eyes, Sally saw what her eyes had not seen: the shooting scene.

She imagined Neal and Hap in the postmidnight dark, leaving the station wagon together, walking toward Roy's house, seeing Roy and her through the unshuttered windows. She saw Hap pale with bewilderment, Neal redden with rage. Neal drew his concealed pistol, aimed for the back of her head, and fired. She fell into blackness. Roy fell as Neal's second shot wounded him. Roy got up, escaped other shots, found his own pistol and—

What pistol? Roy had no pistol, no weapon in the house. Had he succeeded in taking Neal's pistol from him? Had he shot Neal while they were wrestling for the possession of the pistol? And where was Hap all this time? What was he doing? Had the sight of her falling as if she were dead stunned him?

Yes, he was found with Neal, still stunned. The way they had found him in the crashed and burning airliner, in the mass of crushed, dead bodies, including those of his mother and two sisters. God! Hap!

What was he reading and thinking?

She remembered how books had worked their magic for Hap in a time when all else had failed. Books she had read to him, books he later read for himself. She remembered the resurrection of the boy's wonder, imagination, and joy of life. She hoped the magic would work for him again.

She doubted it. It was too much to ask, blood upon blood, death upon death. She was afraid. For Hap.

27

On the road outside the Belanger house, a parked patrol car held two uniformed policemen, bored with the police calls on the radio and their assignment. All they had to do was sit there to keep the press away, to keep an eye out for any sign of trouble in the house.

They were pleasured only by occasional smiles from Ilona, and by regular visits from Sonia, bringing them coffee, sandwiches, and cakes.

On the studio bed in Ronny's room, Hap Hendley, clad in a T-shirt, Levis, and sweat socks, lounged and read J.D. Salinger's *The Catcher in the Rye.* He was Holden Caulfield, leaving the train at Penn Station and going into a telephone booth. . . .

A knock on the door returned him to South Oaks, to the Belanger house, and to himself. His head jerking away from the book and toward the door, he sealed it with the hardness of his stare. There was no one he wished to see or hear, there was no one he wished to be other than Holden Caulfield. No place he wished to be other than Penn Station.

Another knock, a turning of the door nob. Hap quickly hid his face behind the opened book so that whoever had entered would not be able to see the death rays his eyes were sending out.

"Hap?"

Mrs. Belanger's voice. Good, warm voice. He liked her voice, her good looks. He did not like her eyes. They said too much about what had happened, and he did not like that. He liked Sonia better. Her eyes were warm, good grandma eyes. They made him remember Louisiana, and that was all right.

"Hap?" Mrs. Belanger again. "Mrs. Cooper is here. She has some books for you. Larry's books."

The secret word was *books.* He did not like Larry Cooper. Larry was a year older, in college, and kind of stuck up. He liked Ronny Belanger better. Ronny was a year younger. He liked playing one-on-one basketball with him.

Hap lowered the book and turned his head. The sooner he showed his face to Mrs. Belanger, the sooner she would leave and let him get back to Penn Station. He saw Mrs. Belanger, Mrs. Cooper, and Mrs. Lawler. He did not like Mrs. Lawler. He did not know her as well as Mrs.

Belanger or Mrs. Cooper. She had no kids, and she had seen him with his father's blood all over him, and that was the way he believed she now saw him.

"How are you, Hap?" Mrs. Cooper asked.

Hap nodded. The sooner he nodded, the sooner she would run out of stupid questions and leave him alone. To be Holden Caulfield.

"My husband just called me," said Mrs. Cooper. "From the hospital. Sally's going to be all right. She's going to be well."

Hap answered with tears. As he wondered whether or not Holden Caulfield would have cried, he hated himself for being Hap Hendley, for loving Sally, for being glad to hear that she was not dead or dying. He turned his head now toward the window to hide his tears, to stop them. No more tears, not ever again, not even for Sally.

He heard books being dropped on a tabletop. "Good-bye, Hap." From Mrs. Cooper and then from Mrs. Lawler.

"Would you like some chocolate cookies, Hap?" From Mrs. Belanger.

He shook his head. He was Holden Caulfield and he had to think about whom he was going to telephone. No time now for cookies, good as they were. A moment after he heard the door being shut, he returned his tear-stained eyes to the book.

Ilona, Dolores, and Joan went downstairs. They settled down in the living room. They had much to say to each other.

"Well," said Dolores, "at least we can stop worrying about Sally."

"Yes," agreed Ilona.

"Can we?" asked Joan.

"Perry doesn't lie," said Dolores.

"Sally won't lie," said Joan uneasily.

Dolores was confused. "What are you trying to say?"

"We're in trouble," said Joan. "All of us potato peelers."

"Does that matter now?" asked Ilona.

Joan nodded. "Very much. Would there have been any shootings if there hadn't been the potato peelers?"

"No," said Dolores.

Ilona agreed.

"The blame's mine—all mine," said Dolores.

"The trouble's all Sally's," said Joan. "We three only have problems."

"No," said Ilona. "I am divorcing mine. You know that."

Joan said, "I was thinking about your Roger in New York, and what he might think when he reads the papers."

Ilona doubted Joan's fear. "Who would put such a thing in the news-papers?"

"Sally," said Dolores, with understanding.

Ilona, now troubled, asked, "Should I tell Roger?"

170

"Wait," advised Dolores. "Maybe Sally won't be asked."

"Wishful thinking," said Joan. "This is a big story. A sexy, lurid scandal."

"Will there be a big trial?" asked Ilona.

"It depends on the inquest," Joan told her.

"What is an inquest?"

"A session of the coroner's jury," explained Joan, "to hear evidence about the shootings. To determine whether or not Neal Hendley's death was justifiable homicide—"

"Please," Ilona pleaded ignorance.

Joan explained. "If the coroner's jury finds that Roy Sutter killed Neal Hendley in self-defense—do you understand what self—?"

"Yes," said Ilona. "It was self-defense, was it not?"

"I think so," said Joan. "Frank thinks so."

"Doesn't everyone?" asked Dolores.

Joan faced Dolores. "Can you tell me what Lieutenant Fonte thinks?"

"He's Roy's friend."

"He's a detective," argued Joan. "And I saw the look on his face that night. I heard—"

Dolores broke in. "Hap was there! He saw the shootings!"

"How do you know?" demanded Joan. "Has he talked to you?"

"No," said Dolores.

"Will he talk at the inquest?" Joan asked. "And if he does, can you guess what he might say?"

Dolores frowned. "I believe you've guessed, haven't you?"

"Frank and I both have," said Joan. "And we don't like it. Who—which of us can imagine what Hap might say? I also saw the look on Hap's face."

Dolores lost her temper. "You always claim to see trouble! How come you failed to see trouble that rainy afternoon in January when I suggested the conspiracy?"

Joan took the rebuff. "I used to hear it said that a stiff prick had no conscience. I can only add this: my clit had no conscience."

Ilona shuddered. "Please, Joan, not now."

Almost to herself, Dolores said, "The guilt's mine."

"The blood is on all our hands," said Joan.

"Yes," said Ilona.

"And what's our punishment?" asked Dolores.

The doorbell rang. Ilona rose. She remained standing in place when she saw Sonia crossing from the kitchen to the front door. The old servant admitted Fonte.

Seeing him, Joan whispered to the others. "Shall we make a mass confession?"

171

Dolores glowered at her. Ilona left and returned with Fonte.

Facing Ilona, he said, "I'll be taking Hap to the hospital in the morning."

"Must you?" asked Ilona.

Fonte said. "Gotta get on with the inquest."

"Do you need Hap for that?" asked Dolores.

"Badly," said Fonte.

Joan asked, "And what if he doesn't talk? Or can't?"

"He has to talk, one place or another. One way or another," said Fonte.

"Sodium pentothal?" asked Dolores.

"I leave that to the psychiatrist."

"Oh, I hope it doesn't come to that," said Dolores.

"Me, too," said Fonte. "I know about the kid and his problems. But I got a problem, too."

Dolores asked, "Can we help?"

Fonte turned to her. "With the boy?"

"The inquest," said Dolores.

Fonte shook his head.

"The trial," said Joan. She meant to be bolder than Dolores.

Fonte turned to Joan. "Who said anything about a trial?"

"No possibility of one?" asked Joan.

"It's possible." He sighed. "You know that, Mrs. Lawler. You're a lawyer's wife."

"Frank's no trial lawyer," said Joan.

"No," said Fonte. "But the deputy D.A.'s are." Saying no more, he turned and went upstairs. The three women exchanged doleful glances and said their good-byes.

Fonte rapped his knuckles on the shut bedroom door, entered, and found Hap buried in his book. He glanced at the titles of the books Dolores Cooper had brought. Grown-up books, the kind read by bright kids.

There was a seventeen-inch Sony television in the room. Color, too. A Marantz hi-fi unit, an eight-track tape deck, and hundreds of dollars worth of records and tapes. And this kid, this poor, bright, dumb kid was reading. It was a strange sight to behold.

"Good book?" asked Fonte.

Hap's head remained buried in the book.

"Just nod or shake your head."

Reluctantly Hap nodded.

"Like to see Sally?"

The boy shook his head.

Fonte hated himself for getting tough. "You like being stuck with a big needle?"

Hap did not flinch.

"The kind that makes you talk and say things you never want to say to anybody."

Hap made no sign, not even of fear.

"The choice is yours," said Fonte. "I'll be coming by for you in the morning. Think it over."

The boy lowered the book. He gave Fonte the kind of look Holden Caulfield might have given him.

Fonte saw the look before he turned and left. He kept seeing it all day and all night. He knew nothing about Holden Caulfield, but he knew enough about Hap Hendley to make him sick with concern for Roy Sutter.

28

The waking from her after-breakfast nap was more like the beginning of a dream for Sally Hendley. The sun was warm, bright on the shut door, and brighter still on the tranquil face of Hap whose eyes shone on the open pages of a worn book.

She saw him at his best, at his ease with life and with himself. He saw himself as Gene Forrester, the sixteen-year-old student at the Devon School in New Hampshire, the narrator of John Knowles's novel *A Separate Peace*.

Hap was sitting close enough for Sally to reach him by a stretch of an arm, by a touch of a hand. She was uncertain about her voice. He reacted without a change of expression, with a reluctance to remove himself from the action of the novel.

Sally chose to use the book as a bridge to speech. "What are you reading?"

Hap answered by moving the book toward Sally, allowing her to read the title on its spine.

"Enjoying it?" Sally asked.

Hap nodded.

"Good," said Sally. "Haven't they made a movie of it?"

Another nod.

"Did you see the picture?"

A shake of his head.

"What's it about?"

No nod, no shake of the head. Only a nervous movement of the mouth, a swallowing, and then an opening of the mouth, a sound of hemming, and, at last, voice and halting words. It was Neal's voice in a higher octave.

Her mind trembling, her nerves tearing, Sally listened to Hap tell her everything about that part of the book he had already read, and nothing about himself. She listened attentively and tried not to think about anything beyond the book. For Hap's eyes were on her, and she knew he could sense whether or not he was interesting or boring her. Hap always had to be handled with care. Now more than ever.

When Hap was silent again, Sally asked, "Been reading a lot?"

A nod, followed by speech. This time Hap told her about *The Catcher in the Rye*. And what he had to say was good, lucid.

174

Sally proceeded with caution, with questions about his well-being, the room at the Belanger house, the food, the books.

Then Sally asked, "What about school?"

Hap shrugged.

"Want to go back?"

The boy shook his head, shut his eyes, and scratched his brow.

"Whenever you're ready. You tell me when. I won't rush you," Sally said.

Hap opened his eyes. Unable to face Sally, he returned his eyes to the novel. Sally allowed him to read undisturbed for a while. It gave her time to choose her next question with care.

"What time did Dad pick you up last Friday?"

The mention of "Dad" caused him to shut his eyes. His head did not move.

"Were you surprised to see him?" Sally asked.

Hap nodded.

"Dad thought it would be a happy surprise," she said. "He got up that morning feeling well. Strong. I suggested he run up to Ojai and spend the weekend with you at the Inn. When he agreed, I asked him to call the school—to let you know he was on his way. Dad said he wanted to surprise you."

It troubled her that she was only repeating what she had said in their last telephone conversation. Yet it seemed correct as a method, as a ploy to draw him out and bring him to tell her the untold mystery of what had occurred in Ojai. In South Oaks.

"Hap?"

The boy read on. About the Suicide Society of the summer session at Devon.

"Was Friday a beautiful day?"

Hap was deaf to her.

"Was it like you said it was—on the telephone?"

More interested in the novel, he nodded and read on.

"Did you get to play eighteen holes before dark?"

The same, detached response. With each nod the silence deepened and worsened.

"Who won?"

The boy tapped his chest.

"Tell me about it."

The question, it seemed to Sally, only divided the boy's mind. One part of him stayed with the excitement of the novel, the other recounted the highlights of the golf match.

"Then what did you do?" asked Sally.

"I told you on the telephone." He read on.

"Was Dad drinking in the room before dinner?"

Hap shook his head.

"Was Dad tired?"

Another shake of his head.

"What did you talk about at dinner?"

"School."

"What about it?"

Hap said, "Dad was telling me what fun he had in high school, playing football, basketball, and golf. Having all those assistant coaches from all those colleges coming around—sucking around his folks—trying to get him to sign a letter of intent—or something. He said he wished he was my age. In my boots. In my school."

"Did you think that was strange, Hap?"

Hap turned down the corner of one of the opened pages and shut the book. Sally feared that he might rise and leave. Instead he sat there, his eyes filling with awe, his throat and mouth stirring.

He said, "Yeah. I was listening and laughing and smiling when I wasn't laughing. I was liking what Dad was saying. And liking the way he said things. The way he looked at me when he was smiling and talking." Hap paused to swallow. "He looked at me like he was glad to be alive. Like he was glad I was alive."

Although she knew the answer, Sally, nevertheless, believed it was right to force Hap to put it into words. Into feeling. "Hap? Why was that so strange?"

"You know."

"Tell me, Hap."

"Dad isn't—" He broke off, stung by the realization of his father's death. "Dad wasn't like you—but nobody was like you." He said no more.

Sally prompted him. "Go on, Hap."

The boy bit his bottom lip. By the time he had found his words and voice, the teeth marks were discernible. "You always look at me and see just me. How I look right then, how I feel. And you hear just me when it's just me who's talking."

"And Dad?"

"Except for last Friday—up till bedtime anyway—Dad was—well, he was never comfortable with me. I could tell that. I could tell he was looking at me and thinking about Mom and Millie and Nancy."

"That's natural," said Sally. "I mean—understandable."

"I didn't understand. I still don't," said Hap. "He looked at me the right way Friday. If he did then, why didn't he—why couldn't he do it before?"

"It takes time for a man to recover—" Sally broke off when Hap began to shake his head. "What is it, Hap?"

176

"I didn't have the time," he said. "I needed Dad right away. Needed him bad."

Yes, he was growing up, thought Sally. He was correcting his memories, learning values and truths.

Hap had more to say. "I used to feel Dad didn't want me around. His good-byes were always better than his hellos. I think he liked it better when he didn't have to see me and remember Mom and Millie and Nancy."

"Hap, this time you chose to leave Dad and me and—"

"Which time?"

"Going off to school in Ojai."

"Sure," he said. "But I was leaving Dad. Not you. And sure I was happy to see him Friday. I knew how sick he'd been, and I was glad to see him up and around. But I would've been gladder—happier—if you'd come along with him."

"Dad asked me to," she said.

He faced Sally. "Why didn't you?"

She chose the truth. "I thought the two of you might have a beautiful weekend together."

"Why wouldn't it have been more beautiful with you along?" he asked.

"I was a fool," Sally confessed.

"You sure were," Hap agreed.

In vain Sally waited to hear more. She suspected he was about to blame her for Neal's death.

"Hap?"

He stared at the door.

"What went wrong?"

The question prompted Hap to open his book again.

"Shut the book, Hap. Look at me." He obeyed. "Please answer me."

"Try another question," he said.

Until she found a new tack, Sally was silent and uneasy. "After our telephone call—what happened?"

"I was in bed. Studying. Thinking."

"About what?"

"Me and Dad."

"Good thoughts?"

Too choked to speak, Hap nodded.

Sally hesitated. "When did you see Dad again?"

Hap's face darkened as he conjured the moment. "I wasn't sleeping, but the room was dark. I know it was almost eleven-thirty by the time we got in the station wagon. But then the dashboard clock's always a little slow and—"

Sally interrupted him. "Did Dad come back to the room?"

He nodded.

"Tell me what happened. Everything. Everything Dad and you said and did."

"Everything?"

"Including the four-letter words, if there were any."

"Sure were," muttered Hap to himself. Louder and clearer to Sally, he related, "Dad came in, drunk and mad. Hit the lights and said, 'Get your ass outa bed and get dressed. We're gettin' the hell outa here.' I started to ask him where we were going and he jumped on me. He said, 'Shut your fuckin' mouth and get dressed and packed! You got five fuckin' minutes!' I was thinking maybe there was a fire or something, but then I could see that nothing and nobody was burning but Dad."

Sally asked, "Both of you went directly to the car?"

He nodded. "Dad just threw the bags and golf bags in the back, got behind the wheel, and I got in beside him. He was speeding and burning rubber even before we got to the freeway."

"Did you know Dad was headed back home?"

"I figured that when he turned south on 101."

"Did you try talking to him?"

"No, I knew better. He was looking at me and not even seeing me. He was seeing red. I could see he was drunk and mad. We were passing through Ventura when Dad got to talking to himself, or maybe—"

The door swung open. A nurse marched in to bring Sally a glass of orange juice, a warning about needed rest and unwarranted stress. For Hap, she had a dark, curious stare.

When the nurse was gone, Hap said, "I don't like her."

"She means well," said Sally.

"That means nothing. Everyone thinks they mean well."

The observation was relevant, but first things first. "The car, Hap," cued Sally. "Dad talking to himself."

Hap responded. The boy was a good mimic and delivered his intermittent outbursts not in his own voice but, rather, in Neal's deeper, anguished baritone.

" 'Stupid son of a bitch! . . . No good prick. . . . What the hell does he understand about war? . . . What does he know about vasectomies? . . . North Vietnam ain't Germany or even Japan. . . . The son of a bitch can't tell the difference between a good war and a bad war, a right war and a wrong war. . . . Stupid Texas bastard. . . . What the hell does he know? . . . An engine ain't like a human body. . . . Tryin' to shit me that when a doctor cuts you and cuts off a line it's like some stupid mechanic cuttin' a line in an engine. . . . What does that flag wavin' motherfucker Ralph Norwich know about a vasectomy? . . . That prick couldn't spell the word. . . . I shoulda cut out his fuckin' tongue.' "

178

As Hap paused, Sally was able to recall that Ralph Norwich had been a fellow pilot in Neal's bomber squadron.

"What else, Hap?"

In his own awed voice, the boy said, "Dad was driving hard, blinking his eyes like he was having trouble seeing. Around Camarillo he started to hit the brakes. He stopped the car on the shoulder and told me to take the wheel."

Sally had to prompt Hap again. "Did he say anything else?"

"No."

"Did he sleep?"

"No, he kept smoking and coughing, all the way home."

"Then what?" asked Sally.

"I turned into our driveway, hit the button, and the garage door came up. The garage was empty."

"Did Dad say anything then?"

Hap nodded absently. "He said, 'That fuckin' MG! Always somethin' wrong with that little shit of a car!' "

"Did you go into the house?" Sally asked.

"Dad got out," Hap said. "I put the car away and caught up with him at the front door. Dad was ringing the doorbell and banging on the door. He grabbed the keys from me, opened the door. He went from room to room, looking for you, looking for a note maybe. I don't know. In your bedroom Dad looked at the bed—the way it was mussed up, with your nightgown, the pillow, and covers the way they were. He just took everything and threw it on the floor."

Sally asked, "Do you know why?"

Hap thought about it. "It wasn't like you. You're not that sloppy. Dad figured—he must've figured something happened—maybe a phone call—like there was somebody or some place you had to get to in a big hurry."

She sighed. "Then what?"

"Dad went into the den and took a shot of whiskey before he turned to me and said, 'Let's go. You're drivin'.' "

"Did you ask where?"

"Not till I got the station wagon out of the garage."

"And what did Dad say?"

"He asked me if I knew where the Cooper, Belanger, and Lawler houses were. I said I did, and all he said back was, 'Let's go.' "

Sally said, "Tell me everything."

"First," said Hap uneasily, "I drove to the Lawler house on Texas Lane. The house was dark. No MG parked anywhere around."

"Did Dad leave the car?"

"No. He just told me to get on. It was the same at the Coopers and the Belangers. Dark houses, no MG around."

"Then what?"

"Dad said, 'Back home.' "

"Very angry?"

"He was burning, but nothing like—" Hap broke off. He went on in agony. "I was coming down South Oaks Road, heading home. Dad wasn't looking anymore. He wasn't seeing anything but the cigarette he was lighting. He was smoking and coughing when I hit the brakes."

Sally felt the boy's agony, but she dared not disturb the fires of his memory.

"Dad wasn't wearing his seat belt. He had to throw up his hands to keep from going into the dashboard and windshield. He turned on me. 'What the fuck was that for?' I say, 'I saw Mom's car.' Dad says, 'Your Mom's dead! What car? Sally's MG?' " The boy was struck dumb for a moment. "I say, 'Maybe I was just seeing things.' The next thing I know I'm stepping on the gas again and the station wagon's moving. Then Dad yells at me, 'Where the fuck are you goin' now?' 'Home,' I tell him. 'Turn the fuckin' car around!' he tells me, and I do. And he says, 'Stop where you thought you saw somethin'.' "

Knowing where they were in time and place, Sally waited to hear the worst.

"I stopped the car," said Hap, "but I didn't turn my head. I didn't want to look and see what I knew was there. Dad looked. I don't know how much he could see in the dark. Then he asked me, 'Who lives here?' I knew, but I didn't tell him, but then Dad looked like he knew. He reached over, shut the ignition, the lights, took the keys and got out of the car. He went around to the back of the car. He lowered the tailgate and I could see him looking for something in the tool compartment. Finding it. Moving away from the car. Up the driveway. Toward Mr. Sutter's house. I was sitting there, hating myself, hating Dad, hating you. Being afraid for you. Knowing—feeling maybe that Dad was up to no good. And maybe that you were up to no good."

Sally wept. All Hap saw was the night in question.

"From where I was sitting, I couldn't see anything but the MG. Then I heard the first shot and the second. I knew it was Dad firing the target pistol, which I didn't know he had until then. I couldn't see—I couldn't tell what he took from the station wagon. I didn't know he'd hid the pistol there." He paused. "I got out of the car. I walked; I couldn't run. It was like I wasn't supposed to run. Maybe because Dad told me to stay put—maybe because—I don't know. All I know is I walked up the driveway—like you walk in nightmares—and I saw Dad there with the floodlights on him. With him holding the pistol and kicking in the dark window—it was all dark inside the house. Then I saw him climbing up and trying to get into the dark house through the big window he'd kicked in."

180

Hap fell quiet. Sally could not prompt him. She had no voice. Hap's own voice returned, quavering, maddening.

"There was an explosion—like the whole house blowing up. All the glass and wood flying. Dad flying back and falling on the grass. I ran to him. I ran hard. I fell down on top of him. Only it wasn't him, it wasn't anything alive and looking like him. He had no face, no eyes, no nose, no chest. He was just a mess of blood and guts."

The blood ran from Sally's brain, taking her from sight, voice, and awareness.

Seeing only his father's blood, Hap went on. "I tried to put Dad together. Then I gave up and buried my head on his chest, in his blood. And then I saw the lights go on inside the house. I looked in. I saw Mr. Sutter bleeding, holding you, and you were bleeding. The next thing I heard was screaming in my head. People on the plane screaming, everybody screaming. Mom was bloody and dead, Millie bloody and dead, Nancy bloody and dead, Dad bloody and dead, you bloody and dead. And the fire exploded. The flames—"

Hap said no more. A glance at Sally caused him to bolt from his chair and rush to the door.

The smelling salts opened Sally's eyes. The nurse was with her. Hap was gone.

29

Friday, fateful Friday. It was the day the coroner's jury had convened in downtown Los Angeles to hear evidence about the South Oaks shootings. The "true verdict"—yet to be announced—would give the name of the deceased, when, where, and how he had met his death, and who, if it were deemed to be a criminal act, was involved.

At dusk the principal witness turned his sedan into the driveway of Sutter's home. Haggard in appearance, he frowned at the plywood panels nailed to the frame of the shattered, center window.

Inside the house, in the den, sat a gloomy Roy Sutter listening to the KNX news reports. His right arm was in a black silk sling, his left hand held a glass of whiskey.

He tensed when he heard the doorbell. Putting the glass down, he went to the door.

"Hello, Vince," he said.

Fonte entered without a word, without a smile. He followed Sutter to the den, shut off the radio, and went behind the bar to help himself to a much-needed drink.

"Bad news?" guessed Sutter.

Fonte shook his head and poured vodka, into the glass, into his dry mouth.

"Nothing yet?" asked Sutter.

"Sit down and relax," said Fonte. "I'll be getting word here. Pretty soon, I think."

Sutter sat down, unrelaxed. He held his tongue and waited for details.

Fonte had another quick shot before he asked, "How are you holding up?"

"Long day," said Sutter.

"I think we both look it, Roy. But I have a feeling it was tougher for you. Have you done anything besides keeping your ear glued to the radio—and bending your one good elbow?"

"Frank Lawler was here for a couple of hours. He's handling some business matters for me."

"The restaurant deal?"

"Yeah. Here, not in Carmel," said Sutter. "I'm holding off on that."

"Whatever the verdict?"

"Yeah. I figure I better wait and see how things go."

"Look," said Fonte harshly. "You'll be exonerated, no question."

"Vince, how tough was it?"

"I had it tougher yesterday with Snyder."

Sutter understood he was referring to Otto Snyder, a deputy district attorney, who had ideas of bringing about his indictment and prosecution.

"Is that why you never called me?" asked Sutter.

"How the hell could I tell you that the little bastard let me walk out without letting me know if he was gonna fuck you or not?" Fonte took more vodka. "Anyway, he didn't."

Sutter sighed. "Thanks."

"Don't thank me yet," said Fonte, still aggrieved. "I had to let the bastard in on every damn thing."

Sutter winced. "The potato peelers?"

"Everything."

"Did it come out in the inquest?"

Fonte shook his head. "I had enough ammunition. Hell, I don't think we needed more than the kid's statement. But I laid it all out. Your statement, Sally's, and the one I got from General Norwich up in Ojai. The guy Hendley had run into in the hotel bar that fucking night. I was good, hitting and fielding."

Sutter did not understand the last remark.

Fonte explained. "I handled all the questions cleanly. Especially the tough chances. The hard ones hit at me—like what the hell was the Winchester doing loaded in your closet? The coroner—and he must've been coached a little if not enough by Snyder—he kept at the idea that you may've been setting up Hendley for the kill."

"Was I?" wondered Sutter.

"Can it," snapped Fonte.

"Let's talk about it," Sutter insisted.

"No, I got a better idea," said Fonte. "Feed me before I fall on my fucking face."

Sutter held off. He rose and went to the kitchen. Fonte trailed him. Sutter opened his refrigerator for Fonte's inspection.

"Take what you want," said Sutter.

Fonte smiled. "One arm in a sling and you're running a self-service cafeteria."

Sutter watched Fonte use both of his hands to take some cold cuts, cheese, and an opened bottle of Burgundy.

At the table Sutter smoked and nursed his drink while Fonte ate and drank in silence. Biding his time, he let Fonte choose the moment and the subject for conversation.

Fonte was questioning him about the wisdom of selling the Ivy

League, inasmuch as he had seemed to abandon his ideas of a new restaurant in Carmel and a new home in Carmel Valley.

"What the hell are you going to do with yourself, Roy, play golf seven days a week?"

Before Sutter could respond, the telephone rang. His mouth stuffed, Fonte signalled that he would take the call. Sutter took whiskey as Fonte went to the telephone.

"Speaking," said Fonte. He chewed, listened, and said, "Thanks." Turning to Sutter, he said without emotion, "Justifiable homicide. No sweat."

Fonte returned to the table to regard a stunned Sutter with scorn. "Did you hear me or didn't you understand me?"

His eyes blank, Sutter nodded. He rose and went to the telephone. Quietly Fonte observed him dialing his number.

"Room 314, please."

The number registered with Fonte. It was Sally Hendley's hospital room. He spit the food from his mouth into his napkin before he shouted his command. "Hang up!"

Sutter's head jerked toward Fonte. "I'm only calling—"

"Hang up!"

Sutter obeyed.

"Call anybody but Sally."

"You said, 'no sweat,'" Sutter reminded him.

"Call one of the potato peelers. Let one of them tell her."

Sutter dialed the Lawlers' number. Joan answered. She was happy for him, happy to forward his news and love to Sally. He thanked her and hung up.

"Leave the phone off the hook," said Fonte brusquely.

"Why?" demanded Sutter.

"Because I want your damn attention. After I get the hell out of here, you can spend the rest of the night answering the phone."

"My number's unlisted; you know that."

"Your pals know it. Hershey can come on and stay on for as long as he does when he gets onstage."

Sutter removed the telephone from the hook before joining Fonte at the table.

"Vince, you're giving me the heat. I thought it was off. I thought I was in the clear."

"You're in a fog," said Fonte. "Now listen to me, and listen good. I don't want you seeing, calling, or writing Sally. No flowers, no candy, and no sending your love."

Sutter could not believe that Fonte was anything but overwrought, overworked. He had a desperation for laughter, but he sensed that he dare no more than a grin. "Vince, you're great. You talk like I was a

184

paroled convict and you were my probation officer."

Fonte was not amused. "Guess again."

Sutter did. "You're my brother, my keeper."

"Think what you like," retorted Fonte. "Just don't get out of line."

His grin enduring, Sutter said, "Can I *think* about Sally?"

"Yeah, with your head. Not with your heart or your cock."

The grin fled. "For how long?"

Fonte thought about it. "Till the kid goes back to school."

"When will that be?"

"Who the hell knows, Roy. Probably next September."

Sutter groaned.

"Before the damn shootings," Fonte reminded him, "you did make up your mind to keep away from Sally until a year from September."

"I wish I had," said Sutter forlornly. "But aren't things a little different now?"

"Hell, no," said Fonte.

"Hendley's dead."

Fonte hit him. "Hap Hendley isn't."

Hit hard, Sutter stood up and staggered to the bar for more whiskey. Fonte continued to eat and drink wine until Sutter returned to the table.

Sutter tried to build his own case. "I always got along with Hap. We always hit it off."

"Ancient history," said Fonte. "Counts for nothing now."

"Then why did he tell the truth? Why did he give you the ammunition to save my neck?"

"Only because he couldn't lie to Sally," said Fonte.

"No other reason? Don't you give him any credit for character?"

Fonte said, "I think I'm in a better position to judge that than you are."

"You didn't know him until—"

"I know him now," Fonte interrupted. "Listen, I spent a half a day with him—right after he left Sally's room. I took him to Ojai with me when I went up to see General Norwich."

Sutter wanted to know more about Hap.

Fonte told him. "We had a nice drive up to Ojai. I let him alone, and he just sat there on the front seat beside me reading his book. Every once in a while I'd glance over at him, and he looked like he was a million miles from me and the shootings. He was *in* the book—you could see the intensity in his eyes—something you couldn't see when he was looking at you."

"What did that tell you?" asked Sutter.

"Me and you, were we ever that way except when we were checking our scorecards or maybe reading the sports pages?"

185

"No," Sutter admitted.

"The kid's deep. He's what my kids call a *brain.*"

"Isn't that good?" demanded Sutter.

"Not for you, I don't think."

"Didn't you talk to him?"

Fonte sipped wine before he nodded. "All the way back home. First I let him hear what the bartender and the manager at the Inn—and the general—had to say about his old man. Then I had the kid—we were in the car then—tell me word for word what he'd told Sally before she passed out."

Sutter asked, "Did the stories match up?"

"Yeah, they did," said Fonte. "Then we got to talking about the shootings. I put some straight, hard questions to him, and he gave me straight, hard answers."

"Like what?" Sutter took whiskey.

"I asked him how he looked at the shootings, and he said something like this: 'I don't blame anybody but myself.' I asked him how he got to that, and he said, 'I should've never stopped the car when I saw Mom's MG. I knew whose driveway it was, but I didn't think fast enough. I didn't remember how drunk and mad Dad was. I didn't remember there was something between Mr. Sutter and Mom.' And I said, 'How the hell could you? You weren't around. And even the people who were—like me, like your Dad—didn't know.' He didn't buy that. He said, 'I should've remembered those times at the country club. I should've known Mr. Sutter was always so nice to me because he kind of liked Mom. You could tell there was something going on between them even then—not that anything was happening—I mean, that they were doing anything about it. I knew how Dad felt about Mr. Sutter, although the way he did had nothing to do with Mom. Just with the kind of jealousy one guy has for another because he can't stand for the other guy to be better at something he wants to be best at.'" Fonte faced Sutter. "That's a mouthful, isn't it?"

Sutter could only nod. He waited to hear more. Worse.

Fonte returned to his account. "I said, 'You can't blame yourself for not remembering all that. You saw the MG, you reacted, you hit the brakes.' And he said, 'It was dumb, and I'm not dumb. You can't read all I've been reading and be dumb. The teachers at school don't think I'm dumb.' The next thing I said was, 'You're only human, you're young.' He didn't buy that a bit. Listen to this, to what he said, 'Sure, I'm young. That's why I'm different from you and all grown-ups who don't remember how clear and clean they saw things when they were young.'"

Sutter, visibly moved, remained silent. He had no wish to disturb Fonte's haunting memories of his dialogue with Hap.

The detective went on. "I didn't quibble with him. I didn't tell him —speaking for myself—that I was as bright a kid as him. I just asked him what things about the shootings he saw that us grown-ups—even us professionals—didn't see. It took him about a minute to get the words out, and he said, 'Did you ever see the shootings as a duel?' "

Sutter never had. The thought, as sharp as a dueling sword, pierced his heart. "How did you answer him, Vince?"

Fonte said, "I told him I saw a duel as something organized, arranged, between two men or between their seconds. I went on to point out how accidental the whole damn thing was. His old man running into a guy he hadn't seen in years. His old man bringing up a subject like vasectomy, the other guy making it out to be something worse than it was. Things like that—all the little accidents that went together to make the shootings happen the way they did, when they did."

"Did you convince him?" asked Sutter.

"Hell, no," said Fonte. "The kid just shook his head, and I asked him if he knew what a vasectomy was. He nodded, and then he said, 'It had to happen. I'll tell you why. Two men in love with the same woman.' I went right at him, telling him the statistics on divorce and on shootings. Nothing. He's right back at me, saying, 'A man doesn't divorce his wife to turn her over to his enemy, not most of the time. Not if he's my Dad, and you remember how hard life's hit him. Not when there's a gun handy for a man used to using guns and dropping bombs to kill people in war. It just had to happen.' "

Sutter understood Hap too well.

Fonte had more. "Then I asked him this: 'About the idea of a duel, you believe it's a fair way of settling things? Fights? Scores?' And he said, 'There's never been a fair duel. The better shot's bound to win. Unless the worse shot's not using a matching pistol.' "

Anticipating Fonte, Sutter asked, "What did Hap say about the Winchester?"

Fonte was glum. "About what you've already guessed."

"Doesn't he know his father shot Sally and me before I went for the Winchester?"

"The kid knows everything. In addition to books, he reads the papers."

"Then he must've read that I warned Hendley I had the Winchester. He might even have heard me! Did he?"

Fonte shook his head.

Sutter grimaced in agony. "Do you believe him?"

"He believes you."

Dumbfounded, Sutter waited to hear more.

"But," said Fonte, "the kid thinks he knows why his old man *didn't* believe you."

187

"What the hell could he know?" demanded Sutter.

"What you and I know. That you used to sucker Hendley. The way you used to throw up some grass to test the wind in your face. The way you'd take out a four wood for a shot you knew you could make with a four iron. And you'd manage to knock the ball close to the flag. And then Hendley'd get up there and knock his shot over the green and into the woods. The kid remembers all of Hendley's talk about your tricks. Get the picture? The kid thinks that when his old man heard you bark about the shotgun, something in his head must've reminded him about all the times you suckered him, and he was not about to be suckered again."

Sutter emptied his glass. "Did Hap know—had Hendley told him I kept the Winchester in my car—?"

"No, he read that in the papers." Fonte rose, taking the emptied plate to the sink, the wine bottle back to the refrigerator, from which he took an apple.

Sutter quit the kitchen and went to the den, but not to the bar. He slumped into his club chair. Fonte stretched out on the couch, munching away at his apple.

"Is there more?" asked Sutter dolefully.

"The kid's leaving in the morning," reported Fonte. "Flying to Louisiana with the body. He'll be back before Sally gets out of the hospital."

"Then what?"

"He intends to take care of Sally. The way she took care of him, the way she brought him back. Sounds good, doesn't it?"

"If you say so," said Sutter.

"I don't."

Sutter stiffened in his chair. "Spill it."

"That's just what I'm trying to keep from happening. No more spilling blood around here." He bit into the apple again. "Remember how we used to talk about taking one of those European golf tours?"

"Yeah," said Sutter absently.

"Soon as your arm's fit, I think you ought to take off."

"You're chasing me," deduced Sutter.

"For your own good."

"I've got business. The sale—"

"You got a lawyer on it."

"Anything else?"

"Yeah. Let your lawyer close the Carmel deals."

Sutter sensed the suggestion was unwise, as unwise as the letting down of his guard to allow Sally to view the landmarks of his Carmel dream. Now Carmel seemed to be a dirty word. Dirty pictures. Or, at least, dirtied pictures.

All he said was, "No, I better hold off and stick around here."

Fonte looked askance at him. "What'll Sally think? What can she think but that you've given up?"

"I'll tell her otherwise," he responded.

"Not until I give you the word," said Fonte strongly.

"Yes, master."

Fonte looked hard at him. "I don't like the way you said that."

Sutter came back at him. "I don't like anything you said tonight."

Fonte left the couch. Confronting Sutter, he said, "Here's more you won't like. I had one of my men go through the Hendley house—to see if he could find the matching target pistol."

The revelation tore and pained Sutter's guts. "Did he find it?"

"No," said Fonte. "But he did find that someone had been in the house. In the garage he found freshly disturbed dust—like someone had been looking for something."

"Who?" demanded Sutter.

"The kid."

Sutter winced. "Has he admitted it?"

"I never asked him. I don't intend to. My man found all of the papers, magazines, and mail in Hap's room. All of the stories about the shootings had been clipped out and filed in a drawer."

"Did your man find the gun?" asked Sutter.

"No, not even after a thorough search."

"Is he satisfied there's no gun in the house?"

"He is," said Fonte. "I'm not." He tossed the apple core into Sutter's lap and left the house.

30

The sleeping capsule rested in the small paper cup on the metal table beside the hospital bed. In the darkened room Sally Hendley faced the window rather than the light spilling from the corridor through the open door. It was her last night at the hospital, no night for sleep.

Unable to read the stars, she read her own entrails.

The wounds left by the bullet's entrance and exit from her neck were healing. The stitches had been removed; the scars were forming. In time, she was told, they could be removed by cosmetic surgery. But she had no interest in this. She meant to keep the scars. She looked upon them as badges to mark her guilt and shame.

The trauma that had pierced her mind was still lodged there. It blocked out elation about her recovery. She did not know if she had escaped death or if she had only lost the escape of death.

This afternoon she had been permitted to spend a few hours up on the hospital's sun deck. The sun, the blue sky, and the air were good. The San Gabriel mountains to the north of the valley were visible and beautiful until her mind flew over them and on to Carmel Valley. It was still there on every map but her own. Without it, the sky and sun lost their color and warmth.

She was about to return to her room when she saw Dolores Cooper and Ilona Belanger approaching her. She settled back on her lounge to endure their visit. Ilona was leaving in the morning for New York. This was good-bye. She was happy for Ilona, and also happy to be done with her. She wished Dolores would return to Palo Alto. And she was no longer happy to see Joan in the evenings.

The awful thing about it all was her awareness of how good the three of them were to her—better than blood sisters. In truth, they had behaved much better than her own brothers and her parents. The letters from Indiana were written in languages that had no words for understanding and compassion, let alone love. Her first telephone call to her parents was her last.

And yet, here in South Oaks, she had Ilona to give her blood, to take Hap into her home and heart. She had Dolores, fleeing her own daughter and newly born grandson, to run to her and assume all guilt. And she had Joan to give her blood and a lifeline to Roy.

190

Short hours ago Joan had brought word that Roy was leaving for Las Vegas, not for Carmel Valley. It had meant nothing to her to hear that Roy was returning the Winchester to Hershey Barnes. The farewell to arms had come much too late. She was of no mind to accept the stark truth, too often enunciated by Joan, that the shotgun had saved Roy's and her own life.

Dolores had put it best of all. She was able to believe in Dolores's piper, but she could not believe that Roy and she had made their last payment.

It had not mattered that, on the sun deck, Dolores came to tell her it would be wiser to listen to Ilona, who in matters of blood and memory of blood, was more knowing than any of them. Ilona had survived a revolution in Hungary, a revolting life with Bobby, and the revolting experiences of the potato peelers. Ilona was on her way to New York, to happiness, at least a chance for it. And it was Dolores's contention that there was nothing now to prevent her from finding happiness with Roy.

Sally had listened, not smiling, not scorning, and not saying what was on her own mind. Hap.

Hap was not a subject she could discuss with Ilona or Dolores. They believed in their hearts that Hap was a miracle wrought by her. They had known Hap since the days when he was troubling their own sons and daughters. They had observed the change in Hap for the better, his turning from the destructive to the instructive, to the point where Hap was welcomed into their homes, by themselves and by their children.

And there was the second and recent miracle: the shocked, stupored, prep school boy touched by her and returned to communication and communion. Before he had left for Louisiana, Hap warmly embraced and thanked not only Ilona and Dolores, but also Sonia. Hadn't he told Sonia he loved her more than his aunts in Louisiana? Hadn't he told the truth about the shootings? And hadn't he been man enough to shoulder the blame?

To the girls, she had said nothing. But now, in the dark, the matter of blame and of Hap's acceptance of it was a source of terror to which her mind returned.

She saw the blame as a cancer in Hap's blood.

In his nightly long-distance telephone calls to her, Hap had never said anything about the funeral, about Neal, or about what he was doing and thinking in Louisiana. Instead he had directed all of his concern to her: how she was feeling, what the doctors said, when she would be ready to leave, and when he would begin to nurse her back to health. And always his affirmation of his love for her. So little said, so much unsaid but sensed by her.

Yes, tomorrow was to be a day of coming and going. Ilona to New

191

York, to her own apartment and into a marriage that would be deferred until she obtained her California divorce. Roy was driving to Las Vegas. Why? She saw the shotgun, the golf, and the pleasure of Hershey Barnes's company as evasions. She was not concerned that Roy might hit the bottle too hard, laugh too hard, and too easily find the favors of show girls. What did trouble her was that Roy was putting not only time but distance between them.

She had bought the explanations for Roy's decision not to visit her, not to call, and not to write. The word was caution. She might have accepted the word and all other explanations had there been any mention of Hap. The omission had not eluded her. It made no sense to her, not when matched with everyone else's and her own observations of Hap.

She sensed there was more that had been left untold, the telling left to time, to Hap himself.

Yes, tomorrow was a day of seeking and finding. Hap would be arriving at LAX in the morning. In the afternoon he would come to the hospital to take her home, to take her through her period of convalescence. She would play the patient, he the medicine man, a reversal of the roles in the last psychodrama played by both of them.

He would read to her. She would read him, and she would take her pills, sweet or bitter, all of her medicine, all to cure him.

31

The readings began at once, but not in the way Sally had imagined them.

She had overestimated her strength, and for the first week at home she was taking her breakfast in bed and returning to sleep until Hap would wake her for lunch. After that she would change into a sun suit and lounge by the pool. The last days of March and the first days of April were fair and warm. The sun and the applied oil browned her to the point where she appeared in better health than she was in truth.

She and Hap took their dinners together at the dining room table. He set a good table, and they ate well—from a larder stocked by Dolores Cooper from a supermarket, and by Ilona Belanger from her own refrigerator, shelves, and freezer.

Hap was pleasant, relaxed, and yet distant. There was conversation, but no dialogue between them. Each night he had encouraging comments about the progress of her recovery. He asked about the daily calls she received from her own doctor, Dr. Cooper, Mrs. Cooper, Mrs. Lawler, and Mrs. Belanger in New York.

Of her three friends, he was most interested in Ilona. He could not forget her kindnesses to him, her's and Sonia's. He talked about Ilona's children and had only good to say about them. He never mentioned the matters of divorce and remarriage. Bobby's name was as absent from his vocabulary as was Roy's or Neal's.

And yet Sally was aware that, when Hap was not busy with taking care of her and the house, he was not reading any of the novels stocked in the house by Dolores, Joan, and Ilona. Instead he was studying two subjects unrelated to his interrupted school work: Neal's papers and memorabilia, gathered from drawers in the house and from filing cabinets rusting in the garage, and a collection of newspaper clippings pertaining to the shootings.

About these she remained quiet. She merely bided her time and built the strength she knew she would need once Hap decided it was time to probe her for those truths troubling him.

The first morning she was well enough to take her breakfast with Hap, he asked her where she would like for him to read to her. She chose the place, according to the weather. He chose the book, according to what Sally believed was his design, rather than his pleasure.

193

The first novel and the two following it on successive days were works by Americans who were Nobel laureates. Novels of violence. Steinbeck's *Of Mice and Men*, Hemingway's *To Have and Have Not*, and Faulkner's *Light in August*. The last named took Hap two days to read aloud to Sally.

It was late afternoon and they were under the sun, Sally lounging, Hap sitting in a director's chair, when he read the closing paragraph of Faulkner's novel.

Unlike the other times when he had finished a novel, Hap did not slap the book shut, keep his mouth shut, and go outside and spend an hour or so practicing foul and lay-up shots, leaving Sally to hear only what a bouncing basketball might tell her.

Now he faced her. "Which one did you like best?"

The surprise of Hap's voice at this moment took away her own. She feigned consideration before she uttered the answer long known to her. "Steinbeck. The character of Lennie haunts me. I believe I'll remember him longer than any of the other characters in the three novels."

He accepted the reply. He did not debate it.

"Which is your favorite?" asked Sally.

The telephone rang. Hap rose to go into the house.

"Forget it," said Sally.

Hap grimaced bewilderment.

"Whoever it is will call again." She could not tell him how precious the moment and the mood were to her.

But he seemed to understand. He sat and waited for the ringing to die. "The words don't say and mean the same thing for you and me. Make believe the words are hot water, and your brain is a mass of ground coffee beans. Then the book for you is *coffee.* Say my brain is a mass of tea leaves—then for me it's *tea.*"

"Yes, I follow you," said Sally.

Hap went on. "I like the Steinbeck book best because it tells me about violence in California."

Sally shuddered. She understood him too well. "Tell me about the funeral in Louisiana."

"What about it?"

"Everything you care to tell me."

Hap's approach was cautious. "The only thing I liked about it was this girl who was with her father. He and Dad played high school football. I saw a lot of them. She kissed me good-bye when I left."

Pleased to hear this, Sally asked, "Does she make you want to go back there to live?"

Hap shook his head. "I couldn't live there. It's too close to the graves. Anyway, down there they'd expect me to fill Dad's shoes."

"You can, you know," Sally said.

He did not appreciate her confidence in him. "I have my own shoes. My own mind. I don't think like those people. I don't like what they like, and they don't understand what I do about things."

"Things like what?"

"The funeral, for one. Everybody kept saying how great it was, how nice, how lovely. I thought it was cruddy."

Sally was bewildered. "Why, Hap?"

"The preacher gave me a pain with the show he put on," Hap related. "He enjoyed it. He had his audience, and he looked like he had them believing he was talking right to God. No Bible in his hand. He knew all the words. He could see right up there to heaven. But he couldn't see or understand what the hell was going on there on the ground." Hap laughed.

Sally saw it as a boyish, impish laughter rather than an expression of a distraught, maddened mind.

"Like Uncle Carl said afterward, 'That darn preacher could fill a grave with his own bullshit.' "

Sally could neither laugh nor smile.

Hap had more to report and a deepening frown. "And if that wasn't bad enough, they brought in an honor guard from the air base and had them firing blanks into the sky. Like they were shooting down an enemy plane identified as God."

The imagery, the bitterness awed Sally.

There was no stopping Hap now. "Those guys in uniform—they should've loaded their rifles with the real thing and fired right through the coffin. Then all that bullshit about burying a dead soldier might've had some meaning. You know what I mean?"

"No, I don't," confessed Sally.

"A soldier should die from a bullet fired by another soldier," he explained.

Sally questioned that. "One of his own comrades?"

"It happens," he said evenly. "Happened to Stonewall Jackson, and even in World War II it happened with the Army, Navy, and Air Force. Dad told me about one of the gunners on his B-17 bringing down a Mustang. Happened a lot."

Sally observed Hap opening the book and flipping the pages. She hoped that he was going to say something more about it.

Hap went from Europe to Louisiana. "Nobody at the funeral knew what they were burying. The coffin was sealed, and only I knew what was inside. Only I knew some of me was inside there with the—what's the nice word for it?—with the remains. Some of my tears, my drool, my snot, my vomit—"

"Hap! Please!"

He took one look at Sally, went to the pool, dipped a cupped hand,

195

and sprinkled her sick face. Then he sat beside her, soothing her brow with a wet hand and voicing apologies.

"No more about that," he promised. He went on to offer to bring her something to drink, to leave her alone, to take her inside, or whatever she wanted.

Sally decided to endure. She had to read him, more and more. His silence told her of his solicitude for her. His voice and his words were of greater import and urgency.

"Can I say some nice things?" Hap asked with an uneasy smile.

"Please," said Sally.

"The more I think about it, I'd have to say those people down in Louisiana were really nice. They love Dad. Did you catch the present tense?"

She did. She had to wait to catch understanding.

"Dad's still alive to them. They talk like it was only yesterday he was running for all those touchdowns and making All-State. He's their hero, their living legend, and the funny thing is that what Dad did in high school seems more important to them than what he did at LSU or in the war. They were with him, running with him, winning with him. The men and the women. And the women—some of them grandmothers now—they remember Dad, and you can see the girl in their eyes the way they talk about dancing with him, kissing him, and just being around him. Near him. Isn't that something?"

"Yes, it is," Sally agreed.

"I began to understand that better," said Hap, "when I started rummaging through the garage the other day, collecting all of Dad's scrapbooks, pictures, old letters—all kinds of things that made me see what he was. And you know—in some pictures—I'd see myself. Since then I've been looking for Dad in mirrors."

Sally remained closemouthed. She was uncertain whether this was good or bad. She had no doubt that everything he told her had a meaning. A purpose.

Hap studied her, his smile warmer than the sinking sun. "You feeling all right now?"

"Much better, thank you."

"Think you can stand one more recollection from Louisiana? Or have you had enough?"

"One more," said Sally.

"Like I said, they're all nice people, but they just don't think before they open their mouths. And sometimes they talk stupid, and they make you feel the twentieth century has passed right over their heads. Take Uncle Carl—he's sixty now and he's got a mouth full of store teeth, but what he says has bite. He drove me to the airport, and on the way he said this to me: 'You know what, Hap, boy? I should be goin' out west with you. I got me some business out there. I got me a gun that needs emptyin'.' " Hap ended there.

For Sally it all translated to a horror she now desperately tried to shield. "Yes, I understand," she said.

The reply and the composure were met with a clean smile. "You don't agree with Uncle Carl, do you?"

"Not at all, Hap."

He pressed her. "You agree with the law?"

"Yes, I do."

Hap nodded and laughed, ran a hand through his head of hair, and then bothered to explain his laughter. "I was looking at you, and there was something about you that reminded me of this girl in Louisiana. Her name's Bessie Morgan. Anyway, I was remembering the kind of kiss she gave me. Like this."

Sally did not stir as Hap brought his mouth to hers, his tongue dividing her teeth and reaching for her throat. She neither responded nor repelled him. He did not linger beyond the point of demonstration.

"What do you make of that?" he asked, grinning.

Sally was cool. "I like the grin better."

"Doesn't say much for my kissing."

"It said what it had to—about Bessie."

"And about me?" he asked.

"It tells me you've lost your shyness."

"That good or bad?"

"Good," Sally admitted.

Hap's grin widened. "And I wasn't even trying. All right if I try harder?"

Without waiting for a reply, he moved toward her again. She held him off. "Please."

Hap noted the pain in her voice, in her eyes. "My kisses turn you off?"

"Yours or Bessie's?"

"Mine."

"Don't taunt me, Hap."

The grin gone, he said, "Is that what I'm doing?"

Sally let silence speak for her.

It did. "You thinking it's not right for a son to kiss his mother like that?"

"Of course."

He picked up the book and slapped it against his thigh. "I'm not your son. You're not my mother."

"You call me *Mom*," she reminded him.

"That was kid stuff," he said. "No more of that. I'm growing up—and not just in my legs. Let me tell you about guys like me. We get turned on by women like you."

The chill that came over Sally was not caused by a gust of cold wind. "Women like me?"

Hap nodded and sat down. "Yeah, and why not? You're good looking. Sexy. Women your age and a little older—like Mrs. Belanger—you turn guys my age on, much more than girls our own age. And I don't just mean the giggly, goody-goody girls. It goes for the fast girls who pop a pill a day and never worry about getting pregnant."

Sally tried to direct him away from herself. "Have you known such girls?"

"I've been slow about it," he said. "I haven't balled any of them yet. The closest I got to it was last summer—one time when I was swimming over at the Belanger pool." He laughed. "No, not Mrs. Belanger. Karen. We came out of the pool. I slapped Karen's behind with a wet towel. She chased me—into the garage. Well, we fooled around in there, just standing up, kissing, feeling each other, and then, boy, I just popped off —if you know what I mean."

Sally knew. "It happens."

"When you were about sixteen, did you ever make it happen to a guy like me?"

Sally shut her eyes and her mouth.

Hap prompted her. "You trying to remember or to forget?"

"Only your question," she said.

"It's hard to see the truth. Human eyes—even a hawk's eyes—aren't good enough. You have to learn how to see things with imagination. You know what imagination is?"

"Yes," she muttered.

"How about you? Do you look with imagination? Do you think with imagination?"

"I used to daydream," she said, thinking of Carmel Valley.

"When did you stop?"

Sally hesitated. "It happened all of a sudden."

"When the bullet hit you?"

Sally winced and nodded.

"What did you daydream about mostly? Lately."

Silence for a while. Hap did not press her, but Sally pressed herself to find the right way to open her Pandora's box.

"The future," she said.

"How far into it?"

"The happy day you went off to college."

Hap frowned. "What has that got to do with you and your daydreams? They're your daydreams and they must've been about you and what you wanted—what you *imagined* you wanted. Now what was that?"

"Happiness," said Sally. It bothered her to be at a disadvantage with Hap.

"Divorce from Dad?"

"Yes," she said with pain.

Without pain he went on. "Marriage to Mr. Sutter?"

"Yes."

"You never imagined the shooting party, did you?"

"Hap, you called me from Ojai. You said it had been a beautiful day."

"Clear skies for Dad and me," he said without passion. "A clear coast for you and Mr. Sutter. Lucky guy, Mr. Sutter. He had you and me to help him."

"Hap, what are you saying?"

"Your imagination's weak. At least, it was all the time you were in a fury."

Sally was confounded.

There was more from Hap. "I helped Mr. Sutter by seeing with my eyes, and not with my imagination. I saw the MG." He paused. "I know the sound a pistol makes. I know the sound a shotgun makes. I know the sound my voice makes. The pistol . . . the shotgun . . . nothing but echoes of my voice . . . telling Dad about my seeing the MG."

Distraught, Hap stood up. Sally rose with him. Together they returned to the house, to the kitchen. Sally waited for him to say something about dinner, but Hap, when at last he spoke, resumed his speculations.

"Mr. Sutter's got a good imagination. A great one. I remember once—last Christmas, I think it was—when he came over to the practice range at the club, where you and I were hitting some balls. You were listening, weren't you, Sally? You remember hearing him tell me how important it was for me to keep my head steady through the swing. And how much more important it was for me to imagine the kind of shot I wanted to hit. Just to imagine the way the ball comes off the clubhead and rises and takes off for the target. If you look, if you peek, you're dead. If you imagine and make the right swing—that does it. You listening, Sally?"

"Yes," she said, waiting for the next swing at her heart and head.

"The trouble was that Dad had no imagination. No game plan. He couldn't see that there was something going on between you and Mr. Sutter. Dad's lack of imagination killed him."

Sally sat down to keep from falling down. She knew that Hap had more truths to hit at her. She had more reason to believe it as she watched him fix a Scotch on the rocks for her.

After he had served the drink, Hap said, "Yeah, you got to admire Mr. Sutter. His imagination saved him. *And you.*"

Sally drank to Hap's truth, and then drank more to drown a realization of her own. It came not from her imagination, not from her reading of Hap's relaxed face and bright eyes as he scurried to prepare dinner, but from the simple sum of the books he had read to her, the things he had told her today, and the tongue that had found her throat.

The more dangerous game was not ended, the players were now she, Roy, and Hap.

32

By mid-afternoon Sunday the game was resumed. Not Sally versus Hap, but Hap versus Roy Sutter. It happened on South Oaks Road, a hazard born of haphazard.

Sutter's Cadillac was moving northward toward his home when he saw Hap walking against the traffic toward his own home. He was easy to recognize by his long legs and long stride. Braking the car, pulling over to the right, Sutter waited until the boy came alongside.

"Hap!" There was ease in his voice, on his face.

The preoccupied boy turned his head. His expression unchanged, he crossed the road.

Sutter did not wait for him to speak. "Can I drop you off?"

"No, thanks." Hap's ease matched Sutter's.

"How's Sally?"

"Fine."

"She must be," said Sutter, "if you can leave her alone."

Hap said, "She has company—the Coopers and the Lawlers."

"Good. And how are you?"

"Making out."

"Like to talk to you. When's a good time?"

Hap did not balk. "Now, I guess."

"My house or yours?"

Hap did not answer until he was seated beside Sutter on the front seat. "Yours."

Sutter drove on. "Just getting back from Vegas."

"Win any money?"

"I stay out of the casinos," said Sutter.

"Why? You're a gambler."

"I don't like the odds—or the action."

"What kind of action do you like?"

"Golf," said Sutter, to what he believed was the second of the boy's pointed questions.

"Yeah, that's your game."

"Played thirty-six holes every day."

"No shooting?" asked Hap idly, his eyes on the windshield as Sutter took the slow turn into his driveway.

"No, no skeet or trapshooting. No hunting."

"Not ever again?"

"I doubt it." Sutter watched the garage door rise before he eased the car into the garage.

When they got out, Sutter decided against wasting any time by removing his luggage from the car trunk. He went straight to the door. Hap went to the windows, to the grass and plants outside of them.

Turning to Sutter, he said, "Looks like nothing ever happened here."

Sutter could not refute him. He unlocked and opened the door. Hap preceded him inside. As Sutter shut the door, he saw Hap staring at the closed closet door in the entry hall.

"This where you kept the Winchester?"

"Yeah." Sutter opened the closet door. As Hap looked inside, Sutter said more. "I gave it back to Hershey Barnes."

Hap calmly shut the door and turned to Sutter. "How did you get it back from the police?"

"Routine."

"I didn't get the pistol back," said Hap. "Not that I want it."

The boy moved into the living room, looking from the windows to the fresh carpet. Observing him, Sutter decided to voice his oblique question.

"Ever do any target shooting with your dad?"

Turning about and retracing his steps toward the entry hall closet, Hap said, "A few times. I like hitting golf balls better than targets. Is the carpet new?"

"Yeah."

"That much blood?"

"Yeah."

Hap was standing about where Sutter had stood and fired the shotgun when he said, "There could've been more."

"There was enough." There was an edge to Sutter's voice.

Hap faced him. "You were a sitting duck. Sitting there in the light, holding Sally."

"Yeah, I was."

"The target pistol was there on the grass. Blood and stuff all over it. If I had any stuff in me, I guess I would've picked it up and picked you off."

"Lucky me," said Sutter. "How about a Coke?"

"Thanks," said Hap. He followed Sutter to the den.

Sutter was standing behind the bar sipping whiskey and the boy was sitting comfortably on a bar stool playing with his glass. With Sutter.

"Nice room," said Hap. "Nice house."

"Used to be," said Sutter.

"New big window, new carpet."

"Needs new faces." He did not go on to tell the boy that death had visited here once too often.

"I'm a new face," said Hap.

"Sure, you are," Sutter agreed. "You look a damn sight better than you did that night."

"You, too. You looked scared."

"I was."

The boy eyed him intensely. "You still look a little scared."

"You scare me," said Sutter. He poured more whiskey for himself.

"All kids scare grown-ups. That's just the way it is."

"No, it's just you, Hap."

"I always liked you," said Hap. "I still do."

Sutter remained skeptical. "But what?"

"No buts about it."

"I killed your father."

Hap did not blink. "The law says you were *justified*."

Unappeased, Sutter demanded, "What do you say?"

"I said it all," said Hap calmly. "To Sally, to Lieutenant Fonte. It must've carried a lot of weight in the district attorney's office. And with the coroner's jury."

"How can I thank you?" asked Sutter, aware that he was leading with his chin.

"You don't have to," the boy said. "We're even. You saved Sally for me."

Sutter stayed with directness. "I thought I was saving her for myself."

"You did."

Momentarily stunned by the answer, Sutter finally asked, "What are your plans?"

"For who?"

"For yourself."

"I've got nothing to worry about," said Hap. "I'm fixed for life. Loaded. All that insurance money put away for me. Invested. All the blood money—from the plane crash and the crash of your shotgun."

Sutter now felt the pain that had torn through his right arm and shoulder the instant he triggered the fatal shots. "Something about the shotgun bothers you, doesn't it?"

Hap feigned thought. "Probably not as much as it bothers you. From what I know about you, I'd guess you'd rather have faced my father with a matching pistol, like you faced him on the golf course with the same kind of ball and clubs. The shotgun is kind of like a cannon, especially at the close distance you were from the big window."

Frowning now, Sutter said, "I didn't have a pistol—never have owned one. Your father owned two."

Hap drained the Coke in his glass.

"Another?" asked Sutter.

"Thanks, but I'd better get back to Sally. She may be alone by now," Hap said. "Just one more thing: I don't have the matching pistol. I don't know where it is or what my father did with it. I just wanted you to know." He slid off of the bar stool.

Silently, Sutter trailed him to the front door. "Give Sally my love."

"Sure."

"I'd like to see her."

"Sure, soon as she's fit."

"She was fit enough to have company this afternoon," Sutter reminded him.

"You're not company. You're Sally's future," said Hap with reason. "She and I—we've got—we need some time for the two of us. After this is over, we'll be drifting apart. She's got you, and I've got my life to make. Right now, we're doing a lot of reading together, talking things out—like we have to. A lot of healing and understanding we both need. When the two of you get married, I'd like to be there. And I don't want to be there like a guy who wants to open his big mouth when the preacher asks if there's anybody there who knows any reason why these two shouldn't be joined in holy wedlock." He smiled wanly, but it was a smile, and a first one.

Sutter smiled back. He liked what he had heard. "How about a round of golf one morning?"

"I'll wait," Hap said. "I'd like to play at Pebble Beach." The smile faded and gave way to sorrow. "Playing with you at the club'd only remind me of that game you and my father had in the rain. I wish it'd rained harder and sooner that day. I think maybe if the two of you hadn't played that day, Dad'd still be alive. There was blood in the rain."

"Yeah," Sutter agreed.

He watched the astonishing boy open the door and walk away. Once on the driveway, Hap looked back, not toward him, but toward the green grass and the white, freshly painted windows. He shut the door on Hap but could not shut out the doubts from entering his mind.

It was all hard to believe, easy to want to believe. He would wait and see. He would not be a fool and rush into closing deals in Carmel Valley for the house and restaurant. The thing to do now was to bring Vince Fonte up-to-date, to gain his reaction, good or bad.

Then he found himself wondering what Hap was going to report about their encounter to Sally.

Sally was asleep under the sun. She lay face down on the lounge, the brassiere of her two-piece swim suit unhooked, her arms limp until the thud of a body splashing into the pool stiffened them.

204

As her eyes burst open, she saw Hap doing the Australian crawl across the length of the pool. She observed the smooth motions of his driving arms and kicking legs as his tanned body cut the clear water. Reaching the far end of the pool, Hap made his turn and flipped over on his back to do his backstroke. It was then that Sally saw that the boy was wearing no trunks.

She shut her eyes and turned her head away from the pool. For a while she listened uneasily to the fury and nervously fastened the brassiere. She quivered as water struck her back.

Hap laughed. "That feel good?"

"Yes," she lied. "Are you decent now?"

More laughter. "I've got a towel."

Sally opened her eyes and saw Hap standing before her, dripping wet, a towel wrapped about his loins. "Did you take a nice walk?"

"The dip was nicer," Hap said. "Let's go in again—skinny-dipping."

"The doctor said it would be another week before I could go in the pool," she said. It was the truth.

"Okay," he relented. He took the towel from his torso and began to dry himself.

Sally shut her eyes.

"Am I embarrassing you?"

"You're a big boy, Hap."

"Glad to hear you say that," he said sternly. "Now open your eyes. We're going to talk like two grown-ups."

Sally opened her eyes, and she kept them open, despite the fact that Hap was now drying his private parts.

He smiled. "Make believe we're nudists."

She showed her displeasure. "Is that the topic of our talk?"

"No, sex and love."

She turned her head and body away from him. He sat on the lounge and used a free hand to force her face toward him. "Please," she begged.

"No sex," he promised. "Just love."

When she stirred to leave, he restrained her.

"Would you raise up the lounge, please?" she requested. Hap did as she wished. "Now would you draw up a chair and cover yourself?"

Again he acceded, to both demands. When they were both comfortable, at least in posture, Hap eyed her. "Do I remind you of Dad?"

"In what way?"

"Dad's face, Dad's cock."

She frowned rather than wince. "What happened on your walk?"

"I'm asking the questions," he said.

Sally did not abide him. "Are you angry because the Coopers—?"

"No," he interrupted. "That has nothing to do with anything. Just answer *my* questions." He paused. "Whose cock did you like better? Dad's or Mr. Sutter's?"

Sally shied from guilt or shame. The danger, she sensed, lay in the manner of her stand against his assaults. She said, "That has nothing to do with love."

Hap accepted that. "All right, who was a better lover?"

Sally hesitated and chose the truth, the only thing that might save her. "Roy."

"Because he's younger?" he asked without rancor.

"Your father was only two years older when I fell in love with him."

"Then where did the difference come in?"

"Roy gave me a dream. Your father didn't."

"What did Dad give you?"

"Only himself," said Sally.

"Tell me about Mr. Sutter's dream."

She did. She told him about Carmel Valley, about children.

He pouted at her. "Dad gave you me."

"Yes," she said.

"Not that he wanted to, did he?"

"Not at first," said Sally. "But your father did come to admit that I was the best thing that ever happened to you."

"Did you believe him?" asked Hap.

"Of course."

"What do you believe—right now?"

Sally said, "I believe you were—you *are* the best thing that ever happened to me."

"What kind of *thing?*" The rancor was there now.

Sally explained. "The kind of *boy* who made me dream of having more boys like you."

"From Mr. Sutter," he concluded.

"I brought my dream to your father," said Sally. "His answer was the vasectomy. He had his reasons, which I could understand."

"But not accept," said Hap.

"No, I'm too young to give up my dreams," she said.

Hap was not moved. "Dad used to say World War II was the one *good war* America fought. I guess you could say the same thing about the *shootings.*"

"No," she rebuked him. "I'll never say that."

"Why not?" he persisted. "What's to stop you from your dream now?"

"There's blood all over it," Sally said with anguish.

"Aren't babies born with blood all over them?"

She was sick now. "Only the mother's blood."

"Will Dad's spilled blood stop you?"

206

"Good question, Hap."

"Give me a good answer."

"I can't."

"Take a stab at it."

Sally took note of the violence of his language before she said, "Joan Lawler told me that Roy didn't buy that house in Carmel Valley."

"Does that mean he's given up?"

"I won't know till I talk to Roy."

Hap was blithe about it. "I talked to him."

Sally tensed, her back coming away from the lounge. "When?"

He dealt out his words. "I ran into him."

"Tell me about it."

"Nothing to tell," he said.

Sally could not relent. "Nothing at all?"

"Nothing new. He's a nice guy. You know that, I know that."

Sally bewared the boy's aplomb. "It would please me to hear all about it."

"You'll be more pleased to hear it from Mr. Sutter. I won't spoil it for him. Or you."

"Is Roy going to call me or visit me?"

"In good time."

Sally frowned. "In *whose* good time?"

Hap smiled. "Mine."

She shivered with cold. He took his towel, rose, cloaked it about her shoulders, and then dove into the deep end of the pool.

Sally had no eyes to watch him. She tossed the towel to the vacant chair as her mind played with the obscenity of Hap's smile-cloaked, one-word reply.

At one end of the gamut of meanings she found release and relief, arising from a belief that patience was the key to reopen her dream. At the other end, she came upon terror, upon the awareness that Hap had set himself up as her judge, her jury, and her jailer.

She watched Hap now as he stood naked and poised on the diving board, setting his feet and hands, jumping high, coming down upon the board that sprang him into an arc that knifed him into the water.

From where she was sitting she did not see him surface in due time. The water was quiet for too long before horror bolted her from the lounge and took her poolside. She screamed his name.

The water answered. At the deep end of the pool, Hap's head appeared before he came out of the pool and toward her.

Seeing the fright lingering in her eyes, he laughed, "You thought I hit bottom, didn't you? I was just swimming underwater, back and forth. Pretty good, huh?"

Sally retrieved the towel and flung it at him.

More laughter. "Did I scare you?"

"Yes."

"Sorry about that," he said. "I guess I was just showing off." He turned away and started toward the house.

Sally remained, returning to the lounge, not so much for the sun, but for an escape from shadows.

33

The following Friday morning the alarm clock rang an hour earlier than usual in the Lawler bedroom. For them it was a day that held much promise, at least for the sale of their house.

Roark Bennett arrived at the Ventura Boulevard office of Cardwell & Company at 7:44 A.M. The prospective buyers for the Lawler house, a young bank executive from Bakersfield and his wife, were due in one minute.

Before he unlocked the closed door to the office, Roark Bennett picked up the two morning newspapers, the *Los Angeles Times*, and the *Valley News and Green Sheet*. Inside, he turned on the lights and headed for his desk, one of sixteen given to the company's real estate agents.

Seated, he took some cursory glances at the page-one headlines in the *Times* before tackling the eighty-four pages of the *Valley News*. Established in 1911, it was published every Sunday, Tuesday, Thursday, and Friday morning. Ten cents a copy on the newsstands, home delivery by carrier $1.25 monthly.

Still an actor at heart, Roark Bennett searched for his name in print. He found it in the real estate section, in agate type, in his company's two-column ad, following a detailed description of the Lawler house.

With intermittent glances toward the front door, with his anxiety given to the failure of his prospects to appear, he turned the pages of the *Valley News*. White or green, they held small interest for him. It had been a while since the last of the stories relating to the South Oaks shootings had appeared, and that was more of a real estate story—the sale of the Ivy League to make room for an office building.

Other than that, as a man more concerned with Hollywood than with San Fernando Valley, he had been following a series of feature stories entitled "The X-Rated Valley." The reporter, a recent graduate of the University of Missouri School of Journalism, had covered skin flicks, massage parlors, hot-bed motels, the sex press, swinging bars, wife swapping, and such, all larded with quotes from clergymen, educators, psychologists, and lawmen.

This day on page A-13 he found another installment. The subhead blew his mind: "The Potato Peelers."

Unlike the previous stories, this one was a blind item, the people and places nameless.

In the third paragraph he came across an untruth followed by a truth that shook his teeth. At the wrong moment. The door opened and in walked the couple from Bakersfield.

In Century City, some minutes after ten o'clock, the telephone rang in Frank Lawler's law office. Joan, who was in the midst of taking dictation from Frank—a letter to Bobby Belanger's counsel—lifted the receiver.

She recognized Roark Bennett's voice. No hello, no self-identification, merely a pained question: was she alone? When he heard her reply, Roark Bennett immediately gave her what on any other morning but this would have been great news. He had a firm offer, a deposit check in hand. He named the price.

It disappointed Joan. She checked it out with Frank. It was four thousand less than they had hoped for. Joan asked Roark Bennett if they had some time to think about it. He told her to take the offer. Now. When Joan wanted to know why they could not make a counteroffer, Roark Bennett was quick to assure her that this would blow the deal. After all, they were dealing with a banker. He did not tell Joan what else the Lawlers would have to deal with.

In another minute the Lawlers accepted. Their future lay in Century City. Roark Bennett, more than ever, was uncertain about the future. The buyers wanted a thirty-day escrow. That was short enough, yet long enough for South Oaks and the deal to blow sky high again. At least the *Valley News* was not read in Bakersfield. Or by the Lawlers.

Around eleven o'clock in the morning Dolores Cooper was at her writing desk, penning a long letter to Larry, when the telephone rang. It was Perry, calling from the hospital, sounding hostile. Had she read the *Valley News* this morning? The *Times,* yes, the other, no. She had stopped reading it when Larry graduated from high school and was no longer making local news.

Perry shut her up, ordering her to read page A-13. He hung up without saying good-bye. He had not bothered to tell her that the story was all over the hospital, titillating doctors and nurses alike. With one lone exception.

Dolores, meanwhile, rushed from the master bedroom to the guest room—still Perry's room—to separate the *Valley News* from the *Times.* She began to read the story standing up. She was sitting down when the newspaper fell from her hands.

The cleaning woman heard her cries and rushed upstairs to see what was wrong. Dolores dismissed her and returned to the problem at hand: whether to call Sally or Joan.

She was so uncertain, she ended up by making a long-distance call to

210

New York. She spoke to Sonia. Ilona was out for the afternoon. She left a message for Ilona to call her.

Cooler and thinking more clearly now, she was able to recall that the Lawlers did not subscribe to the *Valley News.* The Hendleys did.

She now called Joan and found her alone in the reception office. Frank was in his private office, engaged with a client. Before Dolores could say anything, Joan gave her a report on the sale of her house. And what did Dolores think about the price?

Dolores could not say, she could only read from the newspaper to her, a nervous, faulty reading. And Joan was listening and thinking that everything was turning to shit. The house and the deal, she and her deal with Frank. Now she believed she understood what had been wrong with Roark Bennett this morning. He knew; he had read the story.

But Dolores was still at her. What should they do about Sally? What if Hap read the story?

Coldly Joan considered the questions. She told Dolores not to call or visit her. She herself had stopped by the Hendley house last night and everything was in order. Sally was feeling and looking better than ever. Hap was talking about returning to school in a week or so. All was well, and what had done it was Hap's chance meeting with Roy Sutter.

Dolores understood this, but she wondered if the story might undo it all.

Joan comforted her with odds. What were the chances of Hap reading the paper? If he should read it, the chances would be against his reading the story in question. Perhaps eighty-four to one. And, God forbid, if he did read the story, what were the chances of his understanding it?

Much too good, they both agreed. And, in this context, good was bad.

Roy Sutter spent the afternoon in his office at the Ivy League, discussing financial matters with his accountant. At breakfast he had read the *Los Angeles Times,* the one morning newspaper delivered to his home. The *Valley News,* which carried the restaurant's modest one-column ad in each of its editions, was delivered to the Ivy League.

The story in question had been read by Rick Kelley, Jasper Macom, the chef, and several waiters. To a man, they cared about Sutter, but none wished to be the bearer of bad news.

At about four o'clock in the Hendley house, Sally came to Hap's room to tell him she was going to take a bath and a nap before dinner. The boy, who was putting golf balls into a cup, assured her he would be in his room.

Sally was relaxed even before she settled in the warm tub. Matters were improving. It had been a nice day. All the days since Monday had been good. Not a problem, not an incident with Hap. The critical days between them seemed ended, and the expectations for the future looked good.

She was thinking of Roy and Carmel Valley when she heard and saw the bathroom door being opened by Hap, naked and aroused—in his eyes if not in his penis.

Sally gasped, dropped her wash cloth, reached for her bath towel. She draped it over her shoulders to conceal her breasts.

"Hap, what is it? Please, just give me a minute to—"

"Stay put," he ordered. "It's time for us to rap."

"Here?"

"Sure, in hot water." Hap stepped into the bathtub and eased himself down to where he was facing her, his long legs straddling her torso.

Aware of her danger, physical and sexual, Sally did not stir anything but her own confusion. "What's happened? You've been so—"

"I'll ask the questions," he interrupted sharply. "Save your breath for the answers."

Sally shut up. She believed she could bear his questions.

"What's a *femme fatale?*"

"That's a sinister woman—who brings evil to men. It's French."

"Sure," he said. "That fits. Fits you perfectly."

She was wary now. "Does it?"

Unmindfully he went to his next question. "Are Mrs. Cooper, Mrs. Lawler, Mrs. Belanger, and you *the potato peelers?*"

Sally's sweat was cold. "Where did you hear that?"

Hap told her where and when he had read it. "The story says you were all part of a sexual conspiracy. No names were mentioned," he said. "I figured it out—because it ties in with the shootings."

"Oh, God," Sally moaned. "May I see it?"

"Not now. You sit there and let me see through you."

Sally felt like sliding down into the water and drowning herself. Only her head slipped, and her eyes closed.

"What was the dirty joke about the birthday cake?" Hap now asked.

Raising her head, opening her eyes, Sally saw that she must answer him. And she did.

He listened and was far from amused. "You took the cake from Mrs. Lawler. You took it upstairs to Mr. Sutter."

"Yes," she confessed.

"And Mrs. Lawler went to a motel with a guy she'd picked up in the Ivy League."

"No, it was a vacant house in Encino."

"That's not what the story says."

"It's the truth," she said.

He believed her. "But there were motels—used by all of you."

"Not by me."

"Where'd you go?"

"Only to Roy's house."

212

"Mr. Sutter warned you that you were playing *a more dangerous game.*"

"Didn't the story say I loved him and he loved me?"

"Sure," Hap said. "And all that means to me is that you didn't bother to listen to Mr. Sutter. You didn't take his warning. You just took Dad's life."

"No!" Sally protested.

"Bullshit! You started it! You could've let Mrs. Lawler go up with the cake! You could've let Dad live!"

"Yes," said Sally, weakly, forlornly.

"You should've stuck with the potato peelers. Or wasn't their *rage for sex*—as the story puts it—enough for you? No, you must've had a fury that was worse—the fury a woman has when she's looking for a new lover."

Sally asked, "Did the story say that?"

"No, I read it in a book," he said.

Sally persisted. "Did the story say I took the cake to Roy because I wanted to avoid trouble for the girls and for Roy?"

Hap shook his head. "You sure avoided it."

"I tried," she said.

"So did Dad."

Sally was bewildered. "What does that mean?"

"It means you both failed," said Hap. "You didn't avoid trouble. Dad didn't avoid death. I wish he'd killed you both."

Sally saw that he meant what he had said. Unable to say anything, she sat there wondering what else Hap might say or do. To her. His mouth did not stir again.

With his left foot, the boy freed the towel and found her breasts. His right foot also moved. The toe pressed into her navel before sliding down to her vagina. Fearing that he might be taunting her into a struggle that could end with him drowning her in the tub, Sally remained steadfast.

At last he spoke. "Wash me."

"Must I?"

"You didn't get to wash the blood off Dad," he said. "That's what the womenfolk down in Louisiana would've done for Dad."

Sickened by the thought, Sally felt it would be better to obey the boy, best to occupy herself with a wash cloth. She soaped and washed his legs, ending high on his thighs, sensing the stares he directed to her breasts.

"Turn around," she said.

Without protest, he did. Now she washed his back and his arms. When she was done, he turned to face her again. She tried to wash the wrath from his face, the fire from his arms and chest. And then she tried to hand him the wash cloth and soap.

"You're not through," he said coldly.

Sally froze.

"Come on," he urged her. "You won't find a dildo down there."

Sally shuddered. "What do you know about dildoes?"

"It was in the story," he said plainly. "I figured it was Mrs. Belanger who'd been raped by the dykes."

Sally took Scheherazade's way, trying to hold him off with talk. "You're wrong."

"Am I? Then who was it?"

"Why did you think it was Ilona Belanger?"

"Ronny, Karen, and me were once alone in the Belanger house. Ronny found the key to the window box."

She lied to draw him out. "I don't understand."

Hap obliged her. "It was full of dirty pictures and things. And a dildo. We didn't know what it was called. Ronny called it *a crazy cock.*"

"When did you find out what it was called?"

"In school. One of the guys had one of those sex papers. We sure learned a lot." No blush, no grin. He was still grim. "Who was it?"

"Joan Lawler," said Sally. "It was a horror."

"That's what the story said," Hap told her.

She tried again to hand over the wash cloth and soap. He merely shook his head, put his hands on the sides of the bathtub, and waited for her to go on with the washing.

He had to prod her. "Get on with it."

Sally tried to rise and leave. Hap's left hand caught her by the throat. She gasped for breath.

He loosened his fingers. "Don't. Bathtub accidents are too easy to explain away."

Believing his threat, Sally soaped the wash cloth before she brought it below the surface of the water. When the cloth touched his erection, Sally quickly removed it and went to his lower abdomen.

In a moment Hap said, "All of me. If you don't do it with your hands, I'll push your face down there."

Sally did what she had to do, with her hands. At the climax he had her breasts clutched in his hands.

Without a word, Hap left her in the tub, grabbed another bath towel, and quit the bathroom.

While Sally trembled and wept in her bed, Hap was busy in his own room. A screwdriver in hand, he freed the back panel of his stereo-phonograph console and removed what had been taped inside.

The missing, matching target pistol.

34

For Joan Lawler this Friday was a day passing as painfully as a kidney stone. At six o'clock, from Century City, she reached Roy Sutter at his home.

Puzzled by his pleasure in hearing from her, she took another tack. She failed to mention the story in the *Valley News*, or that the real estate agent who sold her house was the man who had idly coined the "potato peelers" phrase.

Joan did tell Sutter about the sale of her house, her immediate need to begin apartment hunting, and her inability to stop by Sally's or his house that night. He understood. He believed all was well, as it had been all week. Off the telephone, off the hook, Joan still faced the task of telling the truth to Frank.

It took a call from Las Vegas to hit Sutter with the bad news. It came about an hour later, from a bitter Hershey Barnes, unaware that he was the first bearer. It came slowly, with ill-timed black humor.

Barnes announced himself as Sutter's favorite gun caddy. And what would it be for this shot? The Winchester again? Or his own Purdy? Silence and confusion from Sutter. Or was he packing a bag and going off to join Judge Crater?

When Sutter asked Barnes what the hell was bothering him, the latter complained he was shitting green. He blamed it on his reading of a valley newspaper.

Sutter got the pun and asked him to read the newspaper story to him. Barnes refused. He told Sutter to read it for himself; he hadn't the stomach for it. Before he hung up, he told Sutter to call him back from Australia.

It was Rick Kelley at the Ivy League who read the story aloud on the telephone. It felled Sutter.

He went to the bottle before he tried to reach Vince Fonte, who was not on duty, not at home. Mrs. Fonte had a bitter tale of her own, told with tears.

Vince was fit to kill. All on account of garbage. Their West Valley home was threatened. Garbage was being dumped so close that she could see and smell it from her kitchen windows. The neighbors were looking to Fonte for muscle, and he was out using it on the developer of the tract and the politicians who had shut their eyes and nostrils to what was happening. It wasn't fair. It wasn't right.

Sutter heard Mrs. Fonte out and asked her to have Vince call him at home.

It was almost eleven o'clock before Fonte did. *He* was in trouble. He had roughed up the developer, who swore to bring charges against him. If they got him for anything, said Fonte, it would be for manslaughter.

When it came his turn to speak, Sutter had little heart to voice his own problems and fears.

Fonte had read the story at headquarters. He was sick about it. In a way it was his fault, for trusting that little fuck of a D.A. He had had it out with Snyder, who sweated and swore that the kid who wrote the story had double-crossed him. He had been talking off the record. Fonte hadn't checked it out with the reporter yet.

Then Fonte wanted to know if Hap Hendley had read the story. Sutter could not tell him. He did report that it had been a good week at the Hendley house. Things were looking better.

Fonte told Sutter to keep it that way. He admonished him to tend to his business and to keep him posted. And, Jesus, he was damned glad that Sutter had sold the restaurant before the story broke. He wished Sutter could close the doors tomorrow and let the bulldozers go to work.

Sutter reminded him that by the terms of the deal he had to keep the Ivy League running until July 1, at which time the buyer would take possession.

When Fonte failed to understand the reason for this, Sutter explained that the buyer had insisted upon protection. In the event of a delay caused by financial or building difficulties, the buyer had the right to continue the operation of the restaurant under its own management.

Fonte doubted that such a day would come to pass. The way he saw it, from tomorrow on the Ivy League would begin to die. He was back to the garbage before the call was ended.

Saturday and Sunday proved Fonte wrong.

At the Ivy League Saturday was not unlike any other Saturday in April, as the cash register, the cars on the parking lot, and the faces of the patrons proved. The same was true for Sunday.

The weekend in South Oaks was, if anything, quieter than usual. The Coopers were not talking. As for the Lawlers, Frank had moved into the guest bedroom Friday night after Joan gave him the story to read and her confession to hear. For Joan it was a minor triumph. At least Frank had not packed his bags and fled to a motel.

At the Hendley house Sally and Hap were not talking, not taking their meals together, not reading together. They were as quiet as their telephone, save for those times when Hap went out front to bounce his basketball.

Monday was another kind of day. Sunny, warm, smoggy. The mountains to the north were obscured, the mountains to the south were etched in the foul, coppery air.

On this day, for the first time since the South Oaks shootings, Roy Sutter donned his blue blazer and took up his post at the Ivy League. Saturday and Sunday had done little to allay his fears. This, he knew, would be the day of crisis. This day he, not Rick Kelley, had to be at the helm.

By eleven o'clock that morning the storm broke.

The parking lot attendants were the first to sense that something was amiss. The automobiles leaving Ventura Boulevard and turning into the driveway were strange to them, and there was a pattern in the strangeness. The vehicles were older, cheaper, and unwashed.

Sutter, on the inside, noted the early rush of strange faces, pairs and groups of men and women entering the Ivy League for the first time. While the interior was strange to them, his face, because of its exposure in newspapers and on television screens, was familiar.

They stared, gawked, whispered, and regarded him as if he were a figure in a macabre wax museum. But soon he knew that he was not the main attraction. He was aware that they had been drawn here by the prospect of seeing the potato peelers. He saw women who seemed to be volunteers to enlarge the ranks. He saw men who seemed to be willing companions for sex in the afternoon. The regulars were there, in depleted ranks, in dismay. The insurgents, thanks to the story in Friday's *Valley News*, were taking over.

Sutter discouraged friends calling in for reservations. Other friends who came in were sent away with regrets and apologies.

Behind the bar, Rick Kelley was sick of strangers asking for cheaper beers and cheaper brands of whiskey, loading pockets with the restaurant's wide blue match books. He had Jasper instruct his crew of waiters to be on the watch. This crummy crowd was capable of stealing the pictures from the walls, not to mention the silverware.

Kelley's next order of business was to rescue his boss from this ordeal. Donning his own blazer, he went to Sutter and urged him to go home.

Sutter refused. This was part of his punishment, and he would stand up and take it. And there he remained until about four o'clock that afternoon, taking more than enough punishment.

There had never been a busier day at the Ivy League, never a worse one. They stood deep at the bar, drinking and waiting for tables. They stood outside the doors of the restaurant. They stood their ground, despite being told—at first by the instructed parking attendants—that there would be a two-hour wait for tables. They would not be turned away.

Kelley was at the door when Fonte appeared. He spent a few moments getting the lowdown from Kelley before taking more time to survey the disorder in the cocktail lounge and dining room.

For him it was an unhappy "happy hour." Were it not for the familiar decor and the pictures on the walls, he would have guessed that he had wandered into a swinging bar or into a different kind of garbage dump. A good reader of faces and character, he saw that the women were a mixture of housewives from homes north of Ventura Boulevard, divorcées, liberated singles, and some hookers. The men he saw as a group that was unlike the established, well-heeled regulars who could afford the Ivy League's tabs. And the interaction between the sexes he saw as something that might be of interest to a man from the vice squad rather than from robbery-homicide.

When he had had his fill of it, Fonte went upstairs to find Sutter sipping whiskey and talking on the telephone. The detective poured a shot for himself and listened to Sutter tell Frank Lawler to approach the buyer's lawyer. He wanted to shut down the restaurant at midnight. For good.

The call ended, Sutter sucked in his grief before facing Fonte. "I thought you were playing golf today."

"I did," said Fonte. "Got back home and found a message from Kelley."

Sutter frowned. "I didn't ask him to call."

"I know that," said Fonte.

"Vince, did you look around downstairs?"

"Yeah, Roy. There's gold in that garbage."

"Gold!" exclaimed Sutter with scorn. "No, gold is what my old man tried to pan out of the creeks up in Placerville."

Fonte made his point. "They won't let you close down. All they—I mean the buyer's syndicate—all they'll do is rush the escrow through and take this place off your hands. And not to tear it down either."

"I'd burn it down first," said Sutter.

"Take the money and run."

"I got that advice from Hershey."

"Then I second the motion."

"What about Sally?" asked Sutter.

"Leave a forwarding address."

"No, I'm going nowhere—not till Hap goes back to school."

"What's the morning line on that happening soon?"

"Pretty good," Sutter said. He believed it.

Fonte did not. "As of what morning?"

"Last Thursday night."

"Then came Friday."

"Yeah," said Sutter, mouthing a cigarette. "Tell me more."

Vince hesitated. He had a list. "Stay away from here. Don't play with matches."

218

Sutter lit his cigarette and tossed the burning match onto the carpet.

Fonte stepped on it. "Don't fool with guns. Stay away from the Hendley house."

"That about it?"

Fonte emptied his glass. "Thanks for the drink."

Sutter flared up. "I told you that Hap said he didn't have the other pistol."

"Yeah, you did," said Fonte coolly. "I heard you the first time. I'd hate for you to hear the gun go off in your stupid face."

Fonte was at the door before Sutter said, "Okay, Vince. Don't go away mad."

Fonte smiled. "God got us both. He dumped garbage on both of us."

With some effort Sutter matched his smile and waved good-bye. Fonte left him alone with his thoughts.

Staring at the burnt-out match on the carpet, Sutter had some dark thoughts about the Ivy League, the first total commitment he had made. If the restaurant was a part of him—the best part—then he had committed suicide. If the restaurant was not a part of him—but a gift of life from his benefactor, Major Tuttle—then he had committed murder.

From this self-clout, Sutter's mind bounced to two troubling questions: Did Hap read Friday's story? Did Hap have the missing pistol?

35

In the waning sun Sally stalked the garden alone. She was grateful that she had not been troubled again by Hap. Each had given the other a wide berth and a sustained silence.

She tensed when she heard the telephone end its weekend silence. One ring and no more. She imagined that the caller had had a change of mind or a failure of courage.

In another moment she heard the glass door sliding open. Turning her head, she saw Hap approaching her.

He was calm, the hate gone from his eyes, from his voice. "That was Mrs. Lawler."

Sally masked her concern and asked no questions.

Hap spoke again. "She asked me if it was all right to come over. In about an hour or so."

Sally remained wary. "What did you tell her?"

"One word," he said. After a punishing pause, he added, "Sure."

Sally tried not to sigh. "Thank you."

He turned away, took a few steps toward the house, and faced her again. "Like a drink?"

"Yes," she said. "Very much."

Sally followed Hap into the house, into the kitchen. He fixed a Scotch on the rocks for her and took a can of beer for himself. A first for him, at least in her presence. She did not chide him.

Instead she asked, "What shall we have for dinner tonight?"

"I don't know," he said without interest.

"Do you feel like going out and getting us the Monday night special at A Piece of Pizza?"

Hap shook his head.

"I believe we still have some of Sonia's Hungarian goulash in the freezer."

"Later," he said. "I'm not hungry enough yet. Why don't you take your bath before Mrs. Lawler gets here."

Sally checked her alarm. "I'll change into something warmer." She rose and went to the freezer. Finding the right plastic container, she left it on the stove. Then, taking her drink with her, she went to her bedroom and left Hap sipping beer from the can and reading the *Times*'s sports section at the kitchen table.

She thought about locking the bedroom door but dared not, afraid that Hap might hear the snapping of the lock. She went to her bureau, set down her drink, found fresh underwear and socks, and went to the bathroom. She was there for not more than five minutes.

She returned to the bedroom, fastening her brassiere as she crossed to the bureau. The drink was gone. Without turning around, she could sense Hap's presence. Trying not to panic, she set herself before facing Hap. Naked on the covered bed, he held the beer can with one hand, his swelling penis with the other. Her drink was now on the night table on her side of the bed.

"No, Hap," she pleaded.

"It's time to rap again," he said.

"Yes, but not here. Not like this. Joan'll be here soon," said Sally.

Hap grinned. "She can join us. I think she'd like that. I think she can teach us something."

Sally's mind raced to avenues of escape, of struggle. What she feared most of all was being roughed up and bruised by Hap. She had to hide everything from Joan, to keep her from telling Roy about what Hap was doing to her, to keep Roy from killing Hap or Hap from killing Roy.

Standing her ground, she said, "Keep playing with yourself, Hap."

He laughed. "Help me along. Do a striptease. A belly dance. Lick your lips. Anything."

Sally did something. She turned her back on him and his games of pleasure. Opening a drawer, she picked out a sweater and was in the process of slipping it on when she felt his too close presence. As she tried to bring the sweater down over her head, he forced it upward and peeled it from her arms.

Her rage evident, she turned on him. "Please, Hap."

It was not mercy but scorn that he showed her. "It won't help you to cry or scream."

"Don't do it!" Sally pleaded.

"Here or on the bed?"

She slapped away the hand sliding under her panties.

"Here or the bathtub?"

"Nowhere, no time."

Hap kept at her. "The shower?"

"No!"

"The pool?"

"No!"

Swiftly Hap's arms went to her shoulders, one of his legs buckling her knees and causing her to fall to the carpeted floor with him.

Her body pinned beneath his, her mouth free, she tried to talk her way out. "Please, Hap! Don't dirty us!"

Hap voiced anger. "We did that when we dug Dad's grave!"

221

Sally did not quit. "We did no such thing."

"Then who did?" Hap demanded. "Mr. Sutter?"

"No!"

"The potato peelers?"

"No," she said with anguish. "Hap, you have a long life ahead—"

"How the hell do you know?" he interrupted. "That's a laugh when you grown-ups say we kids *think* we know it all. Grown-ups only remember the way things used to be—not the way they're going to be. Nobody knows about that."

"I know my obligation to you," Sally retorted.

"What does that mean?"

"I'm the only mother you've got."

"The hell you are. With Dad dead, I doubt if you're my stepmother. You're nothing to me now." He pressed a fist into the flesh below her rib cage.

Sally gasped. "You're hurting me."

Hap brought away his fist and turned it into a sensuous, exploring hand. "Get into one of your tennis outfits. Like a good potato peeler."

He raised Sally to her feet. She thought it wise to give him the impression that, under duress, she was submitting to him. At the closet, she took her time choosing a tennis dress, thinking the unthinkable: she could change in the bathroom, lock the door, and slash her wrists with a razor blade.

Her tennis dress in hand, she tried to cross to the bathroom. He intercepted her. "Don't forget your socks, tennis shoes, and that blue headband you wear sometimes."

Sally gathered those things before she found Hap blocking her path to the bathroom. "You've been to the john. Change here."

She turned her back on him, slipped out of her panties and into the complete tennis costume. His eyes never left her.

"The bed," he said.

Sally took the long way there, finding and emptying her drink. "I'd like another, please."

"Later," he said.

She went to the bed as if she were mounting a scaffold. Hap came down beside her, lightly kissing her cheeks, her eyes, her nose, and her chin before bringing ardor to her lips and mouth.

Sally tried to play dead. She thought of the dead, of Neal lying dead, decomposing, and faceless in the blackness of his coffin, in the darkness of his grave. The coffin and the grave separated her from the life of Hap's wet lips and wet tongue.

Hap reacted with rages of motion. One hand unzipped the tennis dress, the other reached between her legs. A finger hooked the crotch of the matching panties and strained at it.

222

No longer playing dead, no longer passive, Sally stirred, not in passion, but in an effort to keep the boy's own passion within the first line of her defense. Her right hand found and clutched Hap's penis. He struggled with her, using a knee to separate her knees, and a hand to free his penis and bring it to her vagina.

He gasped the instant he realized he had lost. His free hand was clutching her pubic hair as she masturbated him.

Hap fell away. In another moment he reached for his beer can. She turned from him and wept.

Soon she heard his bitter voice. "Don't fight me. Don't make me hurt you."

Sally tried to reach his unreachable reason. "You can't hurt me. Nothing you do to me can hurt me. Just think of how much you're hurting yourself. Your conscience, your future."

"I feel good," Hap said. "My conscience is buried in Louisiana. My future's now."

"Hap, I'll be all right," said Sally. "And you'll be all right—if you go back to school and put your mind on your plans—"

"What plans?"

"For your life—the long—"

"This is the life. And I never planned it. That's what's so neat about it. I'm making the best out of the worst. You and Dad, you and Mr. Sutter. Where did all your stupid plans get you? Carpenters have plans how to make a coffin. Gunsmiths have plans how to make pistols and shotguns. Gravediggers have plans how to dig graves. Nobody has a plan for happiness. Just for hungers. Desires. I'm taking what I can, when I can. That's me. I grew up the minute I started looking for Dad's face in the bloody mess where his face used to be."

Having held her eyes and ears and heart open to him, Sally said, "What can I do? Tell me what I must do."

Hap said, "You're doing fine. For a start."

"Is the end in sight?"

"I see nothing but you," he said. "And that's all I wanna see."

"If you love me—"

"I just tried to love you!"

"That's not love," said Sally.

"Sex?"

"Maybe that, maybe hate."

"Let's leave it at sex, okay? I'm a horny kid. You're a double-barreled sex object. A potato peeler and a *femme fatale*. Good enough?"

"No," said Sally, her eyes dead. "If you make me believe that's all I am, the last thing you'll do to me is bury me."

Hap laughed. "Made your funeral plans yet? Picked out a coffin? A dress to be buried in? A grave? You see, there you stupid grown-ups go again with your stupid plans."

"I'm serious, Hap."

"So what? You were serious about Dad. You were serious about Mr. Sutter. Get smart. Don't get serious with me—or about me. Or about what we're doing."

"What you're making me do for you." Sally reminded him.

"Not having any fun?"

Her demeanor answered for Sally.

Hap grinned. "How about if I flatter you? Can I tell you I'd rather have you in bed than Mrs. Belanger. And have I got it bad for her. All she's gotta do is smile at me. And when she touches me, I've gotta fight myself to keep from popping off."

Sally let him talk and let him see that she was listening.

"Mrs. Cooper looks pretty good to me at times," Hap went on. "But there's something about her that turns me off. Something not real, something cold. Like she was all mechanical. I'd bet it'd be like balling one of those dummies you see in department store windows. Am I right?"

"No," said Sally.

"How did she do as a potato peeler?"

"Badly."

"Have I got her wrong?"

"Yes," said Sally.

"How did Mrs. Belanger and Mrs. Lawler do?"

"They stopped doing," said Sally.

"Mrs. Lawler's skinny," he said. "She looks at you like she's wondering what you've got hanging between your legs. Just wish she had a little more ass." He laughed. "Sometimes, from far, she looks like the oldest girl in school. That's not so bad, if you think of it like that."

Sally was not thinking, not saying anything. She awaited Hap's next move.

"But—getting back to you," he said, and he said no more.

He turned toward her, brought a hand to her knees. From there it moved upward, stroking her thighs.

Sally did not waste her breath with protests. She lay there on her back, an immobile, mechanical woman whose mechanism was dead. She shut her eyes and mind to Hap's presence, to the touch of life in his hand. Hap tore her panties away before one of his fingers found her clitoris.

Sally was bidding her heart to stop beating, her blood to run dry, and her mind to go blank when Hap withdrew his finger. He mounted her and drove himself and her to climaxes, willed and unwilled, willed and willed. For Sally, her ecstasy was the harbinger of a dread truth.

She was, indeed, a potato peeler.

224

36

The sun had set before Joan Lawler reached the Hendley house and the Datsun's headlights picked up Hap in the driveway practicing his basketball in the dark.

She touched the brake pedal, cut the engine and the lights. The basketball in one hand, Hap used the other to open the car door for her.

"Hi!"

The warm greeting pleased Joan. "Hello, Hap. Did you forget to pay the light bill?"

He appreciated the humor. "It was still light when I got out here."

Joan left the car. "Can you see in the dark?"

He laughed again. "I'm a bat."

"I'll bet," she said. "Where's Sally?"

"Should be in her room. Go on in."

"All right if I turn the lights on?"

"Sure." He tossed the basketball toward the backboard. It fell into the hoop, through the net.

"Good shot," she said, crossing to the door of the dark house.

The door was shut but unlocked. She opened it, stepped inside, and touched the light switches. Lamps came on in the living room, followed by the exterior lights at the front door and at the garage. She heard the sounds of the basketball as she closed the door.

Joan moved through the house until she came to the master bedroom. The door was shut. She rapped lightly. No response, still none when she called Sally's name.

Quietly she opened the door to darkness and silence. When she touched another wall switch, the lamps on the night tables revealed Sally lying asleep on the bed. Uncovered, naked.

On one night table she noted two beer cans, on the other a watery glass and a bottle of Scotch. On the bed with Sally were her tennis dress, matching panties, and brassiere.

When Joan reached down and touched Sally's shoulder, the latter awoke with a start and a gasp of terror.

"It's me," said Joan, reassuring Sally but not herself. She smelled and sensed the worst.

Sally glanced at Joan and shut her eyes. With a weak, hollow voice she asked, "Where's Hap?"

Joan told her before going to the closet and returning with a robe. She cloaked Sally.

"Are you all right?"

Sally opened her eyes. "Yes, perfectly all right."

Joan persisted. "Nothing wrong?"

"Nothing."

"Did you play tennis at the club?"

"No, Joan."

"Been resting and reading?" Joan asked.

"Yes."

"And drinking, I see."

Most uneasy, Sally said, "Hap and I were chatting."

"About books or newspapers?"

"School."

"Everything still all right?"

"Yes," said Sally.

Joan did not hear the ring of truth, but she decided not to press the matter about the story in the *Valley News*. She felt she could be wrong and had no wish to do wrong now.

"Anybody call?" Joan asked.

Sally shook her head. "It's been quiet here."

"The truth?"

"Why do you ask, Joan?"

"Just asking," said Joan. "You seem upset."

"I'm all right," said Sally. "Hap's all right."

Joan changed the subject and told her about the sale of her house. Sally was pleased.

"Is there anything you want me to tell Roy?"

"How is he?"

"Fine."

"Tell Roy I love him—miss him—and hope to see him soon."

"How soon?" asked Joan.

"Tell Roy I'll call him. Very soon."

"Anything else you'd care to tell Roy? Or me?"

Sally hesitated. "No."

Joan broadened her hint. "If you feel like talking—telling me anything—call me, please."

"Yes, Joan."

"Take care." Joan retreated to the door. She watched Sally shut her eyes and nod before she left.

Once beyond the bedroom Joan wondered if she had done right to keep Sally in the dark, if, indeed, she were in the dark.

Outside she found Hap in the dark, the exterior lights at the door and the garage extinguished, the basketball playing still going on.

226

Joan drew a long, deep breath before she went straight to her car. She tossed a casual good-bye at Hap.

He put the basketball down and came toward the car, entering it from the other side, much to Joan's dismay. She did not bother with the engine or the lights.

"Nice car," said Hap.

"Can I drop you off somewhere?"

"No, thanks. How does Sally look to you?"

"A little tired."

His left hand swung over and came down lightly on her right knee. Joan turned on the lights and started the engine.

"Shut it off," Hap suggested.

"Sorry, I'm in a hurry—" She shut up when she felt and saw Hap's hand sliding under her dress. "Don't, Hap."

"Why not, Mrs. L?"

Her stomach knotted, Joan could not speak.

He went on with his hand and his more punishing mouth. "Mrs. L for lawyer. That's you. Mrs. B for businessman or builder. That's Mrs. Belanger. Mrs. D for doctor. That's Mrs. Cooper. And Mrs. P for pilot. That's Sally. Do I get a hundred?"

Joan got her Irish up. "You'll get your face slapped if you don't take your hand away."

His hand climbed higher. Instantly she brought her left hand into play. It fell not upon his face but into his intercepting, right hand. He forced it down to his unzipped fly.

When she struggled, he lashed out with his mouth, "What are you? A face slapper or a potato peeler?"

Joan freed her hand and thigh. "Does Sally know?"

"She knows. I told her Friday afternoon."

"Oh, God! And what have you done to her?"

"What I've been trying to do to you," he said plainly. He now opened the car door and got out.

The instant the door was slammed shut, Joan backed the Datsun out of the driveway. The headlights caught Hap in the act of zipping up his fly.

Shaking, weeping, Joan drove fast, too fast. She caught herself when she was about to turn the car into Roy Sutter's driveway. Now she drove on to the Cooper house.

She found Dolores alone and distraught. Perry was out for the evening, dinner and movies. Alone. So he said.

Joan asked for and got her requested boilermaker. Dolores did not drink with her. She was on Valium and on her second pack of cigarettes of the day as she sat in the downstairs study, coughing and choking on Joan's anguished report.

227

Joan gave Dolores a respite of silence before she confronted her with the problem at hand. "The question is: do I or don't I tell Roy?"

Dolores stood up and paced the floor, wringing her hands, thinking hard.

"Tell Roy nothing," she said at last.

"He's expecting me. Dare I go to his house?"

"No."

"Should I call him?"

"No."

Joan questioned the wisdom of this decision. "Won't Roy suspect something's wrong?"

"He would," said Dolores. "The minute he hears your voice. Have Frank call him and say that everything's all right with Sally."

"I don't know where Frank is tonight. He doesn't get home till late. And what if Roy calls me?"

"Take the phone off the hook."

"He could drive over."

"Stay here," Dolores said.

Joan considered the idea.

"Have you had your dinner?" asked Dolores.

Joan frowned. "And what do we do about Sally? Forget her? Leave her to Hap?"

Dolores lit another cigarette. "Shall we try to get her over here on some pretext?"

"Keep talking," Joan spurred her.

"You and I could go over there. We could say we're taking her to a movie."

Joan shook her head. "You won't get Sally out."

"Would Hap stop us?"

"I believe so," said Joan.

"Could we steal her out of the house?" Dolores asked.

Joan was interested. "How?"

It took Dolores a few minutes to come up with a plan. "We go in two cars. I park down the road. You in the driveway. When we get there, you give me some time to steal around the house. Then you ring the doorbell and occupy Hap while I tap on the glass door to Sally's bedroom. I get her out and take her straight to the airport and put her on a plane for New York. Ilona will take care of her. I can call Ilona. I can pack a bag for Sally. If she's naked or in her nightgown, she can change in the car." She paused. "What do you think?"

"It's wild," said Joan pensively. "Somebody could get hurt. We can't underestimate Hap. He could do anything—after what he's already done to Sally."

Dolores now asked. "Is it a matter for the police?"

228

"That's up to Sally," said Joan.

"How much can she take?" Dolores wondered. "Or will she take before thinking of—Listen, Joan, is it likely that Sally might consider taking her life to save herself from—don't laugh—a fate worse than death?"

Far from laughter, Joan said, "You and I might. But Sally has Roy—something to live for."

Dolores understood. "Listen, I'll fix dinner, you call Ilona. She should be in on this."

Joan agreed. As Dolores went to the kitchen, Joan went to the bar to make another boilermaker.

The telephone rang. Once, twice.

Then Dolores's voice was heard shouting. "Joan, catch that, please! I'm in the bathroom!"

Joan rushed to the nearest telephone. "Hello." There was tension in her voice. "Hello!" It troubled her how much frenzy was now in her voice. She sensed that someone at the other end of the line was listening to her. She sensed it was Hap.

The last and only sound she heard was a disconcerting, disconnecting click.

Ten minutes later the Coopers' doorbell rang.

Still on the telephone with Ilona, Joan did not hear it. Dolores did. She went to the door and admitted a grim Roy Sutter.

"Perry's not home," said Dolores.

"I know," said Sutter. "He called me earlier. Invited me out for dinner. I want to talk to you and Joan."

Wincing, Dolores turned away from Sutter. "Joan! Roy's here!"

Joan heard and broke off her call to Ilona. Gathering her composure she joined Dolores and Sutter in the breakfast room. She was smiling when she greeted Sutter. She apologized for being unable to get to his house.

Not smiling, Dolores asked, "How did you know Joan was here?"

Joan succeeded in laughing. "My car's in the driveway."

Sutter was still grim. "You answered the phone, Joan."

Joan was appalled. "And you hung up on me."

"Yeah," he said. "What's going on? Did you see Sally?"

"Yes," said Joan. "Everything's fine."

Dolores intervened. She asked Sutter to dine with them. He wanted no dinner, no drink, but he sat down.

His eyes on Joan, Sutter smoked a cigarette and listened to the half-truths she told about her visit to the Hendley house. Her hunger killed by tension, Dolores listened to Joan's valiant performance and watched Roy's guarded reactions.

The moment Joan concluded her account, Dolores tried to divert

Sutter's attention. "I can't understand the *Valley News*. It's such a fine suburban newspaper."

"It is," said Sutter. "Don't blame the paper for your troubles. The story was a good one, well written. It fitted in with the series. And you have to credit the paper for not putting it on page one. Blame a deputy district attorney named Otto Snyder."

Joan said, "We blame nobody but ourselves."

Sutter turned to her. It was something other than blame that concerned him now. "I wish you'd be as truthful as the newspaper story."

Dolores and Joan paled. The latter said, "I always try to be."

"You might've fooled me on the phone," said Sutter. "You can't now."

Joan was stern. "I won't try."

Sutter asked, "When did you read the story?"

"Friday," said Joan.

"When did Sally read it?" asked Sutter.

Joan chose to lie again. "I don't believe she has."

"Has Hap?"

"I don't believe so."

Not at all satisfied, Sutter turned to Dolores. "Do you believe Joan?"

"Yes," said Dolores.

Sutter drew on his cigarette and exhaled smoke through his nostrils. He opened his mouth to say, "I wish I could believe you two. But I can't."

Joan said, "I'd swear it on the holy book."

Unmindfully Sutter said, "Let me give you something to think about. Neal Hendley owned a pair of matching pistols. The police have the one he used on Sally and me. And there's a good chance that Hap has the other one."

Dolores groaned. "No!" Joan shuddered.

"Hap could've read the story," said Sutter. Meaning to frighten them, he added, "He could kill Sally."

Dolores put down her knife and fork, took up her plate of food, and left the table for the kitchen sink. Joan drank the last of her boiler-maker.

She said to Sutter, "Hap could kill you, too."

"Sure, he could," he said. "I could understand that. But I'd go to my grave without understanding why you helped him put me there."

Dolores returned to the table with her cigarettes and lighter. She observed Joan's troubled demeanor.

The uneasy silence ended with Joan breaking down and telling the whole truth, beginning with her telephone call to the Hendley house and ending with her leave-taking of Hap.

Dolores, who had heard it all, did not listen as much as she looked for

230

a break in Sutter's poker face. If Sutter was short on emotion, revulsion, and outrage, he was long on concentration, deduction, and understanding.

Now Dolores spoke up. She told Sutter about the schemes Joan and she had devised to rescue Sally. When she was done, she failed to hear a comment from Sutter.

Joan said, "I have another idea. Let me call up Hap. Tonight. Let me offer to take him up to Mulholland Drive. I'll *occupy* him while Dolores takes Sally to the airport. Ilona will pick her up at Kennedy in New York."

"Yes," Dolores agreed.

Sutter shook his head. "That's no good. If Sally runs from Hap, he'll never stop hounding her. Sally's safe as long as she stays put."

Dolores protested. "How safe? With the boy molesting her!"

"That won't kill her," said Sutter coldly. "Running might."

Joan scowled at him. "Won't you die a little?"

"Better me," Sutter said.

Dolores said, "Roy, what are you thinking?"

He took another cigarette. "All this has nothing to do with the potato peelers."

Joan rebutted him. "Everything was all right until the story about us broke. It's what set Hap off. Don't you see that?"

"Yeah," said Sutter. "That and more. Listen to me. On the phone Hap's nice to you, Joan. He's nice to you when you get there. He wants you there to see Sally the way you did. To make sure you get it all, he got you in the car and put you on. He knew Sally told you nothing to tell me. He knew you'd tell me what he wanted you to tell."

"Which I did," said Joan dolefully.

"I'm glad," Sutter said. "I get the message."

Dolores asked, "What is the message?"

"Hap's setting me up," said Sutter quietly. "The way he believes I set up his father."

The reply terrified Dolores and Joan.

Joan spoke up. "And what are you going to do?"

Dolores answered for him. "He's going to leave it to the police."

Sutter shook his head. "No, that's no good. That's not the answer."

"What is?" Joan demanded.

"I haven't come up with it yet."

Dolores said, "Roy, I believe that now you're lying to us."

Sutter shook his head and rose.

"Talk to Lieutenant Fonte," said Joan.

"Maybe."

"Where are you going now?" asked Dolores.

"For a drive."

Joan said, "Make it a long one. All the way to Carmel Valley."

Sutter held a sad smile now. "I'd never get there. Not without Sally."

Joan again. "Damn it, take her!"

"Tonight," added Dolores.

"Over Hap's dead body?"

The question killed Joan's and Dolores's bill of action. It stilled them. They stood up on weak legs and followed Sutter to the door.

Joan asked, "Is there anything you want us to do?"

"Yeah," Sutter said. "Don't call or see Sally—not for a while. I don't want Hap knowing you told me anything."

"I'd never tell him," retorted Joan.

Sutter said, "You wouldn't have to. Hap'd know. He's bright."

Dolores questioned the compliment. "You talk as if you still like him."

"That's the awful thing of it," said Sutter, opening the door and leaving.

37

At the fork of South Oaks Road and Montana Lane, Roy Sutter abandoned his resolve and his course. Instead of driving north and leaving San Fernando Valley by way of Interstate 5, he turned his Cadillac toward the Hendley house.

The car was down to a crawl, his heart racing, as he made the pass. The house belonged to darkness, no exterior or interior lights to burn away its mystery.

The dashboard clock shone like a warning beacon, telling him it was too early for interior darkness and sleep, too strange for the exterior lights at the front door and at the garage not to be guarding the house and its two occupants. If it was not strange, it was purposeful, done by design.

The car picked up speed until it came to the dead end of the lane. Sutter turned it about and soon made a second slow pass at the Hendley house. This time he saw through the darkness and the walls. He was seeing Hap in bed with Sally, seeing a red unlike the red lights flashing on the rear of his car when he hit the brakes.

He lit another cigarette to do something other than killing the engine and rushing inside the house to kill or be killed. In the end he did right. He hit the gas pedal to put distance between him and the house, to put time to work. The challenge was there in the card of darkness. But he needed to find his reason and his advantage.

As it stood now the advantage lay with Hap, as it had lain with him the night Neal challenged him. The boy had the fortress of the house; the boy unquestionably had the weapon. He had only his wits. He had no wish for a shotgun or for a matching pistol. He neither wanted to kill nor be killed. He had to accept his disadvantage, put down Hap's challenge, and free Sally.

The Cadillac sped northward on South Oaks Road. Sutter did not slow down as he passed his own house. It was not the place to stop. Now it was a trap that could envelop him in dreams and nightmares: the failed dream of Christie, the endangered dream of Sally, and the nightmare of Neal and the shootings.

He needed the freedom of roads, the perspective of motion and distance. Or so he believed until he came to Ventura Boulevard to be hypnotized by the red traffic signals. When the lights turned green, he

233

could not cross the boulevard. Instead he allowed an automobile to pass him on the right before he turned right and headed for the Ivy League.

Tonight it would serve as his command post—in his office, at his telephone, where he could be reached and where he could reach people. The idea of taking to the freeway and to the mountains was gone. That was limbo. Tonight that could be hell.

He passed the entrance to the Ivy League, made a right turn at the corner and another right turn into the crowded parking lot. Instinctively he headed for his private parking space close to the restaurant's rear entrance.

The headlights picked up a station wagon parked in his spot, so marked in white letters on the asphalt and by a luminous placard posted on the wall. Engine idling, he just sat there, as undetermined about this minor crisis as he was about his major one.

Suddenly a man's face and then a woman's face appeared in the glare. Their embrace interrupted, they voiced rage and obscenities before Sutter backed away. He found a parking place at the far end of the lot. Emerging as angry as the couple in the station wagon, he cooled off before he reached them. This was no time to seek out trouble.

Sutter avoided the station wagon as he entered the restaurant. He had meant to go straight upstairs to his office, but there was something in the air that drew him to the cocktail lounge, the bar, and the dining room. The place was jumping with dissonant voices, shouts and laughter from strange faces. The dim light was smogged by tobacco. The waiters and bartenders were harried by demands for beer and whiskey. There was no traffic to or from the kitchen.

There was disorder. Rick Kelley was nowhere to be seen. Jasper Macom was the host at the front door. Sutter went to him. The black man sang the blues. He was sick. He was reminded of the night in Montgomery, Alabama, when President Truman announced Japan's surrender, the night the town went crazy. Asked about Kelley, he fumbled his intelligence: upstairs.

On his way to the staircase Sutter was accosted by a glassy-eyed woman. Carefully he gave her the brush, telling her he would be right back.

The door to his office was closed. He made no attempt to see if it was locked. He rapped on the door. Casually.

It was unlocked and opened from the inside by Kelley, drunk, flushed, coatless, unabashed by Sutter's presence.

"Just in time," said Kelley, grinning.

"For what?" Sutter was cool.

"A real cute kid with a snatch full of cake. She's in the john." Kelley turned away, retrieved his blazer, and tried to leave. He could not make it past Sutter's unquestioning eyes.

"You all right, Roy?"

Sutter nodded.

"I'm not. I'm fucking mad," said Kelley. "It's been twelve years since—" He broke off. "What the fuck does anything matter now?"

Kelley left, shutting the door behind him. Sutter idly lit a cigarette and studied the cake plate on the desk top, next to the bottle of Polish vodka and two glasses. He went to the window, opened the shutters and raised the bottom window to clear the perfumed sweat from the air.

He was sitting at his desk, facing the door to his private bathroom. When it opened, he saw a willowy brunette. Still in her twenties, she was braless and wore a see-through blouse, a dark miniskirt, and calf-high, thonged sandals on her stockingless feet. She was as drunk as she was pretty, and she blinked her painted eyes when she saw Sutter.

"What's *your* name, honey?" she asked in a slurred voice.

He had no desire to banter or fool with her. He gave her his real name.

It did not register. "Pour me a drink, Roy."

He accommodated her. As he gave her the drink, he asked, "How long've you been here?"

"In here?"

"In the restaurant," said Sutter.

She sat down on the couch, gulped her drink, and reached under her skirt to scratch. She giggled. "Those cake crumbs itch. Oh, I been here since about six-thirty."

"Who with?" asked Sutter.

"My sister-in-law. My brother works nights. We couldn't make it this afternoon with the others."

"What others?"

"The other women in the neighborhood."

"What neighborhood?"

"Canoga Park," she said. "The other married women—did they dig this joint! Wow! They weren't lying! The paper didn't lie!" She eyed him. "What do you do, Roy? You helping out Rick?"

"Yeah," said Sutter. He rose. "Nice talking to you."

She gave him a wry glance. "You chasing me?"

"Yeah."

She sighed. "My fault. I forgot to tell you I like you. Come over here, Roy, and we'll like each other."

Sutter moved to the door. He entertained no thought of locking it before he held it open for the girl.

She did not rise. She brought her feet up to the edge of the couch, separated her knees, and pressed her blouse against her breasts. "I think you need glasses. Bring two of them and the bottle over here."

"The action's downstairs," he said calmly.

She pouted, sighed, and rose to leave. When she came to Sutter at the door, she distracted him with a wan smile while one of her hands grabbed his crotch. "All that meat and no potatoes?"

He did not bend. "The potatoes are downstairs."

Again the pout. "More potato peelers than potatoes." With a wave of her hand, she went out the door and down the stairs.

Sutter locked the door, returned to the desk, and found a clean glass. He sat there sipping whiskey and not savoring his thoughts about Kelley and the girl in the see-through blouse.

At the end of the Ivy League's charmed life, Kelley had used the girl to help him reenact the beginning of the end. Not out of spite, but out of despair. Not in line with the truth, but according to the fable of the potato peelers in the *Valley News*.

Like him, Kelley was bleeding. Like him, Kelley mourned the passing of the Ivy League. Kelley had been his constant lieutenant in the long struggle to build and maintain the restaurant's reputation. It had been a total commitment for him, too.

Sutter had more whiskey. One drink for Kelley and no more. Now he tried to return his concentration to Sally and Hap, to the crisis at hand. The thought of garbage stayed him, and his mind went to Vince Fonte.

He took note of the hour. It was 8:47 P.M. Drawing the telephone to him, he tried to reach Fonte to bring him up-to-date, to let him judge the actions he had in mind.

Fonte was not at police headquarters, not on duty. He was not at home. Mrs. Fonte was. She informed him that her husband had left a few minutes ago to attend another meeting about the problem of the garbage dump. She was frank to admit that Vince was in a Sicilian rage.

Before he let Mrs. Fonte end the call, Sutter asked her to have Fonte phone him tonight, no matter how late the hour.

Once more he went to the bottle, once again to the telephone. He could not wait for Fonte, he could not abide his own inaction. The action of dialing seemed to be very much in order. It was direct. It was the shortest, straightest, and safest move he could make. So he believed.

In the darkened Hendley house, the three telephones rang.

The second ring woke Sally. She opened her heavy eyes, faced the telephone, and made no move toward it. Instead she turned her head to see if she was alone in bed. At that moment the bedroom door burst open. Twisting her head, she saw Hap, clad in pajamas, pull the telephone jack from its socket.

While the other telephones continued to ring intermittently, Hap sat down upon the bed.

"Did it wake you up?" he asked solicitously.

"Yes," said Sally. "Why don't you answer it?"

"Tomorrow's another day."

236

So saying, he got into bed with her.

"Please," Sally implored.

"Enough for tonight?"

"I'll die," she whimpered.

"Don't." He left the bed.

Sally put a hand over her mouth to muffle her sigh. She watched Hap move away, not toward the bedroom door, but toward her bathroom. Soon the light from there spilled into the bedroom. She heard the medicine cabinet being opened, water running in the sink. The sounds and the light faded.

In darkness Hap moved slowly toward the bed, toward her. "Sit up," he said plainly.

She obeyed.

In the same easy tenor, he said, "Take this glass of water in your right hand."

Sally did so.

"Now take these two capsules in your left hand."

She felt the sticky capsules. "No," she protested. She knew better than to take barbiturates after having had too much whiskey. She tried to explain this to him.

Hap heard her out. "Take your choice," he said quietly. "It's either me or sleep." ·

Sally hesitated. By this time the ringing of the telephones had died. An alarm was ringing in her head when she brought the capsules and the water to her mouth with trembling hands.

Hap took the glass from her, but he did not leave. After she had slid down and pillowed her head, he bent over her. One of his hands forced its way into her mouth, exploring it to assure himself that she had swallowed the capsules. She was gasping for breath before he withdrew his hand.

He now kissed her on her damp forehead. "Sleep well."

And then he was gone, with the telephone and the glass, and with the shutting of the door.

Sally considered going to the bathroom, forcing her own hand down her throat to bring up the capsules in a spew of vomit. In the end, she decided against this, fearing he would hear her and would not hear her entreaties to spare her. She shut her eyes and waited for sleep. For death.

38

Still at his desk, Roy Sutter noted the time: 9:24 P.M. He corked the whiskey bottle, pocketed his pack of cigarettes, and began the execution of his best-laid plan of action.

He took up the telephone, dialed seven digits, listened to five rings before he placed the telephone down on the desk, not far from its cradle. He wanted the Hendley house stirred by his alarms.

As he left the office and went down the stairs, he felt the effects of his drinking in his rubbery legs. Not in his mind. That was as clear as his plan.

Leaving the restaurant by the back door, he stepped into the cool night in time to see a man and a woman entering the station wagon parked in his private space. The man was strange to him, the woman was not. She was last seen in the glare of his Cadillac's headlights.

He put them out of his mind as he walked to his car. He had no time to think of anyone but Hap and Sally. Opening the trunk, he unzipped the big pocket of his golf bag and found a cardigan sweater. His sports coat shed, his sweater donned, he drew a three iron from the golf bag before shutting the trunk.

Behind the wheel, the iron on the seat beside him, he lit a cigarette, started the engine, and began his hard, fast drive. On Ventura Boulevard he found himself glancing at the iron and seeing it as the Winchester. Armed only with this iron, he had lightened the wallets of many suckers who came up against him with fourteen golf clubs.

On South Oaks Road he recalled the not so fine day when Neal Hendley had challenged him to such a match and he had backed off. He could have beaten Neal, but there was no sense to it. He did not need the money. He could not afford the trouble.

In retrospect now, Sutter wished he had accepted the challenge. Things might have worked out differently. He could only have wounded Neal's pride with the three iron. With the shotgun—

He damned the shotgun; he damned the matching target pistols. He had no doubt that Hap was waiting in the house with the missing one.

Certain that the boy meant to kill him, he was equally certain he could not kill Hap. If he had to, he could and would break one of Hap's arms or legs. Hap's idea was to avenge his slain father, his own was to free Sally.

238

The Cadillac turned into Montana Lane and passed the dark Hendley house. Sutter brought the car to a stop on a shoulder of the road. He cut his lights, his engine, and tried to quiet his mind, knowing well that rage would not serve him.

Immobile, he sat in the car, smoked down his cigarette, and allowed his mind to drift to a boyhood memory.

His tenth birthday: he and his father hunting down coyotes in the Sierra foothills, coming upon an old, bearded man, lying dead, attacked by a swarm of carrion buzzards tearing out the old man's stilled heart, hearing the cracks of his father's Enfield rifle, seeing the beating of wings against the hot sky as his father and he built a tomb of stones.

The memory brought Sutter confusion: was he the boy, the father, or the dead man?

By plan, he got out of the car without the three iron. He walked on the road until he came to the Hendley driveway. From there, sensing that he was watched from a dark window, he crossed casually to the front door.

He heard the ringing of the telephone before he pressed a forefinger to the doorbell. No bell sound came through the walls, windows, or door. He attacked the bell's button in various ways. Other than the intermittent ringing of the telephone, no sound, no light, no movement. The bell, he deduced, was either out of order or it had been disconnected.

Now he used his knuckles, lightly and politely at first. No response. He struck the door with a fist. Nothing. With the ring on one of his fingers he tapped the porthole's glass. Nothing.

He stepped back now to regard the draped front windows. He saw no one. Turning away, he went to the garage door and looked through one of the two porthole windows. He saw the station wagon, the MG.

Reassured that Hap and Sally were inside, Sutter took up the next phase of his plan. Warily, he went all around the perimeter of the house, stopping before each dark, draped window and glass door to tap it with his ring. It was like tapping stone. No sound, no movement but his own.

When he returned to the front of the house, he made no attempt to try the doorbell again. Instead he took to the driveway and the road. He opened a car door with no thought of entering or retreating. The door shut again, he started back toward the house, the golf club in hand. He sensed that he appeared menacing holding it with the fingers of his right hand high on the grip.

He now gripped the iron face of the club. Using it as a walking stick, he started up the driveway and toward the front door. Before he used the iron as he had planned, he tried the bell, the knock on wood, and the tap on the porthole window. Nothing, not even a quickening of the wind. Only a realization that the telephone had stopped ringing.

He checked himself when he saw the headlights of a car winding up Montana Lane. He watched the headlights find the driveway of a home across the road. The return of silence and darkness was the signal for the duel with Hap to begin.

Careful to keep himself outside the door's frame, out of the probable line of fire, Sutter returned his fingers to the grip of the club. With one hand, he swung in a wide arc. The club face's toe shattered the double-thick glass.

There was no response of light, voice, or gunfire from inside the house. It was heard across the road by a concerned man en route from his garage to his front door.

The man looked to the Hendley house. He saw nothing in the dark, but he did hear the door being opened and slammed shut. He looked for light and saw none. Not for long minutes. Then it came, the light outside the garage, the light outside the door, the light filtering through the front, draped windows. But all was quiet now, save his mind. Lighting a cigarette, he stood there wondering why someone had to break a window to gain entry into the Hendley house. He knew about the shootings at the Sutter house on South Oaks Road. He knew Mr. Hendley was dead. He would be glad when the house was sold. Pilots, stewardesses, and kids like Hap did not help the image of the neighborhood or the value of his own house.

The man was bothered by this until he heard, first in the distance and then closer and louder, the wailing of sirens. He saw the headlights approaching on Montana Lane, watched a police car stop on the road right in front of him, leaving the Hendley driveway clear for the oncoming ambulance.

39

Out of a clouded, darkening October sky, a Lufthansa 707 descended to a runway on Frankfurt's Rhein-Main airport.

At the terminal the crew of stewardesses, all smiling warmly, made its multilingual good-byes to the disembarking passengers. When, at last, the stewardesses left the jet, all but one of them were smiling, laughing, and joking.

The unsmiling stewardess walked alone to the airline's personnel office. When she confronted a familiar clerk, she was given a verbal message and a letter.

Someone had telephoned yesterday afternoon, asking about her: a male voice identifying himself as a relative of hers, asking for her address.

As the disconcerted stewardess hurried to catch her bus, she studied the unexpected, unwelcome envelope. It was from Los Angeles, from Joan Lawler, addressed to Ms. Sally Foster, Stewardess, Lufthansa Air Lines, Frankfurt, West Germany.

Sally thought of ripping the unopened envelope to pieces. She was angry about a communication with a world from which she had fled in secret, in mystery. But she decided to read the letter in the hope that it might contain a clue to her "relative." When she was seated in the bus bound for the city air center in downtown Frankfurt, Sally began to read:

October 6, 1973

Dear Sally,

It's late Sunday afternoon, a kind of Philadelphia Sunday in Century City. I'm in the office, alone. Having finished my eighth day of work this week, I've been sitting here drinking and thinking about you. Not that I've ever stopped thinking about you, but it was only last Wednesday that I found out where you were and what you're doing. The simple fact that you were alive and doing made my day, and all of my days since.

But it did take me all this time to make up my mind about writing to you, realizing you might not welcome this letter—or any news of what's been happening here. Forgive me if this is so. And if you have no wish to read further, tear up this tearable (terrible?) letter. I'll understand—and go on loving you.

So here goes nothing or something—just a newsy letter. And I'll begin with the best news.

About Ilona: On September 14th she became Mrs. Roger Brennan. Civil ceremony, performed by a prominent New York judge. A family party followed at the Plaza. Dolores and I did not attend, although Ilona did invite us. I believe we were wise to stay away. There were some touchy times. No trouble about the divorce. But Brennan's family gave him a hard time, beginning from the time the New York papers started to print stories about what the hell went on in South Oaks. Names and all. Anyway, all's well now. Karen and Ronny are back in their snooty schools. Ilona and Roger are honeymooning in Europe. Happy ending, happy beginning.

As for Bobby, he's still living alone in the same old house in the same old way. Because of the divorce, he's been in touch—with Frank and me. When he catches me alone, he keeps trying to invite me (alone) to his parties. I keep stalling him, keeping him interested, but I'm only interested in having him throw us a little of his legal business.

About Dolores: Her house was put on the market late in May, sold in July, and vacated in September. Dolores had ideas of moving to La Jolla and going to the University of San Diego. Perry was going to find a bachelor pad in Encino. Both of those plans went to hell when Larry left Cornell back in April and took off thumb tripping, God knows where. So, to try to get Larry back in school, Dolores and Perry agreed to carry on together. They bought a new condominium in Westwood, close to UCLA, where Dolores means to work toward a Ph.D. in psychology. Perry's still got his office in the Valley, but he's planning to move his practice to this side of the hill. Linda's fine, the baby's cute. And, yes, Larry's back at Cornell.

We talk—only when I phone her. She never calls. It's hard—even talking on the phone. No tennis. There are courts, there is no time, no mood. She has her school, her problems with Larry and Perry. I have my work, my problems.

About me: Frank and I are still in business—more the business of law than of marriage. And that's not a complaint. Considering all that's happened, I count myself a lucky girl. We're able to meet the rent payments for the office and for our studio apartment in West Los Angeles. Remember, everything's inflated, except my ego. The upstairs of our apt. has two master bedroom suites. The trip from Frank's suite to mine seems as far as the distance between Dolores's master bedroom and the guest room where Perry used to bed down. I didn't ask, but I gather that Dolores and Perry have the same arrangement.

In June I sold my Datsun to cut down on expenses—and on temptation. One weekend last month Frank had to fly up to San Francisco on business. Left alone and with the Riviera at my disposal, I found myself prowling like a cat, heading for the Valley, driving through South Oaks and trying to make believe it was all the way it used to be. It isn't.

My house now belongs to two senior citizens from Richmond, Virginia, newlyweds, both of whom were divorced from their respective spouses after more than twenty-five years of marriage. They came along about a week after the Bakersfield couple had backed out of the deal. Their reason: South Oaks's notoriety turned them off.

By the way, Roark Bennett was named salesman of the month (July) by Cardwell & Company. He got a good start selling my house and the Cooper house. And, incidentally, to prove the Lawlers have the luck of the Irish, we got six thousand dollars more for our house. The Richmond couple was that anxious. They consider the house "a conversation piece." So much for them.

The Cooper house was bought by a young well-to-do couple from Greenwich, Conn. Tennis nuts. Roy's house is now home for a local insurance man with a wife and two young kids. (I have no idea if you know or care that your house now belongs to a gay couple, one a psychologist, the other a studio set designer. The basketball backboard is gone.)

As I write this, I get the feeling you may have read enough. In case I'm wrong, I'll go on.

Would you believe that Whitney Callender showed up here—at the office— one day last June? His father's still alive. Anyway, he had Frank arrange the purchase of all those old Yale football pictures that used to hang on the walls of the Ivy League. And then he was gone.

Yes, Sally, there still is a restaurant called the Ivy League. I went by it that night. And I just had to go in and see what it was like. For one thing, the new parking attendants are an added attraction. High school dropouts, girls in white boots and short white skirts. Jasper and his crew of black waiters are all gone. In their place are white girls in knee-high black boots and red hot-pants and see-through blouses.

As for the patrons, they're mostly potato peelers from north of the boulevard. The food stinks, the drinks are cheap—as cheap as the place itself. And running the show is nobody but Rick Kelley.

Of course, he knew me, but he was reluctant to talk about "old times." He did say that Lieutenant Fonte never comes around anymore. He also told me that the potato peelers had "taken over" two other Valley restaurants. He didn't seem happy about that or about the fact he had no idea just when the bulldozers were coming to make way for the office building. Nothing lasts, he said.

Like Kelley, I'll skip the "old times." I'm delighted that you're up and doing. I know Lufthansa flies here, but that you don't and won't. Please, remember I miss you, think of you, and pray that you'll write me. Be well.

Shamefully,
Joan

P.S. Loehmann's has opened a new store near the Farmer's Market. I was there last Saturday afternoon, alone. I found this darling pants-suit, and I instinctively turned about to show it to you. I don't know. I just had the feeling the store was back in the Valley and you were with me—like always. Remember? Oh, Gentle Mary, what did we screw away?

With no show of emotion, Sally returned the letter to the envelope, to her handbag. She now turned her eyes to the bus windows, watched night fall, and gave her concern to the "relative" who now knew where she was. This concern was short-lived. The clue was in Joan's letter. Ilona and her new husband were in Europe. Ilona was the "relative." The male voice belonged to her husband.

Not anxious about seeing anyone from California, she was nonetheless pleased that it was Ilona. She would be the easiest to endure. She hoped to find a message and a telephone number waiting for her. She would call Ilona to wish her well. She owed her that.

Leaving the terminal, Sally took a taxi rather than another bus to rush her to her apartment house in the *Innenstadt*.

Her mailbox held no message—only a letter from Paris that told her fortune: next spring she would be a student in a school of fashion design. Happy about this prospect, she floated up in the elevator to the fourth floor. Crossing to her door, she lowered her valise, slipped the key into the lock and turned it. Finding she had locked the door, she lost her smile as her mind unlocked the identity of the "relative" inside.

Sally entered and frowned on Hap, lying on the couch in the living room. The only light in the room came from a bridge lamp playing on the opened pages of a paperback novel, Thomas Wolfe's *Look Homeward, Angel*.

Picking up her valise, Sally shut the door behind her. Hap read on, never once turning his head toward her. She passed through the living room without glancing at him or saying anything. Once in her bedroom, she closed the door, lowered the valise, flung her handbag onto the bed, and went to the window.

She opened it, the cold air rushing against her flushed face and body. She looked out and down. The sidewalk was inviting.

When she heard the bedroom door being opened, she turned to face Hap. He stood there, unsmiling, one hand on the doorknob.

"Hi," he said.

She regarded him with scorn. "Where did you sleep last night?"

"The couch."

"Good-bye," said Sally.

"I've got a room. Steigenberger Hotel Frankfurterhof."

"Good."

"Like to take you to dinner," he said.

"I've had mine."

"Today's my birthday."

"Good-bye, Hap," Sally said coldly.

"I'm seventeen," he said unhappily.

Sally turned to shut the window. She had not remembered his birthday, and she was glad of it.

"What do you say, Sally?"

Her back to him, she said, "I have nothing to say to you."

He persisted. "Nothing to ask me?"

"No."

"Aren't you interested in hearing what happened that night?"

"Not from you."

"Who else could tell you?"

Sally turned on him. "Joan. Dolores. Lieutenant Fonte."

Hap looked sad. "They don't know the half of it."

"I've heard enough," said Sally. "Please go."

His demeanor unchanged, he said, "I came a long way to tell you—all the way from Ojai. I got permission from the school. Got the word of your whereabouts from TWA. Almost two months ago, and I waited. I understood then and still do how you feel about me. I didn't want to see you until today. Until I felt I had a chance for you to listen to a guy seventeen talking about a flipped-out, sixteen-year-old kid."

Unmoved, Sally said, "I see no change in you."

"I'm an inch and a half taller, ten pounds heavier, and ten years wiser," he said.

"Prove it by knowing how to take 'no' for an answer."

Hap hesitated. "To what question?"

"Your unwelcome presence."

He understood. "Okay, I'll split. I'll go from here to the airport and back to school. Just let me tell you what I have to. Do that and I swear I'll stay away from you for the rest of your life."

She tested him. "Did you tell Joan Lawler where I was?"

Hap nodded. "We had a deal. The one who found out first was bound to tell the other."

"Would you tell her—if I asked you to—that you never saw me? That I'm no longer with Lufthansa? That I'm out of reach? No forwarding address?"

"I can't," he said. "I can't lie anymore, not since this morning. I made a birthday vow to myself never to lie again."

"Good-bye, Hap." She spoke with finality.

He shrugged. "Well, I tried. I had to." He returned to the living room. Sally followed him and watched him open a closet door. He put on his corduroy jacket, took his father's trenchcoat and suitcase, and went to the door. Without turning to face Sally, he left.

She caught up with him at the elevator. "Come back and tell me what you have to. I'll listen only so long as I believe you're telling the truth."

Back again in the living room, Sally directed Hap to sit on the couch. She sat in a chair facing him.

"Begin," she said.

"Can I get myself a Coke?"

"Begin," she repeated.

Hap had another question. "At what point?"

"From the time you put me to sleep."

His eyes leaving hers, Hap returned to the night and the hour in question. In a shaky voice, he began to unfold the drama.

"I went back to my room and got the pistol—the one Dad had hidden away. I'd found it by accident one day when I was staying at the Belanger house. I was taking a walk and I came over to our house and started messing around in the garage—just looking for anything to remind me of Dad. I came across the pistol case and a pack of bullets with not much trouble. It wasn't so easy to find the pistol itself, but I did.

"I loaded it, went into the house, and figured out the best place to hide it. I taped it inside my stereo cabinet. I didn't take it out again until after I'd read the story in the *Valley News*."

He glanced at Sally to see if she had any questions. She did not.

He went on. "Anyway—to get back to that Monday night—I held on to the pistol and began to look out for Mr. Sutter. The phone rang again and kept ringing. It was still ringing when I saw his white Caddy pass the house. In another minute I saw him.

"He walked up the driveway and came straight to the front door, looking just like somebody who'd come to visit. He rang the doorbell, but the only ringing he could've heard came from the telephone. He couldn't tell that I'd been to the fuse box and cut off the power. And with the phone still ringing he couldn't tell if we were dead or alive or even there. Then he tried knocking on the door, tapping on the porthole window with his ring until he gave up.

"Then I saw Mr. Sutter go toward the garage and out of sight. I picked him up again as he was going around the house, tapping on every window with his ring. I kept watching him and hoping he wouldn't wake you. Finally he came around front again and just walked away— like he'd given up. Just then I got scared. I realized the telephone had stopped ringing. The first thing I thought was that you were awake, up, and taking the call. I made sure you weren't before I got back to the front windows in time to see Mr. Sutter coming up the driveway again, this time with something in his right hand. First it looked like a shotgun, barrels down. Then it looked like a walking stick until I could see that it was an iron. I thought it was a two iron. It was a three."

Hap paused, his eyes and mind never leaving the scene. "Then I did something that made me feel good about myself. I went back to my room, put the pistol back in a drawer, went to the closet, and got my putter. I figured if it was going to be a duel, I'd make it a fair one. I had the advantage of being inside the house, being used to the dark, so I let Mr. Sutter have the advantage in golf clubs. It would've been too easy to shoot him down.

"I got back to the door just as he smashed the porthole window. The only thing I was afraid of was that the noise might wake you. It didn't. The next thing I saw in the dark was Mr. Sutter's hand coming through the porthole, reaching in, sliding the bolt open, unlocking the door, and then reaching for the light switch right next to the door. He touched it and waited for a light that never came on. Then his arm disappeared, and I ducked into the hall closet, not shutting the door all the way,

246

crouching and waiting. After I heard the front door open and slam shut, I saw Mr. Sutter move into the living room with the three iron back in his right hand. I let him take another step or two into the living room before I sprang at him. I could've split his head open without him knowing it. But I didn't. I called out his name and let him hear it for the last time. He turned on me, body and face—but he never got his club moving.

"I wish I knew what he was thinking. I think maybe he was waiting for the pistol to go off when the back of my mallet-head putter caught him between his eyes. Floored him."

Hap paused to catch his breath. He never raised his eyes to note Sally's vapid stare. Heartbreak in his voice, he continued:

"I brought my bloodied club up again, only to drop it. Mr. Sutter was not moving. Then I did all the things I had to do—the things I'd worked out. I went to the fuse box, turned on the lights all over the house and outside. And then I went to the phone and called for an ambulance and the police. I also called Mrs. Lawler. She and Mrs. Cooper got there about a minute after the ambulance and the police.

"But to go back a bit, I went back to the living room. To Mr. Sutter. He was lying there, not moving, the blood running from his broken face. When the police came in, they found me down over him, bloody mouth to bloody mouth, trying to blow life down his lungs."

Hap ended there. As soon as his voice died, he heard sounds more alarming than gunfire: the clapping of Sally's hands. Staring at her, he saw that she was mocking him. The sight of her now was more sickening to him than the vivid memories of his father's and Mr. Sutter's shattered faces.

"Bravo," said Sally. "A magnificent performance."

He shook his head dismally. "That was no performance for the police. In the end I didn't want Mr. Sutter to die."

"Good-bye, Hap. I don't believe you."

"No," he insisted. "It's true. That's the way it was."

"Your plan was perfect," said Sally coldly. "It worked out perfectly."

"No," he protested in agony.

"Didn't you *perform* for the police? For Fonte?"

"Later I did," he said.

"You surely didn't confess your plot and plan. Why? Were you a little short of contrition?"

Hap hesitated. "I had a good reason not to confess. If I'd told the truth, I would've had to tell Lieutenant Fonte what I put you through."

Sally understood. She had learned as much from Joan and Dolores, both of whom withheld the truth for her sake.

She said. "You didn't fool Fonte."

Hap flinched. "Then why wasn't I held?"

"Don't play stupid with me," she admonished.

He responded smartly. "Sure. There was no evidence. Not against me. And so much going for me. Like having the pistol and not using it. Like defending my home from attack. Like Mr. Sutter being drunk. Like my not lying and saying I didn't know the intruder was Mr. Sutter. Like Lieutenant Fonte telling the newspapers there was bad blood between Mr. Sutter and me."

"Yes," said Sally bitterly. "And there's now bad blood between you and me."

"No," he pleaded.

"You murdered Roy. That's *my* verdict."

"Yours is the only one that counts," he said.

"Is it? And do you agree with it?"

"No."

Sally kept at him. "What's your own verdict?"

"I don't know."

"Are you using your age—your immaturity—as a defense? If you are, it won't wash. You used that up when you shot the Indians on the TV screen."

Hap said, "I don't know. I was thinking I was like Holden Caulfield—"

Again Sally interrupted him. "Please, don't use J.D. Salinger. Not that way."

"I don't mean to," he said, "but it's the truth."

"And your truths are lies to me," Sally contended. "The way you used all of us—especially me—to plot Roy's murder suggests no immaturity to me. It suggests a cold, merciless, cruel, and mature mind—devoid of everything but brute instinct. You see, I've had a lot of time to reason out the unreasonable."

Hap weighed his words before he dared to speak his mind. "When did you reason this? When you were in that sanitarium in Pasadena?"

Sally scowled at him. "Who told you?"

"Mrs. Lawler," he said. "Only last week. A fair exchange of information. After she cut me to pieces."

Sally remained silent. She had no wish to recall her six weeks in Pasadena. Here and now she was thankful to Dolores Cooper for taking her there and putting her in the good hands of Dr. Malcolm Hawley.

"Anything else?" she asked.

"I'd just like to finish with this," Hap said. "I didn't have any idea of avenging Dad until I got to Louisiana for the funeral. Sure, Uncle Carl kept hinting how he felt about Mr. Sutter, about the way he would've liked to avenge Dad. He mentioned old time duels with matched weapons and how boiling mad he got thinking how Dad—with a .22 caliber pistol—had to go up against Mr. Sutter's 12-gauge, double-barreled shotgun. But it wasn't that that put the bug in me. It was something he

248

said when he was drinking hard and making sad talk about Dad." He glanced at Sally. She seemed lost in her own thoughts. "You listening?"

"Yes," she said.

"Uncle Carl remembered me when I was still in the crawling stage. He remembered coming to our house one night with Dad. After Dad had played around with my sisters, he got me out of my playpen. He took me and my uncle into the den. Dad fixed drinks and sat down on the studio couch with his back up against the wall. He put me down and let me crawl to the other end of the couch. My uncle got scared that I'd fall off and hurt myself. But Dad just smiled. At the last second, just when it looked like I was going to fall, Dad reached out, grabbed one of my legs, and pulled me back to him. Then he'd let me go and the same thing'd happen over and over again. Uncle Carl didn't like the idea, but Dad just laughed and told him I'd never fallen off, and never would. Not as long as he was there to catch me."

Sally felt no poignancy, caught no truth. Her expression unchanged, she stared at Hap as if she were still waiting for the end of the tale.

"That's it," said Hap uneasily.

"Is it?" Sally demanded, very much in control of her emotions. "Ask yourself if your father was truly a 'catcher in the rye.' Ask yourself about the time he let you fall. Ask yourself who picked you up. Ask yourself who said yes to life. Ask yourself who said no. Think about it for a year. Look me up on your eighteenth birthday and let me see if you're old enough, wise enough to tell a myth from a truth."

Stunned, down but not out, Hap asked, "Will you be here?"

"Most likely not," she said. "But you'll find me."

The boy was anguished. "Didn't anything I say get to you?"

Sally thought about it. "Yes, two words. *Crouched. Sprang.*"

"I don't get you," he complained.

"These two words bring tigers to mind," said Sally. "The saber-toothed tigers. Millions of years ago, they wandered into what is now Los Angeles in search of water. And they found it shimmering in water-holes that turned out to be black bogs, where they were trapped, where they sank and disappeared."

Hap asked, "What's the point?"

"In the sanitarium," said Sally, "I met a seventy-nine-year-old man who believed he was possessed by the evil spirit of a saber-toothed tiger. He put it this way: 'They let the spirits out when they drilled the oil from the wells below the bogs. They put the tigers in our tanks, and we freed them with the exhaust of our motor cars. And now these evil spirits roam the smog that separates us from God.' "

"The man's not right in his head," Hap remarked.

Sally said, "All the poor man did was strangle his sixty-eight-year-old wife. He believed she was involved in an ongoing affair with a man who'd been dead for thirty years. If he's not right in the head, doesn't your being a murderer make you not right in the head?"

"No," he retorted. "And I'm not possessed, either."

"The old man believes we all are—or were. You, I, your father, Roy, the potato peelers."

"Do you believe that?"

"I believe the old man made as much sense as you did today."

The words hit Hap like shotgun blasts, like a blow from a mallet-head putter. Bleeding, dying, he arose and crossed to the door. He gathered his trenchcoat, book, and suitcase before he faced Sally, who had not left her chair. Her coldness freezing his voice, he turned and opened the door. Before he shut it, he heard Sally's muted, *"Aufwiedersehen."*

Sure, he thought, they would meet again. Next year, some year, some place. He'd find her once he had found the key to finding himself. He'd show her, he'd show them all—all the fucking, fucked-up grown-ups—that he was coming over to their side.

In the street as he moved away, Hap sensed that his feet were leaden and his knees were buckling under something far weightier than his suitcase or book. Was it the weight of his dead father? Of the dead Mr. Sutter?

Feeling he was sinking into a bog, he stopped, looked back at the apartment house, and clutched at the straw of Sally, framed in a high, lighted window.

He raised a leaden hand and waved the book like a flag. Sally was slow about it, but she waved back in a forlorn way. The gesture was enough to pull him out of the bog.

Hap waved once more before he turned and walked away. The ground now hard beneath him, his legs still leaden, he came upon the answer to what was weighing him down:

Sally had turned him into a burdened, saber-toothed tiger crossing a dry wasteland and thirsting for a truth beyond mirages of truth.